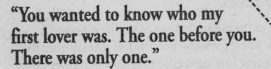
"You wanted to know who my first lover was. The one before you. There was only one."

Tamara saw the shock on Rory's face as she told him. Since she was so inured against having any painful emotions, she wondered why it was so easy to summon tears. They served her purpose—to gain Rory as an ally against her mother. Yet suddenly, perversely, she wanted more than that from him. It was weak to yearn for what could never be—weak to let the idea touch her heart.

It was she who was owed, and she was calling in the debts. If the hook wasn't baited now it never would be.

He would come after her. He would need to know more. She would tell him, bit by bit, drawing him into doing what she wanted.

They would all pay for what had been done to her.

Dear Readers,

One of the magic pleasures of my life is finding a book where the story situation and characters are so intriguing I am compelled to read it from cover to cover, even begrudging time off for meals. I love the on-the-edge excitement of what is going to happen next, the irresistible pull of anticipation and expectation as one dramatic scene is propelled into another and another and I gobble it up, breathless for more.

I especially enjoy stories about families, all the cross-weaving of deep personal interests, finding out where the bodies are buried, what skeletons are in the closet, and the delicious question of when those closely guarded secrets are to be revealed, causing everything to blow up and change. Most of all I love passionate encounters where people's whole lives are on the line and whatever decision is made or action taken will create a turning point from whence there is no retreat.

It is all of these things that I try to bring to my own writing. I hope that you find *The Secrets Within* compelling—I've tried to make it fascinating in its insights and heart-tugging in its emotional intensity.

Enjoy,

Emma Darcy

EMMA DARCY

The SECRETS WITHIN

MIRA BOOKS

ISBN 1-55166-294-9

THE SECRETS WITHIN

For my beloved husband, Frank,
who was determined that this book be written.

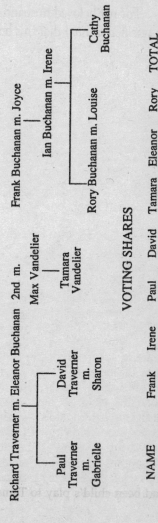

PIONEER FAMILIES OF THE HUNTER VALLEY WINE INDUSTRY

(Commencing with the 5th Generation
of Traverner & Buchanan Families)

TRAVERNER

BUCHANAN

Richard Traverner m. Eleanor Buchanan   2nd m. Max Vandelier

Paul Traverner m. Gabrielle

David Traverner m. Sharon

Irene

Tamara Vandelier

Frank Buchanan m. Joyce

Ian Buchanan m. Irene

Rory Buchanan m. Louise

Tamara   Eleanor   Rory   Cathy Buchanan

VOTING SHARES

NAME	Frank	Irene	Paul	David	Tamara	Eleanor	Rory	TOTAL
Traverner	15%	1%	10%	10%	35%	29%		100%
Buchanan	25%	20%	7.5%	7.5%	18%	2%	20%	100%

ONE

Destroy...

It wasn't a thought. It was a need. A compulsion. A resolution. It burned through Tamara Vandelier's mind, promoting a scorched earth policy that nothing would turn aside.

Four months the doctors had given her mother, four months for the cancer inside her to take its inevitable toll, four months for her to witness the destruction of her life's work and know the depth of her daughter's vengeance for the overweening ambition that had driven Dame Eleanor Buchanan Traverner Vandelier's cold, calculating heart. Eleanor the invincible was invincible no more. She was dying.

Impossible to get to her these past few weeks after the mastectomy. Eleanor had installed herself very privately in St. Vincent's Private Hospital, with security guards at her door around the clock to turn unwanted visitors away. Tamara didn't have to be told she headed the unwanted list.

But Sydney was a big city, not Eleanor's bailiwick, and Australia was full of people who rather relished cutting down tall poppies. The wall of silence Eleanor had instituted at the hospital was easily cracked. Seducing a medical orderly had been child's play to Tamara. He had told her everything she'd needed to know, the prognosis, what steps were being taken, how Eleanor was responding to them.

Then finally, the relief, the elation of this afternoon's news. Eleanor's decision to reject further treatment and go home provided the opportunity Tamara craved for a final reckoning with her mother. The endgame could now be played. To the death.

Eleanor would be home tomorrow.

Tomorrow it could start.

Tamara stood on the top balcony of the beach house. The sea breeze felt clean, smelled clean. This house on the coastline just north of Sydney was the one place her father had built that was hers, not Eleanor's. It was irrelevant to her mother. It had nothing to do with the rich earth and grapes of the great Hunter Valley vineyards that were Eleanor's obsession.

Hatred welled up in Tamara, fierce, dark, all-consuming. She watched the waves form their scalloped edges on the sand all around the curve of the beach, giving the effect of a string of pearls. Pearl Beach. Pearls were for tears, and there would be tears aplenty in the next four months, but not hers. Hers had been shed a long time ago, the summer she was fourteen, the summer that had been life and death.

And now Eleanor would know death, the destruction of her dreams, which would hurt her far more than the mere physical end of her life. She would know the pain of losing what she held most dear.

Tamara smiled. Her plan had a beautiful irony. Her mother would see it, too. She would see what she thought she had destroyed that summer rise again and produce the seed to defeat her, the seed that would be the ultimate card of revenge.

And all the dark, hidden things would be brought out into the light to haunt her last days on this earth, the earth that would no longer be chained to her will. It would be her hated daughter's will Eleanor would see done, the one child she'd given birth to as part of her bargain with Max Vandelier, Tamara the unwanted, the unloved by-blow of ambition.

Love... The old pain twisted through Tamara's heart. She drove it out. Tomorrow she would reclaim Rory. That was the start of it, the core of it. Rory...

She shouted his name as though calling him, then laughed. It was a high, wild ripple of sound that carried on the breeze and drowned in the steady roar of waves rolling in, the inexorable movement of the sea echoing Rory, Rory, Rory. It was as inexorable as Tamara's will to triumph.

Eleanor would never laugh again.

Not even in her grave.

Destroy...

TWO

Surprise woke Rory Buchanan. It wasn't unusual for him to wake with an erection. He did most mornings. Not that it was much good to him. Louise didn't like sex first thing in the morning. She had made that clear to him from day one of their marriage, and it wasn't in his nature to force what he wanted on any woman. Yet here she was snuggled up to him spoon fashion, and her hand was stroking him.

If that wasn't an open invitation, Rory didn't know one. He certainly wasn't about to question it. Nor was he going to move and cut short the sheer unexpected pleasure of it. Normally he initiated their lovemaking. For Louise to be fondling him like this was one hell of a surprise.

Correction. A heavenly surprise.

Her breasts were deliciously squashed up against his back. The heat of her body against his butt was a sure-fire aphrodisiac. With what her hand was doing, he wasn't going to be able to lie still much longer.

She moved, dropping his fully extended organ as she hitched herself up to nibble his ear. 'Come on, Rory. I know you're awake. Do you really want to ignore me? I'm ready for you.'

He growled, happy to give his animal side free rein as he heaved himself over to take her. She didn't want any finesse. He didn't have to contain himself. Her legs quickly wrapped around him, hips lifted, her eyes glittering satisfaction in his excitement. He drove in and opened her up.

It was good. Hot, moist, her inner muscles sucking at him. It was great. For a minute or two he was a steaming piston, revelling in the rhythm. Then he came in an uncontrollable burst and it was over. Far too soon.

It prompted the thought of starting again, making it last longer. The idea was quickly discarded. Better to be content with what he'd had than make a fool of himself. He sighed and gave Louise a rueful smile. 'Sorry about that. Couldn't hold it.'

Her answering smile held no reproach. 'It was fine. Just what I wanted. I like it when you lose control.' She gave him a quick kiss, untangled her limbs from his and headed for the ensuite bathroom.

She always did that. Never wanted to cuddle afterwards or just lie languorously together. Rory didn't mind this morning. The quickie had left him with a warm afterglow. He felt good, relaxed, content. It didn't matter that Louise was so fastidious about cleanliness. She was fastidious about a lot of things. It was one of her character quirks, and it had its advantages as well as its disadvantages.

The thought returned to him when he was combing his hair after his shower. Louise was big on appearances, perfect grooming, clothes coordinated to classy effect, everything just so. She didn't like a hair out of place.

He had conceded to her wish that he go to her hairdresser to get what she considered a fashionable haircut, but no way would he submit to having the lighter streaks in his brown hair blonded more artistically. He snorted at the idea. He didn't mind Louise keeping her long ash-blonde hair perfectly ash-blonde. Such vanity was fine in a woman if it made her feel good. For a man? Well, not for this man. It would have made him feel false to himself.

Though he didn't mind the designer clothes she bought

for him. The quality shirts had a nice feel against his skin. She had a good eye for colour in the silk ties she chose. Since it was mostly irrelevant to him what he wore, it was no big deal to please Louise on this issue. He was always proud to own her as his wife. It was only fair to make her feel proud to own him as her husband.

He walked to the living room in a happy frame of mind. Louise had set the table ready for breakfast. He could smell the bacon and eggs cooking in the kitchen. A cup of freshly brewed coffee was waiting for him. He sat down and lifted it to his lips, enjoying the aroma, the strong, satisfying taste of it.

The glass wall of the living room brought the outdoors right to him, and it was a beautiful morning, blue sky, sun shining, birds flitting through the trees, sparrows, rosellas, Willie wagtails, chirping melodious calls to each other or simply giving voice to their joy in being alive and free.

Rory felt a pleasant hum of wellbeing. He loved this view. He loved this house. This morning he even felt love for his wife.

It was good to be alive.

THREE

Louise cleared away the breakfast dishes, filled Rory's coffee cup, poured one for herself and took it to the other end of the table. She sat with her back to the view. It didn't interest her. Drab gum trees and noisy birds. Why anyone would be entranced by Australian bushland was beyond her. Her interest was focused entirely on Rory this morning.

He looked pleased with his world, all his wants satisfied, his gaze idly wandering over whatever wonders of nature he saw outside. Rory could be stubborn in his resistance to some of her suggestions, but Louise confidently anticipated he would be amenable to her direction this morning. It might be a good idea to give him sex every morning until she had manoeuvred him into full co-operation with her plans. It wasn't any real hardship now she had her goal in sight.

Rory had great potential. She wouldn't have married him otherwise. Though he was certainly one of the most handsome men she had ever met. Quite striking with his toffee hair and amber eyes. He had a smile most women would die for and a body that was magnetically male. With her careful re-imaging, he now carried the instantly recognisable stamp of class. Louise had no doubt she could make him what she wanted him to be.

She smiled as she remembered her first ambition, to go into politics like her father. Jeremy Stanhope, the current Minister for Industry in the federal government, had always lived and breathed power, a heady world she had shared with him since her teens, even before her mother had skipped off to Ireland with a breeder of racehorses. Louise had chosen to stay with her father. She preferred being Daddy's girl to playing second fiddle to her mother.

'Forget politics,' he'd advised her. 'That's not where the power is for a woman. You're too open to attack.'

It had sparked a feminist stand. 'Just because I'm a woman...'

'You've got it made, baby, if you learn to play it right.'

'What do you mean?'

'Tie up with a man who can take you to where you'd like to be in life and work through him. Study history. The most powerful women have been those who knew how to manipulate men and their position. You'll find it more satisfying than being bloodied on the floor of Parliament.'

Louise had liked the concept. She'd taken it to heart.

Her father had inadvertently led her to Rory when he'd pointed out Eleanor Vandelier at the ceremony in Canberra where she was awarded the title of dame for services to the Australian wine industry. 'There's a woman who has her eye on the main chance. Widowed twice on her way up. Got herself one hell of a mansion in the Hunter Valley and now dictates the running of the two most prominent vineyards.'

Louise had noted Eleanor was getting on in years. 'Does she have any eligible sons?'

'Both married. But on her brother's side, the heir to the Buchanan vineyard is still single. Do you want an introduction to him?'

Her father's eyes had sparkled a challenge.

Irresistible.

Seeing what Eleanor reigned over had really clinched it for her. The mansion Max Vandelier had built left the decaying luxury of her mother's old manor house in Ireland for dead. Besides, being intimately associated with two of the highest regarded Australian vineyards that produced world-class wines was a lot classier than messing with horses, no matter how thoroughbred they were.

Rory had been running the Buchanan vineyard for years before she'd met him. He knew the winemaking business inside out. With her at his side to help him, he could certainly handle the responsibilities involved in being head of the family company, directing the business interests of both the Buchanan and Traverner vineyards.

After three years of marriage, Louise wanted her investment of time with Rory to pay off. Eleanor was dying. The position was there for them to take. If they were bold enough.

She sipped her coffee, thinking through the line of reasoning she would use on Rory to get him to do what she wanted today. The opportunities had to be set up. He wouldn't foresee the importance of it himself. He would probably find the idea distasteful. Best to approach the matter obliquely.

She put down her cup. It was time to draw his attention.

'Rory, you haven't forgotten Eleanor comes home this afternoon?'

Spoiling words, souring the sweetness of the morning. Rory didn't want or need Louise's reminder that Eleanor was coming home to die. His grandfather had called from Sydney last night, saying she was refusing any further treatment and he would be bringing her home from St. Vincent's hospital this afternoon.

Ellie, his grandfather always called her. In Frank Buchanan's mind, she was still his little sister who needed his comfort and support. To any objective mind there was nothing little about Dame Eleanor Buchanan Traverner Vandelier. She was a force, a dominant force that belittled others.

Rory didn't care she was dying. He had associated Eleanor with death since the summer he was sixteen. His grandfather was blind to the victims that lay in the wake of Eleanor's ambition. He saw only his sister's achievements. But Rory saw more. He saw the human cost. He found it repellent.

'No, I haven't forgotten,' he answered flatly.

He dragged his gaze from the untainted beauty of nature's innocence and looked directly at his wife, aware she had a purpose in bringing up the subject. She had used *that* tone of voice. It meant Louise wanted something done. It was one of the little nuances he had come to recognise over the three years of their marriage.

Her silk house robe gaped enough to show the soft valley between her breasts. Her long blonde hair was still loose, gleaming with the light behind her. Rory tried and failed to recover the feelings she had evoked in pleasuring him earlier. Was he being needlessly cynical in wondering now if there had been a purpose behind the uncharacteristic closeness and giving?

'I think you should drop by the Traverner vineyard on your way to work this morning,' she said.

Louise was a planner. Sometimes Rory yearned for spontaneity, but Louise's planning usually had his interests at heart. Their marriage was a working partnership. He was reasonably content with it. He just didn't like the feeling of being manipulated or seeing others manipulated. He'd seen enough of it from Eleanor. He didn't want it next to him.

'What for?' he asked.

'To talk to Paul and David. Show some sympathy for what they must be feeling. Eleanor always seemed so indomitable. The news must have come as a shock to them. It's the decent thing to do, Rory.'

She was right. Even a monstrous mother was still a mother, and Eleanor had been the cog around which her sons' lives had revolved, driving wheels within wheels, constant and relentless machinations to safeguard the Traverner inheritance against any possible threat, even to marrying Max Vandelier and selling her soul to hold onto the earth that had belonged to Richard Traverner, Paul's and David's father.

Did they love their mother for what she had done for them, or did they long to make their own way, their own decisions? Might they not see her coming death as a doorway to freedom?

Rory knew he would. But he wasn't Paul and he wasn't David and he didn't really know what they thought or felt about their mother. They were loyal to her. They had every reason to be. They would inherit the fruits of her obsessive drive and ambition.

And that was another cynical thought. Eleanor always soured him. But he liked Paul and David. They had never done him any wrong. They had generously taught him all they knew about winemaking and the business associated with it after his father had died...the summer he was sixteen.

So many questions remained unanswered about his father's death, but one thing was certain. Eleanor had profited by Ian Buchanan's sudden exit from this life. It had opened the door for her to push through the setting up of a family company that tied the two vineyards together.

'Rory?' Louise prompted, losing patience with his silence.

'Sure I'll go,' he agreed. 'It is the decent thing to do.'

In an indecent world, Rory didn't wish to be found wanting in decency. He had once been an idealist. Maybe he still was, underneath the disillusionments that fed his cynifjcism.

'They're probably planning a family gathering to welcome Eleanor home this evening,' Louise casually surmised. Then came the purpose. 'We should be included in it, Rory. I want to be there.'

He had no desire to witness the evidence of Eleanor's mortality, nor extend hypocritical sympathy to a woman he felt the greatest antipathy for.

'She's my great-aunt, Louise. Not my mother. Leave that to Paul and David and their wives.'

'We're family, too,' Louise quickly argued. 'As much family as anyone else. More so. It's your grandfather who's bringing her home, Rory.'

'She asked it of him. She didn't ask anything of us,' he pointed out.

'There's nothing wrong with using some initiative. Particularly in these circumstances.'

'I can't imagine we'd be wanted.'

'I won't be cut out of this, Rory. Eleanor always tries to cut us out.'

So this was what Louise's initial comment had been leading up to. Was it morbid curiosity or a need to be in on the action? He didn't care. It suited him to be cut out of Eleanor's company. He didn't want to be near her any more than she wanted to be near him. He knew why she cut him. He was an uncomfortable reminder of what she wanted to ignore.

He shook his head and stood up, ready to leave, not wanting any further discussion on Eleanor's homecoming. 'It's simply not appropriate for us to be there,' he said, moving down the table to kiss Louise goodbye.

'You're wrong, Rory. I want to see. We both need to see how she is, how much her illness has affected her. Besides, the whole family should be there, showing a solid front. It's a matter of respect.'

His smile was a twist of irony. A solid front?

What about his mad travesty of a mother? Never would she consort with the sinners of the world, and that was how she saw the family.

What of Tamara? She respected nothing and no-one. She would probably turn up with a jazz band, directing a jubilant chorus of 'When The Saints Come Marching In.' If she did, Rory might even be tempted to clap.

'Sorry, Louise. I don't respect Eleanor. I haven't for a long time. She might be the great matriarch of the family, but I will not scrape and bow to her. Not for you. Not for Paul. Not for David. Not for anyone.' He bent and kissed her on the lips. 'Thanks for this morning.'

Her lips tightened under his. He sensed her frustration. Sex hadn't softened him. Her plan hadn't worked. Too bad. Louise had to accept there were some things he wouldn't do, especially the things his soul revolted against. He was already mounting the steps to the gallery foyer when she called out to him.

'You're not thinking straight, Rory.'

He paused and looked at her mockingly. 'Enlighten me, then.'

Her face had hardened with determination. 'Whether you respect Eleanor or not, we must be there to greet her. It's the political move to make.'

Being a politician's daughter, Louise was very big on political correctness.

'She has power over our future, Rory,' she went on. 'She's still head of the company and will be until she dies. She directs the fortunes of both vineyards. When the status quo changes, Buchanan may not be yours to run. Have you thought of that?'

'A gathering of the vultures. Is that what you foresee, Louise?'

'Change usually brings a shifting of allegiances. Once Eleanor's iron fist is removed, who knows what will happen?'

'Don't fantasise, Louise. Paul has been groomed to take over from Eleanor as head of the family company. The job is his. David will run Traverner. Buchanan will remain in Buchanan hands. My hands. Let Eleanor die in peace. If she can.'

'Rory, you only have a twenty percent shareholding in Buchanan.'

'My grandfather has twenty-five percent, and my mother, who never votes, has twenty. How can it be taken away from us, Louise?'

'Eleanor will flex all the power she has now, Rory. We should be there to watch, to gauge her intentions.'

'And curry favour?'

'It can help. Let's prepare for unforeseen contingencies. It may give us some inkling of what Eleanor's inclinations are.'

He let his contempt for the idea show. 'I will not feed her ego by trying to ferret out her wishes.'

'Not wishes, Rory. Eleanor doesn't deal in wishes. She plans, plots and schemes. And we could be on the losing end of every one of them.'

'She's dying.'

'Eleanor will no more accept death readily than she's ever accepted anything that was not to her liking.'

'Let her do her worst.'

His jaw tightened as anger flooded through him. Curry favour with Eleanor? Never! Louise should know him better than that. And she damned well shouldn't have used her body to curry favour with him. He wanted sex freely given. He wanted what he'd once had with Tamara. He wanted love.

The anger twisted into futile bitterness. It was stupid and destructive to recall the Tamara he had loved. She simply wasn't there for him any more. She hadn't come back to him after their one summer together. Never would. She had made that clear to him in a thousand cutting ways.

Instead of Tamara he had Louise. His chosen wife. He swallowed his resentment. It was up to him to make the best of his marriage. He relaxed his jaw and tried a placating tone.

'You have nothing to worry about, Louise. I promise you Eleanor will not touch me or the management of Buchanan. Your future is safe.'

'But, Rory...'

'I'll call on Paul and David. Pay my respects to them. That's as far as I go.'

Louise clenched her hands as she watched him leave. No point in saying any more right now, but Rory's limited vision was intensely frustrating. Sooner or later she would have to widen it. She needed his co-operation to get where she wanted to be, and holding Buchanan was not the end she had in view. She wanted the lot.

It could be done with the shareholdings distributed the way they were. It was simply a matter of influencing the votes the right way. Her father was a consummate numbers man. She'd learnt from him how it was done.

Rory was a fool not to seize the opportunity to observe the family reaction to imminent change. Knowledge was power. Her father had taught her that, too. But Rory had left her no option but to discard that plan. It was just as well she hadn't revealed the rest of her strategy to him. Better to get results first. Then she would make her move and make him see.

In the end, Rory would do her will.

FOUR

Rory took savage satisfaction in ripping through the gears as he drove his Maserati down the hill to the junction that would take him to the Traverner winery. It was no longer a beautiful day. Louise's carping about coming changes had put a nasty dampener on it.

He slowed down for the corner and forced himself to proceed at a moderate speed. He passed a couple of the boutique wineries that had been established since the wine boom of the seventies. Changes, he thought, were a fact of life they'd all been living with for a long time. They were a challenge to meet. That was all.

The past twenty years had seen an enormous surge of interest and investment in the Hunter Valley. It was a far different place to what he had known as a child. There were now over fifty wineries, thirty restaurants, numerous antique shops, working artists' studios, galleries and other moneymaking enterprises that catered for a fast growing tourist industry currently attracting close to a million visitors a year.

Rory cast an expert eye over the rows of young vines in the fields on either side of the road. They looked vibrantly healthy with their new spring leaves. He loved this time of year, the budburst of green completely dispelling the barren look of winter. The quality of the crop of grapes would inevitably be determined by the weather in the four months ahead of them, but there was always something uplifting about spring.

Four months to the next vintage.

Four months for Eleanor to die.

He wondered how long would she hang onto life. No prognosis was absolutely certain. Rory couldn't imagine Eleanor giving up. She wouldn't give up anything. She might try to take over whatever she could, if for no other reason than to make more of her life before she died.

Other people might see her as the grand lady of the Hunter Valley vineyards, admired, respected, honoured by the nation with the title of dame for her achievements in the wine industry, but they didn't know her as Rory did.

Perhaps he should canvas where the rest of the younger generation stood on the future running of the family business, make sure there were no surprises coming from Paul and David. Not that he expected them, but it wouldn't hurt to open up an opportunity for easy communication.

Probably the reaction of the women would be more revealing than that of the men. David's wife, Sharon, had always been cowed by Eleanor. Not so Gabrielle, Paul's wife, who was very much her own person. She didn't compete with Eleanor, but she was certainly not submissive to her. What were their hidden hopes and dreams?

He carefully skirted a horse and sulky, someone out for a morning trot through the countryside in a historic vehicle. Such rides were popular with tourists. The pioneering families of the valley had always used sulkies to visit each other on Sundays. His grandfather had told him many stories about the Sunday gatherings at the Traverners' and the Selbys' and the Buchanans' in the old days.

But those days when the hand of friendship was readily offered in times of adversity were long gone. Rory was disagreeably reminded of it as he approached the former Selby property. He'd been friends with Janet Selby from earliest school days. He'd liked Jim Thurston, too, the man she'd married.

Poor Janet, driven to the wall with one disaster after another. It would always be a sore point to him that he'd failed to get the backing needed to pull her through the worst. She'd been left with next to nothing—no husband, no continuation of the family business, no clear future to pursue.

At least she had accepted the position he'd offered her as his personal secretary. And their friendship had been retained. It was something.

The house Max Vandelier had built came into view. It was an extraordinary mansion, modelled on what Max had considered a grand chateau, an appropriate rival to anything France had to offer in its famous winegrowing districts. Rory smiled over the affectation. In the laconic way Australians had, the valley people referred to it simply as the Big House.

Eleanor had ruled from it for the past twenty-five years, and Paul, as heir apparent, lived there with her, along with his wife and family. Rory suspected Gabrielle didn't like cohabiting with her mother-in-law, though she was always gracious about it.

David at least had had the good sense to get out from under his mother's thumb, building a house for himself and Sharon on the secondary Traverner property along the Broke Road.

Rory passed the lane that led to the old Traverner homestead down near the river and took the turning to Max's entrepreneurial brainchild, the winery with its state-of-the-art technology for winemaking, the underground cellars with their wine-tasting facilities to set the appropriate mood for tourists on a buying spree, the country hotel and convention centre with its French cuisine restaurant. Only Traverner labels were on the wine list.

Max hadn't missed a trick when it came to selling. His

penchant for international business and his desire for prestige had helped build the reputation and profitability of the Traverner vineyard to where it was second to none in New South Wales and a quality name around the world.

Yet what had his only child, Tamara, got out of it? Not much, if Eleanor had her way. Did Paul or David think differently? It wasn't any of Rory's business, yet no matter what Tamara had or hadn't done, she was still family. Without her father's timely investment, there would be no Traverner vineyard. Even if Eleanor didn't care to remember that, Paul and David should.

Rory brought the Maserati to a halt in the parking area outside the winery. He walked to the administrative section and stepped into the receptionist's office, where Cassie Deakin dealt efficiently with all enquiries. She was a bright young woman, invariably projecting a pleasant eagerness to be helpful. She smiled a warm welcome.

'What can I do for you, Mr. Buchanan?'

'Where can I find Paul, Cassie?'

'He hasn't come over from the Big House this morning,' she promptly replied.

'David?'

'He was here but he left a little while ago. He said he'd be at the Big House if anyone needed to contact him.'

'Thank you, Cassie.' He gave her an appreciative smile. 'Have a nice day.'

'Should I say you came by, Mr. Buchanan? Do you want to leave a message?'

'No need. I'll be seeing them. Thanks again.'

'Any time,' she called after him.

He left, completely unaware of Cassie Deakin's seething curiosity. Already the Traverner winery was abuzz with the news that the era of Dame Eleanor's rule was coming to an end. A prompt visit from the manager of Buchanan added another little fillip for more speculation.

Rory's thoughts were concentrated on Paul's and David's

absence from the winery. He wanted to know what was being discussed so privately at the Big House. It was Eleanor's seat of power. Perhaps Paul was preparing for an immediate takeover. A coup d'état. Which would be very interesting.

FIVE

Paul Traverner sat at his mother's desk in the library of the Big House. The personal documents she wanted taken to the old Traverner homestead lay in a neat pile in front of him. Her last will and testament was on top, contained in a manila folder neatly tied with red tape.

The door opened and David strolled in, not bothering with courtesies this morning. He looked at Paul ensconced behind his mother's desk. 'Trying out the throne?' he said flippantly.

'Don't be crass, David.' He rose from the chair in distaste.

'Oh, sit down, for God's sake!' Impatient. Anger simmering. 'You look good there. It's yours, isn't it? She's abdicating.'

'I wouldn't bet on that,' Paul said slowly, uncertain if this was a sudden burst of sibling rivalry. He didn't want it to be. He and David had always been close, supportive of each other.

'She'd be returning to the Big House if she meant to carry on,' David said dismissively, flinging himself into the leather chair he invariably used when reporting to their mother.

Paul moved around the desk and leaned against its front edge, eyeing his brother warily. 'I wouldn't assume anything, David,' he said, using a quiet, calm tone. 'Going to Dad's old home might be to see how *we* carry on and react, now that we know she's dying.'

'Christ!' It was the sound of helpless anguish. David covered his eyes with his hand. He bit his lips. His throat moved convulsively.

Paul straightened, discomforted by his brother's emotion, realising the anger had covered a deep distress. He didn't know how to handle it. Before he could make up his mind what to do, whether to reach out to David or not, the hand came down and dark wet eyes sought answers from him.

'Why doesn't she confide in us?' It was a cry of protest. 'You're coming up for forty, Paul. I'm thirty-eight. Yet she still treats us like children, making decisions without consulting us, giving orders. And through a third party at that,' he finished in bitter frustration.

'If you mean Uncle Frank...'

'Yes, I mean Uncle Frank. She wouldn't even talk to us about coming home. She used a go-between.'

He was hurt. Paul wondered if his mother had shown a softer side to his younger brother. David was built like Uncle Frank and favoured him in looks, more a Buchanan than a Traverner, while he...he was his father's son, expected to live up to a man he'd only known when he was a boy.

'They've always been close,' he murmured, wondering now if his uncle had taken his father's place in his mother's heart.

'We're her sons,' David argued. 'We've always done what she wanted.'

'Maybe that's where we erred, David.'

'Do you think she would have had it any other way?' He gave a dismissive snort and shook his head. 'I'll tell you something, Paul. Despite her edict about no visitors, I went to the hospital to see her. She had a security guard posted outside the door to her private room. He had orders to keep out all visitors except Uncle Frank. I made the guard check with her. She refused to see me.'

Paul gave his brother a commiserating smile. 'You're not alone. The same thing happened to me when I went.'

'You, too?'

'I wasn't required,' Paul said with some irony.

'Why? Why?' It was a need for understanding.

Paul had no answers. 'Maybe she wanted to see how we performed without her guiding hand.'

'That's ludicrous!' David scoffed. 'We're two of the most highly respected men in the business. We didn't earn our reputation by being her puppets.'

Paul shrugged. 'Don't ask me why. I've lost sight of how our mother's mind moves.'

'We've been the backbone of this vineyard for years. We're the ones who make it work. What more performance could she expect?'

'I don't know, but I figure something is expected. Uncle Frank passed on the message that she wants to review her will.'

Fear, fury, frustration. David's body language expressed them all as he argued their position. 'We can't be beaten over the head with that. If we don't run the show, whom has she got? No-one could do it better. We're the best!'

'Together we only own twenty percent of Traverner, David,' Paul reminded him.

'And fifteen percent of Buchanan,' David shot back. 'We've got a foot in both vineyards.'

'Not enough to take over by ourselves. We need both our mother's support and Uncle Frank's to keep control of the business. I don't know what's going on between them, what decisions have been made about the family company this past month...'

'Then maybe we should start making some decisions of our own,' David returned belligerently.

'We need an indication of how she's thinking,' Paul cautioned. 'Let's not act prematurely, David.'

'Well, be damned if I'll let her shut me out again. The time for her grande dame attitude is over. When she walks into Dad's old place this afternoon, I'll be there. And so will Sharon. I won't have my wife shut out, either.'

Paul nodded. 'Gabrielle and I had the same idea.'

'God damn it, they need us! We're the ones in the box seat. Uncle Frank is past it, and it's stupid for Mum to turn to him.'

'Let's sound them out first before acting on what could be false assumptions, David. There's no need for us to rush into taking stands. As you pointed out, we're the key men in the company, regardless of our limited shareholdings. For all intents and purposes, we're in an unassailable position.'

David ruminated on that for a while. Paul could see he was riven by uncertainties. David much preferred to have a clear line of attack laid out for him. To Paul's mind there was no clear line...yet.

'Do you love her, Paul?'

The soft question surprised him. They had never talked about deeply personal feelings. Nevertheless, it was a question he'd been pondering. The spectre of death prompted a reappraisal of their relationship.

Did he love his mother? He'd felt more and more estranged from her as the years of her marriage to Max Vandelier went on, and what had been an action to save his father's vineyard from being sold up turned into something more. And more. Even her second widowhood hadn't changed that. His life and David's were inextricably bound up in hers, yet they were not close to her. She was no longer a mother. She was a matriarch.

'I remember when Dad was alive,' he said sadly. 'It was different then.'

'I guess you remember more than I do.' David brooded

for a minute or two, then said, 'I didn't mind Max, you know. He was good to us, Paul.'

'Yes, he was. It wasn't Max's fault.'

He didn't explain what the fault was. David didn't ask him to.

The knock on the door startled them both.

'Come in,' Paul invited, expecting it to be one of the house staff wanting instructions. Gabrielle had gone down to the Traverner homestead with some of his mother's belongings.

Rory Buchanan entered. He swept them both with an apologetic smile. 'Sorry if I'm intruding on a private meeting.'

'No matter,' Paul demurred.

'I went by the winery to see you—'

'It's hardly business as usual today,' David cut in. Bitterness made his tone even more curt as he added, 'No doubt your grandfather informed you he's bringing his sister home this afternoon.'

'Don't take it out on Rory, David,' Paul chided. 'He has nothing to do with our mother's decisions. I doubt Uncle Frank has much to do with them, either.'

David grimaced and heaved himself out of his armchair. 'Sorry, Rory. It's all been a bit of a blow. No offence meant.'

'They've shared a long life together, David,' Rory said quietly. 'Your mother probably finds it easier to turn to my grandfather at this time.'

It was a fair observation, Paul thought.

'You may be right,' David conceded bleakly. He clapped Rory's shoulder in his usual bluff way and crossed the room to one of the long windows that looked out on the rose garden. 'It's a beautiful day. Pity we have to think about death.'

Paul made an apologetic gesture to Rory.

He nodded his understanding. He was only twenty-eight, twelve years younger than Paul, yet there was a maturity beyond his years in Rory Buchanan.

'I just dropped in to offer my sympathy and let you know

you can call on me for any help I could give over the next few months,' he said quietly. 'I remember all the help you gave me when Dad died. I know it's not the same, but...'

'Thank you, Rory. We appreciate it,' Paul answered for both of them.

'I'll leave you to it, then.' He glanced at David, whose back was still turned to them, nodded to Paul, then moved to the door. He'd opened it and was on the point of making his exit when he hesitated and looked back with an odd expression on his face. Almost belligerent. 'Has Tamara been contacted?'

Paul felt his face tighten. As if they didn't have disturbance enough. They didn't need Tamara playing her usual brand of havoc, not in these circumstances. Besides, why should Rory care about her? Tamara had turned on him viciously after their enforced separation. He was married to Louise now.

'Not as far as I know,' he answered coldly.

A derisive little smile flitted over Rory's lips. His yellowish eyes gleamed their message as clearly as though he'd spoken the words. *You don't want to know.*

Then he was gone, the door clicking decisively shut behind him.

SIX

Janet Thurston felt the unrest that was running rife through the Buchanan winery this morning. Several staff members had stopped her on her way to the administrative offices. Had she heard the news? Would it mean a restructuring of the company? Did she think there would be changes made in management?

Not at Buchanan, she had answered with more faith than certainty. The grim truth was death always brought changes. Who knew that better than herself?

Janet checked her watch again. Rory was over an hour late. He was never late for work in the morning. It was also unlike him not to give her the courtesy of a call to let her know what was happening. It had to be private family business. And what did that mean?

She couldn't help worrying. Rory had never been onside with his grandfather's sister. What if Eleanor tried to take Buchanan out of his hands before she died?

Though Louise would undoubtedly rush into action if there was any threat to her highly self-important world. Rory's wife always had her eye on the main chance, pouring on the charm for people who counted, who might be an asset to know. Anyone who didn't fit that criterion was ignored.

None of the staff at the Buchanan winery liked her. They were of no consequence to Louise, and she let them feel it. Unlike Rory, who took an interest in everyone in his employ.

Janet tried to concentrate on the computer print-out she should be checking. Her mind would not cooperate. Her thoughts kept revolving around Rory.

He was too good for Louise.

Far too good.

Janet wished he'd married someone...well, with more of a heart. Rory had such a big heart himself. All through their school days he'd stuck his neck out, fighting for underdogs, standing up for anyone being bullied. A natural-born leader. She couldn't recall a year when the boys hadn't voted him in as their class captain. She had been invariably selected by the girls.

It brought a smile, remembering the good-natured rivalry, the easy camaraderie between them. They'd had a lot of fun together in those days. The whimsical thought came to her that their liking for each other might even have developed into something else but for Tamara and Jim. Everything had changed for both of them the year they were sixteen.

Her smile widened as she recalled the knowing looks and teasing from their friends when she and Rory had partnered each other to the Year Ten Graduation Ball. The whole school took it as proof they were an item.

Nothing could have been further from the truth.

For months Rory had been more and more taken by Tamara Vandelier, his younger sister's best friend. And Jim had entered Janet's life, employed by her parents as the new winemaker at the vineyard.

Jim. She heaved a deep sigh as those heady days came back to her. Despite his being ten years older than her, she'd fallen madly in love with him. She'd always been in a fever of impatience to get home from school, just to be near him, talk to him, lend a hand with whatever he was doing. Blissful happiness.

Though not such a happy time for Rory, his affair with Tamara ending in a scandalous debacle, followed almost immediately by his father's death in an inexplicable plane crash. Then whatever had really happened to his younger sister, Cathy.

Janet shook her head. Rory would never talk about that, but the rift with his mother had occurred at the same time. He'd stopped talking about Tamara, too, after she'd comprehensively let him down. Impossible to really know the emotional scars he hid behind his cheerful exterior, but the Rory Janet knew should never have married Louise.

Impossible for her to ever become friends with that woman, though Rory remained a good friend. A tower of strength. Helping her and Jim through the unsettled period after her parents had been wiped out by a drunken driver. Then coming to their aid again and again when Jim had been struck down by that dreadful motor neurone disease.

Her heart clenched at the poignant memory of how much Jim had hated being trapped in a body that couldn't perform as he'd wanted it to. Such a terrible way for anyone to die, losing control, bit by bit.

But they'd had six great years of marriage before the disabilities started, she quickly reminded herself. Wonderful years. She'd been lucky. Not many people found the kind of love she and Jim had shared. They'd had many happy times, even during the most trying of circumstances.

Her one deep regret was having left it too late for Jim and her to have a baby. Probably for the best, really. She no longer had anything to pass on to a child. Except love.

'Pretty heavy wool-gathering, Janet.'

Her eyes snapped to the doorway. Rory gave her a teasing smile, instantly lifting her spirits.

'You're late,' she said, stating the obvious.

He winced. 'Eleanor comes home today.'

'Yes, I know. The winery is abuzz with the news.'

He nodded, readily accepting the rumour mill. 'I went by Traverner to see Paul and David.'

'How are they reacting?'

'I got the feeling both of them are in shock. Paul is riding it. David is shaken. Visibly upset.'

'There are a few people here who could do with some calming down,' she warned. 'Maybe a stroll around the staff would help settle things.'

He grinned. 'You're a good watchdog, Janet. Thanks. I'll do it right now.'

He left her smiling. He had a knack of doing that. If she didn't have this job to come to... She owed Rory a lot for his kindness, the pleasure of working with him. He might very well need a good watchdog in the coming months, with Eleanor settling her affairs before she departed this life.

It was something she could do for him. She knew how it felt to have everything taken away from her. She'd hate to see it happen to Rory.

SEVEN

Destroy...

The resolution pumped through Tamara Vandelier as she strode through the Buchanan winery. She wasn't aware of the startled looks she drew from members of the staff, the goggling stares that followed her. Her need to reach Rory gave her tunnel vision.

As usual, she left stunned males and envious women in her wake. Her perfectly proportioned body and beautiful, long legs were on provocative display. She wore a suede miniskirt, dyed fuchsia pink. It snugly outlined the curve of waist and hip and twitched to the cheeky sway of her bottom. The laced fastening at the front left a provocative slit open to just below her crotch. On her feet were strappy suede sandals of the same vivid shade of pink. An elasticised top shimmered around her breasts, moulding them in violet silk.

Her figure was breathtaking, but no less striking was the dynamic vitality of her face. Her glossy black hair was daringly cut into an asymmetrical bob, accentuating the straight black brows and deeply lidded, brilliant black eyes. Her patrician nose, high cheekbones and squarish jawline lent a charismatic strength, while her full-lipped mouth translated into sensual passion. None who saw her ever forgot Tamara Vandelier.

She paused at the open doorway of the executive secretary's office. Surprise caused a slight hiatus in her set course of action. 'Well, well, Janet Thurston,' she drawled, then drove straight to the question that had sliced into her mind. 'Has Rory made you a merry widow?'

'Tamara!' Shock was quickly swamped by a fiery blush as the meaning of the question struck home. 'He gave me this job after Jim died.'

'Convenient,' Tamara observed. 'He'd get more warmth from you than the cool and correct Louise.'

Janet had to be the direct antithesis to Louise. She and Rory had always been friends, and she was looking good, her wavy auburn hair styled into a lovely frame for a face that was highly attractive. She'd darkened her eyebrows and lashes, which lent emphasis to her bright hazel eyes. Her cute retroussé nose was still cute, and Tamara remembered envying her dimples when she smiled.

'It's not like that,' Janet protested. The hot colour staining her white skin flooded both her cheeks and neck. She was clearly mortified that anyone should so misinterpret her position here.

Tamara was satisfied. The decks were cleared. Although nothing would have stopped her, she preferred not to have any innocent wounded. Janet had always been decent to her. She could have been a complication. She wasn't.

'I'm going in to see Rory. Private family business, so no interruptions. Please make sure of that, Janet.'

'If it's what Rory wants,' she replied with defiant loyalty, refusing to be intimidated.

Tamara smiled. 'Believe me. It will be what he wants.'

Janet was dismissed from any further consideration. Tamara moved on, relentless in her purpose. She opened the door to Rory's office without preamble.

He looked up from the computer print-out spread across

his desk. The perfect image of the clean-cut executive, Tamara thought derisively, pristine white shirt, fashionable silk tie, handsome intelligent face, his skin a healthy, glowing tan, his streaky brown hair styled to a longish cut that showed off its springy thickness. Louise had turned him into a yuppie. On the surface. But Tamara knew what lay underneath. She knew Rory inside out.

She had taken him by surprise, as she intended to do. He wasn't expecting her, wasn't prepared for her, yet there was only the barest flicker of interest before the revealing, guarded look cleared his eyes of expression. Shield up, impervious to any more hurt from her.

She gave him her best smile. 'Hello, Rory.'

His self-discipline didn't crack. He ignored the smile and quietly inquired, 'What brings you to me, Tamara?'

The indifferent tone was as much a lie as the steady, blank eyes. It was his defence against the attraction she knew was still there. Tamara pushed the door shut behind her and went straight into attack.

'I want to make love to you, Rory.'

It shocked him into silence. Into stillness.

'Like we did before,' she added to push the old memories to the forefront of his mind.

She strolled forward, slowly enough to give him time to assess her stated intention. Her legs were bare. The front split of the tight little skirt gave her thighs easy movement. The stretch material of her top emphasised her braless breasts. She was obviously accessible. Tamara was in no mood for subtlety. There wasn't sufficient time. Blitzkrieg was the order of the day.

Rory's initial shock diminished to a wary watchfulness. He swung his chair to keep her in his line of vision as she rounded the shorter section of his L-shaped desk. He leaned back, effecting a relaxed posture, pretending a nonchalance he didn't feel.

'What do you aim to get out of this?'

She ran her hands over her body. 'You, Rory. Only you.'

He looked sceptical.

She hitched herself onto the desktop, lifted one leg, placed her foot on his thigh, rested her elbow on her knee and leaned forward, her hand cupping her chin. She used her eyes to project the lust she felt, openly, directly, unmistakably at such close quarters. She doubted Rory would perceive the difference between sexual lust and a lust for justice and revenge.

He was hooked. He didn't move away.

'The straps on that sandal are rubbing my toes. Please unbuckle it for me, Rory?'

She saw the questions in his eyes, the suspicion that this was no more than a kinky tease, the curiosity to know what she was up to, how far she intended to lead him on. She sensed his bone-deep resistance to being sucked in and left feeling a fool.

The slight pinch of his nostrils told her the smell had registered, the strong, musky woman smell that delivered its own message of arousal and excitement. He wasn't to know she had masturbated before entering the winery. The odour was enough to compel an interest, however reluctant it was.

His gaze flicked down and up her thighs. She briefly swung her legs apart.

She wore no panties. Not today. She had deliberately left them off for him.

He worked at ignoring the fact. He studied her sandal as though it presented a complex problem. It did.

In slow motion, tauntingly slow, he unbuckled the ankle strap, eased her foot out of the toe straps and placed the sandal on the desk beside her. Then he sat back, keeping his distance, not taking the bait, his eyes steadfastly fixed on hers, watching for the workings of her mind.

'Why now, Tamara?'

Because my bitch of a mother only has four months to live.

She slid her foot along his thigh and massaged his crotch with her toes. 'Remember how it was with us, Rory?'

'That was twelve years ago,' he stated dryly.

But he hadn't forgotten. No way had he forgotten. Any more than Tamara had. To her it had been the most beautiful summer of her life. And they had ruined it, her mother, his mother. Rory had let them do it. She would never forgive him for conceding to their hypocrisy.

'I was your first lover,' she recalled, hoping the memory would cut deeply.

'There have been a lot since then,' he reminded her, 'for you.' He could not contain the bitterness he felt about her rejection of his fidelity in favour of a promiscuous sampling of other lovers, deliberately flaunted in front of him.

'You're the one I remembered.'

'Bullshit!'

'You always believed the people you shouldn't have believed, Rory, and overlooked the obvious.'

'There is no-one more obvious than you, Tamara. In every damned thing you've done.' His mouth twisted in ironic appreciation. 'Though I must admit to some surprise with this little initiative. I thought if you had ever wanted to get even for your alleged grievances against me, you would have chosen my wedding day.'

She tinkled a light laugh. 'Louise wasn't worth the effort.' She looked deeply into Rory's eyes. They both knew whatever qualities Louise might or might not have, she could never fulfil the promise Tamara possessed.

'She's a good wife. A great wife,' Rory insisted in Louise's defence.

'I'm sure she is,' Tamara said dismissively.

She felt his cock stir. He didn't move away. He didn't stop what she was doing to him. 'I want to feel what I felt when we were lovers,' she said, driving straight to the need no-one else had ever fulfilled.

'You were only fourteen.'

'Eleanor's catchcry,' she mocked. 'How did she convince you we were committing the crime of the century, Rory? How did she make it wrong to you when you know it was right between us? More right than anything before or since.'

That got to him. His jaw tightened.

'Or did your mother muddle your mind with her raving about sin? Did you end up believing what we did and felt together was dirty and sinful, Rory? That we'd burn in hell-fire for—what was her phrase? Rutting like animals?'

'No!' The negative exploded from him, and he jerked his head aside in violent rejection of his mother's perverted form of religion.

For a moment, Tamara lost it, remembering how they had been parted, Irene almost frothing at the mouth as she revelled in shrieking 'Slut!' and 'Whore!' at Tamara, Eleanor flaying Rory for having sex with a minor, then Ian and Uncle Frank brought into the act, the heavyweights to back up the pseudo-maternal monsters.

She dug her toes in under Rory's penis, stroking his testicles, viciously wanting him to remember what had preceded the condemnation scene so artfully and effectively orchestrated by Eleanor. 'Only you can satisfy me, Rory,' she purred at him.

His thighs tensed. His eyes blazed a volatile mixture of desire and hatred. Then very deliberately he shook his head. 'You put paid to our belonging together a long time ago.'

Belonging together was an impossible dream, but if Rory still hankered for it, Tamara had no compunction in dangling it in front of him. 'I didn't believe you had the guts to take me on for better or for worse, Rory. I've changed my mind.'

'Since when?'

'Last night.'

He rolled his eyes at her perverse decision-making. 'I'm married, Tamara.'

'You chose her as a contrast to me in every way. Didn't you, Rory?' she mocked.

He didn't deny it. The cool, elegant, convention-bound blonde he had married could not have presented a more opposite image to Tamara.

She pushed the point home. 'As a rejection of me.'

'Getting married was a rejection of you,' he corrected.

'No. Picking your wife the way you did was the rejection.'

'Did you expect me to remain in love with you? Did you expect me to love Tamara, the tramp? Tamara, the tease? Tamara, the little raver who flaunted her freedom from any normal social constraints?'

He reeled off his offensive list with a fine contempt that was meant to sting, to get under her skin as she got under his. Tamara had grown enough armour to deflect those arrows, well aware she had supplied them herself rather than give her mother the satisfaction of doing it. She couldn't resist giving them a different twist.

'Did I do those things, or were they forced upon me?'

He didn't buy that, but the emission of old pus from old wounds did not continue. 'You made it impossible to resurrect what we had together,' he said flatly. 'You made it impossible for me to respect you. It's too late to change your mind now, Tamara.'

Still he didn't move away from what she was doing. It was certainly possible to resurrect something, whether he wanted to acknowledge it or not. He was fully erect. Was he secretly enjoying what she was doing or scorning the result of her foreplay?

'Your wife doesn't do for you what she should, Rory,' she tested.

'You can get what you want from any number of men, Tamara. Why pick on me?' He shrugged, feigning indifference again. 'I'm just another cock to you. At least my wife considers me more than that.'

Tamara laughed. 'Sure she does. You were a good catch,

Rory. Heir to the Buchanan vineyard. Many people would find compensation in the lifestyle you have to offer.'

Her mockery hit the mark. 'I don't give a damn what you think!'

'Louise is such a fitting wife for you with all her charming airs and graces. Almost a carbon copy of my esteemed mother, Dame Eleanor.'

She couldn't stop the flare of hatred, but it didn't matter that he saw it in her eyes. It gave him pause for thought. All of it wrong, she thought cynically.

Rory Buchanan would die without ever knowing the truth, or why events had turned out the way they did. Tamara felt nothing towards Louise Buchanan, because she was nothing. A non-person was incapable of inciting envy or jealousy or hatred. Contempt, yes, for seeing Eleanor Vandelier as a model to copy. Dame Eleanor Buchanan Traverner Vandelier was a liar and a cheat and a ruthless, manipulating bitch, devoid of feeling and soul.

Destroy.

Four months to live. Four months to die. And die Eleanor would, over and over again before mortality gave her release. The respect, the esteem, the admiration—they were all crap. The reckoning was long overdue. Eleanor was going to face every hidden turd and pay for it.

'All these years you've known I wanted you,' Rory said, an edge of bitter accusation in his voice. 'You've enjoyed parading your lovers under my nose. You've enjoyed tormenting me with your body. So what's the problem, Tamara? It doesn't amuse you any more? You want to raise the stakes? Break up my marriage? Does that have a particularly piquant appeal?'

'Who stopped it between us, Rory?' she countered.

'You know who,' he answered tersely. 'It had to stop once our parents found out. I was sixteen. You were only fourteen.'

'It was you who stopped it. I still came to you. You turned

me away.' Giving her up to his father and Eleanor, and nothing could ever be the same again after that.

'For your sake, Tamara. To carry it on would have only caused more and more trouble,' he argued. 'You had school to finish. I had nothing to offer you by way of a life together. We had to wait.'

'What about the promises you made to me that summer? To make a life of our own somewhere...'

'They were unrealistic. You know it.'

Yes, she knew it. But he'd offered her a dream, let her taste it, feel it, made her believe in it, then dropped it into a freeze tank when the crunch came. His promises were unrealistic, because it didn't suit him to deliver on them. He had chosen to lose her rather than lose his place in his world. Let him face that reality for once!

'I loved you, Rory. You put what our parents thought ahead of me. You put your future with this vineyard ahead of me.'

'It was *for* you, dammit!'

'No. You listened to them and not to me. You turned me away when I needed you most.'

His lips compressed, refusing to justify what he'd done any further, rejecting the guilt she was laying on him, satisfied he had acted honourably and she was the one who had lain waste what they had once shared.

Tamara barely contained the urge to slap him. He had no idea what she had been forced into at the end of that summer while he retreated behind his shield of decency, blocking her out of his life. His ignorance did not excuse him. He'd denied her any access to his mind and heart. He'd cut her adrift to swim or sink alone. The need to prick his blind sense of rightness was overpowering.

'I was pregnant, you know,' she tossed at him.

'What?'

That spun his brain around. He stared at her in consternation, his composure absolutely smashed.

She shrugged. 'Just kidding.'

He shook his head, punch-drunk, not knowing whether to believe her or not.

'Would it have made any difference?' she pushed, deriving intense satisfaction from his inner turmoil. Let him have a taste of what she'd been through. 'Would you have stood by me, Rory, or gone along with a discreet abortion?'

He looked appalled, distressed, completely knocked off his perch of purity. 'Was that kept from me, Tamara?' he asked, struggling for control.

'You didn't answer my question.'

'I would've fought them all for our child,' he cried.

It was what she wanted to hear. It confirmed her reading of Rory's character and strengthened her future course immeasurably. Yet it knifed into the sense of betrayal he had left her with all those years ago.

'For a child of yours, but not for me,' she said in quiet, deadly judgment. The tears came easily, welling into her eyes. 'There was no child for you to fight for, Rory, but if you'd really loved me...'

Relief. Anger at having been stirred. 'I've explained, dammit! Why couldn't you have waited?'

His shield was well and truly down now. He was still vulnerable to her. She pushed her advantage. 'You're the only one I ever loved.'

He exploded. 'Come off it, Tamara! You were incredibly precocious. You knew more than women double your age. Emotionally—'

'Emotionally I was an adult.'

He looked away, disturbed by her tears, not wanting to be disturbed by the distress in them.

She dropped her foot from his crotch, slid off the desk and knelt between his thighs. 'I'll show you how I loved you.'

He grabbed her hand as she pulled on his fly zipper. 'No!'

She raised shiny wet eyes. 'I want to. Let me, Rory.'

'You can't break my marriage,' he said desperately. 'Louise knows about us, about what happened.'

'Fuck Louise! You should have fought for me!' she claimed with a passion that rocked him.

His grip on her hand loosened. The moment of indecision was his downfall. Tamara wasted no time in releasing his erection and taking him in her mouth.

In her mind burned one thought.

Destroy.

EIGHT

Rory Buchanan was hopelessly torn by conscience, by the physical need Tamara incited, by hurts that had never healed, by the sense of loss he had tried to fill with his marriage to Louise.

He shouldn't be letting this happen. It was wrong. He believed in fidelity, in loyalty, yet he couldn't bring himself to pull Tamara's head away from him. Had he wronged her, or was she simply screwing him every which way she could?

The tears in her eyes... Perhaps they were calculated tears. He didn't want to accept the image of a deeply scarred heart hidden under her brutal toughness. Especially not if he'd done the wounding.

Rory gripped the armrests of his chair hard. Her tongue licked exquisite pleasure. Memories swirled over the jangle of guilt in his mind. The first time she had taken him like this, he had ejaculated almost immediately. He hadn't expected it. He hadn't known how to control anything that summer he was sixteen.

Tamara... No girl or woman had ever matched what she had shared with him, what she was doing now. She made him feel unique. Still made him feel unique, although there was no evidence to support it.

He had revelled in every new adventure with her, most of

it sexual, lived in anticipation of the next and the next, thought of nothing else, dreamed of nothing else. Every minute of every day was spent longing to be with Tamara again. He had been obsessed with her, possessed by her, worshipped her, loved her with all the passion of his youth...and lost her out of his own innate sense of rightness and decency.

That was what she had told him. That was what she had said. Why didn't she realise how impossible it had all become after Eleanor had caught them making love? And turned it into a public scandal with her show of outrage.

In hindsight, it had been blindly reckless of them to do what they did that night. Too many watching eyes. All the valley people had been at the Big House for the end of vintage party. They shouldn't have danced together, inciting each other, playing too openly with the sexual excitement that always sizzled between them. When Tamara suggested they slip away, he'd been on fire for her.

They'd had wild sex. Tamara was still straddling him, stoking him for a second climax, her bodice unbuttoned, breasts dangling naked above him as he moved his mouth from one to the other, sucking to drive her as crazy as she drove him, when Eleanor walked in on them and all hell broke loose.

Cathy had told him Tamara had gone to his home again and again the following week, trying to see him, turned away by his parents. Naturally sympathetic to her friend, Cathy had broken the edict of silence, sneaking out to let Tamara know he was at his grandfather's place.

They'd had one meeting. He'd done his best to explain why they had to wait. Then his father had come and taken Tamara back to Eleanor. She'd been crying, pleading, calling him a coward...and he'd been torn in two, drawn to go after her, held back by his father's censure and his grandfather's commonsense advice.

The very next day his father had made some fatal error

and flown his plane into a hill. Suddenly there were family responsibilities that couldn't be thrown aside. Surely that was evident to anyone.

Yet never again had Tamara favoured him with her brilliant, open smile or her wild, joyful zest in living. That was reserved for others, and she paraded them briefly in front of him, one after the other, until he could bear it no longer. He had cut himself loose from her chains, too miserable to care how happy she was with another.

Scorched earth. Nothing left. No tree, no fruit, no flower.

As young as he was, he would have kept his promises if she had stayed true to the love they had declared to one another that summer. If she had waited as he asked her to.

She wouldn't wait.

She was lying about having loved him.

So why was he letting her take him like this?

It was wrong, wrong...

But her mouth still promised all the pleasures a woman could give a man, the swirl of her tongue, the quick lapping strokes, the gentle sucking. He closed his eyes, concentrating on the sensations she aroused. He had tried to teach Louise how to do it right. She never did. Didn't want to. Didn't like it. She readily accepted the way he pleased her, but... It still didn't excuse him from cheating on her.

He should have stopped Tamara. Even now...

No, he needed, wanted...

His body tensed. She was taking his full shaft in her mouth and throat, moving it in and out, fast and hot. He sucked in a quick breath, felt his buttocks clench, the automatic pelvis thrust, couldn't stop the twitch of muscular spasms as the excitement built, straining for release.

It came, jerking into the moist, warm cavern of her mouth. He shuddered as she sucked it from him, intensifying the sheer physical pleasure of being taken with total completion. No withdrawal at climax. Not from Tamara. She went all the way. She made him feel as though she loved every last drop of him.

It made him wish he could wipe out the last twelve years of her life. He wanted her unsoiled, unspoiled, untainted, untouched. He wanted to accept what she gave him without cynicism. He wanted to hold her in his arms and know she was his with all the carefree confidence of that summer so long ago, when youth seemed ageless and a lifetime could be lived in the span of a day.

She looked up and caught him staring at her with the passionate intensity of all the inner turmoil she aroused in him. She rubbed his limp penis across her cheek. 'There never has been anyone like you, Rory,' she said huskily.

His heart clenched against such blatantly deceptive stroking. 'Don't lie to me, Tamara.'

'You were the one.'

'Then why did you...' He clamped his mouth shut. It was one of her damnable games. Like suggesting she'd been pregnant. To let himself be drawn in by it was asking for trouble he didn't need. Tamara and trouble went hand in hand. They were synonyms. It was time to distance himself again.

'I loved you, Rory.'

He stared at her, grimly silent, hating himself for being vulnerable to those words, hating her for uttering them when they could no longer mean anything.

She carefully tucked his penis in his pants and did up his zip. He unlatched a hand from the armrest and gently stroked her glossy black hair, stirred into touching her with the tenderness of feeling she always forced him to suppress. She was bad. She was a wanton, soulless bitch. He wished it could be different.

She rested her head against his thigh. He kept on stroking, reluctant to end the intimacy, however useless it was.

'You make me feel good,' she said, her voice a low, sensual throb.

'You're the greatest actress never to go on the stage,' he derided, letting her know belief wasn't bought with a few cheap words. Not with him.

She tilted her head back, her thick eyelashes half veiling her eyes. 'No-one else ever made me feel good. Only you, Rory.'

'Why?' he asked, wanting it to be true, not wanting to hear another lie.

She paused to consider, her head lowering. 'You made me feel wonderful and beautiful. Inside and out.' She cupped her hand possessively over his genitals. 'You gave me dreams instead of reality.'

His stomach contracted. She knew what buttons to press to get to him, both physically and emotionally. Yet it was true, what she said. There had been dreams, beautiful dreams.

It was also a lie. He knew it. It didn't take twelve years of bed-hopping to know there was only one person who was special to one's life. He withdrew his hand from her hair, sighing his frustration with the treacherous volatility of her responses and reactions.

She lifted her head.

Her face looked so open to him. That was a lie, too. She kept her secrets well. Not even in that summer of intimacy had she shared everything with him. What had tantalised him then formed a grim challenge in his mind now. He needed to reduce her power over him.

'I never asked you before, Tamara.' He'd been too intoxicated by what she gave him to care. But it had to be an essential factor, at least an answer of some sort, and the burning need to wrest some control from her formed a blunt demand. 'Who was your first lover?'

A shiver ran through her body.

He scoured her eyes for the truth, and a shutter came down over her face. Her eyes didn't flinch from his, but they dulled into a flat black. 'You were, in spirit,' she said tonelessly. 'You were the only one who mattered. I needed you.'

No, he couldn't let her get away with an emotional appeal. The sexual experience she had brought to that summer had been beyond the wildest imaginings of his teenage mind. Was still beyond the capacity of most people to even begin to embrace, to know or to learn.

'Who took your virginity?' he bored on, rejecting her evasion, searching for what was real and what wasn't. The hurt she had given him went too deep to ignore.

'You wouldn't want to know.' With an abruptly dismissive gesture she got to her feet, sat on his desk, picked up her sandal and swung away from him to put it on.

Determination blazed through Rory. He would not be dismissed. 'I was blamed for it, Tamara, and I took the blame. I didn't try to justify my so-called crime by telling anyone you weren't a virgin, but I sure as hell want to know who gave you the experience you had.'

Her eyes carved him up with contempt. 'Did you justify it to yourself because you weren't the first? It doesn't matter because she's done it before? Nothing to do with loving each other, Rory?'

'It didn't matter then,' he returned hotly. 'I thought I was special to you. But with all that followed, it made me feel like one of a string.'

'I've told you. You were one of a kind,' she said coolly.

She didn't care about his feelings, except for twisting them to her purpose. 'If there is one shred of truth in what you've said today, you'll tell me who taught you about sex.'

'No.' She glowered at him over her bent knee as she did up the buckle. 'You've made me remember things I'd forgotten, Rory. They're better left unremembered.'

'Like it was better you left me alone until after I married?' he shot at her, frustrated by her intransigence in denying him any real substance to work with.

'Louise is an irrelevancy.'

'To you. Not to me.' He wanted to savage her as she savaged him. 'Not even the best blow job in the world can snuff my wife out of existence, Tamara. You're not good enough. You can't turn my brains to mush.'

Painfully aware he had fallen victim to a dangerous cocktail of emotional and sexual stimulation, he fought to minimise its effect. She'd lost any right to exploit everything there'd ever been between them. As for dismissing the life she had left him to as if it were nothing, Rory couldn't swallow that.

It wasn't nothing and it wasn't irrelevant. It had been his salvation after what she'd done to him, and he wasn't about to let her enjoy some miserable triumph over him and Louise.

'I used you this afternoon. You didn't use me. I took what you had to offer, and I despise you for what you are,' he hurled at her.

'Don't be petty, Rory. We both know we go beyond that.'

Her overriding confidence incensed him further. 'You've given every one of us a reason to hate you. Your mother, your brothers, my wife, my mother. We all hate you, Tamara. Doesn't that mean anything to you?'

'Yes. It means that none of you can forget me.'

'You're beyond reason and reasonableness. You can't be reached.'

Her black eyes challenged him with a knowingness that reduced his outburst to the angry bleatings of a child who understood nothing. 'You justify what you did to me with hate,' she said matter-of-factly. 'My mother justifies what she did to me with hate. My favoured half-brothers, Paul and David, benefit by what was done on their behalf, and they hate me, too. Because there is no justification.'

He shook his head, not comprehending the pattern she was laying out for him. 'You could have been different.'

'I'm not.' She smiled at him provocatively. 'I'm going to the beach house. I'll be there for you and only for you. But don't keep me waiting long, Rory. It's our last chance to be together.'

'No. I won't come, Tamara.'

'Bring your hatred and love with you.'

'Don't play me for a fool.'

'I'm not playing.'

'I'm no longer an innocent boy you can seduce.'

'At least you had the pleasure of innocence,' she mocked.

'Then tell me who took yours from you!'

Her eyes continued to mock, as though his ignorance was his fault. He was sick of what she was doing to him. 'I was a game to you, Tamara,' he said flatly. 'It's still a game.'

'No. What you did to me...'

'Wasn't fresh and new to you then. Any more than it is now.'

Lies! He would not be moved. Not by her tears. Not by her sexual power. Not by the promise she held out to him. She was too damned late with all of it.

NINE

Tamara saw the shift towards entrenched rejection. Rory's eyes snapped with anger, pride, determination. The wounded tiger lashing out, defying capture.

She slid off the desk. She had the means to destroy Rory Buchanan. It was tempting to fling it in his face, smash the whole facade of lies on which his life was built. But he was turning away from her again, and she needed him for her plan to work. She had to deliver the coup de grâce that would put him onside with her.

He wanted innocence. She almost laughed. There'd been no place or time in her life for innocence. Bewilderment, yes. Hurt, yes. And the need to know why, which carved a path through any innocence she might have had. No real childhood. No girlhood, either. She'd been turned into a woman before she realised what it meant. Robbed, cheated, spurned.

Compared to her mother, Rory was an innocent in the rejection stakes. He wanted to claw wounds on her, but he had nothing to hurt her with. She had the claw that would scour past his self-righteous defences. She crossed her arms as though protecting her heart, guarding an inner vulnerability that was long gone. But she evoked it for him, needing to break down his resistance and draw him to her.

'Truth is a two-edged sword, Rory. It cuts both ways.'

He was immersed in thoughts of his own. He looked at her with blank incomprehension.

'You wanted to know who my first lover was. The one before you. There was only one.'

She had his full attention now. His eyes were riveted on hers, hungry for the morsel of knowledge that would choke him and leave him sickened to his very soul.

'It was my father. Who wasn't loved by Eleanor. He started teaching me how best to love him when I was nine years old.'

She saw the shock on his face. She had outgrown the trauma of those early years in her life. She felt she had. None of it touched her. She didn't allow it to touch her. She had crushed the feelings that left her defenceless. When she was so inured against having any painful emotions, she wondered why it was so easy to summon tears.

They fell of their own accord. She let them. They served her purpose, to gain Rory as an ally against her mother. Yet suddenly, perversely, she wanted more than that from him. It was weak to yearn for what could never be, weak to let the idea tap at her heart.

But it did. The emptiness of her life swirled through her. She'd never known what mother love was like. Eleanor shunning her, ignoring her, cutting her off from sharing any sense of any family with her half-brothers. Paul's and David's self-interest had let her do it. They hadn't cared. No sibling love for the cuckoo in the Traverner nest. And her father...her father... Eleanor's puppet to his grave. He had let that calculating bitch do it, too, get away with the murder of love.

Then Rory. He was no better than the others, letting Eleanor win. He had no right to demand anything of her. It was she who was owed, and she was calling in the debts. If he gave away what she'd said, if he confronted Eleanor by himself... No! Tamara needed him on her side.

'So help me God, Rory! If you ever repeat that to anyone, I'll kill you.'

The words spilled out, breaking from something inside her that had slipped from her control. She meant those words. A murderous hatred swarmed into her mind, burning, cauterising the need she would not concede to. Rory had better do what she wanted. He'd better perform. She'd answered him.

She didn't give him time to question further. She strode away from him, straight for the door.

'Christ!'

She heard him rise from his chair. She didn't look back. There was no point. If the hook wasn't baited now it never would be. She opened the door.

'Wait!'

She didn't.

She closed the office door with a slam to punctuate her displeasure and distress at having been forced to the revelation, forced by feelings she didn't want to examine.

She walked out of the winery quickly, leaving Rory to his guilt. He would come after her. He would need to know more. She would tell him, bit by bit, drawing him into doing what she wanted.

They would all pay for what had been done to her. She climbed into her Porsche and slammed its door shut. She was in a door-slamming mood. She revved the engine hard, reversed with a biting of tyres, scything through the gravel, sending it flying.

Rory would come after her.

He had to.

She had just destroyed any peace of mind he might have attained over the past twelve years.

TEN

Rory made it to the parking lot before Tamara left it. As she reversed the Porsche, he sprinted to the only exit in order to block the way out. It didn't occur to him that his actions were ill-considered, damaging to him and to Louise, fuel for gossip amongst his employees. He didn't think of all the startled eyes following them, watching what was being enacted in full view of everyone at the winery. Instinct drove him, blind, heart-pumping, compelling.

Tamara was hurt.

He had to help, protect, comfort. He had to confront and mend what had been done to her. He couldn't let her go. He couldn't let her be alone. If only he'd known, how it would have changed things. He had judged her, condemned her. He'd done everything wrong, turning his back on her when she'd needed him most. He should have talked, listened, understood.

Nausea chewed his stomach. Max Vandelier. Her own father! Who would have believed it? Yet Rory did. It made sense of what he had only vaguely identified before. He believed it.

The wheels of the Porsche were still spinning in reverse when she slammed the gearstick into first and accelerated towards him. Her face seemed to leap at him through the windscreen, vividly imprinting itself on his mind, black eyes blazing wildly, untamed and untameable, her mouth stretched into a teeth-gritting grimace.

She drove the Porsche straight at him.

Death, destruction... They shimmered from her and impaled him where he stood. He saw the violence of being violated, a child consumed by passions, heedless of any consequences, and he knew he formed a powerful focus for all she felt. He found himself gripped by an exhilarating wildness, not caring if she ran him down, daring her to do it. If that was her need, let her take his life.

He didn't try to leap aside. He made no move to avoid the collision. He absorbed the menace and the hatred. He stood firm when commonsense and self-preservation dictated otherwise. It was her choice to do with him what she willed, and he exulted in a surge of fearlessness, challenging her ferocity with a steadfastness he wouldn't let her shake. He felt more alive than he had for twelve long years of sterile summers, his whole being once again inextricably woven into the vibrant tapestry of her life.

The Porsche went past the point of no return. Hitting him was inevitable. Rory's mind registered the fact, but he felt removed from it, as though he had shifted to the place in Tamara's mind that knew no boundaries, no rules, no regulations. Ultimate freedom.

With the flick of a wrist, she placed the car in a skidding broadside. The bonnet dipped under heavy breaking. The back offside wheel ploughed towards the iron stanchion used to chain the parking lot at night. He wondered if she meant to wipe out the back end of the car to avoid hitting him.

There was no reprieve.

With pinpoint accuracy she went to the opposite lock, hand over hand on the wheel. Everything seemed to be happening in slow motion. He watched in fascination as the bonnet of the car inexorably swung towards him.

When the impact came, most of the speed had been scrubbed from the Porsche, but the force of the front guard hitting him was still surprising—sharp, painful, shattering reality. The communion of spirit had soared beyond everything physical.

He was flung into the air and descended heavily on the bonnet. His momentum carried him diagonally across it as the car continued to straighten. He rolled topsy-turvy towards her windscreen. There was nothing to hold onto, nothing to impede his progress. He slithered the last two feet. He went past her, ending up in the air, feet forward, his hands scrambling for some purchase. The windscreen wiper. He grasped it. It wrenched away in his hand.

Incredibly he landed on his feet, staggering under the impetus of his chaotic ride. Somehow he found the balance to whip around and face the driver's side window. The Porsche had halted. Her window was fully down.

'I knew you wouldn't hurt me,' he cried in a rush of giddy triumph.

There was no shock on her face, no apology, no regret. She stared at him, weighing his reaction, her black eyes remorseless and intensely penetrating. 'Don't tempt me,' she warned. 'One day I might.'

He shook his head, buoyed by a confidence that nothing could erode. 'We shared too much.'

'It wasn't the past that made me spare you, Rory.'

'What was it, then?'

'Deep down inside your guts, you approve of me.'

'Yes,' he agreed with mad fervour.

'I need you with me.'

'For what purpose?'

'To be the father of my child.'

The sheer audacity of it took Rory's breath away. The child they hadn't had. The bond that might have changed everything twelve years ago. For her to think of such a thing now... It stunned him. Yet he didn't doubt she would proceed with such an intention, if that indeed was her intention.

'Why choose me?' he asked.

'You're a true hero.' Her smile mocked. Her eyes challenged.

'You've just finished telling me I let you down.'

'Ah, but you'd never let our child down, would you, Rory?' She thrummed the engine. 'I'll be at the beach house. If you're going to get me pregnant, you haven't got much time. It's measured in days.'

She released the clutch on a roar of revolutions and gunned the Porsche up the long, poplar-lined driveway.

Rory looked at the broken windscreen wiper in his hand. Every worker in the place must have seen what had just happened. There would be hell to pay with Louise. She couldn't be expected to understand this. He didn't know that he understood. It didn't seem to matter.

Whatever was happening was way outside his experience. Why would Tamara want to have a baby? He couldn't think of anyone, anywhere, who would be less inclined to want to be a mother. It was against her nature, her way of life, her attitudes, her principles.

There never had been anything maternal about Tamara. The image of her doting over a child in her arms was unbelievable. Yet in a way it wasn't. Tamara would or could be more protective than a lioness with a favourite cub. Whatever she did would be complete, focused and obsessive. The commitment would go beyond protection and doting and nurturing. It would constitute a universe entire unto itself.

If there were to be a child... He felt the ache and the need and the longing in his loins to be the father. No other man. No-one would look after them as well as he would. He was different from the others. He'd put his life on the line for her.

'Rory? Do you need help?'

The anxious question broke into his deep reverie. A light

touch on his arm begged his attention. Reluctantly he turned his head and met the white-faced concern of Janet Thurston. The encounter with Tamara must have sharpened his senses. He'd never noticed Janet had freckles. Natural enough with the fair skin that went with her auburn hair. He simply hadn't seen them so markedly before.

'I'm fine, Janet.'

'Your shoulder.'

He glanced down. His sleeve was torn from its shoulder seam. His flesh was already discolouring. 'It's nothing,' he demurred.

'She could have killed you.'

The fierce cry surprised him with its strength of feeling. Shock, he thought, automatically dismissing it. 'Don't make a fuss.'

'She was insane.'

'No.'

'But—'

'Go back inside, Janet.'

She stood her ground, a slender little figure, her eyes wide. Her pretty, cheerful face was bereft of its customary good humour. It was set with determination. 'I think I should drive you to a doctor.'

'Don't argue with me.' He was terse, not wanting to be held up by her or anyone else. He hobbled around her, heading for his car.

He felt pain, knew it would be worse when the bruising from the impact started to come out. Yet there was a pleasure in the pain. It was a catharsis, a cleansing of wide, gaping wounds, a cauterising of a haemorrhage that had never ceased.

'Where shall I say you are? If anyone asks?' Janet called after him.

He ignored the question, didn't want to think about it, didn't care. Having reached his car he unlocked the door and slid into the driver's seat. The compelling need to find out what was going on, what was really happening in Tamara's mind, wiped out everything else. He couldn't let her go. Not without knowing. The engine kicked into roaring life. He wouldn't be far behind Tamara. His Maserati had as much horsepower as her Porsche.

Gearstick slammed into reverse, foot hard on the pedal, wheels digging into the gravel as he braked to swing the car to the exit. He caught a glimpse of Janet, watching his departure. Her hands were clenched. There was a look of intense helplessness about her. Loneliness. Ignoring her was probably the cause. He didn't normally brush people off.

He knew he should go back to the office. But Janet could handle most things. For today, he didn't give a damn what happened and who was the boss.

Tamara was the only essential. Rory slammed the accelerator to the floor. There was a lunacy to what was happening that somehow made sense. He didn't know how or why. The compulsion ran too deep.

The truth was he'd never really stopped thinking about her, caring, wanting the girl he'd known. Now that she had ripped the door to the past open, he didn't want it shut again.

ELEVEN

Max! The horror of what Tamara had told him seized Rory's mind again as he shot down the long avenue of poplars leading out of the winery.

Had Eleanor known and turned a blind eye to it? Her marriage to Max Vandelier had been an arrangement for money. What kind of wife had she been to him? What kind of mother to Tamara? For Max to have used his own daughter—only nine years old!—to satisfy his sexual needs was one hell of a result.

Rory recoiled from the repugnant image. It didn't fit his memory of Max Vandelier, a big, booming extrovert of a man, genial, generous...which made Tamara's revelation all the more sickening. But it answered so much, Rory had to accept it was true.

He slowed as he reached the end of the poplar trees and turned out of the gateway, then stamped on the accelerator again. The road to Cessnock stretched ahead. Beyond the town the expressway to Sydney would make a smooth trip to the Gosford turn-off. Even so, Pearl Beach was two hours away. He didn't expect to catch Tamara. She was an expert driver in a fast car, but he would arrive directly behind her.

His mind churned with flashes of the past as he sped after her. He hadn't taken much notice of Tamara in her growing-up years. She was Cathy's friend, two years younger than him. Apart from doing the odd, brotherly act for them when asked, he'd been busy with his own circle of friends.

It was Max's death that had jolted him into looking at Tamara differently. Or rather, Max's funeral. That was when it had started, coming across Cathy and Tamara hiding in the garden at the Big House, Cathy trying to comfort her friend, who was in floods of tears.

'Can you help, Rory?' Cathy had pleaded.

He'd thought it was grief, at first, but it had been more than that when he'd persuaded Tamara to talk it out with him. Knowing what he did now... The conversation leapt into his mind, taking on layers of meaning he couldn't possibly have guessed at.

'She'll send me away.' Forlorn hopelessness, the brilliant dark eyes swimming in a sea of desolation.

'Who?'

'Eleanor.'

'Why on earth would she do that?'

'She doesn't have to please my father any more. She's got everything she wanted out of him.'

'You're her daughter, Tamara. I know it hurts that your father's gone, but surely your mother...'

'She never wanted me. She hates me. She always has.'

'But you're family.'

'Not the right family.'

'You belong here.'

'She won't let me. Only my father ever wanted me, and he's dead.'

It had sounded so extreme, yet to her it had been a stark truth.

'You're not seeing this straight, Tamara,' he'd argued in his ignorance.

'Yes, I am. You'll see. She'll send me away. I won't even have Cathy.'

He'd promised her this wouldn't happen. Determined to

fix her misery, he'd laid out her fears to his grandfather, who'd agreed to speak to his sister about Tamara's sense of alienation, however groundless it was. There'd be no sending her away when she'd just lost her father.

It had been winter then, the end of July. Impossible to pinpoint now when feeling sorry for Tamara, being kind, had moved to a compulsion to look out for her, be with her. There was an intensity about her that drew him, an energy he found irresistible, and she was, even at fourteen, alluringly beautiful, and so sexually provocative he was as horny as hell just thinking about her.

He'd lasted until school broke up for the Christmas vacation, believing she was innocently unaware of the signals she gave out to him, but she *had* wanted him. She'd shown him all summer how fierce, how wild, how needful, how all-encompassing her wanting was. And he hadn't cared how she knew so many ways to pleasure them both.

Her father! Her goddamned father! Rory thumped the driving wheel, railing against his blind acceptance of her sexual precocity. He'd been too caught up in that glorious summer of madness with Tamara to look at anything straight. He'd constructed a private, intensely intimate world of their own, dreaming of a future where everything would be perfect for them—a fantasy brought crashing to earth with a vengeance when Eleanor had sprung on them on the night of the end-of-vintage party.

On Max's bed.

Rory groaned. That spine-chilling detail, meaningless to him then, was horrifically significant now. Had Tamara been exorcising her sexual experience with her father, overlaying it with what she felt was real, mutual love? She'd told him the room hadn't been used since Max had died. They were safe there. Safe!

Sweet Jesus! What had he done in not fighting their parents' edict that they be separated? Tamara, pleading with him, tears streaming down her cheeks... He closed his eyes in a reflex action against the image in his mind.

A horn blared.

A truck coming around the corner ahead, the Maserati almost in the centre of the road! Hands wildly correcting the drift of the car, adrenaline racing, fear thumping through his heart, no thrill now in facing death, mind almost numb with the need to escape it.

He squeezed past the truck, rocketing into clear road again. The instability of what he was doing hit him with sobering force. Travelling at reckless speed. Like Tamara. Reacting instead of acting. Going nowhere, but getting there fast. Caught up in Tamara's frenzied world. Letting her draw him into it. Pulling him after her.

He had to stop it. Had to think. He was putting everything at risk—the life he had made for himself, a life with order and purpose and continuity. It was utter madness to shove it all aside as though it meant nothing. Just because Tamara wanted him again. For her own purpose. Her own needs.

He eased his foot off the accelerator, relaxed his grip on the wheel, coasted the car along until there was a wide enough verge to pull off the road and park without interfering with any passing traffic. He lowered the window and leaned against the door, inhaling deeply, needing to clear his mind and get everything into some kind of reasonable perspective.

For several minutes he simply rested, trying to get a grip on himself. The rush of insanity that had carried him to this point had somehow erased the ache in his bruised shoulder, the pain in his leg. He felt them now.

It reminded him Tamara had been giving him pain for a long, long time. That truth was more pertinent—should be more pertinent—than the truth she had used to whip him into this madness of chasing after her. Whipping him one way or another for the past twelve years. Was he a masochist?

Even if he was to blame for not comprehending the breadth and depth of her needs, there was no way back to that summer. It was gone.

So where did he go from here?

What kind of future was possible with Tamara? Only more pain, if he viewed it realistically. What she'd done this afternoon had destructive malice written all over it, now that he looked at it with a cooler head.

He gazed over the fields of vines. They were his love, the one constant he could rely on in his life. Tamara would tear it up and throw it away like confetti.

Louise supported it. She was the ideal partner for him, if not quite all he might have wanted in a wife. The positive aspects of their relationship were readily counted.

He could depend on her to behave sensibly, charmingly and beneficially at all times in any social or business situation. As the daughter of a cabinet minister in the federal government, she had absorbed that training, and she put it to good use on Rory's behalf. He was proud of her savoir faire, proud of her well-dressed, well-groomed, elegant beauty. She never shamed him in public, never put a foot wrong.

Louise always had her father's ear. She was right behind the lobbying for a lowering of taxes on wine exports. She also had a keen eye on how much of the tourism-development dollar was spent on promoting the Australian wine industry, especially in the Hunter River Valley. She knew all about special government grants, government subsidies, government perks, government submissions.

Her keen involvement in his business provided a sharing that gave solidity to their marriage. They had mutual goals, a future based on mutual interests. It wasn't empty. Yet he suddenly felt there was a hole in the middle where there should be substance.

He didn't really know what resided in Louise's heart. Perhaps that was because he kept his own closed, too aware of his inability to feel what he should for his wife. It was his fault. He went through the motions of loving. He hoped she didn't feel the lack of it. If they had a child, maybe the empty place would be filled.

He would love her because she bore his child. Couldn't fail to. It was the most intimate bond of togetherness. He needed that with her. Needed it now. Needed it badly. The sensible thing to do was go home and put it to Louise, persuade her it would be good for them, right for them.

He leaned forward and switched on the engine. The action made him doubly aware of all the sore places on his body. Having checked the road was clear, he swung the Maserati around to point in the direction of home.

It didn't matter that he hurt. There was a far deeper ache needing to be appeased, the ache stirred into painful life by the love that had eluded him, the unanswered void left by the Tamara of his dreams.

He drove listlessly, automatically, safely. His mind kept echoing her words. *The last chance for us to be together.* But they were hollow words, he told himself, teasing words, tempting words, no substance to them. Better to maintain the life he'd built without her. He hung grimly to that conviction.

TWELVE

Gabrielle Traverner was well aware that Rory's wife took her for an ineffective fool, a mere cipher in the family circle. Louise's very first comment to her, 'Oh, you're French!' had been dismissive, as though being a foreigner and having an accent put Gabrielle on some lower level. However, it was typical of Louise to view all other women as lesser beings than herself. Typical also of her to politely cultivate Gabrielle because she was married to Paul and lived in the Big House and could be useful on occasion. Like today.

Louise had wanted to meet Rory's mother. Gabrielle had obliged, curious to watch Louise in action with Irene Buchanan. It had been a masterly buttering-up session. As they drove away from Irene's cottage, Gabrielle wondered how Louise would handle the next step in her bid to win Irene over.

'That poor woman. Why on earth does she live like that, Gabrielle? It's so...comfortless.'

More fishing under the guise of sympathy.

'To Irene's mind, poverty is akin to godliness,' she answered dryly.

Louise frowned. Money wasn't going to work with someone who willingly embraced poverty. Gabrielle waited to hear the next angle.

'She didn't seem upset over the news about Eleanor.'

No emotions for Louise to tug on yet.

Gabrielle gave a matter-of-fact reply. 'Eleanor's fate is God's will. Getting upset would not be an appropriate attitude.'

Irene and Eleanor despised each other. Gabrielle didn't care to let Louise in on that family truth. No doubt she would find out for herself soon enough. And use it for her own ends.

Gabrielle had started visiting Irene years ago, wanting to know more about the family outcasts, wanting to know why. She had thought learning the answers might help her ease Paul out of his mother's clutch. It hadn't.

Now she could hardly bring herself to hope that Eleanor's illness and death would make any difference. It might make Paul even more determined to be the son his mother expected him to be, chained to the heritage she'd ordained for him for the rest of his life. Eleanor cast a long shadow.

Yet her pervasive domination must surely dim, Gabrielle argued to herself. There had to be a chance for her to win back the Paul she had met and married in France. For the past seven years—from the day he'd brought her home to the Big House—he'd been slipping away from her. Not physically. The sexual connection was still strong. Yet the deeper intimacy they had once shared, the meeting of like minds, attitudes, outlooks, that had been lost, and Gabrielle yearned for it with a longing that hurt.

Louise sighed. 'I guess the tragedies of losing her husband and daughter in fairly quick succession turned Irene's mind a bit.'

Irene's mind was more than a bit turned, but Louise could find that out for herself, too. 'It must have been traumatic,' Gabrielle agreed.

They were out of Cessnock and on the road to Pokolbin before Louise initiated the next piece of spadework.

'Does Tamara know what's happened to her mother?'

Tamara always knew. Too many times she had turned up at the Big House in the middle of a social function, embarrassing Eleanor with scandalous antics. It could not be coincidental. She never swooped in on them when nothing was on.

Gabrielle suspected someone on the household staff kept Tamara informed of Eleanor's doings. She had no doubt the renegade daughter had been tracking her mother's cancer and knew of the outcome. How Tamara would respond was totally unpredictable. But interesting. Gabrielle looked forward to it, certain there would be action. If it jolted Paul into a reassessment of where he was, all the better.

'I imagine Uncle Frank contacted her last night, as he did us,' she answered Louise. 'Though he may not have known where she was. Tamara doesn't keep us posted with her comings and goings.' A vast understatement. Surprise attack was Tamara's game, and she played it to maximum effect.

'She's not in touch much, then?'

'No.'

Irene and Tamara—a highly significant block of voting shares in the company. Did Rory know what his wife was up to?

Unlikely, Gabrielle thought. She'd never seen any signs of Rory Buchanan being anything other than a straightshooter. She didn't know him well. Rory had a habit of keeping himself to himself. Nevertheless, Gabrielle instinctively liked him. She empathised with the apartness he felt.

'She's a strange one,' Louise remarked musingly. When Gabrielle made no reply, she added, 'Tamara, I mean. So impossibly rude. And crude at times.'

'Yes,' Gabrielle agreed. If Louise tried using her brand of diplomacy on Tamara, she'd be playing a losing hand. Tamara would wipe the floor with her.

'What does Paul think of her?' Louise persisted.

This was touchy ground. 'Tamara isn't involved in the business. What she does is her own affair.'

'You mean he doesn't care about her.'

Louise would like that. However true it was, Gabrielle was not going to give that information to her. Let Louise find her own ammunition to fire in her quest to win the votes she obviously wanted.

'I didn't say that, Louise. Tamara is his half-sister. Family is family.'

For the rest of the trip home, Gabrielle fended off artfully put questions about Tamara. She knew she sounded like an airhead, but she didn't care, as long as she frustrated Louise. Not that Gabrielle thought Louise would find any joy with Eleanor's daughter. No-one and nothing got to Tamara. She danced to her own beat.

Gabrielle well remembered her introduction to Paul's half-sister. It was mind-blowing. Everyone of any note in the wine business was seated in the ballroom of the Big House. A glittering evening—tables dressed in starched white linen, Venetian crystal, Spode dinnerware, sterling silver, bowls of roses, guests in formal dress, a man in tails playing pleasant background music on the grand piano. The partying had stopped dead as the roar of motorbikes charging up the front steps drowned out music and conversation. Three Harley-Davidsons reared to a halt in the foyer facing the ballroom.

The riders dismounted and removed their helmets, a woman flanked by two brawny men, all of them kitted out in black leather liberally adorned with threatening studs, chains and gang emblems. Everyone stared at them, dumbfounded.

'Hot damn, guys! Look at this!' the woman cried, exuding a wild, magnetic energy. 'My mother's laid on a best-bib-and-tucker party for me.' Her gaze glittered over the company and fastened on Eleanor at the head table. 'You remembered my birthday,' she trilled in amazement.

Eleanor rose frigidly to her feet. 'Your birthday is not until next week, Tamara.'

'Well, I thought you might have preferred to forget it, Mother, so I brought my party with me.'

'So I see.' A larger group of bikers was crowding into the foyer, gawking at the two-storey ballroom with its domed ceiling. And sizing up the guests and furnishings. The tension of trouble looming had everyone frozen in their seats, but Eleanor refused to be intimidated. 'If you'd given me prior notice of your intentions, Tamara, I could have accommodated your friends. As it is...'

'No worries, Mother. I never expect you to do anything for me. My catering van is out near the pool now, and I've got a heavy metal band all primed to jazz up the night.' She swaggered forward, waving her arms. 'What's all this, then? Celebrating an important Traverner event?'

'If you'd been in touch, you would have been invited,' Eleanor coolly prefaced her explanation. 'It's a reception for Paul and his bride, who arrived home from France a month ago.'

'How splendid!' Tamara pranced up to the head table, grabbed Paul's hand and shook it vigorously. 'Congratulations, Paul. Introduce me to your beautiful bride. I just knew you'd choose one of the beautiful people.'

He stood up, holding Gabrielle protectively as he helped her to her feet. 'Gabrielle...my sister, Tamara.'

'Only a half-sister,' Tamara quickly corrected. 'We wouldn't want your new wife thinking she was more contaminated than she is.' She grinned at Gabrielle, her black eyes sparkling with wicked mischief. 'Welcome to the family.'

'Thank you. I hope—'

Tamara cut her off. '*I* hope you know what you're letting yourself in for. The Traverner bloodline is terribly important to Mother. But I see you've got good child-bearing hips.

Shouldn't be any problem for you to produce what's wanted.'

'That's enough, Tamara,' Eleanor broke in with icy reproof.

'Yep! Mother always knows when and where to draw the line.' She swung around, exuberantly throwing her hands high to draw all eyes as she started to the foyer. 'Happy party, people! Anyone who wants to join us out by the pool later on is welcome. Might get rather stuffy in here.'

The bikers trailed outside, the three Harleys giving their exit a resounding kick.

Eleanor took the stunning disruption in her stride.

Paul was furious.

Gabrielle was fascinated.

A month in the Big House had been long enough for her to want to see Eleanor's dominance flouted. Tamara had done it with bold flamboyance. Gabrielle had looked forward to learning more about Tamara. It turned out to be a long exercise in observation. No-one wanted to talk about the black sheep of the family. She was dismissed as of no account. Nuisance value.

Gabrielle was sure Louise had been equally blocked in her quest for hard information about Eleanor's daughter. Her prying now wasn't being rewarded with any satisfaction, either. Tough titties, Gabrielle thought rudely. Sometimes she envied Tamara her brassy boldness. And her total disregard for what others thought. Freedom...

Except Gabrielle did care what Paul thought. Couldn't help caring. For better or for worse, she loved him.

Eventually they turned into the long avenue of poplars that led to the Big House. Louise fell silent, her gaze fixed straight ahead, probably coveting the mansion Max Vandelier had built as she drove towards it. Gabrielle had seen the acquisitive greed in her eyes many times.

Having slowly skirted the huge stone fountain, Louise brought her car to a halt precisely in line with the centre of the massive portico that framed the entrance to the house. They exchanged a few polite courtesies, and Gabrielle alighted. She watched Louise drive off, then turned to mount the steps.

Glancing morosely at the majestic, hand-carved oak doors, she wished this wasn't her home. It would never be a real home to her. It represented too many other things. But her children were here, the Traverner heirs. Paul was here, the king in waiting. No choice. If she had a choice she would happily give this house to Louise just to be done with it.

Should she tell Paul Louise was on the move?

Was Tamara on the move?

Irrelevant, Gabrielle reminded herself. Eleanor was coming home this evening. Eleanor always dictated policy. Eleanor would undoubtedly take care of everything before she died.

THIRTEEN

Louise contemptuously dismissed Gabrielle Traverner—stupid woman—the moment she was out of the car. The problem of Tamara Vandelier taxed her mind as she drove home. An enigma that had to be solved. The aborted teenage affair between Tamara and Rory wasn't exactly helpful. Perhaps an arm's-length deal might be worth trying. She immediately thought of her father. He was very experienced with such deals. She would consult him.

She turned onto the dirt road that led up the hill to Rory's house. It was unreasonably perverse of Rory to have chosen to build his home away from the Buchanan vineyard. This badly accessed hill was where the local artists and potters lived. It had a fine view over the valley, but it did not add to Rory's stature as a winegrower of considerable and growing reputation.

She did not like the house, either, but she hadn't been in Rory's life at the time it was built. She parked her car in the double garage, crossed the front porch, entered the foyer and walked down the steps to the living area, sourly unimpressed by the open-space design with its preponderance of natural wood and huge expanses of glass.

She couldn't complain, because Rory loved it. He said it gave him a sense of freedom, although what he wanted freedom from was beyond Louise's imagination. She wanted possessions around her, possessions she could count, possessions worth having. She wouldn't feel content until she had the premier house in the valley. The Big House. And all that went with it.

She was about to pick up the telephone and call her father when she heard Rory's Maserati turning into the driveway. It was too early for the work of the day to be over. He must have come home for some specific reason, maybe to pick up something he needed. The call to her father would have to wait. She didn't want Rory to overhear what was best kept private.

She went to meet him, arranging her expression to one of wifely concern. He opened the front door before she reached the steps to the foyer. She saw the ripped sleeve and the bruised shoulder and stopped in surprise.

'What's happened to you?' she cried in genuine alarm. The last thing she needed was Rory in a fight and injured.

'I had a run-in with a car,' he said flatly. He shut the door and limped forward.

'Your leg!' Louise started up the steps to lend support.

Rory waved her off. 'A bit bruised. That's all.'

Her concern switched to practicality. 'I've got witch hazel in the kitchen. It should help take out the bruising. Can you manage the steps?'

'I'm not crippled.'

Pride dented more than anything, Louise thought, heading for the kitchen. 'Is there much damage to the Maserati?' she asked.

He followed her, the question about the car unanswered. She wondered if the accident was his fault. He was clearly out of humour about it. So was she, but it was better not to show it. A sympathetic attitude had to be maintained. She needed Rory's co-operation to effect a reconciliation with his mother.

She heard him drag out a kitchen stool and settle on it as

she took the bottle of witch hazel and a bag of cotton wool from the medicine cupboard. She removed the lid from the bottle, picked out a handful of cotton wool and swung around.

Rory was unbuttoning his ruined shirt. There was a look of determination on his face. His gaze flicked to look directly at her. 'I wasn't in the car.'

Louise paused. There was something wrong here. 'Are you telling me someone deliberately hit you?'

He shook his head. 'It was an accident.' He winced as he drew his arms out of the shirt and dropped it to the floor. His shoulder was a massive bruise.

Louise moved forward to treat the injury. 'So what did happen?'

'Tamara came to the winery. We argued over old times. She was upset. I tried to stop her from leaving. She tried to swerve around me, but I got hit by her Porsche.'

He recited the facts in a flat tone that drained them of any drama or importance. Louise paused in her dabbing, her mind racing, her heart squeezing tight. If Rory had ruined any chance of a deal with Tamara...

'Did she stop?'

'Momentarily. It was my fault, Louise. Tamara didn't mean to injure me. I shouldn't have got in her way.'

'Why did you?'

He shrugged. 'It seemed the right thing to do at the time.'

She knelt to roll up his trouser leg and treat the injury to his shin. There was a purpling lump, but the skin wasn't broken. She applied witch hazel as she prodded Rory for more information.

'She must have been very upset with you.'

'Not with me. Other things. What had happened with her parents. Our families.'

Relief pumped through Louise, quickly followed by a surge of excitement. For Tamara to dump her troubles on Rory surely meant she had more confidence in him than any other member of the family, however fragile that confidence was. It suggested there might be some bias towards him that could work for them. Which was all to the good.

'Where was Tamara going?'

She unrolled his trouser leg and stood up. Rory caught her waist and pulled her between his legs. He rested his face against her breasts, his arms sliding around her back to hold her in a close embrace.

'I don't want to talk about Tamara, Louise,' he said gruffly. 'Let's go to bed and talk about us.'

She produced a light laugh. 'Darling, you're really in no condition to make love. Let me go so I can get rid of this stuff in my hands.'

'I want to be close to you.'

Louise gritted her teeth and concentrated on relaxing her body so she wouldn't appear unresponsive. If she went to bed with him, she knew what would happen. She would have to ride him. It was not an appealing thought. She might get out of lovemaking altogether with a little talking.

She tossed the used cotton wool onto the torn shirt on the floor and pressed his head closer to her breasts, using her fingers to stroke his thick, springy hair. 'I guess you're fairly shaken up,' she said softly. 'Let me give you some aspirin, Rory. It will ease the inflammation and pain.'

He sighed and let his arms slide away. Louise stepped back quickly and returned to the medicine cupboard. 'I want to talk about us, too,' she said as she fossicked for the packet of aspirin. 'What do you have on your mind?'

He did not reply.

She swung around, the packet in her hand. Rory's gaze was fixed at her hip level. His mind was definitely below the belt, Louise thought in exasperation.

When he lifted his eyes to hers, the look of deep yearning in them gave Louise a twinge of disquiet. It was not what she expected. It was something beyond sexual desire.

'I want a child, Louise.'

Her antenna for trouble twanged in no uncertain terms. Whether it was the encounter with Tamara or with Tamara's car, Louise didn't know, but Rory had definitely been shaken into a reappraisal of priorities in his life.

She clicked on an understanding smile. 'Well, of course you do, Rory. Every man wants to father a child. It's a natural biological urge.'

She quickly busied herself at the sink, getting him a glass of water, pushing two capsules out of their foil covering, giving herself time to think. She had to get out of this while putting as graceful a face as she could on it. No way was she going to have a child at this juncture of her life. If ever. Children were such messy things.

Rory took what she handed him, waiting until after he'd swallowed before picking up on her generalisation. His eyes probed hers, assessing her receptivity, unsure if the evasion was deliberate or a simple lack of awareness.

'I'm talking about now, Louise,' he said quietly.

She frowned. 'You don't mean right now, do you?'

'Yes. Why not?'

She shook her head. 'We're both so young. A child is a big responsibility, Rory. I'm not ready for it yet.'

'What does it take to be ready? I want the responsibility, Louise. I want to be a father. You can have any help money can buy.'

'But it won't be the same, Rory. Our lives won't be our own.' She whipped the glass away from him, placed it on the sink, then took both his hands in hers. She gave him an appealing smile. 'For one thing, we won't be able to make love any time we like. We'll be ruled by a schedule.'

She tugged him off the stool. 'Come on, darling. It's too soon to be talking about babies. Let's go to bed and simply enjoy being together.' At the moment, that was definitely the lesser of two evils.

He moved reluctantly. 'We've been married for three years—'

'And will be married for a great many more.' She released him and bent to scoop the torn shirt from the floor. 'I'll pop this in the laundry and join you in a minute.'

She left him, well aware he was disgruntled. It meant she would have to make a real effort to satisfy him sexually. It was tiresome, but there was no escaping it. Besides, it was easy enough to simulate passion if she thought of the Big House. Rory was the means to that end.

He was in the ensuite bathroom when she entered their bedroom. The toilet flush was followed by taps running. It gave her time to slide off her shoes and remove her panti-hose, the most inelegant part of undressing, before he appeared. She'd coiled her hair into a neat, sexless chignon for the visit to Irene Buchanan. Rory preferred it loose. She started removing hairpins.

He propped himself in the doorway, watching her. 'When do you envisage starting a family, Louise?' he demanded.

She barely quelled her irritation. 'We do have other family matters to consider,' she reminded him more tersely than she meant to.

'Like what?'

Cold. Very cold. She set the pins on her dressing-table and considered how best to respond as she raked her fingers through her hair, shaking it loose. Continuing to undress showed willingness on her part, even though she sensed Rory had turned off the idea of having sex. It gave her the moral high ground of being caring and obliging.

On the other hand, since there had been a definite shift of mood between the kitchen and the bathroom, perhaps now was the time to do some serious talking, rearrange his priorities. She turned to confront him with a few trenchant points.

'When Eleanor dies there could be a lot of changes, Rory.'

'It won't affect us.' Stubborn. Resistant.

'You intend to stand back and let Paul take over from his mother?'

'He's been groomed for it.'

'To head the Traverner vineyard, yes,' Louise conceded, not wanting to reveal all her plans at once. 'But I see no reason he should be chairman of the Buchanan vineyard. That place is rightfully yours, Rory.'

'The head of the company is chairman of both vineyards, Louise,' he said wearily. 'Failing that, the position would rightfully belong to my grandfather. If you're speculating about separating the vineyards from the family company, forget it. Paul and David and Eleanor together hold sixty-six of the two hundred voting shares. Even if my grandfather would agree on dividing the vineyards into separate entities again, he and I only hold sixty. We'd be outvoted.'

'What about your mother?'

He laughed. 'Not a chance in hell! And I wouldn't want her vote, anyway.'

Louise tried to decipher all the nuances of that laugh. Derision, certainly. But there were dark undertones. Bitterness? Anger?

'Is it you or she who's intransigent about a reconciliation between the two of you?' Louise asked, needing to know what she had to work on.

'Drop it, Louise.'

'Why? You talk about having a family, yet you're alienated from your own mother. You talk about being close, yet you've never told me why you won't have anything to do with her.'

His face darkened. 'Isn't her religious mania reason enough?'

'Lonely people cling to a prop like that,' Louise reasoned. 'When they've got nothing else...'

'She had a family,' he snapped. His eyes blazed with violent emotion as long-held secrets came tumbling out. 'We had God and hellfire. My father worked long hours to escape it. He made the vineyard his life. I took refuge with my grandfather. After Dad crashed his plane and escaped her for good, she focused her soul-saving sadism on my sister.'

'Sadism?' Louise was shocked.

Rory's mouth took on an ugly curl. 'Mental abuse. Physical abuse. Purifying her sinfulness. Cathy stuck it out for eighteen months, then ran away and killed herself with an overdose of heroin. How do you like that for redemption?'

Louise flinched. She hadn't been privy to such private family history. Rory had always glossed over it. For a moment, she was shocked into sympathy. 'I'm sorry about your sister, Rory. I wish you'd told me.'

Guilt haunted his eyes. 'I wasn't there enough for her. I was trying to learn the business as fast as I could. So I ended up losing her, as well as—' His mouth clamped shut. His hand sliced the air with a sharp, dismissive gesture. 'It's over. Finished with.'

'Yes,' Louise quickly agreed. It must have been ten years ago. 'Was that when your mother moved to the cottage in Cessnock?' she asked, wondering if Irene felt guilt, too.

He nodded. 'She wasn't going to get any satisfaction out of me. Ever,' he stated grimly. 'Nothing on this earth will induce me to acknowledge that woman as my mother again.'

'I see,' Louise murmured, seeing only that her plan would be ruined if she didn't break down Rory's resistance. It didn't matter whether the estrangement was justified or not. It was a matter of being pragmatic about the future. Her mind moved swiftly through various permutations, looking for the best line of approach.

Rory pushed off the bathroom doorway and walked towards her, his hands lifted in a gesture of appeal. 'I want my own family, Louise. I want the sense of love and unity a family should have. I want what I never had.'

'Oh, darling!' Louise moved to meet him. She slid her hands up his chest and lifted eyes that begged his understanding. 'That's partly why I went to see your mother today. It all seemed so wrong to me.'

His hands gripped her waist hard. His eyes flared with a dangerous, tigerish light. 'You took it upon yourself—'

'No, no. It wasn't as direct as that. Gabrielle was going, to give your mother news of Eleanor, and she took me with her.'

'I didn't know you were friendly with Gabrielle,' he said coldly.

'It was simply something that came up—' after a masterly piece of angling '—and I saw no harm in tagging along, Rory. As it turned out, your mother was very polite to me. I got the feeling she was pleased I had come, and—'

'No doubt she was,' he cut in acidly. 'Nothing would please her more than to convert my wife to her twisted brand of Christianity. And it is twisted, Louise. Believe me.' Disgust in his grimace. He stepped back and headed for their dressing-room. 'I think I need some fresh air.'

Bad vibes. Very bad. Yet Louise felt she had to break through to him. 'For heaven's sake, Rory!' she cried in quick appeasement. 'Give me credit for some intelligence. There's no chance of my taking her religion seriously.'

'Then stay away from my mother, Louise,' he flung back at her. 'She's none of your business.'

He disappeared into the dressing-room. Louise knew she had to strike now. Irene Buchanan was very much her business. Getting Rory's mother onside was critical to her ultimate ambition. She had to make Rory see the bigger picture.

He'd turned off the idea of sex, so that wasn't going to help her. Reason didn't seem to work. If he wanted a family, then she'd invoke family for all it was worth. She would not let Rory walk away from the action that had to be taken.

Louise moved to the doorway of the dressing-room, prepared to do battle. Rory had stripped off the remainder of his business clothes. He ignored her presence, grabbing a pair of jeans and proceeding to pull them on.

'Your mother owes you, Rory,' she stated. 'From what you've just said, she owes you a hell of a lot.'

His face had *brick wall* written all over it. 'I don't want anything from her, Louise.'

'She's deprived you all your life. It's not fair for her to deprive you of a heritage that should come to you and our children, not only by right of birth, Rory, but by right of all you've done to enhance the reputation of the Buchanan vineyard. For the sake of the family we'll have—'

'If you're talking about inheritance, forget it. My mother will leave everything she has to her church. The works of her God are far more important than the works of man.' He flashed her a mocking look. 'Or woman.'

He zipped his jeans and sat on the valet chair to pull on socks and a pair of casual shoes. He had no conception of the big picture. Narrow and blind, Louise thought in disgust, and stupidly stubborn. It made it all the more difficult to shake some sense into him.

'I'm talking about the vote that will be taken after Eleanor dies,' she pointed out, careful to keep her voice calm and reasonable. 'It's only a few months away, Rory. If you become chairman of Buchanan, you'll be your own man as far as the future of the Buchanan vineyard is concerned. You'll make the decisions. You'll choose future directions.'

'I do that now.' He didn't bother looking up.

'Only after consultation with your grandfather. And Eleanor. And you'll soon be without them, Rory. Eleanor's dying, and your grandfather's older than she is. Are you going to let Paul dictate our future?'

No reply. His head remained bent as he slid on his shoes. Perhaps that had stung his pride.

Encouraged, Louise forged on. 'You should be on equal terms with Paul, Rory. Your grandfather loves you. He'll see the justice of voting you in as chairman of Buchanan once it's pointed out to him. With your mother's vote—'

He stood up, his face still hard and unyielding. 'No way will I grovel to my mother, Louise. Not even for the chairmanship of Buchanan.' He unhooked a sports shirt from a hanger and gingerly pushed his arms into the sleeves.

'Let me deal with your mother. You don't have to do anything if you don't want to.'

His mouth twisted. 'And what do you intend to say to her on my behalf, Louise?'

'Whatever I have to in order to get her vote.'

'Lies?' A brief, glittering glance at her.

'She owes it to you,' Louise repeated, adding the base appeal, 'let justice be served, Rory.'

He started buttoning his shirt, his gaze lowered, his expression shuttered. She hoped it meant he was considering her proposition instead of dismissing it out of hand. The buttoning went on slowly. Without looking up, he asked in a deadpan voice, 'If I agree to that, will you agree to having my child?'

Why was he so obsessed with procreation all of a sudden? Or did he simply need to score a point from her? Louise put on an appeasing smile.

'I never said I wouldn't have a child, Rory. Only that I wasn't ready yet. Once our future is settled, I'll be happy to think about it.'

His fingers paused over the last button. His gaze lifted. There was a piercing quality to his eyes, a concentrated focus she had never seen in him before. It excited her. There might be more to Rory than she had realised.

'*Think* about it? Are you saying our future together depends on my becoming chairman of Buchanan?' he asked, more assessingly than inquiringly.

Louise took the plunge. 'With Irene's support we'd hold eighty-one votes against their sixty-six. Why shouldn't we go for everything, head of the family company and chairmanship of both vineyards?'

'Why not, indeed?'

He looked at her with such weighing calculation, Louise felt they were on the same wavelength for the first time since they were married. No emotionalism. Pure, clear vision of what it took to get what you wanted.

'Tell me how you assess the situation,' he invited.

At last! Open discussion of ways and means!

FOURTEEN

Rory watched the woman he had married with clinical detachment. It was a strange feeling, having the delusions with which he had clothed his life stripped away in front of his eyes. There was a hollowness in his chest, as though his heart and lungs had been removed, though they continued to function. As did his mind, with the sharpness of a scalpel, unblunted by any emotion.

Ambition. That was what he was looking at. Naked, clawing, heartless ambition. Tamara was right. He had married another Eleanor. Worse. At least Eleanor cared about the vineyards. She had lived and breathed them. Louise was only interested in power.

She would say whatever she had to say and do whatever she had to do to get what she wanted. That was very clear to him now. He was simply the rungs of the ladder for her to climb to where she wanted to be. Or was that too sweeping an indictment?

Rory's innate sense of fairness demanded more evidence before final judgment was passed. Or was it hope pleading for some other resolution? Hope had drawn him home to this confrontation, hope for something more fulfilling than Tamara would ever offer him. What a joke!

Well, he'd wanted truth, hadn't he? It was being laid out

for him now. So let Louise hammer every nail into the coffin of their marriage before he buried it. He'd made probably the worst mistake of his life when he'd turned Tamara away from him twelve years ago. He would make no mistake with Louise.

He watched her marshal her thoughts, saw the calculation crystallise in her grey, winter-cold eyes before she spoke.

'There is, of course, Tamara's vote to be taken into consideration.'

'Ah, yes,' Rory agreed. 'There lies the critical element. Tamara's fifty-three votes can swing it either way. And while she's always shown her contempt for all of us by never bothering to use that vote—'

'We have to get to her before they do, Rory.' Ruthless determination. 'We must either persuade her to back us or ensure she will not be persuaded to vote for them.'

Persuade Tamara? Rory almost laughed. No-one had the power to reach Tamara. She was a force unto herself. She chose. He hadn't driven her to the revelation about her father today. She'd used it to draw him after her. He realised that now.

'What do you suggest?' he prompted, curious to hear how Louise would plan her approach.

She did not so much as hesitate. 'Everyone has a want. Everyone has a need. Everyone has a weakness. You know her as well as anyone, Rory. Probably better than anyone.'

A devious, calculating manipulator. Had she graphed his weaknesses, his needs and wants, providing the necessary to keep him satisfied and in her corner? Rory suddenly found the dressing-room claustrophobic. He had to get out of here. He pocketed his wallet and limped forward.

'I wouldn't make that assumption, Louise. Tamara is unreachable in any sense you know. In any sense any of us knows,' he said with bitter irony.

She blocked his passage, her hands sliding up his chest.

'Tell me about her. You said she was upset about family matters. That means she cares. Think hard, Rory. What is Tamara's want? What is Tamara's need? What is Tamara's weakness?' She ran her fingers into the open vee of his shirt. 'She must have one. What did she really want with you today?'

His skin crawled with revulsion. Had Louise ever touched him in honest desire to be close to him? Had she ever given one honest response to him in their marriage? He gripped her waist and forcibly moved her aside. 'Cut it out, Louise. I'm not interested in bed any more. Nor are you.'

'Was Tamara?'

'Yes, she was!' he snapped, his detachment smashed by a flood of fierce resentment at having been fooled and used. He wanted to hit out, to crack Louise's smug air of control over their lives. 'She said she wanted my child!'

Louise laughed. 'Whatever for? Why would she want such a thing?'

Rage blurred his mind. His hands itched to throttle Louise's long, pale neck. She struck at the heart of his manhood. He felt violated to his soul. 'At least she's prepared to give me what you won't,' he flung at the travesty of a woman he'd married. He knocked her hands away from him as he turned to march stiffly from the room. He couldn't bear to occupy the same space as her for another minute.

In the hallway he gulped in a calming breath. Violence was not the answer to anything. He'd brought this situation upon himself with blind pride. Tamara was right again. Louise had been a rejection of her. He'd made his bed and done his best to lie in it, but there was no lying in it any longer.

He reached the open gallery that overlooked the living area. His leg hurt, but he didn't move to the balustrade to use it for support. The pain served to remind him he'd have to pay for how he'd screwed up his life. The moment he mentioned divorce, Louise would go for the jugular.

'I'm prepared to give you a child, Rory.'

He stopped. So she thought his desire for fatherhood was a tool she could use. Let her talk, he thought. Let her give him the ammunition to use against her when the time came. Very slowly he half-turned and looked at her in cynical inquiry.

'What's the proviso, Louise? The condition for your compliance to my want, my need, my weakness? What are you going to exact in return?'

'I want the Big House.'

His head jerked. He hadn't thought as far as that. It not only stunned him, it took his breath away. His chest lifted as he filled his lungs. Then he exploded.

'For God's sake, Louise! We're talking about a child!'

'We're talking about a deal,' she corrected him, boring straight to the essentials. 'Eleanor got the Big House because she was prepared to make the same deal with Max Vandelier. I want that house and all that goes with it. I'm prepared to—'

'Tamara was the result of that deal. Do you want a child like Tamara?' he yelled at her.

'I want the Big House,' she repeated, coldly and flatly.

'I won't have a child under those conditions.'

'Choose as you please. But there's one thing you do have to do if you want to keep me, Rory.'

There was more, he thought incredulously. 'And what's that?' he asked, determined on knowing the lot.

'Get Tamara's vote.'

He laughed in scorn. 'Why would she give it to us?'

'For some reason she wants a child. Give Tamara what she wants and exact what we want in return. It's hardly a difficult procedure, Rory. Before you take her to bed, make her sign a declaration giving you the power to vote her shares by proxy. We'd also need another declaration saying you'll never be named as the father of the child.'

He stared at her, shocked beyond any shock Tamara had

ever delivered to him. 'You'd go that far,' he said, his voice thin with the unbridgeable distance of totally irreconcilable differences. And he'd felt guilty about being unfaithful to this woman. God! She was like a pimp organising terms with a customer.

'Look to the future, Rory.'

Didn't she know him at all? 'You realise you're putting our marriage on the line,' he said, appalled that she had absolutely no conception of the person he was. The marriage was finished. The judgment was in. No possible mistake. Whatever the cost, he would get Louise out of his life.

'I'm offering you a powerful partnership,' she went on with her sickening logic. 'Conventional fidelity or infidelity is irrelevant. Together, we can really put the Buchanan and Traverner vineyards on the map. I can do a lot of things for you, Rory. Public relations with the right people. People of influence. Purposeful hospitality. Promotional socialising. I've got that at my fingertips if you're chairman of both companies, if we have the Big House.'

'That comes first and foremost.' Bile soured his mouth as he saw that the virtues he had listed for Louise were simply part of her master plan.

'Believe it. I was born to be someone important. I am not going to play second fiddle to Paul and Gabrielle. I want centre stage.'

He nodded, mentally clutching at the last shreds of his control. 'I'm glad we've got that spelled out, Louise. It makes everything very clear to me.'

'Tamara is the key, Rory. Do your part in getting me the Big House, and whatever you do with Tamara, I'll give you your child.'

She was as blind about him as he had been about her. He found a perverse satisfaction in stringing her along. 'I'll think about it,' he said, and she didn't hear the mockery.

'You haven't got time to think about it. Tamara might change her mind.'

'You want me to go to her now.'

'Yes. Go to her. Don't waste a moment.'

'And do whatever she requires of me.'

'Opportunity does not have a reverse gear. Remember what I've said. It's up to you to get what we need from her. You've either got the guts to go for it, Rory, or you're not the man I want in my life. Or in my bed.'

Did she think she was some ultimate prize he'd do anything for? The woman was stark raving mad if she believed he was of that ilk. Not even for Tamara...

The hurt, the painful confusion of this afternoon swept back with tormenting force. Tamara, the love they'd once shared, open and uninhibited desire, a child of their mutual need...

He stared at the chilling, computer eyes of the woman he had married and remembered the heat of that long-ago summer. 'Oh, I'll go for it, Louise,' he said passionately. *For me, you ice bitch,* he added in silent venom. *Not for you.* 'I'll go for everything that's gnawed at my guts for years. I've got nothing to lose, have I?'

'I like you when you're like this, Rory. When you're all steamed up and hot. It makes you powerful. Invincible. That makes me hot, Rory. Power is my sexual turn-on.'

'I appreciate the enlightenment. To find out, at last, what turns you on is definitely a turning point in our marriage.'

'It's all gain,' she exulted.

'I'm on my way,' he said, barely able to contain the violence coursing through him. He headed for the front door with haste. He had to get out of here, get away from Louise before he vomited all the vileness in his mouth. He wanted to kill her.

FIFTEEN

Destroy...

The thought, the need, the resolution gathered intensity as Tamara parked her Porsche outside Irene Buchanan's home.

A sign driven into the front lawn read,

God is Salvation
Bible readings
Monday Wednesday Friday
3pm—5pm

Today was Thursday. Irene Buchanan didn't know it yet, but today was the day she was going to earn her salvation. Or damnation. Tamara didn't care which.

She alighted from her car. If everything went to plan, this wouldn't take long. It didn't matter if Rory arrived at the beach house ahead of her. He would wait. He wouldn't drive so far for no result.

Irene's house was no more than a small weatherboard cottage, a public statement that she had shed worldly goods. Being in town and closer to her church was much more godly than residing amongst grapevines grown for the production of demon alcohol.

They were the reasons Irene gave herself for having vacated the old family homestead on the Buchanan vineyard. Tamara wasn't fooled by them. She knew precisely why Irene had shifted after Cathy died.

Suppress the memories. Bury the guilt. Justify everything with a mantle of virtue. That was Irene's way. How could she live with herself if she didn't shovel all the sins onto other shoulders, painting herself as blameless?

Tamara rang the doorbell and waited, ready to move the moment the door opened. She did not intend to give Irene time to shut it in her face. The old harridan could rant and rave as much as she liked, but Tamara was not going to leave until she had driven a few telling stakes into the dark side of Irene's heart.

The front door opened wide.

'May God bless and—' The unctuous benediction stopped in midflow. 'You—you Jezebel! Go away! Don't—'

'Now, Irene, is that any way to greet a repentant sinner? Where's your Christian charity?' Tamara chided as she pushed inside, grabbed the door and shut it behind her.

Irene backed away in alarm, her arms lifted in a high cross, warding off evil. 'Don't mock the Lord, you witch of darkness! Get out of my house! Get out!'

She was a pathetic stick of a woman, her long, thin body covered in a shapeless beige dress, her grey hair scraped into a tight bun. Yet the zeal of a fanatic burned in her eyes, eyes that darted and pried and fed on forbidden things with a sick, self-righteous fervour, eyes that judged and exulted in the judgment, eyes that greedily loved the hellfire she preached.

'We need each other, Irene,' Tamara said with insinuating softness. 'We've been intertwined, haven't we? Ever since—'

'I won't listen to your wicked madness. Lies, lies, lies,' she shrieked, clamping her hands over her ears.

'I've never told on you, Irene. I've never told other people what you did. How you watched in secret, hugging it to yourself and pretending you didn't know. Have you ever wondered why?'

One hand flew out to point in judgment. 'God struck you mute. He turned your tongue into stone. God is on my side. God is strong.'

Tamara laughed. 'Then why do you live in this poor hovel of a house?' She stepped forward, her hands out in mocking supplication. 'Come on, Irene. Show me through your humble home. Show me how your God provides for your needs. Show me how strong your God really is.'

'Heretic! I have no need for wealth. Nor money,' she screamed, shaking her fists in angry defiance. 'It all goes to my God.'

'You'd have a lot more to give to your God if Eleanor didn't hate and despise you, Irene. If she didn't keep you poor as she tries to keep me poor.'

'You're rich. You're rich. I saw your car when I opened the door.'

Irene knew nothing of Tamara's private inheritance from her father, the money Eleanor hadn't fought her for, seeing it as the means for the cuckoo daughter to fritter away her life, far from the realm Eleanor guarded so jealously. The shares in the vineyards reaped little income for those shut out of the business of running the wineries. Irene was aware of that.

The evidence of the car was simply grist to the mill Tamara could use to crush the hypocrisy out of the vituperative woman in front of her. Lies and truth—so easy to mix them to get the desired result. Eleanor had taught her that.

'I had to sell my body to get what I want, Irene,' she said, spreading her hands over her breasts and squeezing their obvious fullness in deliberate provocation.

Irene stared, unable to tear her eyes away.

Tamara slid her fingers higher and began to drag the elasticised top down the line of her cleavage. 'Just as you had to sell your soul,' she hissed.

'You're a creature of evil!'

Tamara pulled the top lower. 'Have you ever fantasised about having my body, Irene? Did you want to be me?'

Irene screeched. 'Filthy, vile, despicable, loathsome harlot!'

'Was there a time when you wanted me? Are there parts of me, Irene, soft parts you would like to touch and stroke?' Tamara goaded. 'Would you like to see all of me?'

'Servant of Satan, whore of hell, you will burn, burn as a beacon to save others from sins of inflamed lust.'

'Feel the ripe fullness of my breasts, Irene. Remember the Song of Solomon? "Graceful thy breasts, as two fawns that feed among the lilies, breasts generous as the grape." It's in your Bible, Irene.'

'To hell and perdition and eternal flame.'

'Do you dream of me at night in the cover of darkness, wanting what I've known?'

A frenzy of screaming. 'Get thee gone, Satan!'

Gasping as though she was choking, Irene turned and ran down the hallway. Tamara pursued at a walking pace.

'You are a creature of evil, too, Irene. You do it differently. I know how you treated Cathy. Your own daughter. She wrote to me. I still have the letter.'

'Go away! Go away!' She turned, her right arm and fingers extended. 'Die!'

Nothing happened.

Irene blundered into a room and slammed the door. Tamara turned the handle and pushed against Irene's weight. She was stronger than the older woman, stronger in body and mind, driven by a force that demanded retribution. A gap opened, despite Irene's frantic resistance.

'You can have your revenge on Eleanor,' Tamara said persuasively. 'You can have your revenge on everyone.'

'You're the same as your mother.' A frenzied cry, the core of hatred shaken from her, beginning to spill out.

'No, not the same. I was just easier to get at,' Tamara stated bluntly. 'I was a substitute fantasy, Irene. It was always Eleanor you really wanted in your sights. She's the one with the power.'

I was the victim, the scapegoat.

Pointless to express that truth. It wouldn't win her anything. The endgame demanded a ruthless pruning of useless facts. She had to attack the heart of self-interest. Tamara pressed on with relentless and incisive logic.

'She took your husband away from you, Irene. Then, after his death, she took over Buchanan, as well as Traverner. That should have been your position. You married the heir to Buchanan, but Eleanor stole all the power and respect for herself. And she fixed it so you couldn't even get the money. There was nothing for you, Irene, because she took it all away from you.'

There was no acknowledgment, no admission, but the hoarse pants coming from the other side of the door had more to do with inner churning than the physical effort of keeping Tamara out.

'Eleanor is dying, Irene. In just a few months you can have as much money for your God as you want. Do you want to know how, Irene? How you can undo what Eleanor did and win yourself enormous respect from your fellow believers?'

'I won't listen to you.'

It was a token protest, dragged out because it was the right thing to say, a defence against the violation of her ingrained hypocrisy.

'I've never told on you, Irene.'

'Lies. All lies.' But there was despair behind the words, not desperation.

'You own twenty percent of Buchanan and one percent of Traverner,' Tamara reminded her. 'Yet here you are, as poor as a church mouse. Do you know what Eleanor does with the profits made over the years?'

No answer. Louder pants, seething with hatred and envy and the hidden resentments that curdled her mind. Tamara knew it. It poisoned the air puffing from Irene's lungs.

'All the money is leached away from the shareholders and spent within the company or stuck away in trusts,' she continued. 'Neither you nor I see what is rightfully ours.'

'That's to build up the vineyards,' came the ragged argument.

Tamara laughed in soft derision. 'While Eleanor lives in the luxury of the Big House. And Paul and David and their wives have everything they want. Rory and his grandfather get the crumbs from their tables, but what about you and me, Irene? Do we have everything we want?'

The push against the door weakened. Tamara shoved. Irene staggered as Tamara stepped into a room as bare as a nun's cell.

'You're content with this?' she scorned.

'It's good enough for me,' Irene cried.

'It's pitiful, Irene. Pitiful, like you.'

'The devil has sent you to tempt me.'

'Is this where you do secret things to yourself, Irene, covered by the darkness and the silence of the night?'

Frantic to escape the taunting, Irene scuttled over to the bed, and like a child afraid of phantoms, plunged herself under the quilt and lifted it over her head.

'Wealth beyond all your possible dreams, Irene,' Tamara went on, relentless in pursuing her purpose.

'I won't be tempted. The Lord is my shepherd. I won't be tempted.'

'The Lord has sent me as his avenging sword.'

The burrowing into oblivion ceased. 'He has?'

'Someone has to do it, Irene.'

'The Lord works in mysterious ways.'

'A sword to cut down those who have deprived you,

Irene. Someone to do the dirty work so you can stay clean. We'll be secret partners, Irene, just as we've always been. But this time, it will be for good. To set aside a great injustice and reap what should have been ours and the Lord's. It can be done.'

'How?'

'Think of your votes combined with mine. We'd control thirty-six percent of Traverner, thirty-eight percent of Buchanan. Think of how little more is needed, Irene, to get control. Uncle Frank, your father-in-law, can give it to us with his vote. His fifteen percent of Traverner and twenty-five percent of Buchanan added to our holdings give us control of both vineyards. We hold the secret that will bend him our way.'

'What secret?'

'You know, Irene. We both know. You could be head of the family company. Think of the reward you could give the Lord. You could sit in Eleanor's place and dispose of the profits from the vineyards as you will. Wouldn't you like that, Irene?'

A little snuffling sound from underneath the quilt.

'Once Eleanor is dead, Rory's grandfather should give his votes to you. You gave him Rory to carry on the Buchanan name. It will be your turn, Irene. He can be made to see the justice in that. Especially with our secret to persuade him it would be the only way justice would be served.'

The quilt was still, absolutely still.

'The reason I never told on you, Irene, was God told me not to.'

It was the only language Irene related to. She would never understand that the silence Tamara had maintained was for Rory. Or was it for herself, because of Rory? Whatever. It had something to do with Rory, whether love or hate.

Irene's God had never been a God of love. The avenging sword was a far more desirable concept.

'I'm the sword, Irene,' she repeated, nailing the point

home. 'When you're ready, come and talk to me. I'll be at the beach house.'

She walked out, closing the doors softly behind her, her purpose accomplished.

SIXTEEN

The stretch limousine rolled slowly and smoothly along the narrow Pokolbin roads. When the Traverner vineyard came into view, Frank Buchanan reached over and gently stroked his sister's hand.

'Almost home, Ellie.'

She stirred from her drug haze, opened her eyes and turned her head towards the side window. The first thing that hit her gaze was the monstrous house Max had built, dominating the landscape, as he'd meant it to.

Max, so extreme in everything he did. Unless it was on a larger, bolder scale than anything that had gone before, it was no good. His vision of greatness knew no boundary. Nor did his passions, his love of life or his seed.

The seed that had spawned Tamara.

The seed of my discontent, Eleanor thought, wincing over the wildness that had proved impossible to control, the wildness that was still running free, unpredictable, unrestrainable, dangerous.

'Are you in pain, Ellie?'

'It lets me know I'm alive,' she answered dryly.

'I'm not sure signing yourself out of hospital and coming home is the right decision.'

She rolled her head towards her brother. 'My life is here, Frank. You know that better than anyone.'

He nodded. 'Why not return to the Big House? You'd have Paul and Gabrielle to look after you.'

She knew she looked old and frail. Her body was mutilated, and her hair had turned white. Physically she was an invalid, but she didn't want to be viewed as one or treated as one. Her mind was still sharper than a shingle splitter's axe.

She would see the family when she chose to, not when they chose to see her. What time she had left was her own. It was precious, not to be frittered away on niceties and nonessentials.

'I'm going home, Frank. The Big House is not home to me. It never was.'

'It would be more convenient.'

'When did I ever do anything because it suited convenience?'

'Never.'

'That hasn't changed. I don't want memories of Max around me.'

Frank didn't argue. He never did. He'd only spoken out of concern for her, not wanting her to be alone in the old Traverner home. But she wouldn't be alone. Apart from the resident couple who would look after her practical needs, she would have her memories of Richard and the life and love they had shared.

She was tired. She was in pain. She wanted to go home to Richard. It was as simple as that, an ache, a need to return to the time when her life had been happy and uncomplicated, or at least to a semblance of it, where the echoes of her years with Richard would be around her.

It was inevitable that other things would intrude, impossible to avoid with the nemesis of Tamara haunting what time she had left. Traverner and Buchanan had to be kept secure. Max's daughter was like a loose cannon shell that had not yet found its target. Eleanor was under no delusion about what the target was. Maximum destruction.

'Have you been in touch with Tamara, Ellie?'

It jolted her. Frank reading her thoughts? She spoke sharply, discomforted by the idea. 'Why do you ask?'

He looked discomforted, as well. 'You told me to inform the rest of the family. I wondered about Tamara.'

'And give her the chance to mock me? Embarrass me? Shame me in public with more of her outrageous behaviour?' Her look was flagrantly derisive, meant to silence. 'I may be many things, Frank. I'm not a masochist.'

He frowned. He was not quelled. When Frank had an idea to express, nothing could put him off. 'It would be good to make peace, Ellie,' he softly suggested.

She almost laughed. He was so far out of kilter with the reality she faced. Impossible to tell him. He hadn't realised what had been necessary to get where they were now. He didn't have her foresight. Yet she loved his essential goodness, and it was important to her—always had been—that Frank think well of her.

She kept her mouth firmly shut.

Frank took it as a signal she was listening. He pressed his point, meaning well. 'All those unsuitable people Tamara brought home with her. I know it offended you, Ellie, and you saw it as deliberately scandalous. I thought...' He hesitated, choosing his words carefully. 'Well, that kind of wild rebellion...maybe it was a plea for acceptance.'

Never. It was war. Frank had no concept of hatred. He was looking for other reasons. Excuses.

'You might have been too hard on her over the affair with Rory,' he added quietly. 'It's worth thinking about, Ellie. I think Tamara was deeply scarred by it.'

I will not feel guilty about it, Eleanor thought fiercely. *I did what had to be done*. Besides, Tamara herself had recognised the losing game inherent in that pregnancy. She had not argued about the abortion. Yet after she had come out from the surgery, the look in her eyes, so piercing, so deadly, unforgettable however much Eleanor tried to wipe it out.

'I have the feeling she's a lost child, Ellie,' Frank murmured sadly. 'Maybe, deep down, she wants to come home. It wouldn't hurt to give it a chance, would it?'

'There's no chance of a reconciliation there, Frank.' It was the truth. She added the excuse she had always given her brother. 'Tamara was spoilt rotten by Max. Ingrained habits don't suddenly melt away at a soft word.'

'I know. I know. But...'

'No. Believe me. There's no meeting place between us.' Except a battleground. 'And I want to think of other things.'

He sighed, disappointed but accepting he'd tried and failed. 'Sorry. Just an idea I had,' he murmured.

'Which satisfied your sense of rightness.' She smiled to smooth over any hurt in the disagreement. 'Some things you have to let go, Frank.'

He nodded, his hands opening in a gesture of letting go. He'd said his piece. Eleanor knew she wouldn't hear any more from him on the subject. She wished she could dismiss it so easily.

It wouldn't go away.

Tamara was the cost of her marriage to Max, the cost of saving the Traverner vineyard for Paul and David. The full cost still had to be met and paid.

All these years that knowing little witch had waged a subtle form of guerrilla warfare, challenging, waiting, the black eyes watching, accusing, scorning, an unremitting relentlessness that would not let go, would never concede defeat. It would be war to the end with Tamara, hard and merciless.

Eleanor grimaced at her powerlessness to stop the chain reaction of hatred, started so long ago, before the child Max had insisted upon had even been born. She had hated every minute of that pregnancy, hated the necessity of it, hated even more the possible result of it. The relief of giving birth to a daughter had been enormous. A girl could be diverted from any interest in the vineyards. Max would not have been so malleable about keeping a son out of the business.

It had still been tricky, with Max so besotted with his daughter and Tamara so incredibly precocious, virtually from the cradle. How soon did a child sense alienation from her mother? Had she instinctively fought for her territory, competing for her father's love and attention and loyalty?

Another memory slid into Eleanor's mind. Tamara at three, the black eyes boring through Eleanor's pose of caring, defying her authority, denying her the right to any say in her life. The deliberate, calculated turn to her father, coaxing support from him. The awareness of the child—at three!—had shocked Eleanor out of any complacency over having had a daughter whose future could be easily manipulated.

The battleground had been laid then. It had shifted many times, and Eleanor had countered every move Max's daughter had made, defusing it of any power, turning it to her own advantage. But Tamara would not go away. She returned again and again to plague Eleanor and let her know it wasn't finished between them.

Paul and David had no real comprehension of their half-sister's driven hatreds, nor would they know how to deal with them. They knew the wine business inside out and loved it as their father had. They were good, solid businessmen. They were not fighters.

It worried Eleanor. It disappointed her. It frustrated her. But there was nothing she could do about it.

If Tamara had been Richard's daughter... She had the mettle Paul and David lacked, much as Eleanor hated to concede it. It was what made Tamara so dangerous. She had to be comprehensively blocked from using the company shares she had inherited from Max. At least the shareholding was diffused, spread over both vineyards. And Tamara's liaison with Rory was beyond revival now he was married to Louise.

So where was the weak spot? What could Tamara do?

'Ellie—' Frank cleared his throat '—I've been thinking. I'll come to the old house and stay with you.'

A whimsical smile curved her lips. No-one else called her Ellie. To other people Dame Eleanor was a formidable woman, no-one's fool, respected for her business acumen and feared by her competitors. Such viewpoints floated over Frank's head. He always used her childhood name. She was still his little sister, regardless of the changes wrought by time and circumstance.

'It's not necessary.' In fact, it might inhibit her from actions that had to be taken.

He looked keenly at her. 'We've been through a lot together over many years,' he reminded her.

Their lives were inextricably woven together. He was not only her brother, he was her friend. He knew her as no-one else knew her. Not everything, but the part of her she liked best.

'I don't know what I would have done without you,' she acknowledged.

He had been her rock of stability, the one person she could always rely on after Richard's death. It was commonly thought she was the stronger because she had initiated so much and was the driving force behind the success of their vineyards. Frank was quiet and taciturn by nature and preferred the background, weighing everything before acting or speaking. Perhaps only she knew the depth and breadth of the strength in her brother's character.

She watched him as he worked at formulating his thoughts into the right words.

'I guess I'm going to have to learn to live without you.'

'I guess you are, Frank,' she said.

He was seventy-six years old, her senior by eight years, and although his features had coarsened with age, he was still an impressive man, built like an oak tree. To her knowledge, no-one had ever picked a fight with Frank. His placid, gentle nature didn't invite fights. His size certainly deterred them.

'I don't want to intrude,' he said hesitantly.

'You never do,' she assured him.

'I'd like to be—well, just to be there for you, Ellie. If you need me.'

A lump constricted her throat. She reached out and took his hand, staring at the age spots on his dry, weathered skin, fighting tears as she slowly linked her fingers with his. Facing death was a lonely business. She wanted her brother with her. She would work around his presence somehow.

'From the beginning to the end,' she murmured.

'I'll see you settled, then fetch my things from home,' he said gruffly.

She nodded, squeezed his hand and turned her head to look out the window again.

Traverner land. One hundred and fifty years of devout cultivation. Two hundred and fifty prime hectares under vine on the lower slopes of the foothills near the Brokenback Range, plus another one hundred and twenty hectares on the secondary property on the Broke Road. It was what she had given her life to. She knew every clod of the heavy red clay with its natural lime. She had worked it with her hands.

The limousine slowed and turned.

There by the sliprail fence, she and Richard had pledged themselves to each other. Forever.

Seventeen years they'd had together. And all her growing-up years before that. She vividly remembered deciding to marry him when she was four years old. Frank had run off and left her stuck up in the mulberry tree. Richard had rescued her.

If only she'd been able to rescue him.

She looked down the rows of vines they were slowly passing on their way to the house. She caught a brief glimpse of the garden bench she had placed where the lightning had struck, ending Richard's life.

Tomorrow she would go and sit there. Tomorrow she would let herself remember that dreadful day. But right now she had to think about the future. She had rescued the Traverner vineyard for Richard and his sons. She would not allow anything to get in the way of securing what she had achieved. Not even death.

'I wish to see Paul and David as soon as I get home,' she said, knowing Frank would make the calls for her.

'They'll be waiting inside for you. Gabrielle and Sharon, as well. They want to welcome you home, Ellie.'

She didn't need a welcome home. She needed to know what had been going on while she was in hospital. She needed to know where Tamara was. She needed to know what Tamara was up to.

The limousine came to a halt.

She looked out at the rambling weatherboard house with its bullnose iron roof and the wide verandas and felt her heart turn over. Richard was here. She could feel his presence everywhere.

She was home.

SEVENTEEN

'I want the chairmanship of Buchanan, Paul.'

David's declaration created a silence that smashed any facade of family harmony.

'We've always been equals in everything,' he went on in forceful argument. 'I say we share the family company equally. So let there be no misunderstanding. You can have Traverner. I intend to have Buchanan.'

Gabrielle looked at the shock on Paul's face and knew David's announcement had not been anticipated in any shape or form. It did not come as such a stunning blow to her. For one thing, the vineyards didn't mean as much. For another, she had sensed something wrong, something more than the unease of how best to act when Eleanor's limousine arrived.

David and Sharon had been tense from the moment they had arrived at the old Traverner home. Sharon, particularly, had been nervous in both her speech and manner. Gabrielle had wondered about it. Now she knew. David had told his wife what he was going to say.

Paul was frozen by the doorway that led out of the sitting room. He had been hovering there, expecting the limousine to arrive at any moment. David stood with his back to the unlit fireplace, his face set and stern. No yielding there. No backward steps to be taken.

He had the same big, sturdy build as his uncle, Frank Buchanan. Like Frank, he had never been known to fight over anything. Never had to. His size was too daunting.

David was ready to fight now, his dark Buchanan eyes steady and determined. He waited for Paul's response.

Sharon rose from the settee and moved to link her arm with her husband's. Gabrielle had always thought her light-weight, petite, fluffy and feminine, a case of opposites attracting when she and David fell in love.

Sharon had one highly individual characteristic. She draped things. She draped a chair or a piece of furniture as a curtain draped a window. She embellished it without being part of it. At this moment, she draped David.

It prompted Gabrielle to reappraise what Sharon's role was in this outburst from David. She was certainly part of it. Her pretty face had taken on a proud, defiant look. She was standing with her man over what they both undoubtedly saw as his rightful claim to a fair division of family property.

Was it a case of the younger brother kicking against the older brother, heir-to-the-kingdom situation? Or a long-hidden jealousy?

Paul was made so closely in the image of his father, tall, lean, blue-eyed, his face not quite classically handsome, yet attractive because it reflected the highly strung temperament of his upbringing and heritage. Gabrielle knew that underneath the show of authority and austerity lay a deeply sensitive heart. He had shown it to her openly, the year he was in France, the year they had met and married, away from his mother.

Men liked him for his directness. Women liked him for the way he looked so attentively into their eyes. Yet Paul was not flirtatious by nature. He appeared to be singularly unaware of his sex appeal. She'd found that intensely appealing. He'd seemed so amazed that she loved him for the man he was, as though she had to overlook shortcomings—almost certainly a hangover from his mother's demands on him.

Somehow, under the influence of his mother, he took on a blindness or tunnel vision, directed solely at the business. He was hurt by David's words. She saw the shock on his face give way to a look of pained bewilderment. He'd had no idea David was discontent with the way they worked together. Although Paul was the senior, he regarded his brother as an equal partner. The division David was proposing cut the bond Paul had believed they shared.

Divide and conquer. Was David taking this action at his own behest? Or was there more to it?

The amalgamation of the properties under the family company was something Eleanor had carefully forged with her brother twelve years ago. Gabrielle could not believe Eleanor would look upon David's demand for division with friendly eyes.

She saw the effort Paul made not to react in any way he might regret later. He would be forcing himself to weigh implications and the options available to him. Gabrielle bled for him.

She didn't move to stand beside him. It would only promote an image of them against us. Paul wouldn't want that any more than she did. She would help him deal with it later, when they were alone. Nevertheless, the need to support him—as she'd always done whenever he felt lost within himself—was paramount. The nexus of silence had to be broken. A distraction was essential.

'Louise,' she said with a startling clarity that drew the attention of everyone in the room. 'Louise is a bitch.'

They stared at her, shocked that such an unGabrielle-like word would fall from her lips. The abrupt change of subject left them confused.

She rose from her chair with dignity and grace and

smiled, looking from Paul to David to Sharon and back to Paul. 'But perhaps I am wrong. Perhaps I should have said Louise is a politician's daughter.' Gabrielle managed to inject acid scorn into the word *politician*.

Paul frowned. 'What specifically are you talking about, Gabrielle?'

She looked David straight in the eye. 'You're not the only one trying to undo what your mother built, David. Louise set me up to approach Irene today.'

'So what?' David asked belligerently. 'What does it matter whom she sees?'

Gabrielle strolled towards Paul and took her place beside him, slipping her arm around his and taking his hand, her fingers stroking their empathy, then gripping tightly, letting him feel her love and loyalty as she spoke a truth that had to be faced.

'The assumption you're working on, David, is that Paul will give you what you want. You haven't done your sums. Paul may be in no position to give anything to anybody.'

She felt Paul's body stiffen, absorbing another shock, momentarily rejecting the idea she was putting forward. It did not matter. Paul had to realise and face it sooner or later. It may as well be now, when it could do some good. The situation was no longer David versus Paul, but Paul and David united against what others might be planning.

'Irene has always abstained from voting,' David argued. 'Unless Louise suddenly gets religion in a big way, which I don't see happening, she and Irene would have nothing in common.'

'Can you guarantee that Irene will always abstain?' Gabrielle softly challenged. 'And Tamara, too? People can change their minds, given the right approach and the right incentive.' She paused for it to sink in, then flatly stated, 'Louise is a dealer. Like her father.'

'What makes you think that?' David asked sharply.

'Haven't you noticed her working the parties at the Big

House? She's even more adept at it than your mother is, David.'

He stared at her, the realisation hitting him that his calculations could be thrown completely awry.

It was the first time any of them had considered that control of the Buchanan vineyard might be taken completely out of Traverner hands. Rory had not been considered a contender for control of anything. He was twelve years younger than Paul, ten years younger than David, and it was David who had trained Rory in the management of the Buchanan winery.

Rory's vote from the twenty percent of Buchanan he had inherited from his father was insignificant by itself. However, if Irene's vote from her twenty-percent holding was added to Rory's...

'Forty percent to our forty-two,' David said dismissively. 'It's no problem.'

'If Uncle Frank continues to vote with us,' Paul said, realising now that nothing could be taken for granted.

David swung on him. 'He's always sided with Mum.'

'Eleanor won't be here.' Gabrielle's quiet words sobered them.

Nothing was going to be the same after Eleanor died. They had to come to terms with that. If David didn't want to stay with Paul, working the Traverner vineyard together, it was going to be even less the same. Gabrielle had a premonition of bad times ahead. She didn't want to be part of it. She hated scheming. She wanted a peaceful, happy life with Paul and their children.

She looked at him in silent anguish. He was a fine man, caring of others, strong in integrity. She loved him. She tried to be all he might want in his wife, given his position of prominence in the valley. Yet she hated the Big House and the kind of life that went with it. To her it had a soulless quality. If they could simply be together, as a family...

'I think Uncle Frank would vote for me,' David said, his

expression one of almost vulnerable appeal to Paul, the fight leeched out of him for the moment. 'I'm as much a Buchanan as Rory is. And don't forget it was me Uncle Frank asked to fill his son's place when Ian died in the plane crash.'

'Until Rory was old enough to take over,' Paul reminded him gently. 'But you may well be right, David. Though if Louise does manage to persuade Irene, then goes after Tamara...'

'Can't we get Tamara's vote?' Sharon piped up.

Paul winced. 'I have no intention of courting Tamara in order to get her vote,' he said in an arctic voice. 'And she'd laugh in our faces if we asked for it.'

'Are we in some kind of jeopardy?' David questioned further, a note of uncertainty in his voice for the first time.

'Work it out for yourself,' Paul said with some asperity, still smarting from his brother's demand even though he recognised there was some degree of justice in his claim to be chairman of Buchanan.

David exploded with irritation and frustration. 'This is a ridiculous situation. Traverner is ours. It's always been ours. Mum is a Buchanan, and we have a right to that, as well.'

Paul watched his outburst with disdain. 'Rights are things earned, not gratuities.'

'God damn it! We have earned it! And no-one's going to take it away from us.' He looked angrily at Paul. 'Irene's never done a hand's turn for the vineyards. Neither has Tamara. Why should they have any say in the vote?'

'Their shares entitle them to it, whether we like it or not.'

'It's an anomaly.' David hunted for a way around it and found none. He looked to Paul for a solution. 'What are we going to do about it?'

The sound of a car arriving heightened the tension in the room.

'Nothing,' Paul said. 'I'm going to do absolutely nothing.' He turned to greet his mother.

'You must do something,' David called after him. 'I insist.'

Gabrielle wondered if David realised what such an insistence revealed. Paul was the planner, the policy maker, the leader. David was brilliant at getting things done once the way was pointed out to him. Essentially he was a follower. Together they were a highly effective and efficient team, complementing each other. With Paul, David felt a strong sense of self-worth. Apart from him, Gabrielle suspected David would quickly come face-to-face with his limitations and begin to feel inadequate.

Paul's back straightened. He stopped and looked at his brother, his eyes colder than Gabrielle had ever seen them.

'If you insist I do something, then I have no choice. I will do something. Tomorrow morning I'll go and talk to Rory.'

EIGHTEEN

Paul set the glass of dark red wine on the table in front of his mother, then showed her the bottle from which it had been poured. 'It's from Dad's last vintage,' he said quietly.

She grazed her fingers over the label and looked at him, her mouth softening into a sad smile. 'It's been a long time.'

He nodded. 'Welcome home, Mum.'

'Thank you, Paul.'

She didn't have to say that the thank-you was for his understanding. It was in her eyes, the dark glow of long memories, joys and sorrows that bound them to a shared life.

Before Max Vandelier.

He turned and served the rest of the family with the wine that had been stored in the Traverner cellars for thirty years. They were seated around the dining table, his mother at the head, Uncle Frank to her right, David on the left, Sharon next to him, Gabrielle opposite her, his own chair at the foot of the table facing his mother. He sat, then raised his glass in a toast.

'To endurance.'

The words might not be in the best of taste, but no-one made a protest. To Paul, it was what his mother's life had been about. There was no place for platitudes now. Only truth.

Nothing could cover up the brutal reality that she was under a death sentence. Her face was thin, engraved with deep age lines. The iron-grey hair, so characteristic of her iron will, had turned snow white. The red dress she wore was a brave statement. It didn't work. Her once indomitable body now appeared weak and fragile.

Paul knew why she had chosen to talk with them here rather than avail herself of the comfort of the sitting room. Dying she was, but there'd be no abrogation of her authority until she'd gone. Simply by being seated at the head of this table, she asserted her position as head of the family and reinforced her right to it.

She was framed by a heritage that had been the focus of her life. Behind her was a magnificent old cedar sideboard. Above it hung a mirror, its ornate cedar frame carved into clusters of grapes and vine leaves. Both pieces had been commissioned by the first Traverner at Pokolbin and passed down through four generations to her first husband, Richard Traverner.

Did she realise her death could put it all at risk?

'Well, David.' She smiled at him. 'Fill me in on what's been happening.' As though she was ready to pick up the reins again, regardless of the physical and mental trauma she must be suffering.

Maybe she had a solution.

He wondered if David would present the problem to her.

Strangely enough, Paul found he didn't care. He felt detached. Since David wanted to dissolve their partnership and be independent, let him state his case to their mother. To Uncle Frank, as well.

Rightly or wrongly, he felt a sense of betrayal, as though the world had shifted and become an alien place. Or had he shut his eyes to what he didn't want to see? How much more clearly did Gabrielle see?

It was so unlike her to put herself forward as she had.

What had prompted her to enter the fray, discarding the air of separateness she usually maintained at family meetings?

He looked at her, wanting to know her mind as intimately as he knew her body. Her eyes were downcast, their thick lashes an impenetrable veil. Her lovely, fine-boned face wore a serenity that concealed her thoughts. Even the long black waves of her hair were completely still, as though sculpted to her head.

She was slowly rolling the glass of wine in her hands, ostensibly warming it to bring out the flavour. He knew the action was a cover for the retreat into herself that so frequently frustrated him.

Gabrielle had the capacity to light up a room with her charm. More often she carried a halo of vulnerable untouchability, as she did now. He felt a violent urge to break it, to reach across, touch her, to make love to her, to drag her out of the private inner world that excluded him.

The tactics Gabrielle had used sliced into his mind. Without pausing to consider any consequences, he cut into the meticulous business report David was giving.

'Louise went to visit Irene today.'

It drew everyone's startled attention. Gabrielle looked at him wide-eyed. He knew precisely what she was thinking. It was not like him to rudely interrupt anyone. It was true. He abhorred such bad manners in others. Right now it gave him a savage satisfaction.

David's lips compressed. He didn't like it. No doubt he would have selected a different approach to their mother. A more private approach. Well, to hell with that!

'Correct me if I'm wrong,' Paul said, looking directly at his mother, 'but I thought you'd be more interested in knowing what's happening among the family.'

No correction came. 'For what purpose did Louise visit Irene?'

There was certainly no damage to his mother's mind. Straight to the point.

'Gabrielle?' Paul invited, challenging her to become involved, to reveal the process of thought that had led to the ripping aside of his blind delusions about the future.

Her eyes searched his intently before she slowly turned to face his mother. 'The news that your operation was unsuccessful apparently prompted Louise to start thinking she shouldn't take time for granted. She felt some effort should be made to effect a reconciliation between Rory and his mother. I agreed to introduce her to Irene.'

Frank Buchanan cleared his throat. 'These are private matters. I won't have any part of them. I'll leave you to talk as you will. No offence to you, Gabrielle.' He drank deeply from the glass in front of him. 'A fine vintage, Ellie. A remembrance of happier times.' He slid his chair back and laid his hands flat on the table as he started to rise to his feet.

A much thinner, whiter hand covered one of his and hung on as he straightened. Paul watched the attachment, wondering how strong it was. Did his mother exert a domination over her elder brother, or was there a dependence on each other as he'd thought there was between himself and David? Did Frank Buchanan ever kick against what his sister wanted?

'Stay with me, Frank. I may need you.' Soft, simple words, more an appeal than a command.

Paul studied his uncle as the old man took the words in, weighing them against his sense of rightness. He had drawn a line. Irene and Rory were his family. He would not have them discussed in a way that could compromise his loyalties.

Paul willed him to stay. He wanted to see how far his mother would respect that line.

Frank took his time in coming to a decision. 'As you wish, Ellie,' he said, but it was not an obeisance to her will. It was an agreement. Paul was quite sure of that as he watched his uncle slowly sit and draw his chair to the table. His mother immediately confirmed it.

'I will deal with the problem of Irene in my own way.'

The pronouncement was pure Dame Eleanor, carrying unassailable confidence and authority. It was also the end of the matter of Irene and Louise and Rory, in deference to her brother's sensibilities.

No dominance, Paul thought. No dominance at all. Frank Buchanan would only take his sister's side if he believed it was right. Paul noticed he retained hold of his sister's hand, lending his strength to hers if she needed it.

It redrew their relationship in Paul's mind. It changed the assumptions he had comfortably nursed. The world he thought he had known shifted again.

His mother looked around the table, sternly reproving, as though they were fractious children who needed her strong hand to keep them in line. 'Are there any other matters that need to be brought to my attention?'

Paul inwardly bridled against the condescension, the assumption they couldn't work things out for themselves, that everything had to be laid at her feet to decide.

No-one replied.

She turned her direct attention to David. 'Are you content with your lot, David?'

The intimidation of her authority was too much for David. He couldn't bring himself to rebel to her face. He hesitated but he capitulated. 'Yes, Mum.'

Paul felt furious with him. If he wanted to be his own man, let him stand up and enforce it, as Uncle Frank had.

'Sharon?'

She glanced at David, looking for direction. He gave none. In a quavering voice, she answered, 'I think my husband is entitled to a more important position.'

Paul stared at her in surprise. Had Sharon put David up to making a claim for himself?

His mother leaned forward, her face jutting out, and in the mildest of tones said, 'What do you suggest, Sharon?'

It was cruel. Like a cat playing with a mouse. Sharon was no Lady Macbeth, pushing her husband forward. She adored David. Whatever she'd said to him would have been out of wanting him to have all he deserved. It was loyalty and love that had spoken, not ambition. Paul watched her struggle for a reply in the face of his mother's obvious readiness to pounce on any challenge to what she had put in place.

'I'm sure if we all put our heads together, we can think of something.' She choked the words out, retreating to safer ground.

His mother leaned back in her chair, the matriarch, the decision maker. 'Perhaps,' she mused. 'Perhaps not.'

She let that sink in.

David sat like a Stoic. Sharon shrank into her submissive shell.

Paul tensed as his mother's gaze shifted to him. He stared straight at her, challenging her to try putting him down in any shape or form. He'd blow the whole bloody business wide open so that no-one could back away from it.

She passed on to Gabrielle. 'What do you want most in the world, Gabrielle? What is your desire?'

There was no hesitation. 'For my children to be happy.'

Paul looked at his wife, wondering if she'd had the answer prepared to avoid contention or whether she spoke the simple truth. She was perfectly calm, apparently untouched by all that had gone before.

In a sudden flash of insight, he realised she had never acceded to his mother's dominance, not in the Big House, not in any personal sense. She stood aside from it, remaining her own person, uninfluenced by the forces that had shaped his life and his thinking.

He didn't like the thought. It made him feel crippled.

'Your children want for nothing,' his mother stated. 'Why aren't they happy?'

'Perhaps—' Gabrielle paused over the word deliberately, looking his mother straight in the eye '—because your children are not happy.'

Paul was unaware of his fingers clenching, stressing the fine stem of the glass in his hand. It snapped. The goblet crashed onto the table, breaking into shards, spilling the precious vintage of thirty years ago across the polished cedar. It formed a dark puddle, like blood.

A surge of some deep instinctive protest drove him to crash the broken base of the goblet down on the table. 'I don't understand this conversation.'

He stood up, raging with so many turbulent emotions he could no longer contain them. His chair tipped over, clattering onto the floor behind him. He didn't care. He glared at Gabrielle, feeling deceived, hurt by her clinical attitude.

'For God's sake! Our children are happy.' He flung his arm out to encompass everyone at the table. 'We're all happy. You couldn't find a family that's happier, more contented, working together.'

He knew it wasn't so, but he wanted it to be true. He wanted what he'd thought he had.

Gabrielle looked at him, her vivid blue eyes piercing in their clarity, pained at giving pain, but determined to follow through what she had started. 'Then why isn't Tamara here, Paul?' she asked quietly. 'Where are Rory and Louise? And Irene?'

He was stumped for a reply. It came to him that Gabrielle had never said a bad word about Tamara. She was especially kind to Rory. She was the only one in the family who visited Irene.

'These are good questions,' his mother said in a mild tone, apparently unaffected by the volatile proceedings. She turned to her brother, ignoring everyone else. 'What do you think, Frank? Are you happy?'

He lifted his other hand over hers and stroked it with

soothing gentleness. 'We'll all be together, close enough, soon enough, Ellie. No need to worry.'

She seemed to grow in strength. She looked around the table. 'You heard your uncle. There isn't any problem that isn't going to get solved. In the meantime, Paul, would you be kind enough to get another goblet and be a little more careful, in future, of your father's precious vintage.'

The older generation reigned. Never mind that the younger generation had carried the load for over a decade. Their contribution wasn't even to be recognised, let alone respected.

'Stuff Dad's precious vintage! I've had enough. Gabrielle—' she looked at him, and he saw a flash of hope in her eyes '—we have our own family to go to.'

'Yes,' she said, rising instantly to her feet, and he felt a burst of fierce pride in himself and his wife. They were an entity unto themselves, and that was the way it was going to be from now on. No dependence on anyone else.

'What on earth are you saying, Paul?' his mother asked, one eyebrow rising quizzically.

He wasn't going to explain himself.

Gabrielle took his hand, her fingers threading through his as they'd done before. He recognised it as a gesture of unity. He didn't know what prompted her to answer for him, but as she spoke, he knew she read his heart better than he did himself.

'He's saying that he loves you. He's saying he's sorry that what's happened to you has happened. He's saying he's worked as hard as his father ever worked and he wants to be recognised as the man he is. So does David. He's also saying enough is enough, and he won't be patronised, and now is the time for change.'

His mother did not look the least taken aback by the statement of truths that rolled off Gabrielle's tongue. If anything, a faint smile seemed to hover on her mouth. 'You speak so eloquently, Gabrielle. It doesn't leave anything more to be said, does it?'

'Yes, there's one thing left to be said,' Gabrielle replied, a deep sadness softening and lowering her voice. 'Welcome home, Eleanor. I'm sure you're tired. We'll leave you so you can rest.'

NINETEEN

Anger drove him. Rory didn't notice the kilometres go by, and time had no meaning. He had a sense of dislocation. Behind him were smashed illusions. In front of him was the lure of lost dreams.

Not that he thought they had suddenly become attainable. He didn't fool himself that the love of his youth could be miraculously fulfilled. Tamara was no more straightforward than Louise had been. But he did want the torment of Tamara eased, one way or another. He felt a compelling urge to get the past and the present straightened out in his mind. Only then could he set a future course with definition.

He tried to give attention to where he was driving once he turned off the expressway to Sydney. A crowd of commuters disgorging from the railway station delayed his passage through Woy Woy. The road narrowed past Umina, and he slowed the Maserati to a careful pace to take the hairpin bend leading to Mount Ettymalong. It was a steep, winding road, demanding concentration until he was over the top and down the other side to the beautiful little enclave of Pearl Beach.

It was a quiet community. The real estate prices made it a rather exclusive community. The village had one general store to cater for daily needs, a public hall, a tennis court,

Pearl's Restaurant on the beach and a café, and the rest was housing. The residents were set on keeping it that way. Even the street names—Diamond Road, Amethyst Avenue, Opal Close, Coral Crescent—reflected the view that this was a jewel of a place to be treasured for what it offered.

Rory had a perverse fondness for the boxy little fibro cottages, built as holiday weekenders long before Pearl Beach had become fashionable. They looked so incongruous, standing shoulder to shoulder against the more elegant homes of the rich and famous who had 'discovered' the hideaway, yet there was a simple honesty about them that appealed to him.

His life was bereft of simplicity right now. He'd finally had some honesty from Louise. What could he expect from Tamara? Another hidden agenda? Was she out to use him, too? Had she given him sex and lies to soften him up for her purpose, as Louise had? If so, no way was it going to work.

He crossed the bridge over the channel linking the lagoon to the sea and climbed the hill on the southern side of the beach. Tamara's black Porsche was parked on the verge beside the house. He slid the Maserati to a halt behind it.

The beach house was a massive concrete and glass structure, built against the hill to face north and running down three levels. It was typical of Max Vandelier to construct something that stood out instead of something that blended in to the surrounding natural bushland. Rory much preferred the more harmonious look of the house adjacent. It was of untreated cedar, the wood silvering with age.

He alighted from the car and was immediately struck by the tranquillity that allowed the sounds of birds and the ocean to be heard. He wondered how often Tamara retreated here, if she found some peace from her restless, hectic life in these surroundings.

He pressed the doorbell.

Impossible to really know what was truth with Tamara. She twisted and twirled like a tornado, touching lives at random, completely careless of what path she took and what havoc she wreaked. But no more of that tonight, he vowed. If she wouldn't be pinned down to answers that satisfied his need to know, then to hell with her, too!

She didn't answer the doorbell. Rory checked his watch. It was getting close to seven. She would have arrived well over an hour ago. He tried the door. It wasn't locked. Was she so confident he would come to her, despite his marriage to Louise?

Rory hesitated, resenting the idea that Tamara might think of him as a dog on a chain she could pull in at any time. He hadn't come to service her. Then he told himself he didn't care what she thought. He'd come because he wanted to and he'd go when he wanted to.

With a seething sense of self-determination he stepped in to the gallery that contained the staircase down to the next level. Hallways on either side of it led to the bedrooms, all with spectacular views. He shut the door behind him and started down the stairs to the main living areas. He knew Tamara was there before he reached the bottom. The glass doors onto the balcony were wide open, letting in the splashing sound of the waves and the salty smell of sea water.

She was curled up on a deeply cushioned cane settee, facing the view, a drink in her hand, ice tinkling. He didn't greet her. She didn't greet him. She was here. He was here. That said it all.

He went to the bar in the corner of the room and helped himself to a double gin and tonic. Mother's ruin, he thought with irony, wondering if Tamara really wanted to be a mother. He took a deep swallow of the strong alcohol and looked at her, a hard challenge in his eyes, not the look of a slave to any woman. Or man.

She studied him. No smile of triumph. No welcoming smile, either. It was as though she was taking a long, detached view of him, assessing his strengths and weaknesses.

'You've changed your clothes,' she commented.

She had changed, too. The soft, baggy T-shirt and multi-coloured leggings made her look like a teenager. A deliberate evoking of memories?

'My tumble on your car ripped my shirt,' he answered nonchalantly.

'You limped.'

'Bruised my leg.'

'Have you had it treated?'

'Louise put witch hazel on it.'

'Louise is a fuckwit.'

'Oh, I wouldn't say that. No, I wouldn't say that at all,' Rory drawled. 'Louise definitely has her wits concentrated on far more than fucking.'

He took a long swig of the double gin, eyeing Tamara derisively. 'Now me...I'd like a good honest fuck. Simply because it's wanted. You once gave me that. I guess the memory of it pulled me here. Maybe I can ignore the fact you want to use me for your own ends, too.'

'It will be your baby as well as mine, Rory. We'll be making it together.'

'Sure! A togetherness project. Which I get left out of once I do the job of impregnating you.'

'No. I won't leave you out of this. I'll never cut you out of our child's life, Rory.' Her black eyes glittered. 'That I promise you.'

There was something ominous in her promise. Tamara had a plan. Wanting a baby was definitely not a spur of the moment impulse. Rory wondered how important he was to the plan.

'Louise wants you to sign a paper saying I'll never be named as the father,' he told her.

Tamara laughed. 'Do you expect me to comply?'

'She also wants a signed declaration from you giving me the power to vote your shares by proxy.'

'How very enterprising of her!'

'If I get these things from you, she'll give me a child. After we're in the Big House.'

'You're hopeless, Rory. You've married a woman in the same mould as Eleanor.'

He bridled under her look of pity. 'Hopeless I might be. At least I'm honest.'

'Do you intend to go back to her?' It was asked with a kind of detached curiosity.

'No. Which doesn't mean I'll stay with you. At the present moment I have a very strong aversion to female bloodsuckers.'

She smiled. There was a gleam of approval in her eyes. Again he felt the tug on his heart, as though the years of crap that had buried their sense of togetherness was simply that—crap. Nothing of any real importance.

He drank some more gin, savouring the enlivening kick of the alcohol. He watched the woman who still held the power to affect him beyond any reasonable stance that should be taken with her. Was it a crazy obsession? Had he inherited some streak of fanaticism from his mother? Tamara was like some dark parasite on his life he couldn't shake off.

'What are you, Tamara?' he asked, curious as to how she saw herself.

She put her glass on the coffee table beside her, uncurled from the settee and strolled towards him, an ironic tilt curling her smile to one side. 'I'm the ministering angel. I won't sign any papers, Rory, but I will soothe your hurts.' She held out her hand. 'Let's go upstairs.'

He shook his head. 'It's not that easy. Not even your expert bag of sexual tricks will work this time. I'm not in a malleable mood. I asked you before—why call on me now, after all these years?'

The smile died. The hand dropped. Her face took on a hard, implacable look, her eyes a flat black. Merciless. 'Use your brain, Rory,' she taunted. 'Work it out. What prompted Louise to drop her mask of wifely perfection?'

So Tamara knew about her mother, knew last night when she had decided she wanted his baby. Who had told her? Probably his grandfather. Yes, his grandfather would consider it the right thing to do, perhaps hoping for some last-hour mending of the rift between mother and daughter.

'Eleanor's cancer,' Rory said out loud. 'The news that she is dying.'

'After all these years.' There was biting mockery in her repetition of his words. 'And even in her death throes she would do everything in her power to stop us from coming together.'

'You did a good job of it yourself, Tamara.'

She turned the mockery inwards. 'Out of love. Out of hate. Out of despair.'

'I waited for you. I was there for you,' he argued, refusing to exonerate her behaviour towards him without more understanding than she was giving him. 'I'd promised you I would be. I didn't look at another woman until you degraded the love I felt for you. Beyond bearing.'

She ignored his bitter accusation as though she was immune to it. Or it had no relevance. Her expression drifted into bleak reminiscence. 'Do you remember what happened that summer before she banished me to a boarding school to keep us apart?'

'I haven't forgotten any of it,' he said tersely, frustrated with her harking back to a time long gone. It was *now* that concerned him.

She shook her head. 'Not us, Rory. Your father.'

The memory of his father's death rushed in on him, the anguish and the confusion and the emptiness, like an extra punishment for what he'd done with Tamara.

'Have you ever wondered how he came to crash his plane into that hillside?' she asked, her eyes focusing sharply on his. 'It was a clear day. No wind. No mechanical or structural fault was found in the wreckage. He was an expert pilot.'

'All I know is it shouldn't have happened. But it did,' Rory muttered grimly. He finished off the gin and set the empty glass on the bar. 'What do you know that I don't, Tamara?'

'Before he drove to the airfield at Scone, he came to the Big House. He was in the library with my mother. She was the last person he spoke to.'

He shrugged. 'So what? It could have been normal business.'

She folded her arms, hugging her midriff. It struck him as a curiously defensive act for Tamara. Bold rebellion was more her style. But she had been badly hurt twelve years ago. Hurt and lost with no-one to turn to because he had acceded to the demands of his parents. And Eleanor.

'I waited for him to come out. Away from my mother,' she said flatly. 'I ran after him and caught him near his car. I didn't want to be sent away from home. I wanted him to let me see you. He shook me off like an insect. He made no response to my pleas. He stared right through me. He got in his car, and two hours later he was dead.'

The old guilt surged in Rory, gnawing with new strength. 'They might have been talking about us.'

'Nothing more certain,' Tamara asserted. 'It was a good weapon for my mother to use. The harm done to her daughter under *his* roof. The betrayal of trust. And so on. She's a wonderful opportunist, my mother.'

'Eleanor didn't fly the plane, Tamara.'

Her black eyes bored into his. 'Your father's death allowed her to move David into Buchanan. It was an easy step then to persuade Uncle Frank into forming the family company. After all, Rory, you were only sixteen—' her mouth curled derisively '—and anything can happen to a teenager. A wild boy like you who'd fucked his cousin all summer.'

A chill crept down Rory's spine. He knew Eleanor was a

manipulator. She would have known about his father's scheduled trip to Canberra that morning. Had she deliberately driven him into such a state of mind that he'd been mentally unfit to fly? Did her obsessive ambition admit no bounds? What Tamara was suggesting was so sick.

He worked some saliva into a mouth gone dry and quietly asked, 'How monstrous is she, Tamara? Did she know about you and your father?'

There was a flare of violent hatred in her eyes before she turned away from him, her head held defiantly high as she moved to the doorway to the balcony. Her gaze fixed on some far distance out to sea. Anger vibrated through her voice.

'She cheated my father. She cheated me. You've thwarted her all these years by following in your grandfather's footsteps, being his true heir in your love for the vineyard and the winemaking. But don't think she won't try to cheat you on her deathbed, Rory. She will.'

The same warning Louise had given. Both women might be reading Eleanor correctly, but they were overlooking the quieter but steadfast strength of Frank Buchanan.

'My grandfather wouldn't allow it, Tamara,' Rory said, confident of his grandfather's love and integrity. They shared a bond of understanding that he couldn't see ever being shaken.

'If I die, my mother is my next of kin. That gives her Traverner, free and clear,' Tamara went on. There was a relentless beat to what she said, like a drum of inevitability. 'Add my shareholding in Buchanan to hers, Paul's and David's, and they have thirty-five percent. She holds the weapon of fear over Irene.'

'Fear of what?'

'It doesn't matter. It's there. And she'll use it. That gives her fifty-five percent. All it takes is for me to die without an heir, and she has both vineyards in her hands.'

The chill deepened. 'You're talking murder, Tamara.'

'An accident. The way I've lived, who would question it?' She swung her head to half-face him. 'Would you, if I hadn't come to you today and you hadn't followed me here and heard me say this?'

She was right. A fatal accident would seem like an inevitable finale to Tamara's reckless defiance of everything normal. Yet had she ever known any normality?

Rory's mind was in chaos, trying to cope with the obscene pattern she was laying out for him. His father, his mother, Tamara...Eleanor moving all of them to her will. Was it a distortion, a horror vision from Tamara's damaged psyche, or the base truth behind all that had lain unanswered? Either way, she believed it, and she was in a position to know more than he did about Eleanor.

'For us, for you and me to be together, Rory, the only chance we had was to run away and cut ourselves off from the family and the vineyards,' she stated flatly.

'Why so extreme?' he demanded, railing against her judgment.

She didn't answer. She continued as though he hadn't spoken. 'After your father died, I knew you wouldn't do that. No matter what I said or did, I knew you wouldn't do it.'

'It would have been wrong,' he asserted strongly, wanting her to respond directly to him.

'Of course.' Her mouth curled and her voice lilted into mockery again. 'Your sense of rightness wouldn't allow it. A true hero steps into the breach. You were suddenly thrust into the role of man of the house. You had a mother and a sister. Your grandfather expected you to fill your father's place at Buchanan. And apart from all that, it was your heritage, Rory, and you loved it. More than you loved me.'

The glib recitation of his feelings made him squirm inside, yet why should he feel guilty? 'We didn't have to run away,' he argued heatedly, trying to force some sanity into her view of the past. 'We only had to wait.'

Violent emotion suddenly erupted from her. 'Don't you yet realise Eleanor was never going to let us join forces?' she yelled, her eyes glittering furious contempt at his inability to grasp what was so clear to her. 'We would have been a threat to her hold on the vineyards. She would have used anything, done anything to drive us apart and keep us apart.'

Rory could feel his jaw tighten with belligerence. 'We could have fought her together, Tamara.'

'You wouldn't have believed me.' She hurled the words at him, her arms flying out in emphatic gesticulation. 'You wouldn't have fought dirty enough.'

'You didn't give me the chance,' he shot back. 'Or the choice,' he added with passionate vehemence.

His hands clenched in mute protest against the impotence of the position she had allotted to him. He wanted to lash out at something. Even if Tamara was a hundred percent right about Eleanor, they could have fought her together. At least to have the option...

'You weren't there for me when I needed you.'

The repetition of that claim inflamed his angry frustration, yet the fire had gone out of her voice. Out of her eyes. She turned her face to the sea again, and her words floated to him thinly, all feeling leached out of them.

'I fought her alone. I was only fourteen. No match for Eleanor. She had too many weapons. She killed my heart that summer. As surely as if she had driven a stake through it.'

She looked at him with a twisted little smile that didn't reach her eyes. 'So you see, Rory, I didn't have it in me to love again. Only to hate.'

And finally he did see. The destruction of dreams.

Out of love. Out of hate. Out of despair.

And his anger died.

She stood in the doorway, wrapped in the hard, protective shell of her aloneness, defying the world she had been born into, fighting it on her own terms, magnificent in her proud, unique, twisted strength. He saw the lost child, the wanton woman, the untameable force that was Tamara Vandelier, and despite the sickness in his soul, there stirred in him a painful tenderness, an urge to cosset and comfort that he knew she would reject.

'Why do you want my child, Tamara?' he asked, scraping the words out of the tatters of what had brought him here.

It was the only question left.

TWENTY

Tamara could feel tears building behind her eyes. Somehow the memories had got too close. She fiercely pushed them back. It was Rory, affecting her in ways she hadn't anticipated. He was strong. She hadn't realised he would be this strong.

Would he have stood with her against Eleanor?

Futile question. They were past that. Get on with the plan. Eleanor was the focus. Tamara couldn't let Rory muddy the course she had set. Sooner or later Eleanor would play her hand, and the shock of it would get to Rory. He'd back off, but he wouldn't back off from the child. The child was the key.

'I want an heir. I don't want my shares in the vineyards to go to a Traverner. Make me pregnant, Rory, and I'll will them to you. For our child. I know you'll do right by our child. If Eleanor lets me live to give birth.'

He flinched. Murder was too monstrous for him to accept, Tamara thought cynically. Yet to her mind there had been three murders that had served Eleanor's ambition. One of them she had complied with herself, not realising the full ramifications of that death. She had only been fourteen, and what Rory thought of her had still been important. Until afterwards.

'If I don't survive Eleanor, you'll get the shares,' she went on. 'I'll leave a document with my solicitor explaining why. It will stop the Traverners from contesting the will.'

'That's if you're pregnant to me,' he said grimly.

'It would strengthen your claim, Rory.'

'To beat Eleanor. It really has nothing to do with me, does it? I'm just a tool.'

Mistake. The shares meant nothing to him. The hard glint in his eyes warned her to change tack immediately or he'd be gone and out of her life and there'd be no getting him back. The sexual angle couldn't be played twice. He'd made that plain from the start. The one certain lever she had was to appeal to Rory's sense of rightness.

'It's true I don't want Eleanor to win. She's taken too much from me.'

'I won't be used, Tamara. Not by you. Not by anyone,' he asserted bitterly.

'She took from you, too. If I had any value to you.'

Hard scepticism flashed from his eyes. He reached for the gin bottle and poured himself another drink. 'I don't doubt Eleanor played her part, but you did a good job of devaluing yourself, Tamara,' he said as he splashed tonic water over the gin.

Nevertheless, she still meant something to him or he wouldn't be here. 'I did love you, Rory,' she said quietly.

His face tightened. He didn't look at her. He added ice cubes, swirled them around in the glass, then drank as though he needed to wash some other taste out of his mouth. It was warning enough for Tamara to be very careful what she said next.

'Any man would do as a tool to get me pregnant, Rory,' she told him. 'You're not any man.'

'True,' he agreed sardonically. 'I'm the man in the right place for you, with the right bloodline to get at Eleanor.'

She shook her head. 'It's more than that.'

'Do tell me,' he invited flippantly.

'If everything had been normal, we would have married, Rory. I would have had your children. To have you as the father of my child now would satisfy my sense of justice. And—' she smiled wryly '—answer a dream.'

He frowned, but Tamara knew his attention was caught again. He could not dismiss her as easily as he might want to. All she had to do was tap behind his pride and pull on the strings that still bound them to each other.

'What dream?' His voice was harsh, his eyes mocking.

She walked to the coffee table by the cane settee and picked up the drink she had abandoned, giving herself time to formulate the most effective words. She took a sip. The ice had melted, watering the gin. It didn't help anyway. Nothing anaesthetised what Eleanor had done to her. The hatred surged again, burning brightly as she swung around to sear Rory with the answers he wanted.

'Eleanor never accepted me as her daughter. I wasn't a Traverner. I was the cuckoo in her nest, and she did her best to shove me out of it. I've been aware of this for as long as I can remember. Can you imagine how it felt, Rory?'

She saw the recoil in his eyes before he glanced at his glass. His lips compressed. A bank of resentments fighting his natural sympathy, she surmised.

'No, I can't. I remember how I felt when you shut me out of your life.' His voice softened slightly as he added, 'But I wasn't a child then.'

It was a concession. Tamara ignored the reference to what she'd done to him. 'She saw to it I had no part in the running of the vineyards. In that sense, too, I was disinherited. It was all for Paul and David.'

'Surely your father could have...' He stopped, hot colour slashing across his cheekbones, her claim of incest recalled, shaming the suggestion he'd been about to make.

She rammed it home. 'I was my father's little girl. Not a son.'

Anguish twisted across Rory's face.

'And *he* wasn't there when I needed him, either,' she said, deliberately evoking more guilt.

It flitted through Tamara's mind as it had many times before. Had Eleanor fucked Max to death? The heart attack had come in bed. He'd been a prime candidate for one, overweight from his hearty appetites for fine food and good wine, plus the strong cigars he habitually smoked.

Fruitless speculation.

Rory still looking discomforted.

Good!

'You wouldn't disown a child of yours, would you, Rory?' she asked softly, knowing the answer. A true hero would never abandon his child.

Several expressions flicked through his eyes, coalescing into a primitive blaze of need. 'No.'

Stupid Louise! She hadn't read Rory's character at all. Still, the desire for fatherhood his fuckwit wife thought she could manipulate played right into Tamara's hands.

She kept her voice soft, appealing to the paternal instinct in Rory. 'I have this dream of you taking our child into the vineyard with you and teaching it all you know, giving it the heritage I was denied, sharing your love of it, the kind of bonding I wish I'd known.'

The ultimate revenge on Eleanor, the child who could take over everything. Let her die with that thought!

'Where are you in this dream, Tamara?'

It jolted her. Where was she? Eleanor would be dead. She hadn't envisaged a life beyond Eleanor. There was a complete blank in her mind. She had been sustained, driven by hatred for so long. What happened when the object of hatred died? It was the end.

A convulsive shiver ran through her. She stared at Rory. If he gave her his child, did what she wanted... 'Where do you want me to be, Rory?'

'Would you love our child, Tamara?' he asked quietly.

Of course. That was the answer. The future. The child

would be innocent. A new life to look after. She could do it right. Not like Eleanor. It would be like a rebirth. A smile of happy satisfaction burst across her face.

'Yes. I'd love it with all my heart, Rory.'

He stared at her as though transfixed. He stared so long her smile faltered and faded. She'd told him her heart was dead. She'd shut him out of it. He didn't believe she could change for a child. And maybe she couldn't. A painful confusion ripped through her mind. Why was she feeling things again?

Damn him! Damn him to hell for not responding to her need. Hatred sizzled over the feelings that confused her. She slammed her glass onto the table and strode to the doorway. She paused there, turning blazing eyes to him, throwing down the last challenge.

'I need an heir, Rory.' Determination steeled her voice, hard, relentless, cutting. 'I want a child by you. You think I destroyed a choice that should have been yours. I hand you this one. If you choose to walk away, there'll be no comeback from me. There are men fishing from the rocks at this end of the beach. I'll make one of them the father of my child. It's up to you.'

TWENTY-ONE

Rory did not leap to answer the challenge. His mind was still dazed and his gut still wrenched by the vision of the Tamara he had once known, the Tamara who had filled the one magical summer of his life, the smile lighting up her face, so joyous and free, her eyes aglow with the wonder of loving.

It wasn't dead and gone. If the thought of their child could bring the Tamara of that long-ago summer alive again, was there still a chance for him? She was giving him a choice, but it sure as hell carried no guarantees. A dream...or nothing.

Worse than nothing, because he knew what lay behind the hard, relentless hatred that drove Tamara's life, and he wouldn't forget it, any more than he'd been able to forget the Tamara he'd loved during the twelve years of nothing he'd already endured.

There'd be no wondering why any more.

And the choice was here and now. It wouldn't come again. Ever.

He searched for some lingering trace of the smile that had transformed her so beautifully, so briefly, capturing the essence of all he had thought was forever lost. There was only a dark, proud ferocity on her face, and the hatred was back in full force, all-consuming, her eyes impaling him with a message—Help me, or you are nothing.

He could no longer blame her for how she thought or acted.

Eleanor...Machiavellian bitch!

Tamara...victim, rebel, locked into a dark battleground with her mother. But when Eleanor died, when she was no more...

Impatient with his silence, scorning his indecision, Tamara broke from her stance near the doorway. She stepped onto the balcony, moving to the railing as though to scan the selection of studs available on the beach below. Not for one moment did Rory doubt she would do what she said. Bold and fearless Tamara, fighting for survival her own way, laying waste what could have been.

Not again, thought Rory, and with all the aggression of his manhood aroused, he skirted the bar in a few quick strides. It would be his way this time. His heart pumped a tempo of fierce determination as he closed the distance she had put between them. No more distance, not in time, not in space.

Through the doorway. Out on the balcony. His arms wrapping around her waist, hauling her away from the railing and against him. Together as they should have been. Together as they would be from this moment on.

'Our child,' he said, staking his claim.

To hell with Louise! he thought savagely. To hell with Eleanor! To hell with the whole damn family! They could all rise against him for throwing his lot in with Tamara. Even his grandfather. But this was *his* life. And he'd fight for it.

There was a moment of stiff resistance, then Tamara let go, leaning into his embrace, surrendering her solitary will to the togetherness he promised. 'Yes.' The vehement affirmation whooshed from her, a burst of relief and elation.

Rory didn't care that she thought she'd won. He didn't care about anything but holding her, keeping her, binding her to him in a union that would give him what he wanted. At least part of it. Part of him and her. A child they would both love.

Tamara tilted her face to the sky, away from the choice that was not necessary now. Rory caught her sense of freedom. They were both free to dream again. He tucked her head under his chin. It made him feel intensely protective.

'I'll hold you safe, Tamara.'

Let Eleanor do her worst! The self-appointed matriarch of the family would not win this time.

'I'd like that, Rory.' Soft, warm words, her body reinforcing them as she snuggled against him, hugging his encircling arms, her hands stroking his as though revelling in his strength.

It fired his purpose, his commitment. He'd show her how strong he was. Without pause for second thought, he poured out his intentions.

'I won't let Eleanor touch us. Or hurt you again. We'll fight her head-on for what is rightly ours. No running away. No backward steps.'

He'd show her she'd been wrong not to trust him. He would stand by her. Through anything.

'A true hero,' she murmured, rubbing her hair against his throat. 'I stood here last night, and the waves rolled in, beating out your name...Rory, Rory...'

His heart almost burst with elation. Despite the years of bitter estrangement, she'd still thought of him with hope, if not trust. She had come to him, playing the games Eleanor had taught her, unable to break the lines of defence she had built for herself. For justice, she said, but it was love she wanted. The love they'd once shared.

But justice had to come first. Only justice would break the bonds of hatred and appease the pain of all the years under Eleanor's evil domination.

'She'll pay for what she did to you, Tamara,' he promised. 'She will know it failed. Before she dies, she'll know that.'

The whole edifice of lies and deceit on which Eleanor had built her power had to be smashed. It was the only way any decent future could be achieved.

'Rory.' It was a whisper to the wind, to the far horizon, to hope, to a love that had been buried beneath deep layers of despair.

The sound of the sea drowned it.

As Eleanor had with her heartless ambition.

To Rory's ears the waves roared another word.

Destroy...

TWENTY-TWO

Janet found it impossible to settle to any work. She kept checking the time, and every passing minute increased her inner agitation. It wasn't like Rory to abandon his responsibilities. He was late to work again, and there had been no word from him since that manic incident with Tamara yesterday afternoon.

The winery was in a ferment of gossip, and his absence fed it. Didn't he realise that? Eleanor on her deathbed, Tamara sweeping in, as violent a catalyst as ever, Rory chasing after her... Janet couldn't blame anyone for wondering what was going on. She wanted to know herself. Besides, apart from political and business considerations, there was the question of how badly Rory had been hit by Tamara's car.

He'd been in shock, limping, completely shaken up. It had been crazy for him to drive anywhere. If she'd had her wits about her she would have followed him in case he ran into trouble. Instead she'd stood there like a dummy, trying to collect herself. Seeing him knocked flying across the car bonnet had shocked her into realising just how much she depended on Rory's cheerful presence in her life.

He meant a lot to her, and she couldn't stand by any longer without knowing something. She reached for the telephone and dialled Rory's home number. The position of executive secretary gave her some rights, especially when the executive himself did not keep her properly informed.

Janet gritted her teeth as Louise's clipped, upper-class voice came over the line. It always raised her hackles. No profit in showing it, though. Louise would not take kindly to hostility from her husband's hired help.

'It's Janet Thurston. Is Rory there, Louise?' she asked matter-of-factly.

Pause. Long enough for Janet to wonder if Louise knew where he was.

'Didn't he call you, Janet?' Condescending tone.

'No. As far as I know he should be here. And he isn't,' she replied flatly.

'Well, some business came up yesterday afternoon and Rory had to fly off. Actually, I'm leaving for Canberra myself in a few minutes. Daddy said some interesting things were happening so I'm not sure how long we'll be gone. But I'm sure you'll handle everything beautifully, Janet.'

It was all so quick and glib. Perhaps it was the truth, but Janet was unconvinced. Rory had never flown off on business without notifying her. 'I'm surprised he was well enough to go anywhere,' she remarked, fishing for more information.

'Oh, you mean his run-in with Tamara's car. Rory said she was upset with the family. Understandable in the circumstances, I suppose, but she really is impossible to help. It was lucky Rory only suffered a few nasty bruises. And that's the thanks he gets for trying to be kind.'

Janet still didn't feel satisfied, yet she really had no grounds for questioning any further. What could Louise be covering up? She knew about Tamara's visit to the winery. Rory had obviously gone home to his wife and told her everything.

'There's nothing for you to worry about, Janet,' Louise assured her. Back to the condescending tone. 'Just carry on as usual. Rory will probably contact you if he gets the chance. Must go now. Bye.'

Janet gritted her teeth again as she replaced the receiver. Louise had that effect on her. How Rory could love such a supercilious woman was completely beyond her understanding. They were certainly not soul mates.

She heaved a sigh of discontent, pulled the desk diary in front of her and wrote 'Canberra' over Friday's page. She wondered what Daddy was up to and why it was such urgent business for Rory. The wine industry hadn't been featured in the news lately, and politicians rarely stirred themselves over anything that wasn't causing headlines.

There was a knock on her door.

'Come in,' she called, shoving the diary aside. At least she had an answer to the inevitable question of Rory's whereabouts. No drama. No dissent in family ranks. Maybe something moving on the federal government front that would affect the wine industry. In other words, business as usual.

Paul Traverner stepped into her office.

Janet stared at him in surprise. David frequently dropped in at Buchanan. He had a personal interest in the winery, having managed it until Rory learnt enough of the business side to take over from him. But Paul... Not once since she had been Rory's secretary had he stepped inside the place. Not to her knowledge, anyway. Nor had she had any personal contact with him since the dark days after Jim died.

The memory of their last meeting slid into her mind—the boardroom at Traverner with Paul and David aligned with Eleanor for the takeover of Selby, Paul doing his mother's bidding, spelling out the terms, Frank Buchanan trying to soften the blow, Rory significantly absent, not wanting to take part.

'Good morning, Janet. How are things with you?'

Friendly question, friendly manner. It didn't fool Janet for a second. A real friend wouldn't have waited this long to make that inquiry. Besides, the projected warmth didn't reach his eyes. Paul Traverner was tense and worried, and the question of her current welfare was not what was weighing on his mind. It certainly hadn't motivated this unheralded and uncustomary visit. Coming on top of Louise's condescension, the glib politeness rankled.

'Do you really want to know?' The mocking words slid out before appropriate secretarial discretion could prevail.

It jolted him. She saw him struggle with a mind shift, his innate sense of courtesy nipping at his set purpose.

Janet silently castigated herself for the pointless little dig. Why should Paul Traverner keep up a friendly contact with her? It wasn't as though they were contemporaries, and she didn't own the Selby vineyard any more. She was just a working secretary. Of no real account to anyone. Except Rory. When he was here.

'Never mind,' she muttered, shrugging off her bruised sense of self-worth. In a lighter, crisper voice she asked, 'How can I help you, Paul?'

He hesitated, his brows lowering, eyes sharply scanning hers. She flashed him a bright smile. It drove him back to his purpose.

'I came to see Rory, but I hear he hasn't come in yet.'

And that wouldn't be all he'd heard, Janet thought, anger simmering. Paul Traverner looked every inch the lord of the manor, with his austere good looks and classy tailored suit, undoubtedly all primed to take over from Eleanor, providing ready continuity to *his* family tradition in the valley. But he wasn't head of the company yet, and she resented him nosing around when Rory wasn't here.

'He's away for the day,' she answered shortly.

'Oh?'

Janet ignored the implied question.

'I'd like to contact him,' Paul pressed.

'Sorry. I don't have a number.'

Paul frowned, the weight on his mind clearly increasing. 'I'm told Tamara was here yesterday,' he said, revealing his

uneasiness about his half-sister's actions and their consequences.

'Yes, she was.'

He waited for her to elaborate. Janet remained tight-
lipped. He was not going to get any speculative gossip out
of her.

'What did she want?'

She raised her eyebrows at the direct probing. 'I have no
idea. It was a private meeting with Rory.'

He sighed in frustration. Again his eyes focused sharply
on hers, searching for a way past her negative response to
him. 'Have I offended you, Janet?' he asked quietly.

The pertinent question put her at odds with herself. Why
was she taking offence at his every word, resenting him being here? He had as much right as the rest of the family to
come to Buchanan at any time, and he wasn't acting unreasonably.

It dawned on her that what she was feeling had more to
do with her own situation than the purpose that had
brought Paul here today. Somehow Paul Traverner personi-
fied the loss of all she had once lived for. His walking in on
her so unexpectedly, when she was feeling down in general,
had triggered an anger she now realised came from a deep
well of unresolved grief.

His visit had to be connected to the changes he would be
anticipating with Eleanor incapacitated, dying. Whatever
eventuated, the situation would not be as drastic or as devastating for him as it had been for her at Jim's death. And
the Traverners had profited by it. Fairly enough in the circumstances, she had to acknowledge, but it hurt. It still hurt.

She looked at him with bleak eyes. 'I haven't seen you
since the takeover meeting.'

The blunt reference to that fateful day disconcerted him.
'You have been invited to a number of functions at the Big
House, Janet,' he softly reminded her.

That was true. Pride had stopped her from attending. She

couldn't stomach watching Eleanor queening it as the grand lady of the Hunter Valley vineyards. Eleanor, who should have known—did know—how it felt to lose everything.

'My family worked that vineyard almost as long as the Traverners have worked theirs. Generations, side by side,' she reminded him, needing finally to voice the hurt she had tried to put behind her. 'And you took it from me.' It wasn't a bitter accusation, simply a flat statement of fact.

Paul instantly recoiled. 'Be reasonable, Janet. We didn't take it from you. You chose to sell it to us.'

'At the time it seemed the best offer. But I shouldn't have accepted it.'

'Why not?'

'I should have found a way to carry on.'

'You know it was impossible.'

'Is that what you told yourself, Paul?'

'You were up to your ears in debt.'

Head over heels in debt from all the care Jim had needed, especially towards the end. She had been in a fog of despair. Jim's death, the funeral, more debts.

'It was the best offer, Janet,' Paul insisted quietly. 'None of the other buyers would have given you the family home-stead free and clear.'

Tears gathered behind her eyes. Did he think a house was all she had cared about?

'We made the takeover as painless as possible,' he added, revealing his total lack of understanding for her position.

Oh, God! She was going to cry. Not in front of Paul Traverner. She pushed her chair away from the desk, stood and turned her back on him, swallowing hard as she walked to the window. She stared blindly out at the view of Buchanan vines stretching into the distance until she'd re-gained enough control to speak.

'I wonder how you'd feel, Paul, if you lost the Traverner vineyard, retaining only the old homestead. And every day you looked out on the rows of vines, knowing they weren't yours any more and they'd never be your children's, either.'

No reply.

For Janet, the silence ached with memories. Somehow it didn't really matter if she reached Paul Traverner or not. She needed to say what she had bottled up inside herself for too long.

'I don't know why... I thought you'd keep the Selby label for the wine from our vineyard. As a mark of respect. Or a sense of history. Or something. But you didn't. Tears of God...aptly named, wasn't it? For the death of an old family tradition.'

'I'm sorry,' he muttered gruffly.

The apology suggested some sensitivity to what she was expressing. Though she didn't expect it to change anything. Too little, too late.

'I was worn out when Jim died,' she went on. 'Your mother was luckier. The bolt of lightning that killed your father was a lot cleaner and quicker than motor neurone disease. I just couldn't manage any more at the time. And the vultures wouldn't wait for me to get myself together.'

'Do you count us as vultures, too?'

His voice sounded pained. She swung around to look at him, to see the truth in his eyes. 'Did you think of offering me a deal, Paul?'

His discomfort was obvious. 'It was discussed.'

'I know it was discussed. Rory put it to a company meeting. I'm asking you, how far did you consider it?'

'We didn't think it was feasible, Janet.'

'You? Or your mother?'

His high, aristocratic cheekbones were all the more prominent under flushed skin. He didn't answer. He didn't have to. Janet knew who'd swung the vote against her.

'Yet Eleanor had been in the same position,' she drove home to him. 'I didn't have a rich man sniffing around, as your mother did. I didn't have anyone on tap who could rescue me. But your family company is rich, Paul. Very rich. It's hard to forget that.'

The pained understanding in his eyes didn't make her feel any better. There really wasn't any point in flogging a dead horse. Stupid to have started it. What was gone was gone. Besides, it was Eleanor's fault more than Paul's.

She took a deep breath, summoned up a smile and let him off the hook. 'Well, I'm afraid you got more than you asked for. I'm not at my best this morning.'

He shook his head, still looking pained. 'I am sorry, Janet. I didn't appreciate...'

She cut him off, not wanting his sympathy. 'Rory is in Canberra. Louise is on her way to join him. I don't know where Tamara is. Anything else?'

He heaved a ragged sigh. 'No. Thank you.'

He left, recognising there was nothing more to be said on either side. Nothing of any use.

Janet wished Rory was here. Surely nothing in Canberra was more important than keeping tabs on what the family was doing. Paul might have come to offer a deal or sound Rory out about how he saw the future of the two vineyards.

The telephone rang, calling her to her desk and her duties as Rory's secretary. She went reluctantly, feeling flat and empty, dropping into her chair and picking up the receiver without any thought or care about who it might be.

'The Buchanan winery. Janet Thurston speaking. May I help you?' she rattled out.

'It's Rory, Janet.'

She sat up straight, instantly invigorated at hearing his voice.

'Sorry I didn't call earlier,' he went on.

'But you're caught up in Canberra,' she finished for him.

'Canberra?' He sounded puzzled, and the pause that followed reinforced the impression.

'I was worried about you so I rang your home. Louise said—'

'Louise.' Harshly derisive. 'Off to Daddy for advice. Smart Louise.'

Not exactly the voice of loving harmony, Janet thought, which was something new. Whatever Rory felt, he'd always shown loyalty to his wife. Rather than pursue what might be a sensitive point, Janet informed him of new developments.

'Paul Traverner has just left. He came to see you.'

'What about?' Sharper, more alert.

'He didn't say. He was disturbed about Tamara's visit here. Somebody had told him about it.'

'So that shifted him.' Very dry.

'What's going on, Rory?' she asked directly. If she was to be a good watchdog for him she needed to know.

'There's movement at the station since the word has passed around, Janet. Paul didn't want to know about Tamara yesterday.'

'Well, he wanted a contact number to get hold of you. I told him I didn't have one and you were in Canberra.'

Laughter. 'Thank you. That'll do fine. I'll be away for a few days. I'll check in with you again on Monday.'

'Rory, what if I need to get in touch with you?'

He hesitated.

'You never know what might come up,' she pressed, wanting to be of real use in whatever was going on.

'True. Then for your ears only, Janet. This is absolutely confidential, and you are only to call me if it's critically important.'

'You're the boss,' she quickly assured him.

'I'm at the Vandelier house at Pearl Beach.'

Janet sucked in a quick breath. He was with Tamara. Had to be. 'Right! I'll keep that confidential,' she babbled, her mind racing to take in the ramifications of this startling piece of news on top of the fact that Louise had lied through her teeth about Rory's whereabouts. 'You realise the winery is fairly jumping with gossip.'

'Let it jump. Any other news?'

'Not of any import.'

'Fine. Talk to you Monday, then.'

Janet sat staring into space for a long time after Rory's call.

He had sounded well and truly disaffected with Louise. But to go to Tamara...

Were old wounds being opened up?

There had been a hard, reckless mood behind much of what he'd said. He'd been hard and reckless yesterday, going after Tamara.

It disturbed Janet. It wasn't the Rory she knew.

She had the sense of many things shifting and big trouble coming. The world as she had known it a few minutes ago had changed.

TWENTY-THREE

Paul wasn't used to feeling shame. It nagged at him as he drove away from Buchanan, tearing at his conscience, forcing him to revise his perception of himself. Why hadn't he seen what Janet had laid out so poignantly?

He'd looked at facts and figures, listened to his mother, dismissed Rory's proposition for a partnership with the Selby vineyard as ridiculously one-sided and actually thought they were doing Janet Thurston a favour, removing burdens she couldn't possibly cope with.

He should have known better.

And what of his mother? She should have known best of all.

Yet he remembered her calling Rory a quixotic young fool for wanting to offer Janet a deal, and her summing up of the situation had been decisive, not one trace of doubt. 'Look at her, Paul. She's given up, defeated. It'll be a mercy to take it off her hands and finish it for her.'

So his mother had ruled. And he'd accepted her judgment without question. Janet was not given a choice. The last of the Selbys had been written off and their holdings swallowed up by the Traverners. All but the family homestead.

Uncle Frank, quietly insistent in the face of his sister's unwavering purpose. 'You must leave Janet her home, Ellie. That girl is in no fit state to find somewhere else to live.'

No fit state. The fight had been knocked out of her and she'd been given no time for recovery. He'd seen a different Janet Thurston this morning and knew she could have pulled through the bad time, given enough help. Rory had known that. Janet was Rory's contemporary. They'd been at school together. Paul realised he should have given Rory's opinion more credit.

The Big House caught his eye. It made him think of Gabrielle and the way she had startled him last night with her comprehension of the situation. She'd always kept apart from discussions of business. Maybe that non-involvement made her see things more clearly. He suppressed the temptation to go and unburden himself to her. The shame was his to carry, not hers. Besides, David was waiting to hear the outcome of the meeting with Rory.

Paul briefly wondered what Rory was doing in Canberra with Louise's father, then shrugged off the niggle of curiosity. If it was important to the business, he'd hear soon enough. Rory was diligent in reporting any relevant lobbying in the halls of power. As long as he was in Canberra, he wasn't with Tamara. Which removed that point of concern.

A more relevant question was how Rory would react if David tried to take over Buchanan. Wouldn't he feel the same as Janet did, having his rightful place snatched from him? Worse, because he'd feel betrayed by his own family. And Rory wouldn't give up, not for a minute. He'd fight. And if that drove him to Tamara and Irene... And Uncle Frank stood up for his family line as he had last night...

Janet's question was a haunting one. How would he feel if he lost Traverner, retaining only the old family homestead?

He drove past the Traverner winery complex. David could wait a bit longer, since there was nothing urgent to report. Paul didn't feel like talking to his brother yet. He needed to get his mind straightened out first, needed to decide what direction *he* wanted to take into the future.

A sense of returning to his roots—or perhaps it was Janet's words prompting him—led him down the dirt road to the home of his childhood. He parked well short of the house, not wanting to disturb his mother and Uncle Frank or alert them to his presence. This journey was a private one.

For a while he simply sat in the car, letting his gaze wander around, triggering memories he hadn't thought of for a long time. They had been a happy family once, when his father was alive, the years of innocence before the catastrophe.

The house hadn't changed. It was a friendly, unpretentious, welcoming house, the wood painted cream with green trim on the windowsills, doors and veranda railings. His mother saw to it that everything was meticulously maintained, even the garden beds on either side of the front steps, planted with shrubs and spring flowers. He wondered what it represented to her.

With a sigh of vexation at the way his thoughts invariably homed in on his mother, Paul pushed himself out of the car. He had to get out from under her influence and be his own man, assert his own values and judgments.

His feet automatically headed for the path to the creek and the old winery. The creek had been his and David's playground during the summers of their childhood. For as far back as Paul could remember he and his younger brother had always been close. Best friends. In harmony with each other.

It had come as a shock last night, David's declaration of a desire for independence. He was used to David following his lead. That was the way it had been ever since they were little kids, him suggesting what to do, David happily agreeing. Why hadn't he recognised his brother's discontent? What else had he blindly taken for granted?

At least two things were now clear to him. His mother did

not always know best, and David could not be counted on to always fall in with him.

It felt as though parts of him were peeling away, leaving him raw and very much alone. Where did he go from here?

He turned his gaze to the old winery. Generations of his family had made their wine there. Most of the other valley families had used tin sheds in the old days, but the Traverners had constructed their winery with thick stone walls, massive wood beams and a high roof. It was built to last. It was a statement of permanence, solidity, endurance. Paul felt a stab of regret that it was no longer in use. Max had built a new winery with all the modern technology available for today's winemakers.

Knowing that only the structure remained, but drawn to it anyway, Paul walked to the main entrance and pushed open one of the heavy double doors. Inside there was nothing but emptiness, yet in his mind were the images of huge oak casks, their dark curved wood dominating the cool dimness, all of them sitting on big, smooth logs on the earth floor.

When he was a child, it had been a place of mystery and magic. He had listened avidly to his father teaching him how pressed grapes were made into wine. He had known then it would be his life, tending the vineyards, bringing in the vintage, loving the land that made it all possible with the miracle of growth every spring.

How would he feel if he lost it?

Probably as empty as this old winery, a shell of a man, bereft of purpose.

Was that how Janet felt?

He closed the door and walked to the oldest part of the vineyard. Here the vines had been planted on five-foot-by-five-foot plots for horse cultivation. His mother had fought Max over his idea to have each alternate row removed for tractors. And won. She'd argued that when the Dalwood vineyard had taken out the alternate rows of its oldest vines, the ones left had been affected, never recovering enough to produce the bounty of former years.

Paul suspected his mother simply wanted them left as they were, regardless of whether they thrived or not. He looked fondly at their gnarled wood as he strolled along. These vines had been planted almost a hundred and fifty years ago, miraculously surviving the phylloxera plague in the last century and still productive today. Although the narrow rows meant more work, Paul knew he would never interfere with them. This section of the vineyard stood as part of the Traverner heritage. Living history.

The deep pride and sense of belonging that swept through Paul brought him to an abrupt halt. No other place could ever mean as much, he realised, wincing as the full comprehension of Janet Thurston's loss hit him. Did the grieving lessen in time?

He rolled his head in silent anguish at his failure to empathise with her plight and inadvertently caught sight of his mother seated on the bench that marked the place where his father had died. Her head was lowered, her arms wrapped around her midriff as though holding in pain. The idea of physical pain didn't occur to Paul. Grief caught at his mind and flooded it with memories, spinning his thoughts back thirty years to the day that had laid waste his father's life and hopes and dreams.

Paul was nine years old, David seven, and it was the first day of harvesting the grapes for the vintage, black clouds rolling over the sky in huge threatening billows, the pickers working frantically. Lightning cracked from the clouds, the thunder so loud it seemed to shake the earth. He and David were frightened by it, but they didn't run away and hide. They had to help the men. The grapes had to be brought in before the storm hit. Their father had said so.

Paul didn't see it happen. There was a bunch of very scary lightning zigzagging down, and his mother screamed. She screamed so loud it could be heard over the thunder. He saw her running and followed her as fast as he could. Something had to be terribly wrong for his mother to scream like that.

Then the hail started, hard balls of ice beating down on his head, shredding the vine leaves, smashing the grapes, but he had to keep running because his mother might need help. The men were running, as well. Two of them passed him.

His father was lying on the ground when he got to where the men had stopped. His mother was kneeling beside him, kissing him in a funny frantic way. One of the men knelt down and grasped his father's wrist. After a few moments he said, 'It's no good, Mrs. Traverner. There's no pulse. The lightning hit him direct.'

But she kept on, the hail bashing down. David came panting up beside him, asking questions he couldn't answer. The men left them there together when their mother didn't take any notice of what was said. He held David's hand and waited for his mother to tell him what to do.

Rain started pelting down with the hail, turning the ground to mush. His mother stopped the kissing and gathered his father onto her lap, her arms around him, rocking him as though he was a baby.

There was no response from his father. He didn't move or speak or do anything he should. His body was limp and his eyes were unseeing. Looking at him gave Paul a sick, empty feeling inside.

David started to sniffle. Paul hushed him and told him they had to be brave and stay by their mother. She might need them to help with their father. But he felt lost, too, because he didn't think his father was going to get better, and if he didn't, there'd be no more playing with him or learning all the important things he knew, or telling him exciting things and seeing him smile. Paul desperately wanted his father to smile at them to show everything was all right.

It didn't happen. His mother kept crying and sobbing out

his father's name, and Paul couldn't bear the sound of his mother crying. He had to do something. He knelt in the mud beside her and put his arm around her waist, trying to give her a hug to show he was there for her. David patted her hair, even though it was streaming wet.

The men came back with a stretcher. They gently took his father and laid him on it. Very slowly his mother got to her feet, lurching as though she didn't have strength to stand. Or maybe it was her skirt clinging to her legs, making it hard to move. It was sopping wet, and mud blotched and streaked her dress as high as her breasts, where she had held his father.

She didn't seem to notice. She didn't bother straightening her skirt. But she'd stopped crying. And finally she realised he and David were there. She looked directly at him.

There was something in her eyes that made him feel a mantle of responsibility falling on his shoulders. He knew he had to take his father's place somehow. He stepped forward and took her hand in his, gripping tight. Then she looked at David and held out her other hand to him.

Together the three of them walked behind the men who carried the stretcher with his father on it, trudging through the rows of ruined vines in the darkness of the black clouds and the battering rain.

So much had been lost that day, his father, the vintage, the income that was to pay the bank loan for the new pressure fermentation tank and the other improvements to the winery and last but not least the mother he had known. She was different afterwards, distant and driven.

Janet believed it was cleaner for his mother, having her husband die in an instant. Paul didn't think so. Somehow, everything was muddy after that. Like her dress after the men had taken his father from her. And, as with her dress, she took no notice of the muddy areas. She walked to her own vision.

He remembered the night she'd sat him and David down

and explained she was going to marry a rich man because it was the only way they could carry on their father's dream. That was important, and they must never forget it. They were Richard Traverner's sons. It didn't matter who else came into their lives. First and foremost, they were their father's sons.

Muddy sentiments.

It had been impossible to ignore Max Vandelier, and it was his dream they carried on. Max's daughter was hell-bent on not being ignored, either. They had both made themselves matter. And it was wrong to say he and David were first and foremost their father's sons. First and foremost they were themselves, individuals in their own right.

Recognised as the man he is. Gabrielle's words to his mother slid through his mind. Paul shook his head. He doubted that was going to happen. But be damned if he was going to be a pawn on his mother's chessboard any more. He would move to his own vision, not hers.

His mother lifted her head and saw him. For a few moments there was an oddly luminous look on her face, and Paul had the uneasy sense she was not seeing him. From the photographs of his father, he knew he looked very like Richard Traverner. Suddenly it was clear why she'd returned to the old homestead. She had chosen to die here. With his father.

Compassion welled up in him as he saw, not the indomitable matriarch of the family, but a woman with white hair and fragile thinness, hugging in the pain of the cancer that was killing her. He hurried towards her, wanting to help. If she was in need... He had the eerie sense of the past blurring with the present. She was his mother.

'Paul.' Her smile welcomed him, though it held the stiffness of pain. The light had gone from her face.

'I thought you might need help back to the house.' He held out his hand to her, smiling to soften any hint of criticism as he added, 'Walking this far after a month in hospital must have tired you out.'

She nodded. 'I'd be grateful for your arm, Paul. Thank you.'

She leaned heavily on him as she stood up, although once she was steady on her feet, the regal bearing he associated with her was back in full force. Nevertheless, she kept her arm linked to his, and the pace she set was slow. She was carefully measuring out her strength.

Paul was acutely conscious of death hovering in front of them. 'I'm sorry about last night,' he murmured. He wished their relationship could be established along more natural lines.

'Stress,' she excused dismissively. 'I can't help how I look, Paul.'

'I know. It wasn't until I saw you sitting on the bench that I realised why you came here instead of the Big House. It's to be with Dad, isn't it?'

'Yes.'

For so long he hadn't felt in tune with his mother. He did now. It was a relief, almost a pleasure. In a surge of filial protectiveness, he said, 'Then forget about Irene and Louise, Mum. The rest of us can sort out whatever needs sorting out. We won't worry you again.'

She flicked him a hard look. 'I'm still head of the family company, Paul. Don't bury me yet.'

Pure Dame Eleanor! Paul grimaced, struggling to reconcile the two faces of his mother in his mind. He tried to find an acceptable course for both of them. 'I meant you can let it go if you want to. I can handle it.'

She shook her head. 'You don't know what you're up against.'

'Well, I'll soon find out, won't I?' he persisted.

'Prevention is always better than a cure, Paul.'

'Then brief me on what you think has to be done.'

'No.'

Blanket rejection. Paul gritted his teeth as resentment stirred, biting into the compassion that had prompted his offers. 'That's hardly a vote of confidence.'

'There are some things I prefer to keep private.'

Hadn't he earned her trust? Why couldn't she confide in him? Anger simmered. To hell with her Mother knows best attitude! He was almost forty, and it was he and David who had contributed most to the success of the Traverner vineyard. They were the winemakers. They made and controlled the business.

'Then let me make this clear,' he said curtly. 'Don't act for me. Or on my behalf.'

She stopped, turning to confront him. 'What is this, Paul? Mutiny?'

He met her challenging gaze with cold determination. 'I'm not a child needing his mother to take care of things for him. I prefer to make my own decisions. And my own mistakes.'

'Very commendable. So what do you intend to do about Rory and Tamara? Do you imagine her visit to him yesterday was a social one?'

Her knowledge surprised him. Her cutting mockery opened his anger. 'Rory is not Tamara's fool. I'll do nothing, because there's nothing to be done.'

Her chin lifted in haughty disdain. 'You suggest I let go. If I have one certainty left in this life it's that Tamara will not let go. Not as long as she has breath in her body.'

'She's entitled to her inheritance. Without Max's investment we wouldn't have a vineyard,' Paul tersely reminded her.

'She won't let it rest there. Consider what could happen if she gets Rory onside with her, Paul.'

If David kept his hands off Buchanan that wouldn't happen, Paul thought with swift certainty. He saw Frank Buchanan coming to join them and realised the old man was probably the source of information on Tamara's visit to the

Buchanan winery. He was revered by the staff there. Someone would have let him know about Rory being hit by Tamara's car.

Paul nodded towards his uncle. 'Rory is your brother's grandson. He's as much imbued with family history as we are. And I'll bet on Rory's integrity against Tamara's mischief-making any day.'

'You underestimate Tamara. She's a threat, Paul. A threat to everything I've built up. I do not intend to let her destroy it.'

He saw the fixed blaze of obsession and purpose in her eyes and inwardly recoiled from it. More mud, he thought, and very deliberately and decisively rejected being party to it. He was his own man, whether his mother wanted to recognise it or not. He was not about to leave her in any doubt as to where he stood and what he saw with absolute clarity.

'You're not doing this for me or David, Mum. Nor for my father. You're doing it for you.'

He unhooked her hand from his arm, stepped back and waved to her brother. 'Uncle Frank will see you safely to the house. If you'll excuse me, I have business to attend to.'

'Paul!'

He ignored her call.

'Your mother wants you,' his uncle said, pausing as Paul passed him with a bare nod of acknowledgment.

'No, she doesn't,' he answered and kept on walking.

TWENTY-FOUR

'What happens to Tamara's shares if she dies?'

Sharon dropped the question into the conversation, killing it stone dead and creating a pool of silence around the dinner table. It was typical of her, Gabrielle thought, to blurt out anything that drifted through her mind. Only with Eleanor did she exercise restraint, having been subjected to the scornful blast of her mother-in-law's eyes too many times to open her mouth on impulse. Significantly, Eleanor was not here to preside over this family dinner at the Big House tonight.

Gabrielle found Sharon's question extremely distasteful. She looked down the table at Paul. He was frowning. His head moved in a negative jerk. Gabrielle was glad he didn't like it, either.

However disturbing Tamara could be, to Gabrielle's mind she was more sinned against than sinning. She knew Paul didn't see it that way. He had no patience with his half-sister, and he much preferred Tamara to do her outrageous gallivanting elsewhere, but he didn't wish her dead.

David answered his wife. 'Mum is her next of kin. If Tamara hasn't made a will—'

'What made you think of Tamara dying, Sharon?' Paul cut in. 'She's younger than any of us.'

'Well, the way she drove her car yesterday, hitting Rory.'

'Rory chose to get in her way. She tried to stop,' Paul corrected her. 'The eyewitness was quite clear about that. Let's not embroider the story.'

Sharon flushed and rushed to justify her train of thought. 'I just meant she lives on the edge. The way she drives, the way she parties and carries on with the most dreadful people, the dangerous activities she indulges in. She flirts with death, if you ask me.'

'That's true, Paul,' David chimed in supportively.

'I wonder why.'

The words tripped off Gabrielle's tongue, and while she usually kept to her private rule of not saying anything contentious, she didn't regret them. Eleanor was not here to dominate the others' thinking. Let them start thinking for themselves, she thought fiercely. Especially Paul.

They all looked at her, Sharon surprised, David puzzled, Paul tilting his head to one side, his eyes narrowed. She sensed his mind was open, weighing, reviewing. The hope kindled by his stand against his mother last night flared again.

'Haven't you ever wondered why Tamara is the way she is?' she challenged all three of them.

'Max spoilt her rotten,' David answered.

'So your mother says.' Gabrielle shrugged and added, 'I've always found it extraordinary that Eleanor allowed him to do so. Tamara is her daughter, as well as Max's. Please correct me if I'm wrong, but it's my impression your mother gets her own way about most things.'

David frowned. 'As I recall, Mum was very involved in the business at the time.'

'Surely Max was, too, with all the building he instigated and establishing the Traverner label in wider markets.'

'Yes, he was everywhere in those days. I guess neither of them had much time for Tamara. Maybe that was why she ran wild,' David mused.

'Were you and Paul allowed to run wild in those days?' Gabrielle asked, moving her gaze to her husband.

'We were older. We had responsibilities,' he answered.

Gabrielle deliberately held his gaze. 'So no-one had time for Tamara.'

'Max got her nannies,' David said.

'A nanny can't take the place of a mother, David,' Sharon said with a sense of her own importance as the mother of his children. 'I can see what Gabrielle is saying. Tamara was left out.' Then in her artless fashion, she added, 'She's still left out, isn't she? Have you spoken to her, Paul?'

'No. I haven't.'

'Well, perhaps you should,' Sharon pressed, clearly not expecting David to do it.

So much for their independent stand last night, Gabrielle thought wryly. Both of them automatically looked to Paul to shoulder anything awkward.

'What should I say, Sharon?' Paul asked quietly.

'Tell her the news about her mother. As Gabrielle pointed out, she is Eleanor's daughter.'

'If Tamara didn't already know, Rory would have told her.'

Sharon frowned. 'At least it would be a sort of gesture, coming from you.'

He shook his head. 'Tamara would not interpret it kindly, Sharon. She wouldn't think I was giving her something. She'd think I wanted something from her.'

'We do,' David said grimly. 'We want her to stay out of things.'

'Perpetuating your mother's policy?' Gabrielle couldn't resist asking.

'You've got some other suggestion?' David snapped, disturbed by the politics of the situation.

Gabrielle looked directly at Paul. 'What's your plan, darling?'

'When Tamara turns up, as she surely will, we deal fairly

with her. The same as we do with Rory, David.' His eyes bored into his brother. 'We don't mess with lines of inheritance. That can only stir bad blood.'

David grimaced. 'Okay. I'm happy with the position of head of sales if Rory will go along with it.'

'No reason he shouldn't,' Paul assured him. 'You're damned good at it, David. Both vineyards can only profit by your expertise in broadening and lifting our sales.'

It was the resolution to David's discontent with his sub-ordinate position that Paul had been hammering out with his younger brother for most of the day and evening. Gabrielle thought it would work well, making David a key man to both vineyards, giving him more self-esteem and responsibility while retaining both Paul's and Rory's support.

'And talking of sales and marketing,' Paul went on, 'when I was with Janet Thurston this morning, she told me how she felt about us dropping the Selby label. It wasn't good, David. She had assumed we'd keep producing it out of respect for her family tradition. That's part of why she sold to us.'

'Why didn't she tell us then?'

'She was bereft and distraught. She trusted us, as long-time valley people, to honour what her family had produced here.'

David nodded thoughtfully. 'They were good people, the Selbys. And Jim Thurston was a fine winemaker for them. It's a shame.'

'Yes, it is a shame,' Paul asserted strongly. 'I think we should do it, David. You could market it as the wine from the old Selby vineyard, adding interest by making a historical feature of the Tears of God label.'

'You're right!' he agreed, his face lighting with enthusiasm for the task, then falling as second thoughts prevailed. 'Mum won't like it.'

'I don't care whether she likes it or not.'

The flat statement galvanised attention on Paul. To David

and Sharon it was a revolutionary attitude. They were stunned by it. To Gabrielle it came as the first promising crack in Eleanor's iron grip. But was it an impulsive act of rebellion or real self-determination?

While David and Sharon stared in shock, Gabrielle studied her husband's expression. It was calm, resolute, self-assured. Was this at last the man she thought she had married, the man she had met in France and left her home and country for? For years she had been waiting for him to emerge again, to lift off the yoke of Eleanor's insidious influence and live on his own terms, to his own set of values. Was it beginning to happen now?

David cleared his throat. 'We've never gone against Mum, Paul. I don't think this is the time to do it.'

'Because she's dying?'

'Well, yes. No reason to upset her when she's only got four months.'

'I wouldn't count on the doctors being right on that score. She's not going to let go, David. Surely you saw that last night.'

'Whatever.' He waved his hand in agitation. 'It'll only be one more vintage. What does it matter if we wait another year to restore the Selby label?'

'It matters to me,' Paul said quietly. 'I will not wait on my mother's death before acting on what I believe is right and just.'

Yes! Gabrielle exulted.

It worried David. He shook his head. 'Mum is not going to like it,' he said again.

'There may be many things she'll initiate in the coming months that we won't like,' Paul retaliated, unmoved by his brother's anxiety. 'I'm telling you now, David. I won't ride with them just because she's dying. I'll judge everything on its merits.'

Yes! Gabrielle's heart swelled with pride in him.

'You think she'll lose her grip?' David asked, even more worried.

'She'll do her damnedest to tighten it. And God help anyone who gets in her way,' Paul said harshly. He eyed his brother with steely resolution. 'I'll be proposing the Selby label at the next company meeting. I think both Uncle Frank and Rory will go for it. It's up to you to choose how you want to vote. I'm not asking you to side with me.'

'Tears of God,' David muttered, looking deeply distressed.

'And well may they fall,' Paul said with a wry twist of his mouth. 'But I will not be my mother's yes-man ever again.'

Free! Gabrielle thought, unable to contain her elation. She smiled at Paul.

He looked quizzically at her.

Her smile grew brighter.

Eleanor's shadow had dimmed.

TWENTY-FIVE

Eleanor dressed with care for her visit to Irene. It was not a matter of pride. It was a matter of presence. Nothing could disguise the physical ravages of the cancer that was inexorably claiming her. Irene would secretly revel in them. But Eleanor did not intend her appearance to suggest defeat. She would not let Irene imagine a diminishment of power.

The plum red dress was a strong statement against her white hair. The prosthesis gave her the shape to carry off the classic simplicity of its elegant line. Jet earrings gave her eyes emphasis, and black patent high heels added the style she had always maintained. A touch of blusher balanced the plum lipstick. Her reflection in the mirror assured Eleanor she did not look weak or sickly or ready to take to her bed and die.

Her general handyman had brought the Daimler down from the Big House, as instructed. Frank was out. She had encouraged him to go to his favourite pub where he usually spent Saturday afternoons, having a few bets on horseraces and drinking with old friends. She neatly evaded any discussion of her need to speak to Irene. She'd be home before he was.

Bill Guthrie was happy to drive her to Cessnock and wait to drive her back again. He'd also keep his mouth shut. He and his wife, Wilma, had a soft job, taking care of the old Traverner homestead, living in it rent-free. There was more work for them now, looking after her and Frank's needs, but she was paying them well for it. She had no doubt they would both do whatever she wanted. They had every reason to be loyal to her.

Once she was settled in the Daimler and on her way, she consciously relaxed, riding the pain she had to live with to keep her faculties in sharp working order. It was a pity Paul was in a snit because she wouldn't share her secrets with him. Wounded ego. She would pour balm on it when a suitable opportunity arose. He would only be shocked and appalled by what she kept to herself. He wouldn't know how to use any of it to his advantage. That was his weakness. Too narrow a vision.

Irene, Tamara...neither of them would respond to Paul's conception of fair play and decency. They had their own privately driven agendas. As, apparently, did Louise. Eleanor smiled. Louise might fancy herself a wheeler-dealer, but she didn't know what she was playing with. The mire of Irene's mind was unfathomable. The only thing that could reach into it was fear.

Nevertheless, Louise's dabbling could prove distracting from the main threat. Better to nip it in the bud. It was important to circumvent any manoeuvring of Irene by Tamara, too. Eleanor was acutely aware that if she didn't strike first, Tamara might well use the weapon of fear herself.

She brooded over Tamara's visit to Rory at the winery. It might have ended badly. But contact had been made. And the timing of it was no coincidence. Tamara was on the move. The question was where would she strike next? And how?

The Daimler pulled up in front of Irene's pathetic little cottage, a relic of cheap housing for miners during the coal boom around Cessnock. Its white paint was peeling, revealing the dried-out old wood underneath. As shabby as Irene herself, Eleanor thought contemptuously.

Bill accompanied her to the front door, helping her up the steps to the porch, ringing the doorbell, waiting with her until Irene appeared in answer to the summons. The grey, miserable stick of a woman stared bug-eyed and slack-jawed at Eleanor, shocked speechless and too lacking in any social niceties to cover up her reaction. Bill made a quick, discreet retreat to the car, leaving the two women alone together.

'Let me in, Irene,' Eleanor commanded, stepping forward.

Irene fell back, still dumbfounded, reacting automatically to the authority Eleanor exerted with voice and action. There was no point in waiting for an invitation that would undoubtedly stick in Irene's throat. Eleanor walked straight into what would have once been called the parlour, obviously the prayer meeting room. One chair was placed between a podium—where a large Bible lay open for reading—and a black iron stand that provided holders for rows of candles. It was clearly the chair for whomever was conducting the meeting.

Eleanor moved to claim it, denying Irene the slightest edge in controlling this meeting. The chair had no cushion. Nor did its hard wooden seat or spoked back support offer any comfort. It did, however, have armrests, putting it a cut above the motley group of battered old kitchen chairs provided for the visiting faithful. As with everything else, Irene carried poverty to extremes.

The threadbare carpet square was probably for kneeling. Even the most fervent servants of Irene's God might find their devotion somewhat tried by varnished floorboards, Eleanor thought, stepping over the tatty fringed edge of the mat with care. Tripping or slipping did not feature in her plans.

Having eased herself into the chair, she placed her elbows on the armrests and leaned back, adopting the imperious air that invariably quelled any argument. Irene had trailed after her. She stood a few steps inside the room, still gawking like a mindless fool, her pale eyes fixed in a glazed fashion on Eleanor's chest.

'Sit down, Irene. We need to talk.'

It snapped her out of her thrall. 'They said your breasts were cut off,' she shot at Eleanor with venomous resentment at seeing her still in shape.

'I don't have to advertise the fact, Irene.'

Enlightenment dawned. 'False,' she sneered and dropped onto the nearest chair. 'Vanity,' she accused, a febrile light leaping into her eyes as she plucked out a sin to start beating her drum.

'You've always had a fetish about breasts,' Eleanor told her.

Chin lifting, mouth pruning. 'I have not.'

Eleanor glanced derisively at the sagging bodice of Irene's drab grey dress. 'A lot of flat-chested women do. But it's more than that with you, isn't it?'

A moment of blankness, then a burst of spitting venom. 'Whore's talk. That's what you are, Eleanor. A whore. Marrying Max Vandelier for his money. Flaunting your body to muddle men's brains.' She broke into a cackle of laughter. 'You can't do it now, can you?'

The sudden ripping away of Irene's usual cloak of hypocrisy surprised Eleanor. Never before had she attacked so openly. Was it in reaction to the touch on suppressed and hidden desires, or was Irene losing her grip on the sanctimonious game?

'God is punishing you, Eleanor,' she raved on. 'He seeded the cancer that's eating you up inside. The avenging sword will cut you down. And I'll dance on your grave. I'll—'

'Oh, I doubt that,' Eleanor drawled mockingly. 'I doubt that very much.'

'You won't be able to stop me,' came the confident jeer.

'I know why your husband killed himself.'

It froze Irene's face. The triumph in her eyes died into a

glassy stare. Her mouth, already open to spew more of her malevolent gloating, remained hanging in a slack gape. Eleanor waited. It took several minutes for her statement to sink into Irene's mind, stir up the buried memories, then get coated with the public lie. Irene rearranged her face into a tight, self-righteous mask.

'It was an accident,' she snipped out. 'The coroner said so.'

'Yes. It was a nice, clean coroner's finding. In everyone's best interests at the time.' Eleanor paused and smiled confidentially. 'But you and I know better, Irene.'

Confusion sharpening to fear, horror quickly withdrawn, hidden. Eleanor could see the thoughts flicking through her eyes, the bolstering of assurance that there was no proof of anything, that Eleanor was fishing in her nasty, sly way.

'I have no idea what you're talking about,' Irene said, puffing out her flat chest as she climbed on her high horse. 'I find your insinuations extremely offensive. And speaking ill of the dead when they can't defend themselves is not a Christian act.'

Adopting the old sanctimonious act, Eleanor thought cynically, and proceeded to puncture it. 'Before Ian drove to Scone and flew his plane into a hill—'

'It's wickedness to say such a thing,' Irene snapped.

'He came up to the Big House,' Eleanor continued relentlessly. 'We had a long talk. You could say Ian unburdened himself to me before putting an end to a life that had become unbearable to him.'

Irene shifted uneasily. 'Why would he talk to you?' she demanded suspiciously.

'Perhaps because I wanted to hear. I wanted to hear everything Ian had to say about Rory and Tamara...and you, Irene.'

A glimpse of naked fear.

Eleanor turned the screws. 'He told me what his marriage to you was like.'

'I was a good wife to him,' Irene flared, leaping to defend her position. 'If he said anything else, he lied.'

'You trapped Ian into marriage.'

'He seduced me. I was having his baby. He had to marry me.'

'Oh, yes. The innocent minister's daughter story,' Eleanor mocked. 'I heard a different version from Ian that morning.'

Irene's eyes flickered. Her hands twitched in agitation.

'Ian was a good catch, and you caught him,' Eleanor went on, employing a calm, matter-of-fact tone to keep Irene on track with her. 'It got you out of your parents' house where everything had to be shared. Even your bedroom.'

'Every woman wants a home of her own.' Harried justification.

Eleanor deliberately slowed her delivery, making every word a telling one. 'You didn't want to make a home, Irene. You wanted freedom. You saw marriage to Ian as a passport to freedom. Not only economic freedom but the space and the privacy and the opportunities to do what you wanted.'

Irene's eyes had the mesmerised stillness of a rabbit caught in headlights. Eleanor paused before shafting home the truth Irene was waiting for but didn't want to hear.

'It gave you the freedom to lead your own secret life. And that wasn't your personal brand of religion, was it, Irene? Ian told me what it was. How you—'

'It's a lie,' Irene said to her. Her hands clenched into fists, and she punched her thighs as she chanted, 'Lies, lies, lies!'

'How often did you have sex with Ian after your daughter was born?'

'Sex is only for making babies.' Self-righteous fervour blazed over the inner turbulence. 'The Bible says so. I did my duty, giving him children.'

'Men have needs.'

'Men are animals.' A hiss of hatred. 'They're sweaty and gross and—'

'And it's only women who turn you on. Women and girls with lush breasts and—'

'Stop it! Stop it!' Irene screeched, leaping from her chair, her hands clamped over her ears. She whirled like a dervish, gabbling, her version of talking in tongues.

Utter gibberish.

Again Eleanor waited. Eventually Irene stopped, panting as though she'd run a marathon. She looked like a scarecrow, hair dislodged from her bun and hanging in wild wisps. Her hands fell to her sides, curling into fists again. Her eyes glittered at Eleanor.

'I saw you burning,' she claimed with rabid satisfaction. 'Consumed by hellfire. Writhing and plucking out your eyes in pain.'

'I'm sure you enjoyed it,' Eleanor said carelessly. 'But while we're both in the land of the living, Irene, I want to get one thing very clear between us.'

'Lies, lies, lies!'

Eleanor pushed herself to her feet, standing tall and straight to impose her will on Irene's darting mind. She would allow no mental bolthole from the threat that had to be hammered home.

'From this day on, if I or my sons require your vote for any company decision, you will give it to us. You will never vote against us no matter what promises anyone might make to you.'

Furious defiance. 'I have the right to do as I like.'

'As you undoubtedly did with your daughter once Ian was gone.'

'She's dead.'

'Like Ian. Both of them suicides.'

'Accidents!' Irene screamed.

Eleanor went for the kill. 'You've now gathered other daughters around you, haven't you, Irene? Daughters of your God. Whom you embrace in love. And touch.'

'You have the filthy mind of a whore.'

'If you ever vote against us, Irene, I will ensure that your standing in the eyes of your church will be destroyed. Your secret life will be a secret no longer. You'll end up a leper in this town. An object of disgust.'

Fear, hatred, rebellion. 'Lies! People will know they're lies.'

Eleanor walked up to eyeball her at close quarters. 'Lies or not, believe me, they'll be made public. And people will say, where there's smoke, there's fire. And they'll look at you and wonder, and whisper, and remember things, and connect them together. Smoke and fire, Irene. You understand fire, don't you?'

Irene quivered.

Eleanor stepped around her and moved to the doorway that led to the front hall. She paused and looked back. 'I understand you met Louise the other day. Rory's wife.'

Irene's head snapped towards her. Her eyes were unfocused.

Eleanor smiled to concentrate her attention. 'Did you like Louise, Irene? Did you lust after her body?'

A choking sound. Convulsive swallowing.

'I think Louise would do anything to get your vote,' Eleanor mused. 'Being with her could be dangerous. Secrets have a way of popping out.'

Irene's eyes were almost popping out.

Eleanor smiled again. 'Much safer to keep faith with me, Irene. You can trust me. I've already kept your secret for twelve years.'

'Get out! Get out!' High-pitched shrieks.

'See you in hell, Irene,' Eleanor said for her own private amusement, then unhurriedly let herself out of the house. She closed the door on a babble of hysterical prayers for her eternal damnation.

Secrets were wonderfully useful, Eleanor reflected with

satisfaction, and she'd only had to use one on Irene to accomplish the desired result.

Fear effectively implanted.

Louise effectively blocked.

TWENTY-SIX

'Ingratiate yourself,' was her father's advice.

Louise pondered it as she drove the last stretch of the Sydney to Newcastle expressway before the turn-off to Cessnock. Ingratiating herself with Irene Buchanan could be a lengthy process. She was in agreement with her father's opinion that an appeal to family feeling would not work. Which meant involving herself in Irene's religion.

Would showing a receptive interest in it be enough? She didn't want to go too public in her pursuit of Irene's vote. Attending church services on Sunday could blow the lid on what she wanted to achieve. The motivation of seeking a reconciliation between Rory and his mother wouldn't stretch that far, not credibly, and telegraphing her intentions to the Traverners was not part of Louise's plan.

Attending the occasional prayer meeting might do the trick. She hoped. If the signboard on her front lawn was anything to go by, Irene held one at her house on a regular basis. Louise intended to check it out. She'd flown to Sydney from Canberra this morning with that purpose in mind. The sooner she started ingratiating, the better. She needed to get Irene onside before Eleanor initiated any new company decisions.

Failing Irene's vote, they certainly needed Tamara's. She

wondered how Rory had fared with the renegade of the family. He'd certainly set out with convincing determination on Thursday afternoon, and he hadn't been home since. Louise had called the house several times over the weekend to check if he had returned. On each occasion the answering service had clicked on, and when she'd played it back for messages, there'd been nothing from Rory. It was thoughtless of him not to keep her informed.

Doing it his way, she supposed. Men, even her father, didn't want to accept or acknowledge that a woman could outthink them. Her father loved giving her the benefit of his experience, and it was always well worth hearing, but he saw her as his student, not his equal.

She had kept the Tamara plan up her sleeve, only mentioning that Rory was negotiating with Eleanor's alienated daughter. Louise wanted a successful outcome before revealing what she'd put in train. Her boldness would surprise her father. He would have to credit her with more go-getting guts than he thought she had.

If Rory didn't get it right... Louise grimaced in vexation. He should have thought to cover his absence from the winery on Friday. She hoped he hadn't blown the Canberra story if he'd called Janet Thurston later on in the day. It was so stupid and unnecessary to fuel gossip over where he was and what he was doing.

Louise wished she knew if he'd gone to work this morning. Calling to find out was impossible in the circumstances. Despite its being Monday, he could still be away if Tamara was driving a hard bargain. Three days and four nights might not be enough to get her pregnant. Tamara would probably want proof of a positive result. Louise knew she would herself before signing anything away.

It was a pity she didn't know more about Tamara. None of the family would talk about her. Even Gabrielle had fobbed off her questions with non-answers last Thursday.

On the very few occasions during the past three years

when Tamara had descended on the family during a social function at the Big House, she had made herself totally unapproachable. Scorn, mockery, contempt, insults seemed to be her stock-in-trade. It was after a particularly cutting snub that Louise had managed to dig out of Rory a mention of the infamous teenage affair. He had flatly refused to give details, insisting it was ancient history.

The one certainty Louise had was Tamara's hatred of Eleanor. It was so obvious to any astute observer. Louise suspected the sudden decision to have a child was tied to this hatred, a case of mocking the dying Eleanor by giving birth to life. Choosing Rory to be the father was probably another perverse decision, a brief resurrection of an affair that had undoubtedly upset Eleanor.

Whatever Tamara's twisted thinking, it was irrelevant, Louise thought dismissively, as long as Rory could get Tamara's vote. And she had to get Irene's.

The Cessnock turn-off came up, and Louise swung her car into the exit lane. She checked her watch. It was only half past two. More than time enough to get to Irene's home for this afternoon's prayer meeting.

Since being Rory's wife might not carry any weight with Irene, Louise figured it was a safer course to establish interest in Irene without attempting any social pressure. The prayer meeting gave her ready entry into the house. She could make the opportunity to ingratiate herself with Irene after the true believers left.

In fact, to ensure not being turned away because of her identity, Louise decided on a slightly late arrival. With others already present, Irene could more easily be swayed into accepting her sincerity. Then enduring two hours of prayers would surely be enough to engage Irene's attention for at least a little while afterwards.

She parked across the street from the ghastly old cottage Irene called home, intent on waiting and observing the faithful followers who came to her door to take part in communal prayer. Probably mad misfits like Irene, needing a prop to give meaning and colour to their drab little lives. Religion, to Louise's mind, was no more than another form of politics, a means of power over people by those smart enough to know how to use it.

The first arrival was a big blob of a woman, so fat she waddled up the path. Her lank black hair was cut in short bob. The hem of her tent dress was lopsided. A baggy brown cardigan looked as if it had been rescued from a dump. Charming company, Louise thought derisively.

The next comers were much older, two women in their sixties or seventies. One was tall and gawky with frizzy white hair and wearing a navy suit that had to be two decades out of fashion. She looked spinsterishly prim and proper. The other had a floppy maroon felt hat crammed onto her head. Layers of receding chins sagged into a blue and grey checked blouse, which manfully covered a battleship bosom and was tucked into a maroon kilt. On her feet were army boots.

Louise rolled her eyes. She had deliberately chosen a subdued and modest outfit, a long sage green skirt and matching tailored shirt, but it was obviously designer wear and the latest fashion. Not that this company would recognise such things. Nevertheless, she was certainly going to stick out from the crowd, which had not been her intention.

As it turned out, there was no crowd. Louise waited until ten minutes past three, but no one else turned up. With a sigh of resignation, Louise sallied forth to do whatever had to be done.

The blob answered the doorbell. Her piggy eyes rounded in surprise. She was clearly not accustomed to seeing a woman of style and elegance on Irene's doorstep.

Louise smiled, projecting a warm, friendly manner. 'Hello. I've come for the prayer meeting. You must be one of Irene's friends.'

The blob nodded wordlessly, her mouth agape at the prospect of Louise joining the group.

'I'm Irene's daughter-in-law. My name is Louise. What's yours?'

'Shirley. Shirley Doggitt.' The blob's face beamed with pleasure that Louise wanted to know her.

Doggitt, Louise thought, was perfectly appropriate. 'How nice to meet you, Shirley. May I come in?'

Dazzled by Louise's charm, the blob was only too happy to give her entry and usher her into Irene's inner sanctum. 'Irene, look who's here!' she announced excitedly. 'It's Rory's wife, Irene's daughter-in-law,' she gushed to the others.

The white-haired spinster and the floppy felt hat gawked at her. Louise nodded and smiled at them, waiting for Irene to turn around and acknowledge her. Her thin, scrawny figure stood stiff-backed, seemingly frozen in the act of lighting the last candle on an iron stand that sputtered with rows of lit candles.

'Louise has come to pray with us,' the blob gabbled on.

'How nice for you, Irene,' the felt hat approved unctuously.

'Yes. Family should be in the fold,' The pious declaration came from the white frizz.

Irene slowly swung around, the taper in her hand still burning. There was something in her eyes that sent a convulsive shiver down Louise's spine. Perhaps it was only a flicker of light from the taper, reflecting oddly, yet Louise had the creepy sense of some dark, turbulent power in Irene. She shook it off, telling herself she was being absurdly fanciful.

'I hope I'm welcome,' she appealed, confident of talking her way past any reservations Irene might have.

After all, she had already won the support of the group.

TWENTY-SEVEN

Louise would do anything to get your vote.

Eleanor's words hammered Irene's mind as she fought the demons that would destroy her prayer meeting, the fear, the hatred, the fury.

Dangerous.

Secrets popping out.

No. Not with the others here. *Leper. Disgust.*

Prayer. Make Louise pay.

Irene smiled. 'God knows what is in your heart,' she said, and the image of the avenging sword hovered enticingly over the shiny blonde head of Rory's deceitful, scheming wife. It was good, it was right to make the liar pay.

She introduced Miriam and Nora and watched them respond to the spurious charm of the snake in their midst. Louise was like Eleanor, smooth and polished, not showing her poisonous fangs. But Irene saw them, hidden behind the flash of white teeth.

She moved to the podium and selected a different page to be read from the Bible, a more pertinent page. It was the signal for the others to settle themselves. Shirley urged Louise into the chair next to her, eagerly offering to share her Bible, completely taken in by the facade of interest and appreciation.

'Turn to Psalm twelve,' Irene instructed, secretly gloating over the truth of the words she had chosen. 'Verse two,' she added as the others found the page. Then she commenced to read.

'"Untruth they keep speaking one to the other. With a smooth lip they keep speaking even with a double heart. Jehovah will cut off all smooth lips."'

She paused and looked straight at Louise's lipsticked mouth, enjoying the moment before continuing to read.

'Psalm eleven. Verse five. "Jehovah Himself examines the righteous one as well as the wicked one, And anyone loving violence His soul certainly hates. He will rain down upon the wicked one traps, fire and sulphur And a scorching wind, as the portion of their cup, For Jehovah is righteous. He does love righteous acts. The upright are the ones that will behold His face."'

Irene's soul soared. It was so uplifting to read the judgment of the Lord on people like Louise, sneaky, vicious, self-serving creatures of the devil. Now to bring her to her knees, make her do penance for the persecution she had planned.

'Let us pray.'

Shirley plopped down from her chair, egging Louise to kneel beside her on the mat. Good, devout, god-fearing Shirley, her innocence protecting her from knowing what Irene knew.

Kneel, sit, kneel, sit, kneel... Irene gloried in the power to make Louise pay, to show up her ignorance, pile on discomfort, strike at the black heart within. The words rolled off her tongue, the strong, exciting words of hellfire and damnation. And the waves started rippling through her body, lovely, warm sensations.

Her eyes were drawn to Shirley's huge, pendulous breasts. *Two fawns that feed among the lilies, generous as the grape...* What would it be like to see her undressed? The pulsing started, excitement so hot, the wet juice of the grape, intoxicating, satisfying...

Louise! Did she see? Could she know?

Fear speared through Irene's secret pleasure, cutting it short. Hatred surged. Frustration. Bitterness. How dare this woman intrude on her life? Coming to take what didn't belong to her. Like Eleanor. Take, take, take. Why couldn't they leave her alone?

Greed. Dishonest gain. A deadly sin that deserved death. God was punishing Eleanor, and rightly so. This woman should be punished, too.

Seething with anger, Irene brought the prayer meeting to an end. She didn't offer the usual afternoon tea. She would not sup with the devil.

Miriam and Nora didn't linger, throwing meaningful looks at Louise as they thanked Irene for an invigorating meeting and expressed the sentiment that a family that prays together, stays together. Irene saw them to the front door and came back to find Shirley still fawning over Louise. She stood pointedly by the doorway to the hall, holding herself rigidly aloof from the sickening sucking up.

The message finally penetrated.

'Well, I'm sure you two have a lot to talk about,' Shirley cooed. 'I won't hold you up, Irene. I'll let myself out. So nice to meet you, Louise.'

'And you, Shirley.'

'Will we see you on Wednesday?'

'If I can make it.'

'Oh, goody!' Puffed up with pride and pleasure, she plodded over to Irene. 'You have such a beautiful daughter-in-law.'

'"And one's very eyes will rot away in their sockets."'

'That's from Zechariah,' Shirley crowed, unaware it was not a Bible test. Glowing triumphantly, she trundled out, closing the front door behind her.

Louise made no move to go, despite not having been offered any further hospitality. 'Such kind people!' she remarked, a slimy smile on her smooth lips.

'Daughter of Lucifer,' Irene snapped, the hatred erupting. 'There's nothing for you here.'

'Oh, but you're wrong. I want to know more.'

Prying for secrets. 'Get out of my house. I'll have no vipers under my roof.'

'I swear to you I come in peace and goodwill, Irene, looking for the light to guide me. I want to see what you see so clearly.'

Liar! 'You mock God with your forked tongue.'

'Look!' White hands supplicating. 'I know you must be disappointed in Rory, but please give me a chance. Maybe I can save him if you show me how.'

Rory. Spoiling everything by taking Tamara that summer. Ian telling secrets to Eleanor. All men animals, rutting animals, dirty...and this serpent woman pretending to be lily-white...

'It must be in your Bible. I'll go and buy one. The same as yours. Which version is it?'

Fury drove Irene after her as the blasphemer walked to the podium, hands reaching out to touch the holy book. 'Filth! Filth!'

It stopped her.

Irene shoved her aside and snatched up the Bible, hugging it fiercely to her.

And the devil fell.

A squawk as she toppled, crashing into the stand of candles, flailing arms, flickering lights, a thud as her head hit the camphor chest under the window, mouth slack, no more sound from it, body sprawled over the black iron frame, splashed with wax, flames licking, catching, fizzing, burning.

Irene watched, fascinated.

No movement. Head lolling. Legs twisted. One shoe half off, its high heel spiked into the fringe edging the carpet. The smell of hair in cinders. Flames racing up the curtain behind the fallen stand. A pillar of fire. Hellfire for the devil.

Yes! Sheer exaltation held Irene transfixed. The smell, the sound, the heat, the sight, flesh turning black as it should, yes, burn, burn, burn. God punishing the wicked. A wall of fire, crackling, cleansing, and the righteous triumphant.

Traps, fire and sulphur and a scorching wind.

The thing hanging on the black frame had invited them all.

TWENTY-EIGHT

Tamara tossed him her beach towel, her eyes dancing with mischief. 'Catch me if you can.'

Rory laughed, watching her with pleasure as she raced ahead of him, nimbly finding sure footholds on the rough rock and log steps leading to the house, wild and carefree as she unsnapped her bikini bra, whipped it off, pirouetted and flung it down to him.

'Slowcoach!'

It spurred him into a chase. He loved the sound of her laughter as she sped up the outside staircase to the balcony. He felt happy, happier than he'd been for a long time. It wasn't the same as when they'd been teenagers, but over the past few days, there'd been flashes of it, moments of intense closeness—a look, a word, a touch—when he'd felt sure her soul moved with his. In a way it was like living with a tantalising will-o'-the-wisp. Now she was here. Now she wasn't.

She was naked by the time he bounded up the last step, naked and perched on the railing, uncaring that anyone might look up from the beach and see her. And he didn't care, either, because she was so captivatingly beautiful.

'I want you,' she sang at him.

He dropped the towels.

'Naked,' she added, her wide grin a teasing challenge, her legs opening to draw him in.

He stripped off his shorts, excited, exhilarated by her daring. Tamara, the bold. Magnificent, compelling madness to couple with her out here in the nude, but the sense that this was time out of time for both of them was strong, and the need to revel in it while he could was intense.

He heard the telephone ringing in the living room and dismissed it. The power of being wanted, no restraint, no inhibitions, was irresistible. He felt the ache in his testicles, the engorgement of his penis, his heart hammering as he responded to her beckoning.

She leaned back, shaking her hair, laughing, risking the long fall to the beach path below. 'Catch me, Rory. Hold me safe.'

He caught her around the waist, and she wound her legs around his hips, pulling him into her, trusting to his strength and balance to keep them both safe as they connected and fused.

'Yes...' Her eyes shone at him, openly exultant, her voice a husky lilt of euphoria. 'Deep, Rory, deep. Pump it into me.'

She arched away from him, flinging her arms out, her breasts tilted to the sky, abandoning herself to his power, wild and free as she had been in their youth so long ago. His Tamara. Rory exulted in the freedom to take her as fiercely as she wanted—he wanted—loving her, absorbing her into his soul again, the spirit of her soaring beyond the ordinary and drawing him with her.

Deep. The cradle of her hips tilted to take all of him, convulsive spasms welcoming him, squeezing him, wanting his sperm in her womb...and he wanted it there, too, seeding the child that would tie her to him. Irrevocably. Regardless of anything the future had in store for either of them, their child would be the heart of their belonging.

Preclimax tension seized him, driving him into a frenzy.

Her heels jammed into his back, urging on his violent need. He came in fast, explosive spurts, and he felt her flooding around him, a warm bath of essences for their baby to be conceived. Would it be this time?

Doorbell ringing.

He hoisted Tamara up, revelling in the soft squash of her voluptuous breasts as he crushed them against his chest. 'Are you expecting someone?'

'No.' She wound her arms around his neck, her mouth invitingly close, her eyes a soft, sexy glow. 'They'll go away.'

He kissed her, losing himself in the sensational passion of her response, her tongue lashing his, fiercely aggressive, a deep invasion that engulfed him in her possession. Her legs slid down, caressing his buttocks, his thighs, behind his knees, and he shook with tremors of pleasure.

'Rory! Rory, are you here?'

The call for him was a shocking intrusion, breaking his intense involvement with the feelings Tamara aroused. His head jerked from her as another call came.

'Rory, if you're here, for God's sake, answer me!'

Janet's voice, raw and urgent, echoing from the lobby. It stilled them both. A sharp question in Tamara's eyes. What the hell was Janet doing here, walking in on them?

'It's got to be important,' Rory muttered.

Footsteps clattering on the wood treads of the staircase leading to the living room.

'Wait, Janet!' he shouted.

Janet felt the blood draining from her face. She sat on one of the stair treads, leaned forward, folded her arms across her knees and rested her clammy forehead on them, waiting for the shakes to subside, waiting for Rory and Tamara to untwine themselves and get some clothes on, waiting to tell him...

Nausea hit her. He'd been doing that with Tamara while... Her mind clamped down on the sickening thought.

It was none of her business. She shouldn't have walked in. If the front door hadn't been unlocked... But the matter was urgent. Critically urgent.

She'd driven all this way, trying continually to reach him, pressing the redial button on the mobile telephone in her car innumerable times, listening to the call buzz, willing him to pick up a receiver. No answer...no answer... Well, she had an answer now.

To more than one question!

She shut her eyes tighter, willing the stark image of his naked embrace with Tamara to vanish. How was she ever going to look at Rory again without seeing that abandonment to physical passion? If only she hadn't started down the stairs... But she'd felt and smelled the sea breeze coming through the opened doors to the balcony and thought... nothing as shattering as the reality.

'Janet.'

Rory's voice, close to her and concerned.

She dragged her head up and forced herself to look at him. He was at the foot of the staircase, wearing shorts now. Her vision blurred over the rest of his body, the long, strongly muscled legs, the sweat glistening on his bare chest.

'I'm sorry if you're shocked by...' His voice trailed off. He was embarrassed...for her.

'Louise is dead.'

That focused his mind on something else. It might be cruelly blunt, but tact didn't seem appropriate in the circumstances. It was what she'd come to tell him.

He stared at her, totally stunned for several seconds before shaking his head as though he couldn't have heard correctly. His eyes sharpened on hers, saw nothing but flat, steadfast fact looking at him, leaving him no room for doubt.

'How?'

'She went to Irene's prayer meeting this afternoon. After

the others left, she stayed on to talk to your mother. I don't know how the fire started. The house burnt down very quickly. Louise didn't get out.'

'Christ!' He covered his face with one hand as he bent his head. Convulsive swallowing. Shoulders hunching over as his other arm wrapped around his chest.

'What about Irene?'

Tamara's voice sliced through the charged silence. It came from the direction of the bar. Janet couldn't look at her. She hadn't really believed Rory would plunge into a torrid affair with Tamara. Not while still married to Louise. She'd always thought of Rory as an honourable man.

She remembered how steadfast he'd been in waiting for Tamara after their aborted teenage affair. He would have married her. She'd rejected him as cruelly as any woman could reject a man. So how could he do this now?

'Janet?' he quietly prompted.

She pushed her mind to the job of informing him of the situation he had to face. 'Smoke inhalation. She's been taken to Cessnock District Hospital. They'll fly her by helicopter to John Hunter Hospital at Newcastle if need be,' she recited flatly.

'Saved from her own hellfire,' Tamara mocked. 'Did she redeem herself or did someone get her out?'

Rory's head jerked up and snapped around. 'For God's sake, Tamara!'

'Let's not be hypocrites, Rory.' It was a hard, brutal retort, slapping him into her world. She walked into Janet's narrowed field of vision and pressed a glass into Rory's hand. 'Fortitude for your stomach.'

She turned to Janet, coming straight at her, up the stairs to where she sat, her black eyes brilliantly magnetic in commanding, purposeful attention. 'Drink this, Janet.' She pressed a glass into her hand. 'It'll take the edge off.'

There was no trace of apology in her expression, just recognition of shell shock. Janet supposed she should appreciate this much caring from her. Tamara was like a primitive force that hit and moved on, leaving others to clean up the debris. Didn't Rory know that? Where did he think this was leading?

Tamara backed off after Janet accepted the glass. At least she'd had the decency to don a large T-shirt that dangled to mid-thigh. Though it was obvious she wore no bra. Probably no panties, either. Hard and reckless.

Janet tossed some of the drink down her throat. It was whisky. It burned her chest, but she didn't care. The sensation was an effective anaesthetic. As Tamara took up a dominant stance by the balustrade between Janet and Rory, Janet could almost view her objectively.

'You'd better brief Rory with all you know, Janet,' she said. 'That's what you came to do, isn't it?'

Janet nodded and turned her gaze to the man who was still her closest friend, to whom she owed her best efforts. 'The call came through at ten to five.'

'Police?' he asked.

'No. Remember Shirley Doggitt? The fat girl at school. You used to stop the boys from teasing her.'

'Thyroid problem.'

'Yes. She'd been at the prayer meeting. Went back when she saw the fire. A neighbour pulled Irene out but couldn't go into the house again for Louise. Shirley was terribly distressed about it. She thought of you.'

It struck Janet that Shirley had probably secretly adored Rory, her kind saviour, the best-looking boy in the school. *My kind saviour, too*, she thought, and looked sharply at Tamara. *Do you know what you've taken? Do you care?*

'So you took the call from Shirley,' Tamara prompted. 'What then?'

Nothing but a relentless probing for knowledge.

Defeated and deflated, Janet turned to Rory. 'I tried to call you here.'

'We were on the beach.'

His eyes looked sick, their usual golden sparkle dulled to a muddy ochre, but he was more composed, accepting what she was saying without any noticeable reaction.

'I thought the police would come looking for you. As a stopgap measure, I called your grandfather. I informed him what I'd heard, told him it might be hours before I could contact you and suggested he act for you on whatever formalities needed attending to.'

'Eleanor will act,' Tamara said derisively.

'You did right, Janet,' Rory assured her.

'Did you tell Uncle Frank where Rory was? And with whom?' Tamara asked.

'No. Rory said to keep it confidential.'

Tamara heaved a sigh of relief. Or satisfaction. It was impossible to tell what went through Tamara's mind. 'It's best kept that way, Rory,' she warned, stating the obvious, in Janet's opinion, yet somehow adding a darker element to it.

He frowned at her.

'You have your wife's funeral to attend,' she went on, punching out what had to be faced. 'Not to mention an inquest and other delicate matters. Unnecessary and immaterial gossip will only make it worse.'

He winced. 'You'll stay here?'

'Yes. I'll come to the funeral. I should know by then.'

Know what? Janet glanced from one to the other, aware of a tense current of understanding running between them. There was nothing to be learnt from their expressions. Rory slowly nodded. He was prepared to leave the issue on hold, but this was certainly not the end of it. Janet caught the sense of intense determination.

'The Canberra story won't hold up,' she pointed out. 'Louise's father knows you weren't there.'

He gave her a rueful smile. 'Thanks, Janet. For saving me on several counts. I'll think about it while I shower and change. Wait for me?'

'Yes,' she agreed, worried that he might mess things up more than they were already messed.

At least Tamara wasn't intent on creating scandal this time. Not until the funeral, anyway. God only knew what would happen there.

Janet studied the glass of whisky in her hands as Rory passed her on the staircase. A pity she couldn't get blind, roaring drunk. Maybe after she drove home. Why not? Her life was looking emptier and emptier. Rory had been her rock, and now he was on a fast track to hell with Tamara. What was going to be left when this was all over?

She took a sip of the firewater, concentrating on the taste and feel of it. It was a relief when Tamara moved away, not bothering to say any more. Janet watched her walk to the open doors to the balcony, then dropped her gaze to her drink again. Tamara might want to recall her most recent intimacy with Rory. Janet didn't.

Another death.

Tamara brooded over it as she watched the waves roll in, forming their habitual scalloped pattern on the sand. String of pearls.

No tears for Louise.

Who could mourn a carbon copy of Eleanor?

But it was another death.

Had Irene perceived Louise's scheming ambition in their after-prayer talk? Fire was Irene's weapon. She might have gone over the edge, turning her fanatical and fevered declaiming into a blazing reality. Accident or murder?

Tamara shivered.

Too many deaths.

Destroy...

It was a two-edged sword. Had Eleanor driven Irene into some blind, hate-filled action against Louise? She needed to know, but it was too late to act now. Eleanor would have already moved, taking Irene under her wing, protecting the family, hoarding more secrets she could use, if and when it became necessary.

The funeral would provide the most fruitful ground for questioning, everybody there together. Tamara smiled. The first family meeting. A most opportune time for revelations.

She slid a hand over her stomach. Surely she had conceived. It was the right time, and Rory had certainly had plenty of shots at it. Her smile widened to a grin. He was the best lover she'd ever had. More than that. The grin faded. A pity it couldn't last.

Or could it?

Was he strong enough to take what would be thrown at him and still stick at her side? Hard to tell at this point. These past few days had been time out of time. To confuse them with reality was a path to disaster. She couldn't afford to let herself go soft, wanting more than was definitely within her reach.

She'd have the child. It was enough. And Rory would do his part. Their child would have what Eleanor would deny them. If it lived.

Too many deaths... The oppressive thought came back and lingered, bringing with it a chilling sense of premonition. Tamara tried to shake it off. She swung away from the view of the rolling sea and her gaze fastened on Janet, still sitting on the staircase, wrapped in misery.

Poor Janet. She'd had it tough, nursing Jim through that rotten, debilitating illness, having her heritage ripped off her by Eleanor. Now she was embroiled in another death, on Rory's behalf, and covering up what she must see as an illicit affair. Caring about people could hurt. Badly.

Tamara didn't stop to examine what drove her—impulse, premonition, empathy. She crossed the room to the foot of the staircase and broke into Janet's air of being lost and alone.

'Stick by Rory, Janet. He'll stay a good friend to you, and he'll need a friend by him with what's coming.'

The low, intense words penetrated. She looked at Tamara, her eyes full of hostile questions. 'He's got you now, hasn't he?'

'Who knows how long it will last?' With Eleanor doing her worst. Which she would.

'You're using him, aren't you? Using him worse than Louise did.' She shook her head. Hopelessness hung around her. 'He's worth more than that. Why can't he see?'

Such deep pain. Somehow it hurt Tamara. It stirred feelings, memories of feelings. A strange, compelling sense of urgency gripped her, spilling a tumble of words that had no reasoning behind them at all.

'You're his rock, Janet. When the time comes, he'll turn to you.'

Janet looked at her in bewilderment. 'Why are you saying this?'

Tamara stared at her, realising what her impulsive words meant. She was beginning to care too much about Rory, what he thought and felt and how devastated he would be when the truth came out.

'Just don't let him down,' she said in brusque dismissal.

Rory came clattering down the stairs, showered, dressed in the clothes he'd worn when he'd arrived. Tamara moved away, leaving him with Janet to settle on an appropriate cover story.

She liked Janet. A good heart. Caring.

She watched the two of them talking together, Rory and Janet, two of a kind, doing the right thing. Integrity. Yes, that's what it was. Integrity and honesty and decency and loyalty. They belonged with each other. While she...

She was alone. Always had been. Except for that brief time with Rory, and it had only been a dream. She recognised that now. Even then it had been too late to have a normal, loving life.

Rory broke away and came across to her, his eyes searching hers, wanting to see what he wanted of her. It wasn't there. She wouldn't let it be there.

'I'll call you later tonight,' he said.

'No. I'll come to the funeral, Rory. We'll talk then.'

'Tamara...' It was a fierce, intense challenge, intent on smashing barriers.

'Let go, Rory. I'll do this my own way.'

His jaw clenched. A determined flash in his eyes telegraphed he'd do it his way, too. Tamara recollected she had appealed to his strength. Maybe that was a mistake. Part of the dream that couldn't be.

Or could it? Was it possible to shut the door on the horrors of the past and go forward? Part of her wanted to believe it.

'The funeral then,' he grimly agreed. For now.

They left.

Tamara poured herself a cold drink and took it out to the balcony. She leaned on the railing where she and Rory had been a short time ago, making their child, she hoped. Tomorrow she would buy a pregnancy test kit. With any luck, the first part of her mission had been achieved.

The funeral. Yes, it was a fitting place to announce the beginning of a new life. A grandchild for Eleanor. Tamara laughed and lifted her glass in a toast to the occasion.

'Destroy,' she sang out in bold bravado, ruthlessly repressing every thought or feeling that might disrupt her set course.

The waves rumbled a long echo.

Destroy...

TWENTY-NINE

As the Daimler turned up Millfield Street, the crowd outside St. Joseph's Church came into view. The grounds and footpath were thronged with people. Cars clogged every available parking space in Cumberland Street and undoubtedly Yango Street, as well. People crossing the road caused hold-ups in the traffic.

Everyone and his dog here for this spectacle, Eleanor thought grimly. Louise's funeral had all the elements to draw them—family tragedy, a whiff of scandal, Jeremy Stanhope with his impressive contingent from Canberra, Louise's glamorous mother from Ireland accompanied by her retinue of horse-world connections and, of course, the dying matriarch of the Traverner and Buchanan vineyards on public view.

'Big turnout,' Frank murmured.

'It's a nice, sunny day. Who'd want to miss the best show in town?'

'It's a mark of respect, Ellie.'

She winced at the gentle reproof. 'I can only think of it as an ordeal to get through, Frank.'

He sighed. 'We certainly didn't need it to happen.'

That was the understatement of the year. The wretched mess had dragged on for almost two weeks with Jeremy

Stanhope turning his baby girl's death into a three-ring circus, grilling the three women who'd been at the prayer meeting and trying to browbeat his way to grill Irene, too.

Well, he'd met a brick wall there. He might be a heavyweight in the federal government, but in the Hunter Valley, Eleanor was held in more respect than any politician. She'd put Irene beyond his reach. Too many family skeletons to be rattled if he got access to Rory's mother. In the end he'd had to accept the written statement Eleanor had produced, setting out Irene's account of the accident, signed and witnessed by appropriate authorities.

'Death by misadventure' was the official verdict, and Jeremy Stanhope couldn't prove anything else. It was sheer pigheadedness, insisting the funeral be delayed until Louise's mother arrived from Ireland and had time to recover from jet lag. Eleanor had dug her heels in on this Friday date. Enough was enough. *Her* family had to be considered, too.

Which reminded her... She turned to Frank. 'How is Rory holding up?'

A slight hesitation. 'He'll be fine.'

'You're worried about him.'

A longer pause for rumination. 'It will all work out in time.'

He was keeping something to himself. Eleanor wanted to know what it was. 'If there's a problem, Frank...'

He shook his head. 'It doesn't matter now.'

Eleanor swallowed her frustration. When Frank was given a confidence, not even a crowbar would pry it out of him. He'd spent many hours with Rory since Louise's death, yet he'd said nothing of what they talked about. It was vexing.

'It was good of you to take over all the arrangements, Ellie. Rory appreciated it.'

What Rory had actually said was, 'Louise would appreciate it,' and Eleanor hadn't liked the flash of hard cynicism in his eyes. Nor had she liked the added comment, 'Having had practice with Max and my father, you know how best to do it.'

Of course, Rory had been offside with her ever since the affair with Tamara. Nevertheless, she'd sensed more than alienation this time. Active hostility. Which was dangerous. Especially with Louise dead and Tamara on the loose.

Max and Ian... Their deaths had been welcome. But not Louise's. Apart from the new situation with Rory, she now had Irene hanging around her neck like an albatross, her madness aggrandised and on a very tenuous leash. A pity she hadn't burnt in the fire. Though that would have given Rory her vote. No, it was better to have Irene under her thumb, at least until she had Tamara's measure.

Bill edged the Daimler forward. As onlookers spotted the car and its occupants, a clear passage was made into the church grounds. The hearse and the formal mourning cars were already lined up on the concrete turning circle. A parking attendant indicated the space reserved for the head of the family.

Eleanor had declined the use of one of the hired limousines. She was not going to the cemetery after the funeral service. Standing by the graveside would be too taxing on what strength she had. Better to rest for the reception at the Big House.

Her arrival caused the predictable stir amongst the crowd, people milling forward, necks craning. Bill held her door open. Frank stood by to lend any support she needed, having already alighted. The buzz of talk quietened, eyes feeding on her altered appearance as she stepped out and straightened up.

A cameraman pushed forward, undoubtedly shooting film for the evening news. The media had already made much of Louise's death. It was a good story, touching prominent people. It was to be hoped it would be a dead story after today.

Eleanor stood tall, head high. Her black crepe dress was a masterly piece of disguise, high-necked, long-sleeved, its cleverly gored skirt both graceful and elegant. It flattered her thinness. The chic angle of her wide-brimmed hat added its touch of class, and Max's diamond brooch was an ostentatious reminder of her status. Dame Eleanor was still Dame Eleanor, and she was letting everyone know it.

She took Frank's arm for the walk into the church, sister and brother, Traverner and Buchanan, the old establishment very much in force, demanding respect and getting it. No-one broke ranks to greet them. That would come later, at the reception. Eleanor had timed her arrival for a few minutes short of the two o'clock service to ensure no delay into the church.

The entry hall was afloat with floral tributes. More than enough to impress anyone. In the greeting room, Paul and David stood beside Rory to one side of the doors into the main body of the church, with Gabrielle and Sharon close by. On the other side stood Jeremy Stanhope and his ex-wife, flanked by their associates.

She nodded acknowledgments but didn't speak, moving straight ahead to take her seat for the service. The funeral director met her at the head of the aisle and ushered her to the front pew to the right of the altar. He murmured his hope that all was arranged to Dame Eleanor's satisfaction.

The organ was playing. The choir sat in the pews designated for them. The flowers were as ordered, white roses, carnations and stephanotis. The dark red jarrah coffin was as splendid as promised.

St. Joseph's might not be a cathedral, but it certainly wasn't a modest little church. Its high, paneled ceiling lent an uplifting air, and the inside remodelling, which had been done since the '94 earthquake, had distinctive and attractive design features, especially the five-sided arrangement of the pews around the altar, giving it the focus of a centre stage.

Jeremy Stanhope could not say they hadn't done his

daughter proud. Apart from which, whether he liked it or not, the Buchanans had always been buried from the Cessnock Catholic church. There could be no quibble on that.

'It's fine,' she declared. 'Thank you.'

'Thank you, Dame Eleanor. Now that you're here, I'll move everyone in.'

She sat, leaving room for Frank and Rory to take their places closest to the aisle. Paul and David and their wives would occupy the pew directly behind them. The priest emerged from the sanctuary and came to offer his condolences. He passed them on to Frank and Rory as they took their places beside her, then moved to speak to Louise's father and mother.

The church quickly filled and settled, hushing as the priest moved into position behind the coffin for the opening prayers. The organist stopped playing momentarily then started on the designated hymn, The Lord Is My Shepherd. The choir was exceptionally good. Eleanor was satisfied all was going well.

Then, incomprehensibly, a whispering started, a rustling of movement. The priest looked up from his prayer book and stared down the aisle. Eleanor did not look around, but it was obvious that someone had come in late, someone who was stirring more interest than anyone should at such a time.

The ripple of sound continued in a forward wave. Involuntary gasps came from the family row behind her. Eleanor looked sideways. A woman...Tamara!

With arrogant confidence in her right to command attention, she stepped past the front prayer stand and swung to face them, Tamara as they had never seen her before, Tamara stunningly dressed in classic clothes that would have done a princess proud at a royal funeral.

Her black suit shouted designer wear with its beautifully tailored jacket, moulded to her spectacular figure and featuring stark white lapels. Its black buttons had inset circles of white. The narrow skirt was a modest knee-length. Sheer black stockings ran to beautiful Italian black shoes, which were crisscrossed with strips of white. Her handbag matched. A finely woven black straw hat dipped to show off a spray of white camellias. Dark red lipstick and nail polish added the perfect touch, subdued, tasteful, yet emphasising star quality.

A sharp pang of regret hit Eleanor. This was the daughter she might have had, a daughter to be proud of. Then the reality of their total alienation from each other crushed the absurdly inappropriate feeling, and her mind clicked to red alert. This was Tamara in full battle regalia. The timing of her entrance had the stamp of surprise attack written all over it.

She stopped in front of Rory, offering her hand.

He stood and grasped it.

'A new life has started, Rory,' Tamara said quietly, soberly.

His fingers tightened around hers. Impossible to read their expressions in profile, but Eleanor had the strong sense of a pact being formed. It smacked of 'The queen is dead, long live the Queen,' with Tamara presenting herself as the candidate for the throne.

'Thank you for coming,' Rory murmured and released her hand.

Tamara moved on and politely offered it to Frank. 'Uncle...'

He stood and took her hand warmly in both of his. 'Good to see you, my dear.'

Frank was obviously still wishful of a reconciliation and wanting this startling show of dignity and goodwill to be a positive sign for it. The moment Tamara stepped in front of her and gave her a mocking little smile, Eleanor knew it wasn't.

'Hello, Mother.'

'Tamara,' she acknowledged, acutely aware of the spotlight her renegade daughter was drawing onto all of them.

Having ratified her spectacular entrance, Tamara skirted the prayer stand. Instead of going to the second pew to sit with Paul and David, she placed herself in a more prominent position by moving into the front pew beside Eleanor. She sat and crossed her legs, dangling one elegantly clad foot in Eleanor's direction. It was not coincidental. Eleanor was acutely aware of that. It was a statement of victory, won with ease and eclat.

Eleanor didn't hear the hymn come to an end or the priest begin the prayers. Her mind was sifting through the significance of Tamara's actions—the dominating play of her late arrival, the handclasp with Rory and the pertinence of the words spoken, the deliberate choice of putting herself in front of her half-brothers.

Rory and Tamara flanking Eleanor and Frank. Eleanor didn't like it. The new establishment taking over from the old?

Not while there was still breath in her body!

Tamara had come in with guns blazing today, but one surprise attack did not win a war. It merely demonstrated the intent to fight. And a fight to the death it would be, Eleanor silently vowed. She would not give up an inch of her hard-earned territory.

THIRTY

It was a simple matter for Tamara to commandeer a place in the limousine hired for the Traverner family. Blocking her out of it would not have looked good to the crowd outside the church, especially when there was room for six people. She waited until the others were settled in the passenger compartment, then followed them into it as a matter of course.

Surprised, David and Sharon automatically shuffled along the bench seat to make room for her. Tamara deliberately chose to sit on their side so she would be facing Paul, the heir apparent, and his wife, the enigmatic and always intriguing Gabrielle. The chauffeur, unaware of having admitted the cuckoo into the intimate family nest, obligingly closed the door behind her, sealing her initiative as a fait accompli.

'Well, isn't this cosy?' She beamed a smile around both couples as she settled back and relaxed for the drive to the cemetery. 'All of Mother's children together.'

The comment did not bring forth expressions of joy and pleasure. David looked uncomfortable and suspicious. Gabrielle observed her with quizzical interest. Paul maintained an impassive face, reserving judgment until her purpose became clear to him. Sharon, without Eleanor to quell her, opened her mouth.

'Didn't you come in your car?'

Tamara raised an eyebrow. 'Aren't I welcome, Sharon?'

She flushed. 'I only meant... Well, how did you get to the church?'

'In my Porsche. I had one of the chauffeurs park it for me. Do you want to find it and shovel me out?'

'No, no, of course not.' She retired, flustered.

Have disposed of fluffy-headed Sharon who could hardly be called a worthy adversary, Tamara turned her gaze to her main target. 'What about you, Paul? Do you find my presence offensive?'

'No,' he answered equably. 'Though I wonder why you came today.'

Direct and to the point. Tamara sharpened her knives. 'Oh, I thought I might as well get in a dress rehearsal for Mother's funeral. After all, it's supposedly only three and a half months away.'

A gasp from Sharon. A thunderous look from David. Gabrielle watching, absorbing. Paul... Tamara gave him another smile.

'Though I'm not supposed to know that, am I? Nobody bothered telling me.'

It amused her that they hadn't figured out she had an informant in the Big House. And in the winery. She made it her business to keep tabs on them all...Eleanor's family.

David rushed to excuse them. 'We assumed you were notified as we were.'

She cut him dead. 'I wouldn't assume anything where I'm concerned, David.'

The limousine pulled out to take its place in the funeral cortege. It moved at a snail's pace, befitting the sombre occasion. With any luck, the trip to the cemetery at Nulkaba would stretch to ten or fifteen minutes. Tamara kept a challenging gaze trained on Paul, applying moral pressure.

David was irrelevant. He followed Paul's lead. Always had. It was Paul she wanted to suffer. She wanted to crack his loyalty to his mother wide open. She wanted to strike at the heart of him, the heart he'd closed to her—his little sister—all his smug, safeguarded life. Mother's blue-eyed boy, performing oh, so faithfully to Eleanor's devious and damnable tune.

'I'm sorry I didn't contact you, Tamara,' he said quietly. 'It was remiss of me.'

'Par for the course, being remiss about me, wouldn't you say, Paul?'

He held her mocking gaze for several moments before replying, 'Yes, I would. And I regret that, too.'

Tamara wasn't expecting such an open admission, and it was given with every appearance of sincerity. It forced a reappraisal of the situation. David might still be in Mummy's pocket, but where was Paul? She looked at his wife, serene Gabrielle who quietly but firmly trod her own path under Eleanor's roof. Had she effected a change of perspective in her husband?

'I've never seen you look so beautiful, Tamara,' Gabrielle said softly, her lovely eyes reflecting nothing but genuine admiration.

'How kind! But then you always are,' Tamara mused. 'Thank you.'

She noted that Gabrielle wore navy. Sharon wore black, conforming with what was expected of her at a family funeral, but Gabrielle wore navy. Not a loud statement, but a statement nonetheless. She did not mourn Louise's passing, and she would not pretend to.

There was power here, Tamara suddenly recognised, a quiet power but one that had to be taken into consideration. She needed time to ponder the significance of Paul's new attitude towards her and how it could be used. Meanwhile there were urgent questions to be addressed. She changed tack, glancing around inquiringly as she moved onto more fertile ground.

'I notice Irene isn't with us today. Where has she been stashed?'

'She hasn't been stashed anywhere,' David protested irritably.

'Come now, David,' Tamara sweetly chided. 'Let's not be picky. Irene was discharged from the local hospital. She's certainly not at her burnt-out house. I doubt Rory would take her in, given the circumstances. Are you telling me Mother hasn't stepped in and—'

'Yes, she did,' Paul conceded. 'Irene is convalescing in a private nursing home.'

'How very convenient,' Tamara drawled, 'keeping her out of the way until Louise's father goes home. It neatly avoids any washing of our dirty linen in public.'

'What do you mean by that?' David growled. 'The fire was accidental. Louise tripped and knocked the candle stand over.'

'And Irene was the only witness.'

'What are you getting at, Tamara?' Paul asked, frowning.

Her voice dripped with scepticism. 'Does anyone here believe Louise went to Irene's for a prayer meeting because she'd suddenly got religion in a big way?'

A pregnant silence.

Sharon broke it. 'She said she wanted a reconciliation between Rory and his mother.'

'Indeed! I wonder why?' Tamara asked sweetly. 'After all these years. Reconciliation, votes, Mother dying, power grab...'

'Stop playing cat and mouse, Tamara,' David snapped.

'Did you tell Mother about Louise's sudden wish for a reconciliation, David?'

He looked discomforted. He darted a glance at Paul, unsure of himself, unsure where this was leading and not liking any of it. Paul held his tongue. The limousine turned off the main concourse into Allandale Road, which would take them straight to the cemetery.

'I told her,' Gabrielle dropped into the tense silence.

Tamara smiled. Maybe, just maybe, she had an ally in Gabrielle, albeit an unwary one. Or Gabrielle had questions in her mind that she wanted answered, too.

'So we have a lot of guilty parties sitting here, haven't we?' Tamara said silkily.

'Of what are we guilty, Tamara?' Paul asked, a weighing look in his eyes.

'Why, Paul, didn't Mother say she would talk to Irene?' She saw the hit strike home.

'And once she talked to Irene,' she continued with purring confidence, 'Louise was walking straight into the fire when she went to do her reconciliation number.'

'That's plain crazy to jump to such a conclusion,' David leapt in.

'Why has Irene been stashed away, David?'

'She's still in shock.'

'And goodness knows what she might say.' Tamara paused to let that sink in. She was enjoying herself immensely. 'Has any one of you spoken to Irene?' she asked, hammering in the nails with relish.

'When we first heard the news, I went to the hospital. In case she needed anything,' Gabrielle stated evenly. 'I was advised she was very distressed and not up to having visitors.'

'Which is perfectly reasonable,' David argued.

'Mother is so good at keeping hospital visitors out,' Tamara tossed into the fray. 'Was there a security guard outside Irene's door?'

No reply.

They passed the Cessnock geriatric nursing home. Not far to the cemetery now.

'This is all supposition, Tamara,' Paul commented

heavily. 'We don't even know if Mum did speak to Irene before that Monday.'

'I'm sure it's within your capacity to find out, Paul. Or perhaps you'd prefer not to know,' she deliberately mocked.

'It doesn't prove anything.'

She subjected him to a long, blistering look of scorn. 'Your mother has been blocking any risk to your inheritance from the day I was born. You can dismiss what I say as supposition if you like, Paul. You certainly turned a blind eye to what she did to me, so I don't really expect anything else from you. It's more comfortable like that, isn't it? Letting Mummy do the dirty work so you and David get everything.'

His jaw tightened.

Tamara let the thoughts linger, hoping the knife was twisting in his gut.

The limousine turned into the entrance to the cemetery and drew to a halt beside the gateway to the section traditionally reserved for Roman Catholics. The Buchanan plot was a short walk away. Tamara had not been allowed to attend Ian Buchanan's funeral, but she had visited his grave. A long time ago. She knew where it was.

'There's really only one problem left,' she mused.

'And what's that?' David obligingly asked.

She smiled at him. 'I'm not dead.'

She saw a look of guilty alarm spring onto Sharon's face. Tamara instantly knew its cause. They had discussed her death, speculating on its advantage to them. She felt a sickening hollowness in her stomach. Hatred swiftly fired her belly again.

The chauffeur opened the passenger door on Tamara's side.

She cast a bright smile around her silent companions. 'Well, let's go bury Louise.' Then she stepped into the sunshine and walked away from them.

She couldn't afford to be careless. She had the child now, the child who could take over everything, Frank Buchanan's great-grandchild. Frank stood beside Rory near the gateway to the burial ground. He'd accompanied his grandson in the mourning car after seeing Eleanor off from the church service. Tamara walked straight up to the grand old man of the Hunter Valley vineyards and slid her arm around his, offering him an appealing smile.

'I don't have an escort today, Uncle Frank. Do you mind if I hang onto you?'

He patted her hand, his eyes warm and kind. 'I'd be honoured. And may I say you're a credit to the family today, Tamara. A real credit.'

A simple, honest old man. Tamara almost felt ashamed of fooling him. But she didn't. Eleanor had been fooling him for a very long time.

She turned her gaze to Rory. The father of her child. His eyes met hers in a searing look of resolution that jolted her heart. Another honest man. In another life, in another time, she could have loved him. She almost did. But there was Eleanor. And Eleanor dominated everything.

There was no choice.

Destroy...

THIRTY-ONE

Paul felt as though he'd been sledgehammered. From all directions. Across the bonnet of the limousine he stared at the old church that stood adjacent to the cemetery, St. Patrick's, non-denominational now, set in beautifully kept gardens and used for weddings. It had been the Catholic church before St. Joseph's was built. His parents had married there.

What might have been if his father hadn't died when he did? Futile thought. What drove his mother to do all she'd done? Her love for Richard Traverner, the need to pass on the old heritage to his sons? Did that override a sense of humanity? Did it preclude any separation of right from wrong? Did it leave no room for anything else?

Tamara's words haunted him. 'From the day I was born.' 'For you and David to get everything.' 'What she did to me...'

He shook his head. He didn't know what his mother had done to Tamara. He'd only ever seen the way she was, an angry, destructive child, demanding attention, any kind of attention, a hate-filled child lashing out, causing trouble, mischief-making, a spoilt brat messing with his things. He'd avoided her. He'd hated her. He'd shut her out of his life. And justified it all the way.

Gabrielle had looked further than he had. Gabrielle. He felt her arm hooking around his and looked at her, loving her, feeling helplessly torn between two visions of the world he'd known, needing her support, her love.

'It's not finished, Paul,' she said quietly. 'There's time to build something else if you want to.'

How did she read him so well? A lump in his throat prevented a reply. He nodded.

'What do you make of that?' David growled, wanting him to smooth over all Tamara had said and implied.

Sharon shuddered, clinging close for comfort and protection. 'She's scary, David. I don't like being with her.'

'Get used to it, Sharon,' Paul tersely advised. 'Tamara is not going to go away. Not this time.'

'She's here to stir trouble,' David concluded, glaring at Tamara. 'She'll have everyone talking about her again. Look at her, making up to Uncle Frank. And dressed to kill.'

'Oh, don't use that word, David,' Sharon pleaded, shuddering again. 'Was she suggesting that Irene actually killed Louise?'

'Forget it, Sharon. It's nonsense. As for Mum being involved...' He frowned at Paul. 'You don't believe that, do you, Paul?'

'I intend to find out.'

He could hear his mother saying, 'Prevention is always better than a cure, Paul.'

David looked startled. 'You can't believe anything Tamara says. She was always a rotten little liar.'

Was she? The record of his mother's voice played on. 'She's a threat. A threat to everything I've built up. I do not intend to let her destroy it.' Tamara's voice. 'From the day I was born...'

Paul looked directly at his younger brother, weighing both voices in his mind. 'Maybe we didn't listen. Maybe we didn't see. I won't take anything for granted any more,

David. I'm going to listen. And look. And make up my own mind.'

Gabrielle squeezed his arm.

'Jesus, Paul!' David gestured in frustration at the indecisive reply. 'What's got into you?'

He half-smiled at his brother's confusion. 'It's very simple, David. I want the truth. When I know what that is, I'll act on it.'

'The truth! I'll give you the truth,' David expostulated wildly. 'Louise is dead and Tamara's here, all togged up like a film star, smarming over Uncle Frank. And guess who else is in her sights over there? Rory. Who's now a widower. We could be in deep shit, Paul.'

Consider what would happen if she gets Rory onside with her.

Paul remembered their teenage affair, remembered how Tamara was exiled to boarding school, remembered her wild plunge into over-the-top outrageousness with its underlying manic quality, shouting, 'I don't care.' But maybe she did care and had cared. And nobody cared back.

'Well, let's wait until the shit hits the fan, David. I'll deal with the fallout as it comes.'

'That might be too late.'

'Then we'll be living in interesting times, won't we?'

David couldn't live with the uncertainty. 'You've got to do something.'

'I will. I'll find out what our mother has done. In the meantime, we go and bury Louise. And let's hope, David...let's hope our mother doesn't see to it that we end up burying Tamara next.'

David's jaw dropped open. Both he and Sharon goggled at him, deeply shocked. Then David recollected himself and sputtered, 'That's a hell of a thing to say!'

'It's what Tamara was saying. The final solution. By which we get everything,' Paul said flatly. 'Would you want it like that, David?'

'No.' He shook his head vehemently. 'No.'

'Then we live with Tamara. And when this is over, I want to be able to live with myself.'

'You mean when Eleanor dies?' Sharon asked, not catching all the nuances of what was being said.

'It will play itself out in its own time. Before or after Eleanor's death,' Gabrielle put in quietly.

Sharon was still confused. 'What will?'

'Tamara's last-ditch stand,' Gabrielle answered.

'You've lost me,' David muttered, frowning heavily.

'And me,' Sharon agreed.

Paul's attention was sharply caught. Gabrielle saw things he didn't see. He wanted to know her vision of his world. He watched her as she spoke, no line of doubt on her face, no concern that she might be wrong in her voice.

'It's Tamara's last stand against Eleanor. For justice, vengeance, retribution—call it what you will.'

So simple, so clear when spelled out like that. Paul was once more amazed at his wife's perception.

'I thought she started it magnificently in the church today,' Gabrielle went on.

'You sound as though you admire her,' David commented critically.

'I do. Tamara knows what Eleanor is capable of, but she's fighting anyway. Openly, defiantly, boldly. I do admire her. Anyone who stands up to Eleanor has a lot of guts.'

The realisation hit Paul that Tamara had been doing that all along, fighting his mother with child's weapons, teenage rebellion, contemptuous capriciousness—and now the last-ditch stand.

From the day I was born.

A threat to everything I've built up. I do not intend to let her destroy it.

A chill crept down Paul's spine.

It would be a fight to the death.

But whose death?

'They're moving in,' David said, nodding towards the graveyard. 'We'd better join them.'

To bury Louise.

They started walking. 'Thank you,' Paul murmured to the wife who walked at his side.

She looked up. 'What for?'

'For being you.'

He saw happiness flood into her eyes, and his heart lifted. It reminded him of when they were newly married, on their honeymoon in Paris. Such blissful, carefree days, filled with the joy of being together. He'd thought it would always be like that.

Somehow it had become muted over the years, the brilliant edge of it fading. He'd vaguely put it down to a natural withdrawal into separate areas of responsibility, motherhood for Gabrielle, his involvement with the vineyards. Yet he had missed it, yearned for it, felt frustrated over not being able to reach it.

He wondered now if Gabrielle had retreated from him because she had seen him in the shadow of his mother, a yesman without the strength of character to stand up for himself. Or for his wife. Joy could be eroded by disappointment.

He silently vowed he would not disappoint her again. Whatever eventuated, he knew Gabrielle would see it through with him. Together they were strong, strong enough to stand up to anything either Tamara or Eleanor threw at them.

THIRTY-TWO

The mourners—if they could be called that—had all been formally received and passed to the ballroom, where Eleanor was holding court, seated on her matriarchal throne. Having performed this formal duty, Rory was more than ready to sink a few drinks to take the taste of hypocrisy out of his mouth. He was sick to death of maintaining appearances. He wanted this farce of a funeral to be over so he could be with Tamara.

He swung his gaze over the crowd, looking for her showstopping hat. Before he could spot her, he caught sight of Jeremy Stanhope, breaking away from his group of cronies from Canberra and heading straight for him, shouldering his way purposefully through the crowd. He was a big, portly man, his mane of white hair a sure publicity draw, instantly recognisable.

Rory tensed. He'd had more than enough of Louise's father in the past two weeks, pushing and prodding and generally making everything more difficult than it had to be. Rory's sympathy for his grief and anger at losing his daughter had been stretched to the limit.

His face was florid, his pale eyes watery bright, sure signs he'd been overindulging in alcohol, probably all day.

'What the hell's going on, Rory?'

Rory struggled to keep cool. 'Is something amiss?'

'Louise told me Tamara Vandelier was a hellion who stuffed up everything. A wildcat who clawed indiscriminately. That's not how it looks to me.'

They were all seeing a different Tamara today. *A new life begins.* Did she mean hers, his, or was she telling him a child had been conceived?

'Tamara wears many faces. She does whatever suits her at the time. She surprised me, too,' he added truthfully.

Her late and dramatic entrance at the church had been mind-spinning and breathtaking. Her stunningly classy outfit gave her instant star status, and she was certainly out to shine, throwing down the gauntlet to Eleanor by sitting beside her in the front pew. Her appropriating a place in the mourning car with Paul and David must have been a conscience-slapping exercise, reminding them that she did, in fact, belong there with them.

Rory suspected it was another act of one-upmanship on Eleanor at the cemetery, yet he was secretly gratified that Tamara had gone out of her way to charm his grandfather, attaching herself to him and acting with superb deference to the sombre occasion in every respect. All eyes had been focused on her in a stupor of fascination. And, of course, she had been scoring points. Rory had no doubt about that. The question was, what did it herald?

Jeremy tapped his chest, his eyes narrowing confidentially. 'Well, I tell you one thing. She's bent on taking over from the old woman. She's been stealing her thunder ever since she walked into the church.'

Was it Tamara's public declaration that she was here to stay this time?

'You could be right,' Rory agreed, picking up a drink from the tray of a passing waiter. He sipped, trying to swallow his frustration at not knowing Tamara's mind. She hadn't answered any of his phone calls to the beach house. Her designer clothes suggested she had been in Sydney.

Jeremy nudged him and lowered his voice. 'Now you know why she wouldn't negotiate with you. Had her own plan.'

'It would appear so.'

Jeremy Stanhope was used to yes-men. The safest course was to agree with him. Louise had told her father during her weekend in Canberra that Rory was spending the time with Tamara in a bid to persuade her to pledge her shareholder's vote his way. To keep the story absolutely straight, Rory had admitted to Jeremy he'd still been with Tamara when his secretary had brought him the news of Louise's death. It was agreed that this be kept confidential in the delicate circumstances.

'Did you get in her pants?'

'What?' Rory almost spilled his wine.

Jeremy gave him a sly, man-to-man look. 'A woman built like that. Shit, Rory! It's enough to give *me* wet dreams.'

It was clear that fidelity meant no more to Jeremy Stanhope than it did to his daughter. Sex was an acceptable and everyday weapon in the powerbroker's world. Rory covered his distaste for the crude question and answered matter-of-factly.

'Take it from me, Jeremy. No one has a hope in hell of bedding Tamara unless she picks them.'

He nodded, his eyes narrowing. 'It figures. A ball crusher like her mother. Wants control. That's what she's doing today, taking control. Better watch her, Rory. She might have been on the outer edge all these years, but she's come in for the kill.'

'Thank you for your advice, Jeremy.'

Rory wondered if the Traverner family was reading Tamara's command performance as clearly as Jeremy Stanhope.

'Louise would have spotted it, too,' he said mournfully. 'Smart girl, Louise.'

'Yes.'

'Need watching, both of them. Don't let Eleanor or Tamara screw you out of what's yours, Rory.'

'I won't.'

'Good boy. Good boy.' It sounded maudlin. He clapped Rory on the shoulder and headed to his familiars, having done his ex-son-in-law the favour of pointing out where the dangers to his future lay. He probably thought of it as finishing up his daughter's business.

In actual fact, he'd touched on one question that was very much on Rory's mind. Did Tamara intend to screw him?

Today's act was very much a solo one. Admittedly Louise's funeral was hardly the place for them to make a stand. But what if she had all she wanted from him—the child—and he was now irrelevant to her? Baggage to be discarded. She certainly wasn't waiting for him to make a togetherness impact on Eleanor. She was forging ahead on her own without any consultation with him.

He finished his glass of wine then realised he'd better limit his alcohol intake. He needed his wits about him today.

'I brought you something to eat, Rory.' Gabrielle, looking after him as she always did whenever he came to the Big House.

He smiled at her as he took a sandwich from the gourmet selection offered on the plate. 'I hope Paul appreciates you.'

Her face lit up. 'I think he does.'

Curious. She looked genuinely happy. He couldn't remember ever seeing Gabrielle so open. Maybe she had bloomed since Eleanor had vacated the Big House. Six weeks of having Paul to herself must have made a difference.

He ate the triangle of bread and smoked salmon as his thoughts returned to Tamara. He wished she would be open with him. 'It must have been an interesting ride with Tamara in your car,' he said to Gabrielle, wanting some hint of the direction Tamara had taken with her half-brothers.

A rueful smile. 'Well, she certainly stirred the pot. As usual.'

'Anything in particular?'

'Airing family matters.' A cautious answer. 'I think it did some good, actually. She's quite an amazing person.'

So Tamara had thrown down the gauntlet to Paul and David, too. Rory raised an eyebrow. 'Do I hear a note of approval?'

Gabrielle studied him for several moments before replying. 'Doesn't she merit approval today, Rory?'

'No question,' he answered quickly. 'I've never seen her dress or behave so appropriately.'

'A class act,' Gabrielle agreed.

'But what's the punch line?' Rory asked quietly.

'The same as it's always been. Eleanor.' She shook her head at him. 'Don't tell me you don't know that, Rory.'

'Of course.' He managed a wry smile as he helped himself to another sandwich. 'I hope Eleanor is appreciating the change.'

'Time will tell,' Gabrielle said as she moved on to look after other guests.

Time would tell a lot of things, Rory thought darkly, but he was impatient for it to pass. Gabrielle had hit the nail on the head. Everything Tamara did was aimed at Eleanor. He didn't really feature in her life unless he joined her in that enterprise. He knew it. He had to accept it. He just wished Tamara wasn't so damned efficient at going it alone.

The reception dragged on. Rory politely accepted condolences from most of the valley people. Louise's mother claimed him for half an hour or so, gushing on about her life in Ireland and what a pity it was he and Louise had not visited her there, but she could see Rory had a world of his own here.

He watched Tamara play the daughter of the house to the hilt, graciously circulating, working the crowd as Eleanor had always done, seeing that people had food and drink, playing hostess as though she had been designated the role, while Eleanor undoubtedly fumed with frustration, her physical weakness tying her to a chair, her usual dominant presence diminished by this limitation.

Tamara, naturally, took full advantage of it. And she looked so damned beautiful, Rory burned to have her in his arms again, to strip off her actress clothes and revel in the naked freedom of loving her without barriers. He wanted to drive Eleanor out of her mind, possess her as completely as they had once possessed each other. He promised himself he'd make it happen. Somehow. They belonged together.

Eventually the crowd dispersed. Louise's parents and their separate retinues were the last to take their leave. They had formed their own little enclave at Kirkton Park, one of the more recently established country resorts in the valley. Since their plan was to depart for Sydney tomorrow morning, the final courtesies had to be performed.

Some of Rory's tension eased as he watched Jeremy Stanhope's limousine travel down the drive, away from the Big House. The last car. Its tail-lights winked a bright red as it paused before proceeding onto the main road. There was no oncoming traffic. The limousine turned, headlights scything through the gloom of twilight as it picked up its pace and disappeared from view.

Gone.

Rory walked slowly up the steps to Max's grand portico, the ostentatious facade of a house Louise had coveted in her greed for the power it represented. Rory felt a surge of hatred for it. His father had gone to his death from this house. Max, Louise...where had their ambition got them? Eleanor, sitting on her throne like a black widow spider, spinning her deadly webs.

But not today. It was Tamara spinning the webs today.

A new life has started... Did it mean what he hoped it meant? Had a child been conceived? Could she know so soon? Nothing was certain with Tamara. Nevertheless, before this day was over, he intended to find out if she was pregnant with his child. There would be no more keeping his distance from her, either. He'd had a gutful of propriety.

The clean-up staff was at work in the ballroom.

'Where's everyone gone?' he asked.

'The private sitting room, Mr Rory. Coffee is being served there.'

'Thank you.'

He hadn't realised he'd lingered outside for so long. He strode towards the more private section of the house, determined to make his claim on Tamara in front of the whole family, if necessary. He didn't care what they thought or what they feared. He and Tamara would make their own family.

THIRTY-THREE

Rory opened the door into the sitting room and entered quickly, aware of a zing of anticipation coursing through him and impatient for the answers he craved. Faces turned to him, Eleanor's stern and guarded, his grandfather's tired but placid. All four of the Traverners wore expressions of watchful expectancy, as though they had been waiting for him to resolve some issue. Tamara had a provocative little half-smile on her lips, her brilliant black eyes gleaming satisfaction.

'A cup of coffee, Rory?' Gabrielle asked, moving smoothly to cover any sense of impasse.

'Yes. Thank you.'

Apparently Tamara had ceded the role of hostess to Paul's wife in this strictly family milieu. As Gabrielle leaned forward to oblige, Rory moved to take the cup from the large, square, marble coffee table that formed the centrepiece for three chesterfields.

Gabrielle and Paul occupied the end sofa, David and Sharon the one on the right. Tamara was by herself on the left. Eleanor and his grandfather sat in the two matching antique chairs, which flanked the marble fireplace. An intimate family gathering.

Their dark clothing looked stark against the peach and

cream furnishings. Rory was struck by the imagery of birds of prey, waiting to feed. Who would lead the pecking order? he wondered, as he settled himself beside Tamara. He noted she was the only one of the women who had not removed her hat.

'I thought it all went very well, Rory,' Sharon piped up nervously.

'I'm sure Dame Eleanor appreciates your approval, Sharon,' he said dryly, nodding acknowledgment to the woman who had organized everything. Except for Tamara's grab of the spotlight.

'Jeremy Stanhope was satisfied?' Eleanor asked.

'Insofar as it was a fitting funeral for his daughter, yes.'

'The flowers were lovely,' Gabrielle remarked.

'A very impressive show,' Rory agreed.

That dispensed with the niceties. The men didn't bother with inane comments. Rory sipped his coffee, waiting for Tamara to fire the first salvo. She had not remained in full battle regalia for nothing. She let the silence linger long enough for maximum impact. Her timing, Rory thought, was impeccable.

'Well, now that we've buried Louise,' she said brightly, 'I think we should take this opportunity, with all the family gathered together—' she paused to heave a sigh '—bar Irene—a pity about Irene not being here, but—' a brilliant smile '—the rest of us are—Mother's nearest and dearest—and we should drink a toast to her homecoming.'

She was up and on her way to the cocktail cabinet before anyone drew breath to comment or protest.

'We've already done that, Tamara,' David growled.

'Oh, really?' She swung on him in surprise. 'Why wasn't I invited?'

No reply.

'Were you there, Rory?' she asked.

'No.'

'Then I hope you don't begrudge us drinking to Mother's health, David.'

He subsided, grim-faced.

Tamara lifted a bottle of champagne out of an ornate silver ice bucket. It was already open. She poured it into Max's Baccarat flute glasses. 'So good of you to provide this bottle of Veuve Clicquot for me, Paul,' she continued. 'I'm sure you and David toasted Mother with the best of Traverner vintages, which, of course, was eminently suitable. It's just that I always associate champagne with celebration.'

'Celebration, Tamara?' Eleanor queried, a fine contempt threading her voice. She wasn't fooled by the act.

Tamara pressed on, ignoring the tone. 'We're all so pleased you're still with us, Mother. And managing so splendidly.' She looked up from pouring the fine French champagne and smiled at her deadly antagonist, but there was no smile in her eyes. They glittered a mocking challenge as she added, 'Without your guiding hand, Louise wouldn't have been buried so beautifully. And smoothly. No hiccup anywhere. You truly do have a masterly hand at such things.'

Eleanor appeared unmoved, but Rory sensed a rise of tension in the room. The four Traverners were unnaturally still. Something simmered below the surface of what was being said. Tamara might be play-acting, but he had the feeling she was knowingly stroking sensitive chords.

'It's good that it's over,' his grandfather said heavily.

'You're right, Uncle Frank,' Tamara agreed. 'And I have some news that I hope will cheer everyone up. Rory, will you help pass the glasses around?'

He did her bidding without hesitation. Tamara was clearly on a roll, and he wanted to see where it led. They all did. She had centre stage, and not even Eleanor was contesting it at the moment. Though it could be the lull before the storm, the waiting to see what was to be hit.

Rory didn't resume his seat on the chesterfield. Having

placed glasses of champagne in easy reach of each member of the family, he strolled to the cocktail cabinet, preferring to be on his feet when the real action began. He had no doubt Tamara was about to launch an attack on Eleanor. The preliminaries had already been orchestrated.

Tamara moved aside, placing herself apart from him, standing in solitary domination of the scene. She looked directly at Eleanor and lifted her glass. 'To Mother, who I know will face her last months as strongly as she's faced everything else.'

Gloves coming off, Rory thought, noting that nobody picked up a glass to echo the toast. Tamara drank alone. Whether the others found her words too distasteful he didn't know. He didn't want to drink to Eleanor, so he didn't.

'Thank you, Tamara,' Eleanor said dryly. 'You are quite excelling yourself today.'

'The best is yet to come, Mother. I appreciate how grim it must be to be looking down the barrel of death, so I hope you'll find my news really uplifting.'

David cracked. 'What news?'

Tamara's attention did not waver from Eleanor. 'A new life. Another grandchild for you, Mother. I'm going to have a baby. Now doesn't that take the taste of death away for everyone?'

It was a king hit.

The boldness of the announcement took Rory's breath away. And everyone else's. There was no rush of congratulations. No word was uttered. Not even a gasp. Wall-to-wall shock reverberated through the silence.

'Though I must say Louise's death got to me,' Tamara blithely said. 'So I went and made a will this week, naming my baby's father as sole beneficiary.' She turned to her older half-brother. 'I lodged it with the family solicitor, Paul. If anything happens to me, you'll know where to find my last will and testament. I also left instructions for DNA tests to be carried out if any question is raised over the father's identity.'

It was true then, Rory thought dazedly. Tamara would not have gone into such legal details if it wasn't true. She was pregnant with his child.

'Who is the father?' Sharon blurted out.

'I am,' Rory heard himself say, automatically laying claim to his child without giving any consideration to reactions or consequences.

Tamara swung around, and he saw in an instant she hadn't been going to name him. There was a wry, quizzical look in her eyes, as though he'd blown the situation and wouldn't know how to handle what came next.

But he did. He knew precisely what had to be done. He set down his glass, stepped forward to stand beside her, and slid his arm around her waist, doubling his claim as he announced with pride and conviction, 'I'm the father, and if Tamara will have me, we'll be married as soon as it can be arranged.'

No backward steps.

Full frontal attack.

'Good God, man!' David burst out, hitching himself forward and throwing up his hands in protest. 'You've only just come from burying your wife!'

'My marriage to Louise was over before she died,' Rory stated flatly. 'Not that it's any of your business, David.'

'Then why did she go to Irene?' Sharon asked, looking totally befuddled.

'Louise marched to her own drum. Whatever she did, it was not for me.'

'Do you imagine Tamara is having this child for you, Rory?' Eleanor coldly challenged.

'No, I don't,' he answered with cool equanimity. 'Tamara is having my child because she wants it. And I want it, too. Do you have a problem with that, Dame Eleanor?'

Her mouth thinned.

Rory gave her no chance to formulate another remark. 'What about you, Grandfather? Any problem?'

'No, my boy. It's your life,' he answered quietly.

'Yes, it is.' His gaze stabbed at Eleanor. 'And this time Tamara and I will be making our own choices.' He swept the others with a look of fiery resolution. 'So like it or lump it, people. Neither Tamara nor I have to answer to any of you for what we do in our private lives.'

She'd wanted the gauntlet thrown down. He'd thrown it with a vengeance. He turned to her, feeling wild and reckless and free. 'Are you all done here for tonight, Tamara?'

She caught his mood and laughed at him. 'Yes, Rory. I believe I am.' She picked up her handbag from the chesterfield. 'Good night, everyone.'

'Rory.' It was a sharp demand for attention from Paul.

They looked at him in surprise as he rose to his feet. His austere, handsome face was a study of determination. His eyes held a glint of defiant purpose as he moved forward and thrust out his hand.

'You have my good wishes. Both of you.'

Rory took his hand, appreciative of the strength of mind behind the gesture. 'Thank you, Paul.'

'Tamara.' As Rory released his hand, Paul offered it to her. 'I didn't say it before. I'm saying it now. Welcome home.'

Tamara didn't move. Paul's hand remained out for her, resolution stamped on his face. Rory was acutely conscious of everyone watching, a riot of feelings screaming through the silence. This was a stand of mammoth ramifications, overturning years of hostile rejection.

Gabrielle stood and moved to her husband's side. 'I'd like us to be friends, Tamara. If you can find it in your heart to reach out,' she said quietly.

Tamara's sharp intake of breath was audible. 'Do you know what you're doing, Paul?' she asked, a hard edge to her voice, not prepared to give facile acceptance to a move that might only be political in the circumstances.

'Yes,' he answered firmly. 'I'm making my own choices.'

Slowly her hand lifted and slid into his. 'You may rue it,' she warned.

His face relaxed into a whimsical half-smile. 'I may rue many things. Not this.'

'Then for this I thank you.' She nodded to his wife. 'Gabrielle. It's nice to feel...welcome.' It was a cautious statement, wary of insincerity.

Gabrielle smiled, warmth and kindness in her eyes. 'I hope the baby is a building stone to happiness.'

In a lightning change of mood, Tamara laughed. 'Well, who knows? We might have a wedding.' She turned an ex-ultant smile to Eleanor. 'It would be much nicer for you to arrange than a funeral, Mother.'

No reply. Eleanor was staring at Paul, a fury of disbelief in her eyes. Tamara had not only fired some powerful broadsides, she'd broken the ranks of the faithful. A twofold victory in her battle against Eleanor. Rory judged it time to leave.

'Grandfather, I deeply appreciate your understanding and support.'

He nodded. 'Good night to both of you. God bless.'

'Thank you, Uncle Frank,' Tamara said sweetly.

It underlined the silence from her mother.

Rory swept Tamara out with him, feeling they'd carried the day. His grandfather was with him. He was the only one whose opinion mattered. But Paul—well, it was certainly a bonus to have Paul onside. Best of all, Tamara *was* pregnant with his child.

THIRTY-FOUR

Eleanor could barely contain her rage. After all she'd done, for Paul to suck up to his serpent half-sister at this juncture was an act of treachery. Or cowardice. Was he running scared with the threat of Rory and Tamara joining up against them? Didn't he realise Tamara would crush him as soon as look at him? That triumphant laugh of hers should have rung a klaxon of warning bells through his head.

And Gabrielle, slyly sweeping along on the sidelines until she perceived her mother-in-law's position weakening. Was she behind this turncoat gesture of welcoming Tamara into their midst? Stupid, stupid woman. If Tamara had Rory's child, she would see to it that it cheated Gabrielle's children of their inheritance. That was what it was all about.

Pain sliced through her body. It took every ounce of her strength not to groan and double up with it. She closed her eyes, fiercely willing it to ease.

'Mum...are you all right?'

David's voice, anxious, uncertain. David, who was useless to her in this fight against Tamara. No vision, no guts.

'Eleanor, can I get you anything?'

Gabrielle, deceptively soft.

'Ellie?'

Frank. God damn him for keeping so much to himself!

She didn't want them fussing over her. She hated every facet of this debilitating condition. And Tamara, of course, had capitalised on it in every direction today, while she had to sit and suffer it, powerless to stop what was going on.

But she wasn't completely powerless. The wheel would turn. It would be Tamara powerless next time. Having shown her hand, Tamara had left herself open to ambush.

'Ellie, do you need your pills?'

The pain was receding. She opened her eyes, sweeping them all with a hard, bitter look. 'Enough is enough. Take me home, Frank.'

'I'll call Bill Guthrie from the staff quarters,' Gabrielle said, moving swiftly to the door.

Eleanor braced herself to move from the chair. David rushed forward to help her. Frank lent his support, as well. There was no point in refusing to lean on their physical strength. That, at least, they could give, and she needed it. Sharon flapped around like a hen without a head. Paul remained aloof, although there was a look of pained compassion in his eyes. It won no points with Eleanor. It deepened her inner rage at his disloyalty.

'A house divided will fall, Paul,' she told him.

His chin lifted. The compassion winked out, a sheet of steel sliding over it. 'Then let there be no division,' he answered.

He had rocks in his head if he thought Tamara would toe that line. There was obviously no talking sense to him tonight.

Grimly holding onto control of all the savage turbulence within her, Eleanor made the painful journey out of the Big House. Bill was waiting by the Daimler, the back door of the car open for her. She stepped in and settled heavily onto the seat. Frank quickly joined her. Both Paul and David had accompanied her outside, but she deliberately ignored their polite good nights, viciously wanting them to feel the weight of her displeasure.

The trip to the old Traverner homestead was completed in seething silence. Frank and Bill helped her up the steps to the veranda. She shook off their assistance as she entered the house.

'Shall I call Wilma to assist you to bed, Ellie?'

'No.' She walked into the dining room. 'If you want to do something for me, Frank, you can pour me a port. God knows I need a stronger drink than French champagne.'

'Port it is, then,' he said equably, letting her curt manner and bitterly derisive tone wash past him.

Her brother's passive attitude infuriated her further as she made her way down the table to sit in Richard's chair at the head of it. Not that it was any comfort tonight. His sons weren't worthy successors. Tamara could run rings around them. She'd certainly been the circus master today and would continue to be if she wasn't stopped.

Eleanor broodingly watched her brother choose a bottle of liqueur port from the selection in the old dresser where the fortified wines were kept. How could he give Rory and Tamara his blessing? Was he going senile?

The bottle was uncorked. Only one glass filled. Frank's walk was slow and ponderous as he brought it to her. Not until he'd pressed it into her trembling hand did he pass a comment, and then it was a useless piece of advice.

'It's no good getting yourself upset, Ellie.'

It snapped the last threads of control. Resentment flooded her mind and spilled into accusation. 'You could have given me warning of this.'

He shook his head. 'I had no warning of what would unfold today. How could I have?'

'By putting two and two together, Frank. In this case, one and one.' She took a gulp of port to fortify herself and leaned forward to blast her brother's foolish blindness. 'You've been with Rory on and off these past two weeks. Don't tell me he didn't confide in you. You've always been close.'

'He discussed the situation with me. In confidence, Ellie.'

'So you knew he'd left Louise.'

He nodded. 'It was Louise who lied about him being in Canberra. Covering up. She thought Rory would come back to her.'

Eleanor snorted. 'Not likely once Tamara got her hooks in. She's the devil incarnate, that one, and she'll ruin his life, Frank.'

He pulled out a chair and sat down, eyeing her with concern as she poured more port down her throat. 'Ellie,' he said, a quiet, serious insistence in his voice, 'Rory loves Tamara. He loved her when he was sixteen. He still does. You're not going to change that.'

'It's lust, not love,' she jeered, enraged by his blinkered sentimentality. 'She's got him by the balls. Do you think I don't know my own daughter?'

It drew a heavy sigh. 'I'm telling you what Rory feels.'

'He's a fool. She'll lead him by the nose to get what she wants. Already he's inviting scandal, talking of marriage when he's barely buried his wife.'

'We've weathered scandals before this,' he reminded her. 'You married Max very shortly after Richard died.'

'Oh, don't throw that at me. You know very well I had to.'

'No. You didn't have to, Ellie. You decided to. There's a difference.'

'And lose the vineyard?' she scoffed.

'I offered to negotiate with the bank, putting up Buchanan as security. We would have survived. Remember the bumper harvest the following year?'

'And we could have had another hailstorm and ended up with nothing. I wasn't about to risk that, Frank.' She swigged some more port.

'I know. I understand, Ellie,' he soothed. 'The point I'm making is you made your decision. Rightly or wrongly, you made it. You can't stop the children from making their decisions. They have as much right to go their own way as you did.'

'The difference is I knew where I was heading. I went into marriage to Max with my eyes wide open. Do you think Rory's are wide open?'

'Tamara is pregnant with his child. It's a good enough reason to marry.'

She banged down her glass in furious frustration. 'You can say that after seeing Ian tied to Irene for the same reason? Why the hell do you think he flew into that hill, Frank?'

'Perhaps there were many reasons,' he said sadly. 'I wasn't there to know.'

She knew. She knew, and she didn't regret it one bit. But she did feel a niggle of guilt for the grief it had given her brother, who'd never done harm to anyone. 'Fetch the bottle for me, Frank. I want another glass.'

He frowned. 'Do you think that's wise with your medication?'

'If I want to drink myself under the table that's my decision. And I have the right to make it. Isn't that what you've been telling me?'

He hauled himself to his feet and fetched the bottle, placing it in front of her without another word. But he didn't pour for her. She uncorked the bottle and defiantly helped herself, flouting his passive resistance. That was the trouble with Frank. Too damned passive!

'The line of least resistance,' she mocked. 'Even Paul took it tonight. I thought he'd know better.'

'Perhaps he sees it differently to you, Ellie,' Frank said quietly. 'Tamara placed herself with the family today. Not against it.'

'It was an act.' She shook her head in disgust. 'A performance you swallowed, hook, line and sinker.'

'It could have been a plea for acceptance. She responded positively to Paul's and Gabrielle's acceptance.'

'And warned him he'd rue it. They were the truest words she spoke.'

He rested his arms on the table and linked his hands, his fingers slowly rubbing over the age-spotted skin. His head was bent, conveying an air of sorrowful resignation, his eyelids lowered to half-mast. The body language was plain to read. He'd said his piece. He was not going to argue with her. He would sit there until she drank herself under the table, if need be, and then he'd help her to bed.

'You're not going to do anything to stop it, are you?' she taunted, unwilling to let him retreat from a situation he should have actively discouraged.

He sighed and slanted her a weary look. 'You stopped it when they were young and there's been grief on both sides ever since. If you don't recognise that, I can't make you see.'

'It was Tamara who made the grief. And she will again.'

He went back to studying the skin on his hands.

Eleanor drank some more port. Frank didn't know the facts. He had no idea of the deadly contest between Tamara and herself. He would not be her ally in this. If it was to be stopped, she had to do it herself.

She knew how to destroy Rory's feeling for Tamara. It meant using secrets that could then be used against her if she wasn't extremely careful. But did that matter if it put Tamara beyond the pale as far as Rory was concerned?

Tamara had to be isolated again. Isolated and neutralised. Though there would still be the child to worry about. If Rory was alienated from her, would Tamara go through with the pregnancy? Yes, if only to spite Eleanor, a life to haunt her death. The child was a problem. She could get Rory to reject Tamara, but she couldn't see him rejecting his own child.

And Rory was now the beneficiary of Tamara's will. It gave him far too much power. With Tamara's shareholding and Frank's backing, Rory could become head of the family company. Add on Irene's vote and he could take complete control of Traverner, as well as Buchanan.

No way would she allow that to happen. Rory did not have one drop of Traverner blood in him. She would have to renegotiate the company shareholdings with Frank to safeguard against such an intolerable outcome. At least she'd had the foresight to secure Irene's vote. Tamara could not take that away from her.

The child, the will...was Max laughing in his grave? Eleanor gritted her teeth. She'd gone through too much to see it all lost now. His damned daughter was not going to triumph at the end.

'Tamara is your daughter.'

The quiet statement from Frank startled her. 'She's Max's daughter.' It was an automatic retort.

Frank pulled himself off the table and leaned back in his chair, looking at her with eyes that suddenly knew too much. 'Was that her sin, Ellie? Being born of a man you didn't love?'

She felt her skin go cold. Was Frank about to turn against her, too?

'Tamara is *your* daughter,' he repeated with pointed emphasis. 'Rory is my grandson. I love him very deeply, Ellie. He, and the child Tamara will bear him, are my future. I wouldn't like you to forget that.'

He stood and placed his chair very precisely under the table. 'I'm sorry, but I don't feel up to sitting with you. It's been a long day for me. I'll tell Wilma to see to your needs. Good night, Ellie.'

And for the first time since he had left her in the mulberry tree for Richard to rescue, Frank walked out on her, slowly, heavily but decisively.

THIRTY-FIVE

Rory's Maserati was right behind her as she parked in front of the beach house. She'd insisted on picking up her Porsche at Cessnock, wanting the freedom her own transport gave her, but he'd stayed linked to her, tailing her all the way, making it an exhilarating drive.

Tamara felt ridiculously light-hearted as she locked the car and headed for the house. Impossible for her to keep Rory, yet he had stood with her, defying what anyone thought, throwing a commitment to marriage in Eleanor's face. Incredible. Marvellous. Soul-stirring.

He caught up with her on the path to the front porch and scooped her off her feet, hoisting her against his chest, grinning like a loon.

'What do you think you're doing?' she demanded, her heart skittering madly as she rescued her hat from being crushed between them.

'I feel like carrying my bride-to-be across the threshold.'

'The door is locked.'

'Well, maybe I'll just kick it in.'

She laughed, adoring his swashbuckling recklessness. 'In a door-kicking mood, are we?'

'Going to smash them all down.'

She flung her arms around his neck and kissed him, loving the wild energy coursing through him, wanting to taste it, savour it, revel in it. Her true hero, a shining knight, all primed to slay dragons. His mouth was hot and urgent, his tongue lashing over hers, hungry, passionately possessive.

He eased his hold, letting her slither down his body, his hand cupping the curve of her buttocks, pressing her to his burgeoning erection. So hard and thick, wanting her. And she wanted him just as fiercely, not for the seed that would seal her triumph over Eleanor, just Rory himself, the boy she had loved, the man he had become, the hard pulse of his flesh inside her, spinning her into the dream world where only she and he existed.

She wrenched her mouth from his. 'Let's go in and get these clothes off.'

'Yes,' he hissed, both of them panting with excitement as she dropped her arms and swivelled in his embrace.

He held her against him, kissing the nape of her neck, one hand moving swiftly down the buttons of her jacket as she fumbled for the right key on the key ring. Wild with impatience, she finally managed to unlock the front door. Rory lifted her into the foyer, kicked the door shut behind them, carried her with him into the master bedroom. In a frenzy of touching and kissing, they tore off each other's clothes, exulting in the delicious sensuality of soft flesh, taut muscle, naked skin.

They fell on the bed in a tangle of limbs, taking intense pleasure in the rub of their bodies as they moved to fit, to join, to blitz each other with the power of their need, hot, hard, explosive, a mash of fiery desire that drove them to the racking tension of climax and melted into ecstatic relief.

Then the sweet aftermath of intimate togetherness as they caught their breaths and their hearts slowed to a more regular beat, contentment sweeping in to replace the frantic soaring of excitement. Rory, kissing her with slow, sensual pleasure, trailing his mouth down her throat, swirling his tongue around her nipples, nibbling them, sucking them, moving lower to tease her navel, then rest his cheek on her stomach as he caressed her inner thighs.

'I wonder if it will be a girl or a boy,' he murmured.

She smiled. She ran her hands over his beautifully muscled shoulders, enjoying the fine texture of his skin, loving the feel of him, the father of her child. 'I can have a scan done at four months if you want to know,' she offered.

Four months.

No, she wasn't going to think of her mother tonight. Not tonight. It would spoil this feeling of blissful freedom with Rory.

'It doesn't matter.' He kissed her stomach and propped his head up to smile at her, his eyes warm and golden. 'How did you know of the baby so soon?'

'Well, I should have got my period yesterday.'

He looked shocked. 'You might only be late.'

She laughed, her eyes dancing with teasing delight before letting him off the uncertainty hook. 'I've always been as regular as clockwork, Rory, and I did a pregnancy test three days ago, the earliest time for a result. It was positive.'

He relaxed into a relieved grin. 'You're happy about it?'

'Yes.'

She slid her hand over her stomach. Whatever else the future held, she would keep this baby safe. Nothing bad was going to happen to this child. She'd fight to give it the best possible life.

The memory of the confrontation with her family drifted into her mind. For Paul to openly wish her well...

'You're frowning. What's wrong?'

She swiftly unwrinkled her forehead. 'Nothing. I was just wondering why Paul came down on our side tonight.' She couldn't believe her pointed stirring had caused such a turnaround. Not so quickly. Rebellion must have been simmering, requiring only some extra heat to bring it to the boil. Eleanor must be spitting chips. 'Have you been talking to him?'

Rory shook his head. 'Not about you. Nor about the family business. Maybe he wanted to the day he came over to Buchanan, before Louise died.'

'You should talk to him, Rory. Find out what's going on there.'

'Monday will be soon enough.'

'What about tomorrow?'

Determination flared into his eyes. 'I'll be here with you.'

'Sunday?'

'I'm staying.'

'You're spending the whole weekend with me?'

'Start thinking forever, Tamara.'

Forever?

The tantalising vista of a future shared with Rory shimmered through her mind.

He gave her a wicked grin and dropped down to tease her clitoris, exciting her into a heaving mass of exquisite anticipation. As the nub swelled and throbbed he stroked her cleft, tantalising her with caresses, moving slowly inwards, finding her G-spot and driving her to another convulsive climax before rearing up and filling her with the thick, hard shaft she craved. She wound her legs around him to hold it in, arching for ultimate depth, feet digging into his buttocks, urging him to stay...forever.

He felt so good, so warmly solid, steady, in control, gloriously sure of where he wanted to be, with her, in her, surrounded by her. The sweet, fulsome glory of it was like champagne in her blood.

'Remember,' he whispered, starting to withdraw.

She clutched at him to bring him back.

He surged forward again. 'Skinny-dipping in the creek...'

She closed her eyes and sighed her satisfaction. 'Yes, yes.'

'The silky slide of the water...'

'Mmm.'

'The feeling of weightlessness...'

Waves of intense pleasure rippling through her. Adrift in bliss.

'Then lying in the long grass afterwards, basking in the mellow heat of the afternoon sun.'

So warm, melting again and again, Rory's soft croon reinforcing the mesmerising rhythm.

'And you ran a feather over me, and kissed my nipples, and took me in your mouth, and I died of happiness.'

She smiled, remembering. 'Then you started at my toes and worked up, tasting everything...'

'And the joy of it all was boundless.'

'Yes.'

He went on, conjuring up the dream again, floating it past her, renewing it inside her, weaving it around her, making it feel real, pulsingly alive, reachable, all things possible.

It was easy to believe in it, easy to lose herself in it, together, forever.

THIRTY-SIX

The revelation came to Irene that she was the avenging sword. It bloomed in her mind, clearing the confusion Tamara and Eleanor had induced with their lies. Dirty whores. Both of them. They, too, would reap fire and sulphur and a scorching wind.

It gave Irene intense satisfaction to think of the blackened thing. 'For Jehovah is righteous, He does love righteous acts.' She now knew she had been delivered from the fire to carry on His work, to strike down greed and vanity and forked tongues.

The devil's minions had taken the thing to its final resting place. She had seen the funeral on television last night. It was a sign that it was time to leave this nursing home, time to take up the position of eminence that belonged to a Chosen One.

She picked up the telephone by her bed and dialled the number Eleanor had written down. It was for the old Traverner homestead, not the Big House. That, too, was a sign. God had directed Eleanor to move out, to go back to where she had come from. It was part of His plan.

Wilma Guthrie answered the call. Irene demanded to speak to Eleanor, knowing she wouldn't be refused. Her confidence soared as Eleanor's voice came over the line. The grand dame had to do her bidding now.

'What can I do for you, Irene?'

Those words played like trumpets of glory in her ears. 'I'm fully recovered, Eleanor. I don't wish to stay here any longer.'

A pause. 'Very well.' Eleanor was thinking. 'Frank is staying here with me. I'll arrange with him for you to go to his home until other, more amenable accommodation can be arranged in Cessnock.'

Shunting her aside again. 'That doesn't suit me, Eleanor.'

An impatient sigh. 'Irene, do I have to remind you your house was burnt to the ground?'

She bristled at the terse, superior tone of voice. 'God said I was to go to the Big House,' she claimed with fierce fervour, seeing a bright vision of her future path.

In a few more months Eleanor would be dead. The Big House could be turned into a temple of the Lord instead of a monument to sin. That would earn the respect of her fellow believers. She would never be regarded as a leper then. The rewards of the righteous would be manifest.

Shirley would look up to her. Poor Shirley had never known anything like the luxury Eleanor had hoarded to herself. Maybe she would invite Shirley to come and stay with her. A disciple, helping to minister whatever fulfilled important needs.

The vision blurred as the silence on the line penetrated her consciousness. Eleanor was resisting the commands of God. Eleanor thought she could rule this earth. Another daughter of Lucifer. Those who did not bow to the will of Jehovah would feel the avenging sword.

'Eleanor,' she cried, calling on the might of heaven to strike the unbeliever.

'You're right, Irene. The Big House is more suitable.'

Submission!

'But not until Monday. Louise's father has friends who

are staying around for the weekend. We don't want to invite unpleasantness, do we? I'll have Frank come and take you to the Big House on Monday.'

'Yes,' Irene agreed exultantly and put the receiver down. The empowerment of God tingled through her.

THIRTY-SEVEN

and Eleanor had reacted badly. No, I don't want to fill
the vacancy for a while. I just want time, and now you
go on back to your work.'
'Yes, Madam.' Quiet solemnity until she was out of sight,
then a triumphant toss of her curly dark head.

THIRTY-SEVEN

Gabrielle stood at one of the tall windows in the library,
watching the driveway, wanting to catch Paul as soon as he
came home for lunch. The staff at the Big House was all ears.
Comments about Tamara's appearance at the funeral and
her uncharacteristically dignified behaviour at the reception
afterwards were on everyone's lips, and there was an avid
curiosity about how the family was reacting to it. The library ensured privacy.

Gabrielle wanted to know how Paul had fared with
David this morning. The atmosphere had been very tense
between them last night after Eleanor's departure. The idea
of a marriage between Rory and Tamara had thrown David
into a panic. And, of course, he'd been under his mother's
heel so long that any open break with her line of thinking
alarmed him.

Paul's car turned into the avenue of poplars just as the
telephone rang. Gabrielle hurried to the desk to answer it,
quickly rattling out her name and hoping the call would not
hold her up for long.

'It is the housekeeper's duty to answer the telephone,
Gabrielle.' The grand dame at her frostiest.

Gabrielle automatically pitched her tone to obliging

warmth, neutralising the cutting ice of authority. 'Do you wish to speak to her, Eleanor?'

'Irrelevant since you're running the household. Kindly have a suite prepared for Irene. She will be moving into the Big House on Monday.'

'For how long?' Gabrielle inquired lightly, hiding the instant recoil she felt at being landed with Irene as a live-in guest.

'For as long as I want, Gabrielle.'

The line was disconnected. The matriarch had given her orders. It was her house. Gabrielle had no right of veto in who came and went. Or stayed. The short hiatus of freedom for her and Paul under this roof was over.

The news of Irene's advent was depressing on many levels. Apart from the political angle, there was the undeniable fact that Irene's brand of preaching was social death, and she was not a happy person to be around. Gabrielle could take her in small doses, but she didn't want her children subjected to those doses.

She replaced the receiver and went to intercept Paul as he came in. He surprised her by immediately sweeping her into his embrace and hugging her tightly. 'I love you,' he murmured with intense feeling.

She eased back to meet his eyes, seeing the warm glow of memory and sharing it with him. Last night's lovemaking had been very special. Her smile acknowledged it.

'Let's move in to the library,' she suggested.

'Good idea.'

She laughed, her heart lifting with the pleasure of being truly his wife again as they closed themselves into the library and resumed their embrace, kissing with an ardour that had been wonderfully refreshed by the new understanding flowing between them.

'Did you talk David out of his jitters this morning?' she asked when she'd caught her breath.

'Not quite.' He grimaced. 'His latest proposition is to talk to Uncle Frank and offer him a deal, swapping our fifteen percent in Buchanan for his fifteen percent in Traverner. He argues it would safeguard our holding Traverner, if nothing else.'

'How do you feel about it?'

'I don't think this is the time to rush in and do anything. It would demonstrate a lack of trust. Besides, I don't believe Uncle Frank would turn against me and David. He knows how much we've put into Traverner.'

'Well, you can tell David he doesn't need a safeguard,' Gabrielle offered with ironic appreciation of Eleanor's Machiavellian manoeuvring. 'Your mother has already stepped in.'

'How?'

'She called a few moments ago. Irene is to be accommodated here from Monday.'

His head moved in a roll of distaste. His arms fell away from her, and he stepped aside to walk off his distress at this development. He reached his mother's desk, stared at it for several seconds, then slowly turned around, a sick look on his face.

'So an arrangement was made,' he said heavily. His mouth twisted as he added, 'For what consideration?'

'I couldn't begin to guess.'

'She visited Irene the Saturday before Louise died. I tricked Bill Guthrie into admitting it yesterday afternoon.'

'It doesn't mean Louise's death was anything but an accident, Paul.'

'I know. But a bias against Louise would have been put into place. Against Tamara, too, no doubt. My mother would be very thorough on that score.'

Gabrielle nodded. 'She would cover every contingency.'

He sighed. 'I don't want to be associated with this, Gabrielle.'

'We're not in a position to turn Irene away, Paul.'

He frowned, ruminating over the dilemma. He shot her a

beetling look. 'How would you feel about us moving out of this house?'

A joyous hope zinged through her heart. 'Do you mean it?'

'Would you mind?'

'Oh God, Paul!' she exploded with long held, pent-up emotions. 'I've hated this house almost from the time I walked into it. If you're prepared to let it go...'

He looked stunned. 'Why didn't you tell me?'

'How could I? You were proud of it. It was part and parcel of your life. You were tied to it in the line of inheritance, mother to son.' She gestured helplessly. 'It was what you brought me to.'

With understanding came pain. 'Was it a better choice to resign yourself to it and retreat from me, Gabrielle?'

She shook her head sadly. 'It wasn't a choice. Your mother ruled...everything. You accepted that, Paul. Without question. All I could do was wait and hope it would be different some day.'

'It shall be today,' he said with grim determination, striding down the room to wrap her close to him, affirming togetherness. 'I'll see what I can buy or rent this very afternoon.'

Gabrielle wound her arms around his neck and kissed him with a wild and wonderful sense of blissful freedom. 'I love you,' she whispered.

'A home of our own,' he promised.

'Yes.'

THIRTY-EIGHT

Holding the fort for Rory was fast becoming a treadmill of worry, Janet reflected as she walked into her office. She flopped into her chair, feeling mentally bombarded by the new rumour doing the rounds of the winery. Why was Paul Traverner looking for a place to buy or rent? If he was. Had Tamara announced her intention to take over the Big House?

Janet did not know what the line of inheritance was. Everyone had assumed Paul would follow on from his mother, but it had been Max's house, and Tamara was Max's daughter. Eleanor's daughter, too. She had certainly claimed that position at Louise's funeral. The whole valley was abuzz about it.

Amazingly to Janet, there hadn't been so much as a whisper of Rory's connection to Tamara since the shocking news of Louise's death, not before or after the funeral. She hadn't brought it up with Rory, either. Since Louise's death he'd only made the occasional visit to the office to deal with loose ends. Business. They hadn't discussed anything personal. Janet still found it difficult to come to terms with his involvement with Tamara.

Well, today was Monday, a new week, a new phase in

Rory's life. She wondered what he was going to do with it, whether he would come to work today.

'Hi!'

'Rory!'

He stepped into her office and closed the door behind him. 'Can I smile at you and not be frowned on?' he appealed, already smiling as he strolled forward.

'Feel free,' she invited, aware of the strain he must have been under with Jeremy Stanhope sticking his nose into everything.

'Thank you. And thanks again for your loyal support, Janet.' He hitched himself onto the other side of the desk, his eyes dancing with warm happiness. 'I know it will probably shock you, but I can't keep it to myself. I'm going to be a father.'

Shock was an understatement. Her heart dropped like a stone. Her overloaded mind zeroed out for several seconds, then reeled over the implications. 'Do you mean—?'

He nodded. 'Tamara's pregnant. We're going to have a baby.'

A baby. It locked him in with Tamara. Irrevocably. Dear God! Did he know what he was doing? There was no way out of this. A baby. And Rory was looking at her as though he expected her to be pleased for him.

'I—I'm sorry.' She rubbed her forehead. Her head ached. 'I can't seem to take it in, Rory.'

She pushed herself out of the chair and turned her back on the eyes she couldn't meet, walking distractedly to the window, her hands gesturing her sense of helplessness. 'This... None of it seems right to me. We've known each other all our lives. Been close friends. Shared good times and bad.'

She half-turned, anguished with painful confusion, needing him to answer it, wanting him to be the Rory she thought she had known. 'I guess I had a sense of security in having certain expectations of you. Depending on a response I could count on. Now...' She hesitated, not wanting to offend him.

'Go on,' he encouraged gravely.

'Oh, Rory! I know it's none of my business,' she cried. 'It's just that a fortnight ago you seemed securely married to Louise. I didn't like her but...' It sounded too bald, too critical to recite his actions to him. He could read it all in her eyes, anyway. 'Would you mind telling me what happened?' she pleaded.

His mouth twisted. 'It wasn't a marriage of love, Janet. It was...expedience, on both sides. I didn't fully realise that until the day Tamara came here. I went home to Louise.' His face tightened. 'With Eleanor dying, Louise had set her sights on the Big House. She actually wanted me to commit adultery with Tamara in the hope of gaining her shareholding vote.'

It was sick. Yet oddly enough, Janet wasn't shocked. It fitted what she'd always felt about Louise. 'But that's not why you did it,' she murmured, sure Rory wouldn't stoop that low.

'No. When I went to Tamara it was to sort out a lot of things.' His eyes took on a faraway look, then slowly sharpened into bitter hardness. 'I can't tell you what was done to Tamara, Janet, but believe me, it wasn't good. She needs me.'

For what? Some dark purpose of her own, after which she'd discard Rory as of no further use? Janet shook her head, distressed by what she saw in store for him.

Rory frowned at her reaction. He slid off the desk and skirted it, walking towards her, his hands gesturing an appeal for understanding. 'I love Tamara, Janet. It's like it was for you with Jim, standing by him through his illness. Nothing really changes what you feel. It lies there, underneath the worst that can be done to you, waiting to be tapped when needed.'

Tears welled into her eyes as Rory recalled for her the terrible ache of loving Jim and not being able to change anything. If Rory felt that kind of love for Tamara all these years, despite what she'd done, Janet could only feel intense sympathy for him. He was going to hurt all the more when Tamara threw it away again.

'I'm sorry you've been so upset by it.' He squeezed her shoulder in affectionate concern. 'Your friendship has filled many holes in my life, Janet. I wouldn't like—'

'It's okay.' She dashed the moisture from her lashes and swallowed hard, trying to regain her composure. Maybe he would be happy for a while. If it had always been Tamara for him, no matter what, who was she to judge what was right or wrong for him? At least he'd have the baby, a child to love, and Rory had so much to give. She struggled to smile. 'You'll make a great father.'

Relief spread into a grin he couldn't contain. 'A new world for me.'

She hoped so. She really did. An anxious thought struck her. 'Does Tamara want to have the baby?'

'Yes. Very much.'

No doubt there. It wasn't fair of her to seed any, either. 'That's good,' she said, privately thinking she could well murder Tamara if she didn't go through with having Rory's child.

'I've asked her to marry me, Janet.'

Another shock to absorb. Did he have no doubts at all? What was Tamara telling him? 'Will she?'

'Provisional. If I still want to marry her after the next vintage.'

At least Tamara wasn't rushing him into what might prove to be another disastrous marriage, and the test of staying power worked both ways. 'Well, that's only four months away, and it's reasonable, Rory, what with Louise's death and everything.'

He shook his head, his face sobering into serious concern.

'It has more to do with Eleanor's death. I can't get through to Tamara that Eleanor won't stop us this time.'

Janet frowned. Was that why Tamara had said this new relationship with Rory might not last? It seemed far more likely it wouldn't last because Tamara didn't intend it to. She hadn't denied Janet's accusation of using Rory, and Tamara's pattern of behaviour was essentially destructive. Janet didn't know what had been done to Tamara, as Rory said, but Tamara herself hadn't exactly lacked in the doing department.

'Does Eleanor know you're together again?' she asked, careful to keep her thoughts to herself.

'Oh, yes.' He gave a short, mirthless laugh. 'They all know.'

'How?' Not a murmur of it anywhere.

'After the funeral, when the reception was over, Tamara announced to the family she was having a baby. Another heir for Eleanor.'

Bold as brass. 'That must have gone over like a lead balloon,' Janet couldn't help commenting.

Rory nodded. 'And I told them it was my child and I intended to marry her.'

After Tamara's initial announcement Janet wouldn't have expected Rory to do less. He *was* an honourable man. He would always act in an honourable way. Had Tamara counted on that, using him in a power play?

Janet could well imagine the consternation, with the lines of inheritance to both vineyards being involved. A merger, one might say, of considerable consequence. Tamara had a purpose all right! She wasn't having Rory's baby out of love.

'What was the reaction?' she asked.

Rory's smile was wry. 'Shock.'

The shock waves were still rippling, Janet figured. Hence the silence. Her mind raced to the immediate problems she foresaw. She doubted Rory had even paused to put damage control in place. Love could be terribly blind. She couldn't blame him for seizing his chance at it. But at what cost?

'How did your grandfather take it?'

'Fine. I'd already told him about leaving Louise. And what I intended with Tamara.'

Janet's concern eased a little. Rory wasn't flying completely by the seat of his pants. Buchanan was safe if he had his grandfather's approval and Tamara's backing. Though Tamara's intentions were highly questionable.

'Eleanor will see a marriage between you as a threat to her interests,' she warned.

'Undoubtedly,' he said dryly.

Janet had an intuitive flash of Rory fighting for the underdog. The question was, how dirty would Eleanor fight? Suddenly Tamara's intensity as she had urged Janet to stick by Rory, be his friend, took on more meaning.

Tamara was challenging Eleanor, but she wasn't confident of a favourable outcome. Maybe in some twisted, backhanded way, she did care about Rory, at least enough to urge Janet to stand by him for the fallout.

The concept of fallout reminded her of another factor to be counted. 'Rumour has it that Paul is looking for another place to live. I don't know if it's true.'

Rory cocked his head, considering. 'Paul stood up for us the other night.'

'Against his mother?' Janet could hardly believe it.

'Yes. Interesting, isn't it?'

Rory drifted to the other side of her desk, pondering the repercussions of Paul's shift in loyalty. Janet automatically followed, stopping by her chair, feeling swamped with all she had to take in and sort through if she was to look after Rory's best interests. Tamara was right about one thing. He needed a friend to stand by him.

The telephone on her desk rang. She reached over and picked up the receiver. 'The Buchanan winery. Janet Thurston speaking. May I help you?'

'Put me on to Rory, please, Janet.'

No announcement of who she was. No polite request, either. Dame Eleanor Buchanan Traverner Vandelier didn't bother with such niceties. She commanded.

'Just a moment, please,' Janet countered, taking cold satisfaction in putting Eleanor on hold as she covered the receiver with her hand. 'It's Eleanor, wanting you. Are you here or not?'

Rory reached out his hand. Janet gave him the receiver. She found herself holding her breath as he lifted it to his ear. The look of ruthless determination on Rory's face was spine-chilling. She didn't need a sixth sense to know he was geared for a showdown, any time, any place. He wanted one.

'Yes, Eleanor,' he invited.

A short pause.

'On what matter?' he questioned.

The answer visibly jolted him. His mouth thinned into a grim line. He took his time replying, or Eleanor was elaborating on her theme.

'I look forward to being enlightened, Eleanor. I'll come now.'

He replaced the receiver and gave Janet a deadly little smile that was enough to kick her heart into a faster beat.

'Well, that didn't take long,' he said.

'What didn't?'

He unhitched himself from the desk. 'The counterattack.'

He knew, Janet thought dazedly. He was not acting out of blind love. He knew what Tamara was up to and he was backing her all the way, regardless of where it led and what it did to him.

'You'll keep holding the fort for me?' he appealed.

'I'll do my best.'

'Thanks, Janet.' He headed for the door.

'How long do you think you'll be gone?'

He opened the door and paused to look at her. 'I don't

know. However long it takes to throw Eleanor's firepower in her face.'

It was a brave statement.

Hard and reckless.

Janet slowly sank onto her chair. She had been right about the world shifting. She was even more right about big trouble coming.

THIRTY-NINE

Eleanor was waiting for him on the front veranda of the old Traverner homestead, ensconced in a well-cushioned cane armchair. His grandfather was conspicuously absent. So were Bill and Wilma Guthrie.

'Good of you to come so promptly, Rory.' She wore a smug air of satisfaction.

'I wouldn't miss this for anything, Eleanor,' he replied, projecting satisfaction right back at her.

He made himself comfortable in the matching cane armchair that obviously awaited him. On the table between them stood a jug of water and two glasses. Hospitality enough, Rory thought, for the meeting of antagonists.

Her eyes assessed his body language. Rory deliberately adopted a relaxed pose, hooking his elbows on the armrests, legs sprawled out, shoulders at ease. He figured indolence drained any sense of importance out of this visit.

'The truth about my father's death,' he stated baldly, repeating what she'd said over the telephone and inviting her to get on with it.

Matriarchal concern came to the fore. 'You need to know what you're getting into, Rory. It's not in Tamara's interests to tell you since you're very much part of her revenge plan.'

Did Eleanor think he was being led around by his cock? If

that was how she saw him, she was taking a position of severely underestimating him. 'So you're going to be my best friend again and save me from being led astray,' he mocked.

'Yes.' She managed a sad look. 'Not that I expect you to appreciate it. What I'll tell you will hurt. It would hurt Frank, too, if he were ever told.'

She paused, pain pinching her face. For a moment, she looked like a lonely old woman, bereft of all that had made her life worth living. Then he saw the fierce flash of will in her eyes, an intense vitality denying death.

'My brother is very dear to me, Rory. I want your word that what I say to you this morning remains between ourselves.'

Damage control. She didn't want to risk alienating his grandfather. Did she really care about hurting her brother or was she thinking about his block of shares? It must have rattled her when he'd given his blessing to a marriage she'd do anything to prevent. Paul, as well. The solid family front was cracking.

'I won't give my word to you on anything, Eleanor. Not without knowing what I'm giving it on.'

Her mouth tightened. In vexation, she snapped at him. 'Your most recent decisions hardly rate my confidence in your good judgment.'

'Then you'll have to risk it, won't you?'

She retreated to a lofty approach. 'Or I could let you go to hell with Tamara.'

'Hell with Tamara is fine by me.'

She shook her head. 'You're a fool, Rory. She's using you.'

'I'm a man now, Eleanor. Not a boy.'

She leaned forward earnestly. 'Frank loves you. It's for his sake I don't want to see you destroyed by Tamara.'

Rory remained unmoved. 'Very noble of you. Shall we get back to truth now?'

The direct challenge visibly incensed her. Rory didn't

care. The days when the weight of her experience and authority demanded respect were over.

'Are you certain Tamara's pregnant?' she shot at him.

'Yes.'

'To you?'

'Yes. Not that it's any of your business, but you'll only make a fool of yourself casting doubt where there's none.'

Her mouth curled in derision. 'It's not the first time Tamara's been pregnant.'

Rory absorbed the jolt, keeping his eyes focused on the gleam of malice in hers.

'And not the first time she's wanted to palm her child off on you as the father.'

Tamara's words sliced into his mind. *I was pregnant, you know.*

It triggered a vivid recall. His heart contracted, remembering her watching him as she tossed off the loaded remark, testing his feelings, asking what he might have done. His reply—'I would've fought them all for our child'—had evoked the response, 'For a child of yours, but not for me.' Tears filling her eyes, tears catching at his heart, twisting him around.

Yet whose child could it have been, if not his? There had been no-one else for either of them that summer. Rory was absolutely certain of it. Unless, after their last meeting at his grandfather's place, when he'd let her go instead of fighting for her... No, he couldn't imagine it, not after the intensity of feeling they had shared.

Nevertheless, something must have happened. Eleanor would not be so confident of her ammunition if there was any doubt. It also answered why Tamara had acted as she had, scorning his fidelity because he hadn't been there for her at the critical time.

'So what did you do, Eleanor?' he asked quietly.

'Tamara was only fourteen. As her mother, what would you expect me to do, Rory?'

Banished to boarding school. Or was it a home for unmarried mothers? Somehow it didn't matter to him who the father was. She had wanted the baby to be his. Maybe, because she had felt rejected and let down by him, she'd had sex with someone else and instantly regretted it. If it had been a spur-of-the-moment, lash-back-at-him impulse, she might not have even known whose baby it was when she found herself pregnant. It might have been his.

'What happened to the child?' he asked, a harsh edge of urgency creeping into his voice.

'I arranged for an abortion.'

Not adopted out. Not given the chance to live. He felt sick. 'Did Tamara have counselling or did your judgment prevail?'

'Tamara agreed to the abortion.'

'She was fourteen, Eleanor.' *And I'd deserted her when she needed me most.* His mind writhed with the despair she must have felt. Pressure from her mother. No-one to turn to.

'It was for the best.'

'Sure it was. Like it was best for her to be shunted off to boarding school afterwards, to live alone with the memory of the abortion. That's great motherly concern, Eleanor.'

'Tamara was out of control here, and you might recollect we had your father's death to deal with,' she retorted in terse justification.

'Ah, yes. My father's death,' Rory drawled. 'Perhaps you could have let my grandfather handle that while you looked after your own family.'

He paused, then slid in his knife. 'On the other hand, you *were* looking after your own family, weren't you, getting rid of Max's daughter and sliding your son David into my father's place at Buchanan.'

Fury flared in Eleanor's eyes, but she quickly controlled it, curling her mouth into an ironic smile. 'You had some better solution to bridging the gap Ian left at Buchanan, Rory?'

He shook his head. 'You moved too fast for me in those

days, Eleanor. I was only a kid, too unprepared and inexperienced to beat your manoeuvring. I have no quarrel with David's filling in for my father, but you got more than his foot into Buchanan. You set yourself on top of it. You couldn't have done that with my father alive.'

'Buchanan has profited through the family company,' she answered loftily.

'Not as much as Traverner.'

'You have more to inherit now than you would have had under Ian.'

He laughed in her face. 'If my father was alive, my mother wouldn't have a vote and she wouldn't be in your keeping. Don't expect me to believe you're my benefactor, Eleanor. Nor do you intend to be.'

'I see Tamara has been working her usual tricks to get you onside with her. She has a fine hand at twisting the truth.'

'We all have a different perception of truth, Eleanor. I'm waiting to hear yours. About my father's death.'

'I don't suppose Tamara mentioned that at the time Ian died, I followed the only possible course to save the family from a far worse scandal than your affair with her.'

'A scandal in your eyes might not be a scandal in hers,' Rory said dryly.

'Then judge for yourself.'

He saw the axe about to fall in her eyes before she mouthed the killing words.

'It was your father who got Tamara pregnant.'

Shock held Rory absolutely still, even as it rebounded off the inner walls of his body, catapulting through him in wild thumps, leaving its trail of carnage, mind, heart, lungs, stomach. The need to repulse such a vicious imputation surged through him, demanding voice. Blaming a dead man who could not defend himself was a truly evil act. Eleanor was everything Tamara had said she was.

Yet the savage mockery in her watching eyes warned him there was more. She was waiting for a protest, waiting to hack it into bloody pieces. Rory held his tongue. He could wait, too. Let her state her case first.

A pause before she struck the second blow.

'Your father had been having sex with her for years before Max died. Tamara cut him off then, threatening to tell me if he ever touched her again.'

No, it was Max. Max! Eleanor was twisting the truth to get at him, washing her hands of what had been done to Tamara by the man she should have satisfied herself. But her eyes were still waiting to feed off his reaction. Instinct urged him to suppress what he knew until she'd fed him all her poison.

Her fangs sank more deeply as she went on. 'When Ian was faced with the fact she'd gone from him to you, still being sexually active, he was incensed into taking another chance at having her. Replacing you as her sexual partner.'

The pregnancy! Doubt hit Rory hard. Max had been dead so could not have made Tamara pregnant. Someone had. But surely to God, not his father. The idea of his father replacing him, having Tamara before him, after him...no, it was too obscene to accept.

Besides, Tamara had said it was Max. But that was after he'd relentlessly badgered her to tell him who had taught her about sex, demanding an answer, refusing to believe anything she said unless she satisfied him on that score. Had she condemned her own father rather than his, sparing him the horror of the real truth?

Was this the dark, shameful secret that had driven her onto such a destructive path all these years? He'd forced her to face it again. Her flight from his office, the moment of madness in her car, the violence of her feelings directed at him. Was it because he was inextricably linked to his father, her molester?

He frantically reasoned it couldn't be his father. He would have seen something. His mother or Cathy—

someone would have noticed such an obscenity going on. Years of it.

His reeling mind started picking up details of a damning pattern—his parents' separate bedrooms, his frequent escapes to his grandfather's home where his mother couldn't berate him, Tamara staying overnight with Cathy.

God! He remembered Cathy yelling at him, 'You know nothing!' when he'd tried to reason her out of her morose and erratic behaviour before she ran away from home. With Tamara gone, his father gone and his mother acting like a jailer to Cathy, he hadn't been able to give much solace to his sister. But maybe there had been worse things preying on her mind.

His stomach convulsed. Bile in his mouth. He forced himself to swallow it. Be damned if he'd give Eleanor the satisfaction of being sick in front of her.

She was watching him, certain of her facts, revelling in the sure knowledge she could beat him down if he tried to refute them.

'If you don't believe me, Rory, ask your mother,' she hammered with soft, deadly force. 'Irene knows the truth, too.'

Rory gritted his teeth against another upsurge of bile. Tamara had said Eleanor held the weapon of fear over his mother. Was this it? His mother and Tamara's united in an unholy bond of silence. Shame. Guilt. The perpetrator dead and the victim shuttled off, out of sight, out of mind, the evidence of a child disposed of with absolute finality.

Hatred burned through him, a fierce, bitter hatred. He wanted to lash out and strike with terrible force. His memories of his father were tarnished forever. Yet he had no doubt blame could be attached to his mother, as well.

A pity she hadn't perished in the fire. And Eleanor... Eleanor doing her maternal worst by Tamara. Eleanor couldn't die fast enough for Rory.

'I'm sorry to have upset you so deeply,' she said with spurious concern. 'If it helps, there is some mitigation for what

your father did. He claimed that even as young as she was
when it started, Tamara had actively encouraged him to
sexual play, and I'd have to concede she was highly precocious in that sense.'

At nine years of age?

'When she was very young she hid under our dressing table and watched her father making love to me. Her excuse
was she wanted to know. Apparently she set out to know
more from your father.'

'You believe that?' he curtly challenged.

She misread where his mind was focused. 'Your father
confessed the whole unsavoury affair before he died. I have
tried to forgive him.'

Pure acid speared off his tongue. 'By transferring guilt to
your daughter.'

Eleanor heaved an impatient sigh. 'Tamara was no innocent young child, Rory. You, of all people, should appreciate
that.'

'You're implying she seduced my father.'

At nine years of age!

'Ian said she was willing. I have no reason to disbelieve
your father, Rory. He was giving me a deathbed confession.
It was directly after he had unburdened his conscience
that—'

'He went and flew his plane into a hill.'

She nodded. 'A tragic accident.'

'Bullshit!' He remembered Tamara's description of his
father's state of mind just prior to getting into his car to
leave the Big House. Unreachable. Looking right through
her. Rory wanted—needed—to know it all now. 'Precisely
when did my father make Tamara pregnant, Eleanor? Give
me the time and the place.'

She hesitated.

Rory sensed she was calculating how much to say and
what slant to put on it.

'The truth, Eleanor.' He bored in.

'Tamara had defied my authority and gone to see you at Frank's place. Ian found out about it and went to collect her and bring her home. I don't know precisely what happened. Tamara said he forced her. She was hysterical.'

Oh, Christ! Rory closed his eyes as the memory of that afternoon hit him again, painted now in new, hideous colours. He could see his father insisting Tamara go with him, Tamara crying, pleading, calling him a coward for letting them be separated, his father shutting her in his car, taking her away, taking her...

He opened his eyes and shot Eleanor a venomous look. 'She had every reason to be hysterical, wouldn't you say?'

Eleanor heaved a much-put-upon sigh. 'Perhaps you're unaware of what Tamara can be like when she doesn't get her own way.'

'No sympathy from you for her distress?' he asked, seeing Tamara bereft of any support, abused and dying inside. *She killed my heart that summer.*

Eleanor grimaced. 'To my mind Tamara would have tried anything to get back with you. She accused Ian of raping her, and in the next breath blamed me for having separated you from her. Everything was my fault. She lashed out in every direction, and I had no idea what the truth was.'

'When did you start believing her?'

'In the end, she detailed what Ian had been doing with her since she was nine. It was too comprehensive not to believe there had to be some truth in it.'

'So you called in my father.'

'Yes. The next morning. I couldn't overlook Tamara's accusations.'

'You put him on the mat.'

'I had to ascertain the truth.'

'And he confessed.'

'Everything.'

He stared at her, seeing what Eleanor must have seen that morning, the advantages to herself of exiling Tamara from the family, convincing her there was no way back to Rory, getting rid of his father. No sympathy. No caring. Sew it up tight and lay it to rest.

'What did you say to him, Eleanor? Kill yourself or I'll reveal all? An honourable death or jail?'

That was a hit! He saw it get swallowed up as she regrouped. 'Is it easier to blame me for what your father did, Rory?'

'Since you have no problem in calling your victimised daughter a little slut, I'm sure you had no problem in calling my father every bit of nastiness you could lay your mind to. Do you want to pretend you didn't tongue-lash him that day?'

'Naturally my sense of decency was outraged, and I let him know it. But to suggest—'

'You had him by the balls and you squeezed.'

She stood up in high dudgeon. 'You are being most offensive. I set out to show you Tamara's true character.' Her hands flew out in emphatic gestures. 'Did she tell you about her sexual adventures with your father? No! Did she tell you she had your father's child aborted? No!'

Rory leaned forward, slamming his hands down on the table, a helpless rage blazing from his eyes. 'That could have been my child, Eleanor.'

'And what if it wasn't?' she retorted fiercely. 'Tamara wanted to live a lie with you. At least I saved you from that indecency.'

'The baby was a Buchanan, either way,' he retaliated just as fiercely. 'Living a lie with me would have been a more decent life than how she lived after you finished with her that summer.'

'You would have happily accepted your father's leavings?' Eleanor jeered.

'I didn't have to know. But I'm sure you would have told me, Eleanor. Did you bargain your silence for the abortion?'

Another bullseye.

The reaction was sheer fury. 'You fool! Tamara lies about everything. If you have any sense at all, you'll have nothing more to do with her.'

Rory rose from his chair, bristling with primitive aggression, hearing Tamara's words in his mind. *I was only fourteen. No match for Eleanor. She had too many weapons.* He towered over the heartless woman who had done all she could to destroy the girl he had loved, and so much more—the years wasted, the life he and Tamara could have had together.

'I hope the cancer inside you works slowly. I hope it makes every day you live a torture. And when you do finally die, Eleanor, I hope you meet up with my father's spirit. And the spirit of the child you had taken from Tamara. I hope they haunt you for eternity.'

That knocked her speechless.

'In the meantime, say or do one more thing against Tamara, and I'll wreak such havoc on all you hold dear, you'll end up with nothing. Except pain. And more pain.'

Her face lost colour. She groped for the armrests of her chair and shakily folded herself into it. Rory felt no guilt, no pity, yet some unquenchable spark of humanity made him lift the jug and pour her a glass of water. He waited for her to drink it.

She revived quickly enough, her eyes turning to him with vicious intent. 'I thought you had something of Frank in you, Rory. I was wrong. You're as madly obsessive as your mother and as sex-crazed as your father.'

'I'm glad you're feeling better, Eleanor. I want you to keep remembering that this time you failed.'

He turned his back on her and walked away.

'I trust you'll have a much longer life for remembering, Rory. I'm sure Tamara will make herself unforgettable.'

She always had been, Rory thought, and kept walking.

FORTY

Tamara paid for the white-fleshed peaches, her favourite fruit, and left the Pearl Beach general store in high spirits. It was a glorious spring day, the sun was warm on her skin, the sea was sparkling, and life had thrown her some bonuses she hadn't expected or anticipated.

She still marvelled at how Rory had stepped forward to claim his child and her in front of Eleanor and the rest of the family. Then Paul and Gabrielle giving their seal of approval. She hoped Rory would find out what was behind this amazing shift in attitude today.

Louise's funeral had definitely been a triumph for her. And Rory loving her afterwards, all weekend, wanting to marry her, blithely dismissing the bad years as though they had never been. It made her feel so good. Happy. Like flying on the wings of a dream. Even knowing it would almost certainly crash down to earth the moment Eleanor hit back, Tamara couldn't help hugging the feeling for a while.

She crossed the road to the beach and paused on the strip of mown grass between the road and the sand, enjoying the dapple of shade from the trees, the swoop of seagulls over the waves, the brilliant blue sky. It was so idyllic here if she shut everything else out. The past two days had been perfect with Rory. She'd been tempted to stop him from going to the winery today, to hold on.

Unrealistic.

He'd given her what was needed to beat Eleanor. And the child was something to hold onto. Strange how differently she thought about it now, perhaps the effect of Rory's attitude, his joy and tenderness as he spoke about a son or a daughter. She had envisaged an instrument of power, not really a person at all.

Heaving a rueful sigh over her fluctuating emotions, Tamara walked on, taking the shortest route along the beach to the house. It might be a good idea to buy a book on all the right things to do during pregnancy. She wanted the best for this child. Definitely hers and Rory's baby this time. The memory of the abortion slid into her mind, and she instantly kicked it out and slammed the door on it. There had been too few beautiful days in her life. This was one of them.

She lifted her head, sweeping her gaze around the cloudless blue sky. Heaven. A figure on the balcony of her house caught her eye. Her feet came to an abrupt halt as recognition blasted her bright sense of pleasure.

Rory, who should be at work in the Buchanan winery. Rory, staring out to sea like a man who saw nothing but his inner thoughts. Rory, who had left her with happiness emanating from him, who now stood like a stone statue, a monument to what might have been.

Destroy...

A two-edged sword.

Tamara knew with heart-sinking certainty that Eleanor had wielded it today.

Rory knew the worst of what she'd kept from him, and the dream that was only a dream was over. No chance for it. Stupid, hopeless hope.

No decent man will ever want you.

The words that had carried her into the abortion clinic twelve years ago came back to haunt her again. Rory was a decent man. She'd played on that, hadn't she? Deliberately and ruthlessly. So she had nothing to complain about. She had known all along it was inevitable Eleanor would strike back.

So why was she feeling pain? Lock it away. She couldn't afford to be crippled again. She needed impervious armour against Eleanor to win. And she would win. Had to. Or her life meant nothing.

Control was the key. If she hadn't lost control all those years ago, Eleanor would not have had the weapons to beat her. In shock, in grief, in rage she had handed the weapons to Eleanor, not realising how they would be used against her. If she'd stayed silent, blocked out what Ian had done, just as she'd blocked out all the other years with Ian, no-one would have known it could be anybody else's baby but Rory's when she found out she was pregnant. Rory would have fought for her then. Uncle Frank would have stood up for her, too, for his own flesh and blood.

She'd lost—Eleanor had won—because she'd been weak and hurt and bleeding for Rory's love, which they had taken away from her, and she didn't know about the pregnancy to come. She hadn't meant for Ian to die. She'd just wanted them to let her have Rory back.

No point in letting it get her down again. None of it could be changed. Eleanor had won then but she wasn't going to win now. No grief to play on. No shock. And the rage would be kept strictly under control.

Her formidable willpower rose above the leaden weight in her chest, and she forced her legs to move on. Love and marriage weren't for her. She knew that. Futile to mourn what could never be. The important thing was having achieved her objective. Rory's child. Eleanor couldn't kill this one so easily. Tamara fiercely vowed she would safeguard this baby to the bitter end of her fight against Eleanor.

She trudged across the sand, not bothering to look up again. Rory had to be shut out of her mind. What was finished was finished. She had successfully completed Act One. Act Two had to be stage-managed with the same surprise element and finesse.

Sooner or later Eleanor would call a shareholders' meeting. The future had to be settled before she became completely incapacitated. Tamara thought of the ammunition she had ready to fire. The beauty of it was Eleanor wouldn't see it coming, confident in the belief her tracks were covered. After all these years, why wouldn't she be?

Secrets were never safe. Eleanor thought she had a monopoly on keeping them and using them when they served her purpose. The prospect of ramming home the same tactic gave Tamara savage satisfaction. And if Irene came to the shareholders' meeting in Eleanor's corner, she would rip her apart, too.

Hatred. It was the one constant that could always be counted. It was the longest pleasure. It burnt away the foolish weakness of wanting to be loved. It was the best armour against rejection and the strongest incentive to live. With hatred she could walk alone, untouched by anything. She could face Rory and his decency and not feel a thing.

She climbed the path to the house and went up the outside staircase, cloaking herself in complete immunity to any hurt. Her mind dictated what had to be done. Confront, dismiss and get on with the plan.

The balcony was empty. Tamara shrugged off the tension that had crept up on her. The glass doors were wide open. She headed straight inside, determined to cut the scene short with Rory and send him on his way. This was her house, and she didn't need a rehashing of the past.

'Hi!' he greeted from behind the bar. No smile. The rattle of ice cubes was a welcome sound. 'I saw you coming and made you a drink.'

'Kind of you.'

Tamara set the bag of peaches on the coffee table, walked over to the bar and hitched herself onto one of the stools.

Rory placed a long lemon squash on the counter in front of her. She'd already sworn off alcohol for the baby's sake.

'Thanks.' She flicked her gaze up to meet his. 'Had a nice chat with Mother?'

The acid sarcasm stilled him in the act of lifting his glass. Anguish in his eyes. For several tense seconds he desperately searched the black, impenetrable barrier of hers, then gave up, his lashes sweeping down as he slowly set his glass on the bar.

'Do you hate me, too, Tamara?' he asked quietly.

The pain didn't surprise her. The question did. She thought about it and decided to answer honestly. After all, she had nothing to lose with Rory now.

'I did hate you. I don't any more.'

'Despite who I am? And what I didn't do?' His lashes flew up and his eyes seared hers with the unbearable knowledge Eleanor had loaded onto him.

Her guard cracked as something in her moved, demanding to reach out to him and ease the hell he was suffering. 'You are uniquely you, Rory. You were apart from what your parents did.' Bitter irony curled her mouth. 'How could I have loved you if you weren't?'

He shook his head. 'I don't know. I don't know how to make up to you for...' His throat moved in a convulsive swallow. He looked away, sickened by the images that had to be running through his mind. 'Was Cathy part of it, too?'

'No.' A wave of sadness hit her, widening the crack in her guard. 'Cathy was my friend. The only friend I ever had. I was afraid he might turn to her if I didn't do what he wanted.'

'Oh, Jesus!'

'He didn't touch her, Rory. She would have told me.'

It was Cathy's damned mother who'd done the damage, but Tamara decided not to load that onto Rory. Cathy was dead and gone. No one could help her now.

'She wrote to me, you know. When I was in my prison

boarding school. She told me she couldn't bear living with her mother any more. Then the letters stopped.'

Rory looked at her with eyes that ached with regrets. 'Cathy was right when she said I knew nothing. So blindly entrenched in trying to do the right thing...' His grimace derided his good intentions.

'Don't whip yourself, Rory,' Tamara shot at him, compelled to be fair in this last farewell to him. 'And don't let Eleanor do it, either. You're not to blame for what happened.'

Still he looked anguished.

Tamara had done enough answering. No more, she decided. No-one had the right to demand she live through it all again. Rory had been generous to her. She'd be generous to him.

'Just wash your hands of it, Rory, and walk away. You have my blessing to blame me for everything.' She smiled as she slid off the bar stool. 'I'm sure my mother did.'

'Tamara...'

She waved dismissively as she headed for the balcony. 'I free you of any sense of obligation to me. And don't worry about the baby. I'll take good care of it. You can leave me with a clear conscience.'

'I don't want to leave you,' he yelled.

Her armour was hard and solid again, ready to deflect anything. She swung around, deliberately striking a provocative stance. 'Come off it, Rory. It's over. You're never going to look at me again without seeing the little Lolita who fucked your father and got rid of his kid.'

He slammed his fist on the counter as he rounded the bar. 'Do you think I believe the crap Eleanor fed me?' he thundered.

Tamara made no reply. The aggression emanating from him was electric. The play of passionate emotions on his face held her riveted.

'I'll tell you what I see when I look at you, Tamara. I see a child who was rejected from day one. I see a victim who was helplessly caught in a web of obscenity. I see the girl I loved, and I rue the day I let her down when she needed me most. And I see the woman you are now and know my life will be unbearably empty without you at my side.'

Did his vision really encompass so much? Was there hope? She cast around for doubt, unwilling to leave herself unprotected, afraid this couldn't be true.

'Part of it was my fault, Rory. I wasn't a complete innocent. I was curious. I let your father do it. And then...then sometimes I liked him cuddling me. It felt like he loved me. It's all right for you to hate me instead of him.'

'No. No!' he cried vehemently. 'You were a little girl lost. He was a man who should have had the decency to keep his hands off you. I won't let you put blame on yourself, Tamara.'

He was coming towards her, his eyes ablaze with conviction. She fought off its mesmerising power. He would change after he thought about it some more. This was the heat of the moment. She held up her hands to ward him off. The words, so indelibly burnt into her psyche, formed her last and ultimate defence.

'My mother said—'

'To hell with your mother!' His hand flew out in fierce dismissal, then slapped onto his chest. '*I'm* saying. Me. Rory. What she says is for her, not for you.'

'No, it's true. I know it is.'

'Tell me then.'

She didn't want to. It burst from her, beaten out by the battering strength of his challenge, the truth he would have to admit and concede.

'No decent man would ever want me.'

That stopped him. Yet why was he staring at her with a look of appalled horror? 'Is that what she planted in your mind?' Harsh, angry words.

'I can't wipe it out, Rory,' she pleaded, needing it ended.

'Don't you realise it served her purpose?'

Purpose? She stared blankly at him.

'It made you feel bad about yourself. So bad it didn't matter what you did any more.'

That was true. But the other was true, too.

'The cruel bitch! She didn't want you to get attached to a decent man. Didn't want you to marry or have children. She lied, Tamara.'

Lies. So many lies. She shook her head. Where did they begin and end?

Rory grasped her arms, violently intent on breaking down every barrier between them. '*I* want you. I'll never stop wanting you. Just say you want me, Tamara. Say it!'

She couldn't. There was an impassable lump in her throat. Her vision blurred as tears sprang into her eyes. Her chest was impossibly tight. There was a welling of nameless things from deep within her, a turbulent swirling, a frightening sensation they would all break out and she'd never be able to put them back again.

The armour she had clutched to herself for so long slid out of her grasp. Her willpower crumbled. All the strength she had harnessed over the hate-filled years seemed to drain out of her body. She started to choke. Tears gushed into her eyes, unstoppable.

'It's all right,' Rory soothed, releasing her arms and wrapping her in a strong embrace. 'It's good to let it go, Tamara,' he murmured, gently pressing her limp head onto his broad shoulder and stroking her hair and back, holding her very securely as she sagged into uncontrollable weeping.

Her mind was a mess. Needs she had kept rigidly suppressed ran rampant, shuddering through her in a chaotic chorus. *Hold me, help me, want me, love me, don't turn away.* And from the desolate loneliness of her soul rose the beat of one name, reaching back to a magical summer of promise. Rory...Rory...Rory.

'I'm here for you,' he answered, strong and tender and

truly caring. 'No-one will ever part us again, Tamara. I promise you.'

A damburst of tears, relief at his belief in her, joy that he could still want her, grief for the lost, ruined years, the waste.

'Be free of all this,' Rory urged softly. 'Free as you've always wanted to be, Tamara. Free to be happy, to love and be loved. You do want me, don't you?'

'Yes,' she choked out. 'Yes.' A sigh of surrender to his will, his direction, his path. Together. 'I love you, Rory.'

His chest rose and fell. 'God knows why.'

She nestled closer, her lips brushing his throat. 'You're my true hero,' she whispered, and there was not the slightest trace of mockery in the words. She felt them deeply. He'd proved it. Only a true hero could still love her through the pain of all she was.

FORTY-ONE

$\Longleftrightarrow$

Eleanor seethed over the meeting with Rory for the rest of the day. It was a bad day for her in every sense. The tablets she took after lunch should have knocked her out for a couple of hours. They did succeed in dulling the physical pain. They didn't touch the torment of failure that raged in her mind.

It was late afternoon when Frank returned, having collected Irene from the nursing home and settled her in at the Big House. Eleanor joined him in the sitting room, wanting the diversion of hearing that one of her initiatives had been successful.

Frank's report of the accomplished mission was matter-of-fact, his manner ill-at-ease. He didn't like Irene, but she was his widowed daughter-in-law, and Eleanor knew he felt a sense of family duty towards her. What he would feel if he knew the truth...

At least she still had that up her sleeve and she doubted Rory would disillusion his grandfather about Ian. Not unless he was pushed. She should have given more weight to what Frank had said about Rory loving Tamara. Yet it was still incomprehensible to her that the attachment could run so deep. Years of sluttish behaviour from Tamara should have wiped out any feeling Rory had for her. The only rational explanation Eleanor could come up with was that Rory had to be justifying what he'd done in falling into Tamara's sexual trap again.

Time would sort it out, but time was what Eleanor didn't have. The baby was a major complication. It was questionable whether Tamara would actually go through with the pregnancy. It didn't fit her capricious nature. Nevertheless, Eleanor couldn't discount it. Hatred lent strength of purpose. If Rory stuck by Tamara, there could be ructions in the family company that would destroy what had been established.

Eleanor brooded over how best to block the next probable step in Tamara's game plan. She was tempted to sound Frank out about which way his vote would go if it came to a crunch over who was to succeed her as head of the company. It was an opportune time. They were alone in the sitting room. It would be another hour before Wilma served dinner.

He was hunched forward in his chair, elbows on his knees, hands nursing the glass of sherry he always had at this time of the evening. He undoubtedly needed it after the large dose of Irene he'd had today. Eleanor decided it was probably wiser to leave serious discussions until the morning when they'd both be less frazzled. Her meeting with Rory had not left her feeling on top of anything.

The sound of a vehicle arriving brought Frank abruptly to his feet. 'That'll be Paul. I'll let him in.'

'Why didn't you say Paul intended to visit me?'

He shuffled his feet uneasily, wanting to go, pausing out of courtesy. 'I didn't know he'd come, Ellie. Thought I'd suggest it. That's all.'

Frank wanting to make peace between everyone, Eleanor thought sardonically. Or at least mend fences. It was only a few days since the funeral. Paul's pride probably made him reluctant to take the first step after her terse show of disapprobation. Nevertheless, he had to be made to realise how critical it was for them to remain strongly unified against sabotage from Tamara.

Paul entered the sitting room alone. The tactful withdrawal by Frank was welcome to Eleanor. It allowed her to speak freely to her son without giving offense to her brother. Paul shut the door behind him, ensuring their privacy and obviously wanting it himself.

'How are you, Mum?'

It was more a polite greeting than an expression of concern. He was certainly not rushing to close the distance that had opened up between them.

'I'm glad to see you, Paul.' He was her favoured child. Nothing changed that. Richard lived on in him. Intent on helping him unbend by offering a friendly gesture, she waved to the decanter on the table closest to Frank's chair. 'Help yourself to a sherry if you'd like one.'

'No. I won't stay long.'

He walked to the fireplace and took up a stance in front of it, directly facing the settee where she sat. It signalled he had no intention of bending. There was a resolute set to his face.

'Can I get you anything?' he asked.

She shook her head. 'I trust Gabrielle has made Irene comfortable?'

'I believe that's the housekeeper's responsibility.'

Very cool and distant.

Eleanor recollected her somewhat curt conversation with Gabrielle and barely stopped herself from rolling her eyes. Petty politics. She had more than enough to contend with. Tact, at this level, should not be necessary.

'I see,' she said with a weary sigh. Paul's wife was definitely coming out of her shell and having an influence on his thinking. 'If Gabrielle wishes to change the way I ran the Big House, she may do so,' Eleanor conceded. It was a trivial matter relative to the far more important issue of succession in regard to the vineyards.

'Gabrielle has no desire to run the Big House at all. It's

yours. I've come to tell you I'll be moving my family out of it this week.'

It shook her. It struck at the foundation of the dynasty she thought she had established. It displayed a further departure from her rule. It was a public desertion of all she stood for. It could not be tolerated.

'That is totally inappropriate, Paul,' she snapped.

'You mean it's not what you want.' He let that viewpoint linger for a moment, then added, 'I doubt you've ever considered what I or Gabrielle want. I'm sorry if it upsets you, but we prefer to have a home of our own where we have the prerogative of deciding whom we welcome into it and whom we don't.'

Irene!

Gabrielle had taken umbrage at having Irene thrust upon her and was forcing Paul to make a stand. The past seven weeks of being mistress of the Big House had obviously gone to her head. Eleanor fumed over the absurd quarrel. Private quarters could easily be arranged for Irene in the Big House, limiting the intrusion on Gabrielle's territory.

'Since when did Gabrielle find Irene so offensive?' she scoffed.

'*I* find her offensive.'

'Then why didn't you discuss the matter with me before coming to this ridiculous decision?'

His face visibly tightened, mouth and jawline. Eleanor was sharply reminded of Rory's words—*I'm a man, not a boy.* Tact could be more important than she'd thought if Paul was feeling she should be treating him differently.

'Would it have changed anything?' he asked, his air of cool distance from her increasing. He was standing very much on his dignity.

'Not as far as accommodating Irene, no.'

'Exactly.' He nodded knowingly. 'You do what you want, Mum. I'll do what I want.'

She lost patience with him. 'You're being cantankerous at the wrong time, Paul.'

'I didn't come here for an argument. I'm doing you the courtesy of informing you I've made new living arrangements for my family. The running of the Big House is all yours. Or you can pass it over to Irene. I don't care.'

'For God's sake! Can't you see this is a pro tem thing? The Big House is yours to inherit.'

He shook his head. 'You know, Mum, I thought like that for a long time. You led me to take it for granted, and I did. But I view it differently now. If you want to talk inheritance, that house should go to Tamara.'

'Are you out of your mind?' She heard her voice becoming shrill, but she was beyond controlling it. 'You want to see Tamara and Rory in the Big House, lording it over the valley and the vineyards?'

He frowned, not liking the image. Eleanor thought she had finally got through to him until he looked at her in critical assessment and asked, 'Is that how you saw yourself?'

She exploded with frustration. 'It's what I made of it. I, through my own force of vision and commitment.' Outrage spurred her into flaying him. 'And you have none if you'd let it go to Tamara.'

'Perhaps I prefer the substance of the vineyards to the status of the Big House,' he answered quietly. 'In any event, Max built it. And Max was Tamara's father, not mine. That's all I have to say.'

He bowed his head in a farewell gesture and started moving to the door. Eleanor could hardly believe it. Paul was walking out on her again without so much as a by-your-leave. She was losing her grip. No. Tamara was somehow taking it away from her. Rory, Frank, even Paul being seduced to Tamara's side. It had to be stopped. She had to make Paul see what was happening.

'Wait!'

He was almost at the door. He half-turned and looked at her, his face closed to any further argument.

'Why are you turning against me, Paul?' she demanded, driven by the need to hold his loyalty.

'I'm not. But I can't say your way is my way. I tried to tell you that. I'm sorry you don't want to hear.'

She did hear him this time. She heard the sadness in his voice. It sent a shiver of fear through her. Death suddenly felt very close, and what she needed to hammer into place was slipping out of her control.

'It looks like I've taken things for granted, too,' she quickly conceded. 'Since you don't see yourself following in my footsteps, it will be easier on both of us if you tell me what resolution you have in mind for the continuation of the family company.'

He was in no rush to reply. He looked at her as though weighing whether it was wise or productive to say anything, given her attitude of belittling his judgment.

It infuriated Eleanor that the trust between them had been broken when she most needed it to be rock solid. She was certain Paul wouldn't have come to this impasse on his own. Tamara had to be behind it, suborning Gabrielle to her purpose, as well.

'Perhaps you think it should be handed to Tamara,' she goaded, determined to find out how far the alienation went.

'Now that *is* ridiculous,' he replied, grimacing in impatience at such an extreme view. 'Tamara knows nothing of the wine industry.'

'Rory does,' Eleanor tersely reminded him.

'Rory doesn't have as much experience in some areas as either David or I. Both he and Uncle Frank are aware of that.' It was a slow, measured opinion.

'So whom do you see succeeding me as head of the company, Paul?'

Eleanor could see his reluctance to reveal his vision to her, aware that if she was not receptive to it the current breach between them might become irredeemable.

She saw the recognition that it had to come to this point sooner or later in his eyes. He moved to face her more directly. His inner tension was evident in the tight clench of his hands.

'I believe the family company needs a new structure,' he started, choosing his words with care.

Eleanor sensed a mute appeal for her understanding. She made no comment, waiting for him to commit himself to more explicit detail.

His expression changed to one of deference and appreciation. He lifted a hand in an open gesture of giving as he continued. 'You pulled the vineyards through a time of vast change and growth in the industry. You can be justly proud of that, Mum. We're in a strong position because of all you did.'

The sugar coating for the pill, she thought, watching him relentlessly, determined to force him to the wall.

He sighed, sensing he hadn't reached her. Resigning himself to the inevitable, he pressed on. 'To my mind, the need for one person to oversee and direct everything is gone, and the business is too big for any one person to fill that role.'

'What you're saying is your shoes aren't big enough.' She threw the words at him, hating his weakness.

Again his face tightened into hard, austere lines. He looked at her with a cold expression that clearly said she had slapped him down for the last time.

'You're right,' he told her. 'My shoes aren't big enough to tramp over the rights of others. Now if you'll excuse me...'

'Tamara will make mincemeat of you,' she jeered, seeing the nemesis of Max's daughter closing in on her, aided and abetted by the inability of her son to grasp the reins she could no longer hand to him. 'Before you even see what's coming she'll have Rory set up in my place. And where will you and David be then, Paul?'

She pushed herself up from the settee, too agitated to remain seated. Her authority had to be reestablished. 'You'll be her lackeys,' she declared with stinging intent. 'Make no mistake about that. If I hadn't secured Irene's vote—'

'And how did you do that, Mum?' Paul cut in, his shoulders lifting in a more aggressive stance, his eyes flashing a sharp challenge.

It was so incredibly stupid to direct what strength he had into putting her on trial. Eleanor attacked him with all the fury of her mounting frustration. 'Nothing falls into your lap, Paul. Maybe that's something you have to learn the hard way. I've made it too easy for you over the years.'

'Yes, you have,' he agreed. 'But the handouts stop here.'

'That they will.' *David*, she thought. *It will have to be David.* At least he wasn't blindly intractable. 'And to clearly demonstrate the error of your way, I suggest we call a meeting of the directors of our family company. The business agenda will be forward planning.'

'Fine!' he shot back at her. 'When do you want to hold it?'

'Well, I wouldn't like to interfere with your house-moving operation.' Bitter sarcasm laced every word. Her disappointment in him was so intense she could barely stand the sight of him. 'Let's say a fortnight from today. I trust you won't be too busy to get the official notices out.'

'Count on it.'

'I will, Paul. And when you finally see Tamara reveal *her* forward planning, as she undoubtedly will, you can start counting the cost of your fickleness.'

He shook his head. He dragged in a deep breath and slowly expelled it, his eyes searching hers in sick hopelessness. 'I mean nothing to you as a person, do I?'

She was too angry to reply.

'All these years since Dad died, I knew it wasn't the same. I tried to make it up to you, learning all my father had known. And more.' He lifted his head as though seeking helplessly for answers. 'I'm your son. But that's not enough for you. Not enough to simply love me for being me.'

Maudlin talk. Eleanor inwardly recoiled from the spongy emotionalism. If Paul couldn't see she'd done it all for him—safeguarding his heritage, ensuring it, building it, expanding it for him to carry it on—what greater evidence of love did he want?

A moistness glittered in his eyes as he brought his gaze to her. 'You've only ever seen me as an instrument of your will.' A dull, dead comment.

Her heart contracted, rejecting all he was saying. It was wrong. Paul's soft core was ruining what could be, if only he had the guts to grasp it.

'Good night, Mum. I hope you can sleep well on the course you've chosen.'

He turned his back on her and left.

Richard's son.

Her most loved child.

The chill of death seeped into her bones. Pain, the harbinger of death, sank its vicious teeth into her. She stumbled onto the settee, grabbing a cushion to clutch, rocking over it until the intensity of the agony eased. Hell could not be worse than this, she thought, bitterly railing at the train of circumstances that had led to this wretched moment.

She could hear Tamara laughing.

Rory, Paul...both of them her fools.

Eleanor consoled herself with the assurance she still had David. David would follow her lead. He hadn't been suckered in by Tamara's performance at Louise's funeral, and he wanted a more important position. Sharon had blurted that out.

She still had time to teach David what had to be done to take over from her. She would live as long as she had to in order to achieve that. David was as strong as Frank. Once he had the bit between the teeth, he wouldn't let go.

And Frank would stand by her. He always had. To the death, he had promised her.

Besides, Tamara couldn't take control of Traverner without Irene's vote.

Irene would stop Tamara.

FORTY-TWO

Irene paused in the centre of the ballroom, bathed in the circle of light shining from the dome overhead. It was the grace of God, blessing the Big House, cleansed now of all those who had occupied it during the years of sin. With Paul and Gabrielle and their children gone, it belonged solely to her, and in her keeping it would radiate the power she now had.

She smiled as she thought of Eleanor waiting for her. Eleanor could wait. She wasn't mistress here any more. The housekeeper might still do her bidding, informing Irene that Dame Eleanor wanted to see her in the library, but the housekeeper wouldn't be here much longer. Shirley could take her place.

It was curiosity and the desire to exert her new domination over the self-styled matriarch that drew Irene to the library. She viewed the figure sitting behind the big desk at the end of the room with a thrilling sense of contempt. Paint and pretence. An eaten-up old mannequin, white-haired and wizened.

'How are you, Eleanor?' It pleased Irene to be gracious from her lofty position as the Chosen One.

'I see Louise's death doesn't hang heavily upon you, Irene.'

'The will of God was done.'

'Unfortunate that the will of God also burnt your cottage.'

Stupid Eleanor, tied to grubby, earthly things. Yet that also served a higher purpose. The wasting witch could easily provide the transport required for the believers to come and worship in this holy place.

'I am at home here,' Irene declared, fired with the conviction that Eleanor was a mere servant, an instrument of supply to the greater good.

'I've always thought poverty as a virtue was vastly overrated,' Eleanor drawled. 'Though I'm sure you won't let luxury spoil you, Irene.'

The snide tone of voice was the bleat of a beaten foe. Irene let it float over her. She sat and smiled, knowing Eleanor was damned for eternity, seeing the dried-up shell that would burn and blacken when the devil took her. But the labour of servitude had to come first.

'I require a minibus, Eleanor.'

Eleanor considered the demand, as though she had a choice, before asking, 'What for?'

Irene decided to humour her. 'So I can hold prayer meetings, as usual. This is too far for people to walk.'

Another pause for consideration. 'I will not tolerate your hanging out a sign on the front lawn.'

'It won't be necessary.' The word would spread. Irene knew the Big House would become a great temple, attracting more and more followers.

'Well, we have something of more immediate concern to attend to first. I trust you received notification of the directors' meeting called for next week.'

'Garbage mail,' Irene said scornfully.

'I take it you have no wish to attend?'

'I will not consort with unbelievers.'

'See you keep to that stand, Irene. I've brought a proxy form for you to sign.' She pushed a paper across the desk and pointedly placed a pen on top of it. 'Since you don't wish to use your voting capacity, I'll do it for you. In accordance with our *secret* agreement.'

A black, formless shadow suddenly hovered at the edge of Irene's brilliant inner vision, a threat that couldn't be borne. She stood up, defying it, clinging to the path of the righteous as she walked to the desk and confronted the corruption behind it.

'You will get me the minibus,' she commanded.

'Write your signature between the pencilled crosses, Irene.'

'The transport must be provided.'

Eleanor leaned forward and tapped the page. Her black eyes blazed. 'I'll be happy to see you happy, Irene, as long as you keep to your word. I'll loose the dogs of hell if you don't. Now sign the proxy form.'

The power Eleanor wanted was purely temporal, meaningless in any spiritual sense. Irene picked up the pen and signed the worthless piece of paper.

'I want the minibus. Today, Eleanor.'

'Purchases of vehicles require considerable paperwork. You'll have it within a week.' She folded the form and put it in her handbag. 'Can you handle a minibus, or am I expected to supply a driver, as well?'

'Shirley can drive it.'

'Ah, yes, Shirley. Your…protégée.' Eleanor rose from her chair. 'Don't make yourself too comfortable, Irene, and please do be discreet. I wouldn't like to have the house staff upset.'

'I don't mind if they leave. I can get plenty of helpers,' Irene boasted, already seeing the expansion of her initial plan. Shirley first, then Miriam and Nora.

Eleanor tucked her handbag under her arm. 'Trained staff are hard to come by. Don't rock the boat, Irene. You won't be sailing in it alone for long.'

It pricked Irene's exultant bubble of confidence. She watched the mangy marionette walk stiffly to the door. Her chest tightened with explosive hatred for the superior air Eleanor always adopted. 'Paul and Gabrielle have gone.' She flung the words after her. 'And they're not coming back.'

Eleanor half-turned as she opened the door, lashed into submission by the whips of truth. 'I have no quarrel with their departure, Irene. And you're welcome to stay on with your minibus. Even with Shirley, if needs must.' Her mouth curled in sly nastiness. 'But there is a limit to your autonomy here.'

'No! God provides!'

'Yes, I know. According to His will. It happens to be *my* will that David and Sharon move in to the Big House. At the appropriate time.'

The mocker left.

Irene stared at the closed door. It seemed to pulse and grow with the power to deny her the promised land, mocking the vision of plenty. A scream tore through her mind. She ran to the door and beat it with her fists, reducing its size, pulverising its capacity to darken the portal of God's gift to her. She felt her blood pounding through her temples, feeding her brain, expanding it, opening it to the full knowledge of the might of Jehovah.

She rested, her body becoming still, the bonds of the flesh transcended by a brilliant burst of enlightenment. The glory of absolute certainty billowed through her mind, dispelling the disturbing turbulence of Eleanor's evil shadow. This was God's house. God's will was stronger than Eleanor's.

Hadn't the spawn of the witch already been banished from His holy temple? Eleanor would not be permitted to bring in more of her evil seed. The door would be closed to all her kind, just as it had now closed on her. The unclean would never be admitted again.

She was the Chosen One. She was the keeper of the flame, and anyone who defiled the vision would burn. So it was decreed. She could see the avenging sword, pure and glittering against a pillar of fire. It was hers to grasp and to wield in the name of Jehovah. His will would be done.

FORTY-THREE

Paul was intent on checking that everything was in readiness as he and David entered the boardroom. His secretary was reliable, but he was acutely conscious of leaving nothing open to criticism this morning. Refreshments were set out on the sideboard, coffee and water simmering on a hotplate. The oval table was arranged with seven chairs as ordered, pens and pads neatly in position.

'By the way, Sharon said to ask you what are we doing about Christmas this year.'

Paul stared incredulously at his brother. They were on the verge of the most important business meeting of their lives, and he was worrying about Christmas?

'It's only a few weeks away,' David gabbled. 'We've always had it at the Big House. It'll be Mum's last Christmas, Paul. We should do something special. But with you and Gabrielle in your new house and Mum down at the old homestead...'

'No doubt our mother will tell us what she wants,' Paul answered curtly. 'For God's sake! Pull yourself together, David. We've got other things to concentrate on.'

'I know. I know. I'm sorry. It's just... Do you think she'll approve our plan for the future?' he asked for the umpteenth time.

Paul controlled his impatience with his brother's need for reassurance. David was tense and worried. There had never been a directors' meeting like this one, possibly the last their mother would attend, and the decisions made this morning would set a future course that would be new to all of them. The sense of being at a critical crossroads was very strong.

'It's not a matter of her approval. We have the votes, David,' he stated evenly. Having placed the minutes file on the table in front of his chair, he moved to the sideboard. 'Want a coffee?'

'No, thanks. My bladder's working overtime as it is.'

Paul poured himself one, determined to appear calm and confident. He didn't doubt his strength to stand firm no matter what his mother threw at them, yet the prospect of open and bitter confrontation was having a gut-wrenching effect. To have his long relationship with his mother end in conflict when she was looking death in the face did not sit well with him.

'Can we trust Tamara?' David burst out, riven with anxieties now the moment of truth was close.

'She won't go against Rory,' Paul answered with certainty.

In their meetings over the past fortnight, there had been no hint of discord between Rory and Tamara. It had been a touching revelation to Paul to see his half-sister glowing with happiness. The magic of loving and being loved, he thought, newly aware of how precious the feeling was. Gabrielle had the same glow about her now they were settled in a home of their own.

'It's such a turnaround from her,' David fretted, still gnawing at the worries besetting him. 'I don't feel comfortable with it.'

'I'd say the feeling is mutual,' Paul commented dryly. 'Tamara doesn't trust us. She's had no reason to. If we stick to the agreement we've made with Rory she'll vote with us. It's as simple as that, David.'

'I hope so,' he muttered.

* * *

Rory waited by his Maserati in the parking lot, not liking the sense of separation. Tamara's insistence on coming in her own car and in her own time this morning worried him. It smacked of raising protective barriers again. And setting up an independent escape route. Did she still think Eleanor could part them?

He didn't realise how tense he was until relief washed through him at the sight of her black Porsche turning into the lot. She parked beside him, and he was opening her door before she'd even switched off the engine. Her smile as she stepped out lightened his heart.

She looked stunning. Her red suit could be classed as business clothes, but on Tamara it was power dressing to kill. Rory couldn't help grinning. Even if the Traverner boardroom was awash with blood on the floor this morning, Tamara would rise above it. So would he. They were invincible together.

'Am I the last to arrive?' she asked.

'No. Grandfather and Eleanor aren't here yet.'

'Good!' She reached into the car and lifted out a black leather attaché case. 'I prefer to set the scene this time.'

He looked at the businesslike case and wondered if it contained ammunition to fire at Eleanor. 'What have you brought?' he asked, not wanting to be caught unprepared when solidarity was essential.

'Insurance.'

He looked quizzically at her, inviting more explanation.

'My mother is not going to let go without a fight, Rory. You might think you're handing her a fait accompli. I'll believe it when it's done.'

He stepped back to pick up his own briefcase as she locked her car. 'What do you see going wrong, Tamara?'

She shrugged. 'Anything or everything.'

'You don't trust Paul and David?'

'They'll both be put under enormous pressure.'

'It *is* Paul's plan,' Rory reminded her.

'Domination is insidious. They've been under it for a long time. She'll be ready for this, don't forget.'

It was an ominous warning. Rory chewed over it as they headed for the administration block. What other secrets did Eleanor have to deal in? As far as he knew, Paul and David had led fairly exemplary lives. No skeletons in their cupboards. She'd already done her worst with Rory. They didn't need his grandfather's vote for the plan to go through, so there was no reason for Eleanor to pressure her brother. Which left Tamara.

The realisation hit him. Tamara was donning her armour again. She didn't believe he could protect her, and maybe he couldn't. She might have referred to David and Paul in saying domination was insidious, but it also applied to herself. The bond of hatred between her and Eleanor spanned Tamara's entire life, and it ran too deeply for him to root out. A few weeks of love and trust could not override twenty-six years of deadly warfare.

They entered the building, and Cassie Deakin greeted them from the reception desk, goggling at Tamara as though she could hardly believe her eyes. 'They're in the boardroom,' she informed them.

'Thanks, Cassie,' Rory replied, ushering Tamara to the staircase.

Rory noticed Cassie's hand hovering over the telephone. It was the first directors' meeting Tamara had ever attended, and coming on top of her performance at Louise's funeral, it would obviously feed speculation about the old order changing. Janet was not wrong about the vineyards seething with gossip. The results of this meeting would undoubtedly be hot news on the grapevine.

This was the ultimate showdown. One way or another, Eleanor had to be finished today, her power broken. Irretrievably. It was the only way to put the evil behind them and go forward.

Paul was sipping a cup of coffee when they entered the boardroom, looking commendably cool in a situation fraught with difficulties. David was clearly on tenterhooks although he managed a firm handshake.

'We won't be needing seven chairs,' Tamara said, moving straight to the end of the oval table and leaving them all somewhat startled as she removed the third chair on the right-hand side, then repositioned the third chair on the left-hand side to directly face Eleanor's at the head of the table. She laid her attaché case on the table in front of it, making a stark statement of one-on-one confrontation with her mother.

Paul recovered first, frowning at the rearrangement. 'You're assuming Irene won't be attending.'

'Mother won't risk it,' Tamara answered dryly.

'How do you know that?' David demanded, suspicious of her intentions.

'Because *my* mother cannot be counted on to react rationally to anything,' Rory drawled, trying to lower the tension running between Tamara and her half-brothers.

Paul nodded thoughtfully. 'Mum said she'd secured Irene's vote.'

'Proxy,' Tamara agreed. 'It would be the only safe way.'

'It doesn't look good, you sitting there, Tamara,' David protested. He stepped forward to his chair. 'You should be with us on the Traverner side of the table as it was set up, and whether Irene comes or not, we should leave the empty chair for her on the Buchanan side.'

She looked at him, her black eyes glittering with implacable purpose. 'I'm not a Traverner, David,' she enunciated with cutting precision.

Her gaze moved to Rory, still implacable as she stated her singular position. 'And I'm not a Buchanan.'

The sense of separation sliced into him again, and he silently railed against it as he watched her chin lift in defiant and independent pride of the heritages they took for granted and were intent on reinforcing today.

'I'm a Vandelier.'

Max's daughter. Not Eleanor's. The message was loud and clear. The cuckoo in the nest was now a fully fledged bird who could place herself apart and stand unsupported by any of them.

Her hands curled around the backrest of the chair, digging in. 'I find it entirely appropriate that the two people who bear the name of Vandelier face each other at this meeting,' she declared. 'It adds a piquant touch to the divisions in our family.'

'You're not alone, Tamara,' Rory asserted, concerned she might feel so. His eyes projected unwavering love.

She gave him a wry smile. 'It's not over yet, Rory.'

It wouldn't be over until Eleanor was dead. He knew that. He'd known it from the first night he'd promised to hold her safe. He wasn't sure now if he could deliver on that promise. Tamara was taking up battle stations. Rory had little doubt Eleanor would publicly maul her to protect what she wanted to hold. If it came to that, he knew he would have no mercy for anyone's sensitivities. He might not be able to shield Tamara, but he'd stand by her, whatever fight erupted.

Paul's cup and saucer clattered onto the sideboard. He looked disturbed. 'If you've got a private agenda, Tamara...'

'Your plan is a fair one, Paul. It has my support,' she assured him. She gave him a searching look, perhaps wondering how much he comprehended. 'We've been on a long journey to this time and place,' she said quietly. 'It's been a journey paved with greed. My father's. Your mother's. It has to be confronted now and finished. That's what this meeting is about.'

'Well, you've lost me,' David muttered.

'She's right, David,' Paul said without hesitation.

David looked at him in bewilderment. Rory caught the

derisive flash in Tamara's eyes and knew what she was thinking. David was the weak link. Eleanor would attack the plan through her younger son. Rory cursed himself for not having foreseen it. It meant they needed his grandfather onside.

The telephone rang. Paul whirled to pick up the receiver. He listened, said, 'Thanks, Cassie,' and replaced it. 'They're on their way up,' he stated flatly.

Rory skirted the table to his chair, on Tamara's right and directly opposite David. Paul moved to his place, between David and where his mother customarily sat. There was an air of nerve-tearing suspense in the room. The battle was about to commence, and Rory suspected none of them would emerge from it unmauled.

Justice.

It wasn't a thought. It was a need. A compulsion. A resolution. It burned through Tamara Vandelier's mind as she watched the boardroom door open to admit the woman who had diseased her life.

No more, she promised herself. Rory loved her. Paul and David, in a different way, had been their mother's victims, too. She saw that now. The desire for vengeance had dissipated with the promise of a new life with Rory. And their child. But there had to be a final reckoning and a righting of what Eleanor's ambition had wrought. Only then could they all move forward and leave the past behind.

But the hatred hadn't gone. It welled out of the wounds Eleanor had inflicted as Tamara watched her mother walk to the head of the table, unaided by Uncle Frank, who followed her into the boardroom.

She wore royal blue. The colour of winners. The colour of queens.

Paul held her chair for her, ever the courteous gentleman. David greeted her too brightly, revealing his nervous state. Uncle Frank acknowledged all of them in his warm, kindly

manner. Rory smiled at him. He loved his grandfather.
Eleanor sat, ready to play what she undoubtedly believed
was a winning hand.

She looked down the table at Tamara. Their eyes met and
held in deadly challenge. Neither of them were under any
delusion about today's proceedings. It was a duel that
spanned the past and the future.

'Would you like a coffee or tea, Mother?' Tamara asked,
moving to the sideboard to play hostess.

'No, thank you,' came the predictable response. Eleanor
would take nothing from Tamara.

'Uncle Frank?'

'I'll have tea. Black and weak, thanks, Tamara.'

She smiled. Rory's grandfather always did his best to
smooth rocky paths. She made his tea and took it to him as
he settled in his chair between Rory and Eleanor.

'Anyone else?' she asked brightly.

Negative replies.

'Then I'll just get myself a coffee.'

It was only a niggle, to keep Eleanor waiting, but Tamara
wanted her to feel the threat of having her domination taken
away from her. There was the rustle of papers being looked
at as she served herself. No small talk.

She carried her coffee to the table, set it down, opened her
attaché case, removed the sheaf of documents she had
brought, snapped the case shut, lifted it onto the floor beside
her chair, then sat down, having successfully made herself
the focus of attention.

'Right!' she declared, casting a look of sparkling interest
around the table. 'If you want to declare the directors' meeting open, Mother, it seems we're all ready.'

No-one more ready than I am, Tamara silently promised the
woman she would charge in front of this family tribunal today.

Justice.

FORTY-FOUR

Eleanor disdained the call to leap to Tamara's beat. She waited for the focus of attention to settle solely on her, idly perusing the papers Paul had sent out as though familiarising herself with their contents. She refused to be distracted by Tamara's cheap tactics—the placement of her chair and the hostess game. She had one purpose at this meeting, and she would not allow her energy to be sapped by irrelevancies.

Frank, Paul and David were, as they always had been, the important factors in her equation for success. She did not discount the possibility that Paul could find himself caught on the horns of his principles and fall in with the line she had planned. David, however, had to be won first.

He was under stress. His shoulders were bunched forward. He kept his gaze fastened on a pen he rolled continually between his fingers. He didn't want to look at anyone. Whether he was simply disturbed by the inevitable change heralded by her death sentence or unhappy with Paul's proposed new structure for the company—perhaps both—David, she was sure, would prefer a continuity that had her blessing.

He had always sought approval. He blossomed under it. It fired his energies, and he performed above expectations.

More importantly, once set a goal, David stuck to it with a tenacity that would not be shaken. He did his best. Tamara would not be able to confuse David. There was much to be said for a straight-line mind.

Whatever influence Paul had exerted on his younger brother, Eleanor had little doubt she could override it. David wanted a more important position. Sharon would not have suggested it without knowledge of her husband's wishes.

Eleanor smiled. Tamara was not the only mistress of the surprise element in attack. Eleanor had deliberately re-frained from conducting a tug-of-war with David's loyal-ties, waiting for today's meeting before unveiling her inten-tions. An unheralded nomination would have the effect of pitting brother against brother, undermining Paul's plan be-fore it could be tabled.

Should Tamara propose Rory in David's place, Paul would swing against them to protect his own interests. Frank would go along with weight of experience. Rory, he would reason, was not seasoned enough to head the com-pany.

It would work.

And Tamara, having shown her hand and been defeated, would be a tiger without teeth. Though the child she carried was a threatening issue. Eleanor dismissed it from her mind for the time being. It was not an immediate problem.

'I take it Irene is not attending today,' Paul said, as she set the papers aside.

Irritated by his casual breaking of her domination of the silence, Eleanor turned a cold face to him, raising her eye-brows in mocking reproof. 'Since you didn't see fit to set a place for Irene, it would be embarrassing if she did decide to attend.'

Out of the corner of her eye she saw David grimace and shoot an angry I-told-you-so glance at Tamara. It warmed Eleanor's heart. Paul, however, didn't turn a hair.

'It's no trouble to accommodate her if she does turn up,' he answered, his eyes demanding a definite reply from her.

'Irene sends her apologies.'

'Well, that will be a first,' Rory drawled sardonically. 'Better record it in the minutes, Paul. My mother sends her apologies.'

Eleanor automatically cast him a quelling look.

He returned a false smile, his eyes boring deep and abiding hostility at her.

Tamara's fool. And her willing tool. Eleanor dismissed him contemptuously, annoyed with herself for having even glanced his way. An unwelcome diversion, momentarily putting her off her stride.

'Are we to understand that Irene's vote can be discounted from any motions put forward today?' Paul asked, forcing a premature disclosure that Eleanor would have preferred to keep up her sleeve for a more telling moment of truth.

She hid her displeasure and adopted a matter-of-fact course. 'No, that is not the case, Paul. Irene has given me her vote by proxy.'

She tabled the document for anyone to check its authenticity. If it was a bombshell to hidden hopes, there was a marked lack of reaction. It was as though they had all anticipated this move and confirmation of it came as no surprise. All except Frank. He leaned forward, frowning, and slid the paper over for his perusal.

'Another first,' Rory pointed out derisively.

This time it rang alarm bells in Eleanor's mind. Rory could have been talking to Frank about his and Tamara's plans, persuading his grandfather towards their point of view. She remembered Frank saying they were his future. Had she miscalculated her brother's long-held fealty to her?

'What's this, Ellie?' Frank was puzzled and disturbed. 'Why would Irene be interested in voting? She doesn't give a damn about the vineyards.'

There was nothing hidden in Frank's eyes, and she knew

he didn't know how to be deceptive. They were open and honest, reflecting his feelings. The cramp in her chest eased. He would listen and assess for himself, as he'd always done.

'I'm dying, Frank,' she reminded him gently, appealing to his empathy with her position. 'Change unsettles people. Irene trusts me to make the best decisions for her.'

His frown deepened. 'She's not in her right mind, Ellie.'

'All the more reason to take matters out of her hands.'

He shook his head, too perturbed by this turn of events to let it slide. 'I'd prefer you not to use this,' he said gravely. 'It might be legal, but it's not right.'

His opposition shook her. It was totally unforeseen. The time he'd spent with Irene, bringing her to the Big House, must have impressed on him how far off the planet his daughter-in-law was. Eleanor was acutely conscious of everyone listening, gauging the consequences of this contretemps. It was imperative she soothe Frank's sense of rightness.

'I have great faith in your good judgment, Frank. I'm sure it will prevail,' she assured him.

'Just so you understand how I feel, Ellie,' he replied, shooting the paper over to Paul for filing.

It was not a propitious opening to what had to be put in place. Eleanor took several slow, deep breaths to calm herself, knowing the apparent weakness would be interpreted, by those who counted, as a sign of her painful condition. Tamara and Rory could think what they liked. David, who was uppermost in her mind, showed concern.

With an air of bravely soldiering on, Eleanor proceeded to the formal acceptance of the minutes of the last meeting. As chairperson, she could and would take control of what happened around this table. Having announced the agenda— forward planning—she launched straight into her planned strategy, determined on sweeping Frank with her before he could be sidetracked by anyone else. She aimed her speech directly at David.

'My resignation as head of our family company will come into effect at the end of this meeting.' She softened her voice. 'Quite simply, I am not well enough to carry on.'

It drew an anguished look from David, which she caught and held, offering a brave smile to retain his sympathy and attention.

'I have thought long and hard over whom I should nominate to take my place. As I see it, there is only one person with the necessary breadth and depth of experience and knowledge to hold the company together and make it work to everyone's advantage.'

David glanced at Paul. Apart from that one movement there was absolute stillness around the table. Eleanor waited for David to look at her, wanting to compel a belief in himself as the better choice. He frustrated her by retreating into a study of his hands, ready to accept what he assumed would be Paul's leadership. Eleanor decided to snap him out of his premature resignation immediately.

'That person is my son, David Traverner.'

His head jerked up. His eyes flew wildly to Eleanor, to Paul, back to Eleanor. Shock, incredulity, then a gushing flood of embarrassment as the impact of her rejection of Paul hit him. His hands lifted in obvious agitation. 'Mum, I—'

'Hear me out, David,' she commanded, aware of the electric silence her surprise announcement had caused and knowing she had to win her brother's support. 'You are thoroughly acquainted with every facet of the management of Traverner. Your stewardship at Buchanan after Ian died demonstrated your ability to take over in a crisis and produce top management there.'

She turned to Frank, intent on his seconding her nomination. 'You'd agree with that, wouldn't you, Frank?'

His face was deeply pensive. 'I appreciate very much all David did to pull Buchanan through a very difficult personal time for Rory and myself,' he said slowly.

The qualified answer lacked the conviction Eleanor needed. She swung straight into more argument, again targeting David for praise that would lift his self-esteem to the necessary level for taking what was being offered.

'I would like to point out David's added expertise in the area of sales. He has been particularly effective in expanding our markets, and I confidently anticipate the sales penetration he has achieved will accelerate under his guidance and authority.'

Instead of looking pleased by this acknowledgment, David vexed Eleanor by once again glancing at Paul as though urgently needing his direction. It was the attitude of a follower, not a leader, and had to be corrected right now. Eleanor turned to Paul in direct and deliberate challenge, knowing he would not put his brother down.

'Do you have any quarrel with my decision, Paul?'

He returned a level gaze. 'You have the right to nominate whomever you like.'

'Do you agree that David has the qualifications I've listed?'

'Yes.' Unequivocal.

'You'll give him your support?'

She could see only a bleak sadness in his eyes as he answered, 'David and I have always supported each other.'

Loyalty. He didn't want to beat her. He didn't want to beat David. He would work around it all. Somehow.

Eleanor smiled, scenting victory. 'Then I move we put it to the vote.'

'Not quite yet, Mother.'

Precisely paced words, shot from the foot of the table like whip cracks and slicing through the momentum Eleanor had built.

Tamara.

Eleanor relaxed in her chair as all heads turned to the source of interruption. It did not surprise her that Tamara had entered the fray at this point. There had been no other option. The call for a vote had to force her hand, and it should work in David's favour. Confident of manipulating whatever Tamara proposed to her own advantage, Eleanor chose to draw her out.

'You have some objection, Tamara?'

'Since you have declared your position vacant, Mother, nominations should be called for from all of us,' she said in a tone of sweet reason. 'We each have the right to put forward a name for consideration.'

Rory.

Eleanor graciously nodded her acquiescence. 'If you believe someone else is more suitable, by all means nominate your candidate.'

'Thank you. I nominate Frank Buchanan.'

She wasn't the only one jolted. No-one was prepared for it, not even Rory. Heads swivelled from Tamara to Frank. Consternation on Paul's face. David looked lost. Rory seemed to be swiftly reappraising. Frank looked completely startled, his face running through a gamut of expressions from confusion to dismay.

He leaned forward, gesturing an apology to Tamara for disappointing her. 'Thank you, my dear. I'm honoured by your respect but I'm far too old to take up such a demanding role.'

Eleanor reached across and took his hand, squeezing it indulgently, relieved and reassured by his good sense. 'Would that we were both young and vigorous again, Frank,' she said fondly. 'It's good we have David, who's familiar with the running of both vineyards.'

'Mother asked David to hear her out, Uncle Frank,' Tamara persisted. 'May I claim the same courtesy?'

He sighed and shook his head. 'A waste of time, my dear.'

Rory pressed his arm, his eyes urgently intent. 'Please, Grandfather, we need you to listen.'

Frank hesitated, not understanding. 'Well, no harm, I suppose. What do you want to say, Tamara?'

Eleanor was sure her brother would not relent. She withdrew her hand and sat back, prepared to watch the interplay between Tamara, Rory and Frank before bringing it to a close. This had to be a ploy to work Rory's name forward. Once that was done, she would pounce, cementing David's and Paul's loyalty to her.

'We all appreciate the time pressure Mother must be feeling, Uncle Frank,' Tamara started sympathetically. 'The sense of urgency to settle what has been so important in her life.'

Frank nodded, accepting the suck-in without question.

'She has only had a little over a month to ponder a future course. That's not very long.' Tamara let the statement hang for a few moments to collect grave consideration. 'And given the span of years Mother has been in charge, the idea of her not being there takes quite a bit of adjustment.'

'Yes, it does,' Frank agreed heavily.

Eleanor had to concede Tamara was clever, intuitively homing in on the right strings to pull. But presentation was one thing, closing a deal quite another.

'The fact of the matter is, Uncle Frank, while Mother was coming to her decision—unilaterally—' deliberate pause to hammer that point '—Paul—' Tamara nodded to him in a friendly fashion '—David—' he was encompassed by an open wave of her hand '—and Rory—' another wave included him '—were working out what they thought would best serve the family company.'

Tension ripped through Eleanor, bringing a sharp spasm of pain. David looked relieved. Paul was leaning forward, alert to the opportunity Tamara was opening up. Rory was concentrating on Frank, willing him to give support, and Frank was captivated by what Tamara was telling him.

'Now maybe they'll need an older and wiser head to watch over the structure they've agreed upon,' Tamara pressed on persuasively. 'Someone they all respect and will listen to when sorting out any difficulties that arise. You wouldn't need detailed knowledge, just the general feel and experience you've had from all your years in the industry. Like a sounding board. It wouldn't be for long, Uncle Frank. Consider it a holding brief to bridge—well, the gap...'

Tamara winced effectively.

Eleanor seethed. It was a holding brief until she was dead and gone and Tamara could more easily push Rory into the gap.

And Frank appeared to be drinking it all in, sampling the taste and considering its possible value.

'Paul?' Tamara looked at him appealingly. 'If you'd explain to Uncle Frank how it will work—'

'No!' The word exploded from Eleanor's throat. She slammed her fist onto the table, like a judge's gavel, demanding order in the court. 'It's madness!' she cried vehemently. 'A company like this cannot be run by a consortium. It will fragment into factions.'

Her violent rejection of the idea caused a frozen silence.

Frank rallied first. 'Ellie, I'd like to hear what the boys have discussed,' he said quietly. 'It may not be workable, but their ideas deserve a hearing. They're fine young men who've been carrying the business on their shoulders for years now.'

'Under my direction,' she fiercely reminded him.

'Yes.' He nodded, collecting his thoughts. His eyes begged her forbearance as he slowly added, 'But there comes a time when pupils can surpass what their teachers can give them, Ellie, and it's wrong to hold them back.'

'This is not in the best interests of the company, Frank,' she insisted. 'You know I've carried it this far, and I will not see it wantonly broken up.'

She flashed a savage look at Paul. 'The road to hell is paved with good intentions. It's strong leadership that takes a company forward, not a mixed bag of self-interests that inevitably leads to disputes and dissension.'

'It's not a mixed bag,' Paul retorted swiftly. 'It's a clearly defined structure. I would argue it's self-interest that can weld partnerships together.'

'And drive them apart,' she shot back at him before switching the whole force of her authority to David. 'I hope you're taking this in, David. I've put my faith and trust in your strength to hold this company together.'

He looked intensely uncomfortable.

'I know you will not let me down.' She hammered the words, needing to put steel in his backbone. Then, in appeal to his pride, she hung what had to be his secret dream before his eyes. 'You are ideally suited to take over from me, David. You have the management skills and the tenacity to get things done. And Sharon will certainly grace the Big House as your hostess for any occasion. You can move in at your convenience, once this is settled.'

He shook his head dazedly, took a deep breath and faced her with eyes that ached to conciliate but a jaw set in grim decision. She'd won him. Triumph zinged through her mind. She felt a fleeting regret that it wasn't Paul, but David was also Richard's son.

'I'm sorry, Mum. I can't accept.'

FORTY-FIVE

Tamara watched the powerful domination of Dame Eleanor Buchanan Traverner Vandelier begin to disintegrate. She felt no pity. She felt no triumph, either. In a strangely detached way, she saw justice being done and felt satisfied.

David and Paul were both hurting, but they would emerge from this crucible more whole as people in their own right than they'd ever been before. Their mother was struggling to fend off the devastation of the dynasty she had so ruthlessly fostered. David's rejection of the sceptre she had tried to thrust upon him was a killing blow.

'You have to accept, David,' Eleanor commanded in a voice that shook with force riven with despair.

'I'm sorry, Mum,' he repeated, shouldering the wretched task of standing firm against her wishes. 'I don't want to be set over Paul. I wouldn't feel right about it.'

'Right?' It shrilled off her tongue. 'How *right* are you going to feel when Tamara closes you and your equally blind brother out of any control over the vineyard your father died for?'

Passion and poison erupting, carelessly unguarded. Tamara felt her heart catch. The final attack was starting, no holds barred. Her emotional detachment shattered as the bitter years flooded into her mind, her long-festering, help-less hatred sharpening into a shaft of purpose.

Destroy...

'Tamara has nothing to do with the deal we've set up with Rory,' Paul asserted.

'Tamara *owns* Rory. He's her puppet,' Eleanor cried heat-edly. 'And just you add the Buchanan shares—Frank's, Irene's, Rory's—to hers and see what you and David have left, Paul.'

'Now, Ellie, that's uncalled for,' her brother interjected, visibly upset.

'I'm no-one's puppet, Eleanor. Which you should know,' Rory threw in, his tone laced with warning.

'You've both been conned,' she lashed out in fury. 'I tell you all, you'll rue the day you let Tamara into your lives.' Her swinging gaze hit Tamara and stopped in a blast of rage. 'I wish to God you'd never been born.'

Tamara was vaguely aware of shocked reactions to the bald truth Eleanor had blurted out.

Frank crying out in protest, 'Ellie, you don't mean that.'

Paul gesturing an appeal. 'For pity's sake, Mum...'

David shaking his head.

Rory slamming a hand on the table in disgust.

It all floated past Tamara, meaningless. The truth had been spoken, the truth she had always known. The truth she had lived with. No escape from it. Ever.

Hatred surged, driving Tamara to her feet in a blaze of red and black. The words flew from her tongue, seared with bitterness and scorching a path between her and the woman who had once carried her in her womb.

'A pity you didn't kill me at birth, Mother. You've been doing a damned good job of it ever since.'

A blur of faces turning to her, mouths hanging open but not speaking, frozen in time. Tamara's focus centred on Eleanor, only Eleanor, as the killing memories beat through her mind, memories of so many bits of her dying—lost innocence, constant calculated rejection, cold, heartless judgments, the forbidden baby, all the doors relentlessly being shut on her, the frenzied search for something, anything, the long, deep chill of outcast loneliness.

Her hands balled into fists, knuckles hard on the table as she leaned forward, her body straining with the force of her emotion. 'But I'm alive, Mother.' The words throbbed from her heart, drummed from her mind. 'And I'm here, Mother. And you can't block me out. And you can't kill what I'm going to say. Or do. Not this time.' She straightened up, breathing hard, implacable in her need for blood. 'There's nothing that can stop me this time.'

Whether consciously or unconsciously, the four men drew back from the table, out of the line of fire, witnesses but not participants in this argument.

Eleanor seemed to move in slow motion, settling back in her upright chair, her shoulders squaring, her chin tilted in proud disdain, her eyes hard beads of shiny jet, ready to deflect whatever arrows Tamara shot at her.

'You have the floor, Tamara. By all means, say what you must and do what you must,' she invited coldly. 'I have no wish to stop you from spilling out all you've stored up for us. I'm sure it will be enlightening.'

'Be certain of it.'

Eleanor nodded knowingly, expecting the outcome to vindicate the accusations she had made and the stance she had taken.

This was the showdown Tamara had dreamed about for so long, the final accounting. She banked down the hot flow of emotion pumping through her. Ice was what she needed. Cold, hard ice sharpening her mind and freezing her heart. She'd learnt the lesson long ago. Control was the key to winning against Eleanor.

She was not a lost child any more. She was not a frantic teenager. She was not a crippled person hurtling down paths of destruction. She was a woman with a future, loved

by a decent man and carrying the child that would start a
new family. Her own.

Eleanor's authority couldn't crush her now. Nor could the
secrets that had been held against her. Rory knew them.
They no longer had the power to take any more from her.

But so much had been taken. Wilfully and wickedly
taken. And Eleanor would find other ways to get at her,
push her away, kill. The baby—nothing bad must touch this
baby. Eleanor had to be comprehensively destroyed today,
stripped of all support so she could never strike again.

With a sense of clear purpose, Tamara picked up the
photocopied document that lay on top of the pile of papers
she had brought with her. Begin at the beginning. Acutely
aware of the order of attack marching through her mind, she
ignored Eleanor and turned to address her half-brothers.

'When your mother married my father to save the vineyard your father died for, a bargain was struck between
them. In return for the huge investment my father was to
make, your mother was to bear him two children. Not one.
Two.'

It was news to both of them. Paul frowned. David glanced
questioningly at his mother, who affected stony-faced bore-
dom with this piece of family history.

Tamara tossed the document to the centre of the table.
'This is a copy of the marriage contract signed by both of
them.'

No-one reached for it.

'If it's of any relevance,' Eleanor drawled, 'I was over
forty when I gave birth to you, Tamara. There were complications. I had a hysterectomy and couldn't bear any more
children. Max understood.'

'And luckily for you, Mother, the one child you did give
him was a daughter,' Tamara answered with pointed emphasis. 'It would have been much more difficult to divert
Max from bringing up a son to be a winemaker like your

sons, taking his rightful place in the great Traverner vineyard.'

'Pure speculation,' Eleanor said dismissively.

Tamara picked up the next document from her pile and tossed it to the centre of the table. 'A photocopy of the medical record of your hysterectomy, Mother. It states the surgery was elective. It wasn't necessary, and there was no health reason for it.'

Eleanor's face tightened. Her eyes snapped with anger. 'It's illegal to steal confidential medical records. You had no right to—'

'Just gathering irrefutable evidence of how you cheated both my father and me to keep Traverner for your sons.'

'You're always so extreme, Tamara. I'm appalled you would go this far to dig up something against me.' Her gaze skimmed the others for support.

Tamara denied her any by simply stating, 'It's true.'

There was a shifting in seats, Paul and David looking to their mother to defend herself, Frank Buchanan glancing worriedly between his sister and the daughter she'd openly rejected.

Eleanor sighed in a show of barely held patience. 'I had a difficult pregnancy with you, if you must know,' she said haughtily. 'It was unreasonable that I be subjected to another one in my forties. Any woman would feel the same.'

'There are women in their forties wanting and having babies every day, regardless of how difficult their pregnancies are,' Tamara retorted.

'That's now,' Eleanor snapped. 'We're talking about over twenty years ago when it wasn't nearly so common. In fact, it was considered risky.'

'You didn't want to risk having a son. That was the true reason, wasn't it, Mother? You wanted your sons by Richard Traverner to be the ones carrying on from their father.'

Another sigh, punctuated by a roll of the eyes. 'I've said

all I'm going to say on this subject. Your harping on it only shows the depth of your paranoia.'

'Oh, I wouldn't call it paranoia when you've openly stated your wish that I'd never been born,' Tamara drawled.

A dismissive wave. 'You try everyone's patience.'

Tamara held her fire for several moments, letting Eleanor believe she had regained her authority. The deaths marched through her mind, igniting the hatred. The baby that could have been Rory's, Ian, Max, and long before that fateful year, sealing Eleanor's intention to kill for her precious Traverner line, the secret Eleanor thought was safe. She was about to find out otherwise.

'What was the sex of the baby you had aborted, Mother?'

Apart from an indrawn breath from Rory, everyone could have been turned to stone. The silence gathered intensity as it went on. Truth or lie? The question had to be answered.

Tamara watched Eleanor like a hawk. The initial shock was quickly shuttered, her eyelids masking the regrouping of whatever forces she could find to establish credibility. Any victory over Eleanor would be hard won. Not for one moment did Tamara believe her mother would crumble without one hell of a fight.

Eleanor's lashes lifted to allow the venomous gleam of narrowed slits. Snake's eyes. 'You know as well as I do, the sex of the baby was not determined, Tamara. You were only a few weeks' pregnant at the time.'

The bitch! Retargeting the hit, turning it into a ricochet. Tamara quickly regrouped, realising she'd let her hatred cloud the forming of her question, giving Eleanor the leeway to strike back. If there was to be damage done, it would go both ways. Gloves off.

Control, Tamara screamed at herself. Control everything!

Confusion on Paul's and David's faces. Consternation on Uncle Frank's. Rory tensing, ready to spring to his feet and stand by her.

Tamara smiled to defuse his concern. 'I don't mean the abortion you arranged for me when I was fourteen, Mother.'

'Shit!' David breathed.

Paul jerked forward, clearly disturbed as he swung his gaze from Tamara to Rory.

'Ellie, is this true?' Uncle Frank asked, frowning, agitated.

'It's true, Grandfather,' Rory answered. 'Eleanor told me herself a couple of weeks ago.'

'Tamara chose to have it,' Eleanor stated, her eyes telegraphing the threat of more revelations, leaving Tamara with no doubt she was prepared to wade into the mud, boots and all, uncaring whom she hurt as long as it turned the tide of opinion against her hated daughter.

'You didn't give me much of a choice, Mother,' Tamara mocked. 'After all, you had to look after your priorities. Another Vandelier was not wanted.' She pointedly switched her attention to her half-brothers. 'Paul's and David's heritage had to be safeguarded.'

'What the hell!' David spluttered. 'We had nothing to do with this.'

'We didn't know, Tamara.' Paul gestured an appeal. 'I'm sorry.'

She didn't care that they knew. It was better they did. Let Eleanor's sons know what was done for them—all for their bloody heritage! Let them understand what had been done to her, the price she had paid for being born.

'That abortion eliminated one heir to the Vandelier line of the family,' she told them. Having focused their minds on the critical line of her attack, she turned her gaze to Eleanor, aiming the big gun. 'But that was not the first elimination, was it, Mother?'

The ice mask did not so much as crack. 'I have no idea what you're talking about.' The shield not only remained in place, it deflected. 'If you had a previous abortion, it was not to my knowledge.'

Tamara shook her head. *Not my blood*, her eyes silently

promised her deadly antagonist. *It's yours that's going to be spilled today.*

'Not me, Mother. You,' she said, to make the point absolutely clear. 'I'm talking about the pregnancy you had terminated before you got your doctor to agree to the hysterectomy.'

Tamara paused, relishing the taste of vengeance before striking the blow that couldn't be evaded.

'Your second child by my father.'

Destroy...

FORTY-SIX

The indictment hung in the air, radiating all the undertones and inferences Tamara had loaded into it, the weapon wielded, hitting its marks with wave after wave of devastating connotations.

Paul and David were unhinged from their secure little worlds. They didn't know where to look, what to do. Rory remained still, but Tamara sensed the strength of his support, the will to fight with her and for her coursing through him. His grandfather watched the sister who had been his longest companion in life, pained bewilderment carved on his kindly old face.

The haughty composure Eleanor had maintained was rattled. Her mouth was a tight, grim line, eyes glazed, their focus turned inward. The secret she had buried all these years had been unearthed, and she had no ready line of defence for it.

Tamara had no mercy. 'Was it a boy, Mother? Or couldn't you stomach the risk that it might be?'

Red blotches appeared on Eleanor's white cheeks. Her eyes blazed bitter hatred. 'How dare you throw this in my face? You know nothing about it. And the reasons you give are so outrageous, I won't discuss them.'

They all stared at Eleanor, assessing her response. Frank

cleared his throat and leaned forward, resting his elbows on the table, his expression a plea for understanding.

'Ellie, this is a very serious matter Tamara has raised,' he said gravely. 'I think we'd all feel more comfortable if you answered it.'

A glare of defiance. But not even Eleanor could wave aside the stench of blood spilled in the cause of holding and building what she wanted for the Traverner vineyard. The need to assert her standing in their eyes forced her to speak, to justify her actions.

'I did fall pregnant to Max a second time, but there was something so wrong—'

'No, there wasn't,' Tamara cut in, ruthless in her drive to have the truth laid bare. 'It was a perfectly healthy pregnancy.'

Eleanor cracked, spitting out her rage at being forced to the wall. 'For God's sake! What could you possibly know about it? You weren't even two years old at the time.'

'Your doctor told me everything. Quite unwittingly. He thought I was you, Mother.'

'Grayson?' A waver of uncertainty. Then an opening she charged through, the light of battle in her eyes again. 'He has Alzheimer's disease. Confused and off his head.'

Tamara held firm, keeping the upper hand with resolute control. 'About the present, yes. But not about the past. The past comes in very clear flashes. When I sat with him in his nursing-home room, he thought he was talking to you in his surgery.'

'The fantasy of a sick man,' Eleanor jeered.

'Truth, Mother. A secret guilt that had preyed on his mind all these years. He needed to talk it out with you. Get it off his chest.'

'I tell you something was wrong,' she shrilled, beginning to lose her grip. Her gaze flicked wildly around the table in search of sympathy. 'I was sick and frightened. I had my life to consider, too.'

It raised no response from her sons or her brother. They were all too stunned to rush to her support. Or too shocked to give it.

Furious at having been forced to justify herself, she targeted Tamara with blistering hatred. 'Why you have to drag something so personal and private into this boardroom—'

'Did you respect what was personal and private to me when you had your conversation with Rory, Mother?'

'You can't fool me, Tamara. You're using him. It was in Rory's best interests to know what I told him.'

'I love him. And he loves me,' Tamara said quietly, feeling again the strength of the bond she and Rory shared, deeply rooted in the joyful freedom of one beautiful summer and spanning the long, desolate years to this time of intense togetherness. 'You can't break us apart again, Mother.'

'Ellie.' Uncle Frank shook his head in distress. 'I asked you to let them be. This is all so wrong, so wrong...'

The protest drove Eleanor to a deeper fury. 'You don't know Tamara as I do. None of you do. I made a perfectly understandable and reasonable decision not to persist with a pregnancy that could put me at risk. Tamara is turning it into something else because she wants division in this family.'

Her voice throbbed with conviction. She eyed Tamara with the ferocity of a lioness protecting her pride against an enemy. 'I know you, Tamara. You aim to take Traverner away from us. And this is your way of going about it.'

The irony was, that had been Tamara's original resolution. Eleanor had read it correctly. Not surprising, when it was Eleanor who had seeded the motivation for it. But Rory's love and Paul's decency had spurred a change of direction.

'You've got it wrong, Mother.'

'You can't bluff me.'

'I'm not trying to. You know as well as I do what you've done—cheating my father, cheating me of the brother I might have had, keeping me out of having any part of the heritage you guarded so jealously for your sons. You shut the door on me from the moment I was born, and it's your fear of the door being opened that's speaking now, the fear I might somehow take Traverner away from you.'

The defence came swiftly and hotly. 'You admit you feel robbed, however neurotic that is. You've made the opportunity with Rory to take over both vineyards. With ruthless haste, I might point out for those who have ears to hear. And the fear, as you call it, is well-founded recognition of your twisted mind, Tamara.'

'Twisted.' Tamara smiled. 'Thank you for that word, Mother. I hope those with ears to hear will remember it.'

'They won't be smiling when they do.'

Tamara picked up the last sheaf of papers in front of her. To her they were tainted with too much blood. She wanted a fresh new life, a future where Eleanor had no reason to touch her again and no power to rally support to do it, either. This was the final parting point, a reckoning that was fair to Paul and David and to herself. Eleanor's authority was broken. This would destroy it beyond any recall.

She threw the papers into the centre of the table.

'There are my shares in Traverner. You can have them. You and Paul and David.'

Eleanor was silenced, staring at Tamara in stark disbelief.

Not so the rest of the company.

'No.' Paul jackknifed forward to shove them back to her. 'It's unacceptable.'

Rory leaned forward urgently. 'Tamara, are you sure you want to do this?'

'There is no need to prove anything,' Frank told her.

'I haven't finished,' Tamara cut them off.

Eleanor gave a high-pitched laugh. 'No. I'm sure you haven't.'

'In return for having me out of Traverner altogether, which will allow you to die in peace, Mother...'

Tamara paused, her eyes challenging Eleanor to recognise that the battle was at an end. With this pact, the ground being fought over was eliminated.

'I want the old Selby vineyard.'

The deal surprised them all, coming as it did out of nowhere. Tamara had not even discussed it with Rory. The idea had only come to her this morning as she drove past the old Selby place and remembered how Eleanor had taken it from Janet.

It offered a truce. But there was no response from Eleanor. It was as though all her fighting spirit had been demolished by this one stroke. She was left empty, her face void of expression.

Tamara turned to Paul. 'Do you consider that an equitable exchange?'

He searched her eyes to see how serious she was, then slowly nodded. 'More than equitable, Tamara.'

'What do you want it for?' David asked in bewilderment. 'You've never been in the business.'

'I can learn, David,' she answered with quiet determination. 'I intend to offer Janet Thurston a partnership. It will give her back a fair slice of her family heritage, and it will give me the chance to build something of my own.'

'It would give Janet back her Tears of God,' David murmured, then swivelled to Paul, leaning close to discuss the situation privately with him.

'It's a wonderful idea, Tamara,' Rory warmly approved. 'Janet will work her head off for this. It means so much.'

For a moment she allowed herself the luxury of feeling bathed in his love.

'A fine solution,' his grandfather agreed, nodding approval.

He turned to his sister, whose utter stillness cloaked her in some withdrawn inner world. Her sons' conversation did not impinge on it. Nor did she appear aware of anything

that had ensued since Tamara had unequivocally over-
turned the basis of her arguments.

'Ellie,' he called softly.

Her mouth compressed.

'Please listen to me.'

Her head turned marginally his way, her reluctance to
concede anything implicit in her bearing. Her eyes flicked at
him impatiently.

Her brother gestured an appeal. 'You must now see there
is no threat to everything you've worked for. Show that you
can be generous, too, Ellie. The Selby vineyard has no meaning to you in the same sense that Traverner has.'

Yes, let it be over, Tamara thought with a wave of longing. The soul sickness she had carried all these years needed
lifting. She wanted to come home. Paul had welcomed her.
David was accepting her.

Look at me, Mother, she wanted to cry. *If you could only have
accepted me as your daughter, not an intruder who threatened
your personal world, it could have been different. Was there really
a need for all this pain? I might not have been so bad if you'd let me
into your life. All I wanted was love. And the sense of belonging.*

But Eleanor didn't look at her. Her face suddenly twisted
in anger, her eyes flashing sharply at her brother. 'Don't you
realise it's breaking off an asset that belongs to the family
company?' she protested, scorning his plea for generosity. 'I
acquired the Selby vineyard for good reason. It provides us
with...'

The words rolled on, beating out the obsession for possession that still drove her, regardless of cost. Tamara couldn't
bear it. It was never ending.

She snapped.

'You can't let go, can you, Mother?'

It stopped the dreadful drum of words, but the controlling ice had melted in Tamara, releasing another torrent of
pent-up bitterness.

'You can't give anything up. Not fairly. Not squarely.

You'll cheat and you'll manipulate and you'll murder anything I care about, right to your grave. Your greed, your lies, your filthy ambition—'

'That's enough!' Paul cut in, rising to his feet.

Tamara looked wildly at him, not realising she was shaking. 'You don't understand,' she cried. 'You haven't lived through what I have.'

'No, I haven't,' he said gently. 'But it stops here, Tamara. You can trust both David and me to balance the ledger in all fairness to you. Please. I'm asking you, let our mother be now.'

The adrenaline-fired energy drained out of her as she looked at the woman who would deny her everything. There was no pleasure in the hatred she had borne for so long. No pleasure in vengeance. As for justice... Why had she ever thought she could wring that out of Eleanor? Her heart ached for what she had never had, never would have. Tears welled into her eyes.

'She is not my mother, Paul. She never was. I was only ever Max's daughter.'

The painful emptiness of loss was echoed in Paul's voice. 'I'm sorry you don't have the memories I have. I hope we can make good memories for you from now on. I'm not the brother you might have had, Tamara, but I am your brother. So is David.'

'Yes,' David gruffly agreed. 'I'm sorry for not...not—'

'Oh, it's not your fault, David,' she cried, and rolled her head wearily to Paul, who stood as his own person now, the brother who had extended his hand to her in fair friendship. 'So where do we go from here?'

Paul turned to his uncle, as Tamara had done earlier. 'Uncle Frank, will you accept the nomination for head of the company?'

The old man of the vineyards hesitated, glancing around their faces. 'If it's what you all want, then yes, I will, Paul.'

'Anyone against?'

No reply.

Eleanor shook her head as though she couldn't believe it was all being taken out of her hands swiftly and efficiently by one of her own sons.

'You're it, Uncle Frank,' Paul softly declared. 'Anyone against Tamara swapping her Traverner shares for the old Selby vineyard?'

No reply.

'That goes through, too.'

Rory stood, moving quickly to slide his arm around her shoulders and hug her close to him. It was good to feel his warmth and strength and love, knowing she could always lean on it.

Eleanor stared at them, her black eyes completely expressionless, looking straight through the coupling that had finally defeated her. Her face was pinched and pale, disturbingly lifeless. It was as though the driving force that had sustained her will to hold on had died.

Destroy...

Tamara shuddered. A death before death.

She hadn't meant to do it. The plan had been different today. Yet the gun had been loaded and the trigger had been pressed and this was the result.

'Ellie, would you like to go home now?' her brother asked caringly.

No reply. No sign he was heard.

He rose to his feet and shuffled around the table, gently squeezing her shoulder in concern. 'I'll help you,' he promised.

'Are you all right, Mum?' Paul asked anxiously, moving to her other side.

His voice penetrated. She flinched from him as though his nearness pained her. Paul hesitated, unsure what to do, the anguish of wanting to help stamped on his face.

'Frank?' A tremulous cry of need from Eleanor.

'I'm here for you, Ellie,' he answered.

She clutched at his arm, and he helped lift her to her feet. As she swayed shakily against him, he moved to support her with both arms.

Paul moved swiftly to the door, opening it wide. David hovered close by in case he was needed. Neither of them was spared so much as a glance.

Slowly, painfully, Frank Buchanan steered a steady course out of the boardroom. For his sister. Who was dying. Yet Eleanor had no word of reconciliation for any of them.

The battleground was silent.

It was over.

FORTY-SEVEN

Rory wasted no time getting Tamara out of the boardroom. She seemed drained of vitality, her body leaning limply against his as he swept her downstairs and out to the car park. He kept his arm around her, holding her close, uncaring what Cassie Deakin or anyone else thought. Tamara needed comfort. More than her energy had been depleted in that final, bitter outcry to her mother.

She made no protest when he helped her into the passenger seat of the Maserati. She sat listlessly passive while he fastened the seat belt for her. Her head rolled towards him, and she gave him a faint smile.

'Where are you taking me, Rory?'

'Home.'

They didn't speak during the short journey to his house on the hill above the valley. No quarrel about leaving her Porsche behind. No quibble over giving rise to gossip. They had moved beyond holding some discreet line. Being together was all that mattered.

He pulled the car up in the driveway outside his garage, wanting to take Tamara into his home by way of the front door.

'This is the house you shared with Louise,' she said flatly.

He met the slight query in her eyes with unflinching directness. 'She didn't share it. She lived here with me, but this house meant nothing to her. I had it built before I met Louise.'

Her smile was tinged with warmth this time. '*Your* home.'

'Yes.'

'You're taking me into it.'

'Yes.'

'*I'll* be happy to share it with you, Rory.'

He reached over and squeezed her hand. She had the air of a little girl lost, hauntingly vulnerable, trusting him to make everything right for her. 'It's been waiting for you, Tamara,' he said gently. 'As I have. All my life.'

She returned the squeeze. Tears filmed her eyes, adding a poignant brilliance to the swim of emotion. 'I need you. Without you, I'm nothing.'

Eleanor, still preying on her mind. The refusal to acknowledge the ultimate peacemaking offer—the handover of the Traverner shares—was the ultimate rejection and a denial of any truce between them. Eleanor, cruel tyrant, reviling Tamara to the end.

'You may feel that now, Tamara, but you could never be nothing.' He smiled to reassure her. 'You're a force to be reckoned with. Haven't you just shown that?'

She looked uncertain, disturbed. 'Maybe I went too far, Rory.'

'No. You did what you had to do. Don't torment yourself about it. Eleanor had it coming to her.'

'I left her with nothing.'

'That's not true. You gave her a chance. She could have accepted what you offered. She chose not to. She chose to turn her back on Paul and David, too. You didn't leave her with nothing, Tamara. She *chose* nothing rather than admit she was wrong.'

'What if I got it wrong, Rory?'

'You didn't. She couldn't deny any of it.'

She heaved a deep sigh, trying to unburden herself. 'I thought I wanted how it ended. But it was...awful.'

Eleanor, defeated, routed, finished. The lack of any concession from her underlined what Tamara had been up against all her life. Rory felt no pity for Eleanor, not an ounce of compassion for the woman who'd given none to her daughter.

'She's not alone as you were alone, Tamara,' he gently reminded her. 'She has my grandfather with her. He'll look after her.'

'Yes.' She sounded relieved. 'He's a good man, your grandfather.'

'I think so.'

'Decent. Like you.'

'You're not alone, either. You have me.'

It dragged her out of the darkness swirling through her mind, her eyes seeing only him and all he offered her. She managed a tremulous smile. 'Thank you for being here for me.'

'I always will be.'

He leaned over and kissed her, wishing he could root out the deep imprint of her years with Eleanor. He suspected it would never really be erased. All he could do was overlay it with the happiness he hoped to spread over the rest of her life. Bringing her home with him was a start. The house was something fresh and new to her. It would be new to him, too, with Tamara in it.

'Let's go inside,' he murmured.

'Yes,' she answered huskily.

They left the car and entered the house. Rory took her by the hand to lead her into his living room. She trailed slowly after him down the steps from the foyer, looking at the high, cathedral ceiling, warmly panelled in boxwood, then swinging her gaze to the wall of glass that overlooked the valley.

'It's wonderful, Rory. You must love walking out here in the morning.'

'Yes. The trees are full of birds then. And in the evening.'

She moved ahead of him, crossing the room to the floor-to-ceiling windows for a more comprehensive look at the view. Rory followed her, pleased and proud that her first impression was so positive.

'It's so...alive.'

'I'm glad you feel it, too.'

She turned and curled her arms around his neck, pressing her body into his. 'I need you to fill me, Rory. Now... please?'

Fill the sense of emptiness, the nothingness Eleanor had left her with, take her with him as he should have taken her with him at the end of that summer, away from Eleanor and his father. She wanted the healing joy of love, needed to feel it permeating her body and soul.

He kissed the lost child in her with tenderness, the woman in her with all the passionate love he'd held waiting for her, only for her. Her red dress of battle was thrown aside. He wanted her naked, newborn with him. He laid her on the sheepskin rug in front of the fireplace and filled her with all he was, giving until she felt replete and her eyes shone with happy contentment.

'We'll have a great life together, won't we?' she whispered.

'Every minute from now on,' he assured her.

'And this is our home.'

'Yes.' He grinned at her, happy that she was happy. 'Welcome home, my love.'

FORTY-EIGHT

Janet couldn't help smiling as she watched Tamara engage their waiter in a discussion of the sweet courses on the menu. She had never known anyone with such an amazing appetite for life and everything in it. Somehow it was infectious. She could hardly believe how much her own life had changed—infinitely for the better—since Tamara had swept into it.

Here she was at Robert's, arguably the finest restaurant amongst the vineyards in the Hunter Valley, celebrating the signing of the partnership papers with a superb lunch and having a marvellous time. It was typical of the warm and wonderful things that had been happening to her over the past two months.

Paul and David had both extended the hand of friendship. They were going to produce the Tears of God label for her this coming vintage, before the changeover of management of the Selby vineyard was effected. At Gabrielle's and Paul's invitation, she had shared Christmas dinner with the family, Eleanor having absented herself from any festive celebration. Sharon had insisted she come to her and David's New Year's Eve party. And there'd been so many exciting meetings with Rory and Tamara, setting up plans for the future.

She no longer felt lonely or depressed. Life was meaningful again. It had a new shape and purpose, something to work for, something to dream about, something to achieve. She still missed Jim, but she knew he would be happy for her. It had deeply distressed him that his illness had been so draining on her, in every sense, but especially the financial aspect, leaving her with nothing but insurmountable debts. He would be blessing Tamara for what she'd done.

'Janet, you'll have to help me out,' Tamara said with a wistful sigh. 'I fancy the orange gateau with chocolate sauce, but my friend here—' she inclined her head at the hovering waiter '—reckons the passionfruit mousse with the raspberry coulis is to die for.'

Janet laughed. 'Okay. Order them both and we'll swap half each.'

'You don't mind? If you really want something else...'

'I don't care. I'm happy to taste whatever's put in front of me.'

Tamara laughed and handed the menu to the waiter. 'There's a recommendation for you.'

'Thank you, madam.'

'Our pleasure,' Janet replied and heaved a contented sigh as the waiter left them alone again.

'Feeling good?' Tamara teased.

'Feeling somewhat bloated. I'm not sure I can fit any more in.'

'You'll be tempted.'

'Undoubtedly.' Her gaze roved over the massive beams and open rafters that supported the vast ceiling and dropped to the huge sandstone fireplace at the end of the room. 'I love this place. Great ambience. Great food.'

'Great occasion,' Tamara chimed in.

'Yes. Especially for me, Tamara. It's like being handed back my life.' Janet looked at her quizzically. 'Do you mind telling me why you decided to do it?'

She winced. 'A long story, Janet, and not a happy one. Let's just call this a new start. For both of us.'

'You didn't really need me,' Janet quietly persisted, too curious about Tamara's motives to let the matter drop entirely.

Tamara looked at Janet consideringly, her brilliant black eyes losing their sparkle, the fascinating mobility of her vibrant face oddly still. When she spoke, her tone was deeply pensive, as though she drew the words from a level of knowledge she rarely examined.

'Needs come from reasons that don't always make sense to other people. I trust you, Janet. You're like Rory in many ways. It makes me feel secure having you as my partner.'

Trust was important, Janet reasoned, yet she had the feeling there were far more layers to Tamara's reply than she was revealing. She couldn't be speaking of financial security. Her inherited wealth from Max was substantial, and she had Rory's backing, as well. Janet wondered if it was emotional security Tamara sought. Most of her life seemed to have been barren of it.

Eleanor. It all revolved around her. Janet was sure of it. With Eleanor's retirement from the scene, the shift of power that had emerged was the talk of the whole district, let alone the vineyards involved. But it was more than that. It was as though the doors of a prison had opened wide.

Tamara had blossomed into a different person. Rory was happier than Janet had ever seen him. Paul and David seemed to have taken a new lease on their lives. The Big House... Janet broke into laughter.

The sparkle came back to Tamara's eyes. 'What's so funny?'

'The Big House being turned into a church.' Janet shook her head in bemusement. 'I'm amazed Eleanor is allowing Irene to do it.'

Tamara shrugged. 'I doubt she knows. She's not seeing

anyone but Uncle Frank, and I don't think he cares to talk about Irene.'

'Surely her sons...'

'No. She won't see them, either. Complete shut-out.' She grimaced. 'Neither Paul nor David toed her line. She won't forgive them that.'

'But she's dying.' Janet found it difficult to comprehend anyone retaining such a cold, relentless attitude when there was so little time left. Yet when had Dame Eleanor ever shown finer feelings?

Again Tamara sobered into that odd stillness. 'It's not over until she does die,' she said flatly. 'Who knows what she might still do?'

Eleanor had certainly not imbued everyone with peace and light in her lifetime, Janet thought. 'I'm sorry. Let's talk about happier things. The wedding. And the baby. You're obviously not suffering too much from morning sickness.'

Tamara brightened. 'Rory takes care of it. He brings me a cup of tea and biscuits in bed each morning. That was Sharon's advice, and it works.'

'I bet Rory loves doing it, too.'

She laughed, glowing with happy pleasure. 'He's so determined to make everything right for me. This insistence on a proper wedding with all the frills is hardly appropriate.'

'Come on, Tamara, it's every girl's dream. Rory wouldn't do you out of it.'

'But me in full bridal regalia?'

'You'll look beautiful. Besides, you've always been the bride of Rory's heart.'

'Oh, Janet!' Her eyes glistened with a sheen of moisture. 'That's a lovely thing to say.'

'It's true. So you can't do him out of his dream.'

A big sigh. 'Well, you're going to have to help me get it right. I'll probably need advice on everything.'

And she didn't have a mother who would give it. If Janet

could have spat in Eleanor's eye at that moment, she would have. Tamara hadn't had a mother worth shit, as far as she could see.

The waiter returned with the ordered sweet courses, and they looked divine. Janet was certainly tempted. Their taste more than lived up to their presentation, a delightful end to a superb meal.

Over coffee, Janet listed what had to be considered for a proper wedding. Rory had set the date, the first Saturday in March. The grapes would have been picked by then, all going well, and the wineries would be in full production. It was only two months away. Time would fly by. Shopping trips were planned.

They left the restaurant in a happy mood, strolling down the covered walkway to the adjoining cottage, a historic landmark at Pepper Tree. Built in 1876, it was kept as a museum of the furniture and lifestyle of the pioneers in the valley. They wandered into the old sitting room, commenting on the low doorways and little windows.

'People must have been shorter in the last century,' was Tamara's opinion.

In the dining room, a well-worn butcher's block was set on a sideboard. Janet ran her fingers over the smooth dips in the wood. 'This has seen a lot of carving.'

'Mm. Yet it's still so solid. They built things with a sense of permanence, didn't they?'

'They were here to stay,' Janet murmured. 'Like my family.'

'I've never had a sense of roots. You have, don't you, Janet?'

'Yes.' She smiled wryly. 'That's why it hurt so much when I had to sell up.'

Tamara nodded. 'Whatever happens, you'll stay on now. That's the good thing about our partnership. It's rooted in permanence.' Her smile was wry. 'As much as anything can be.'

'What are you afraid of, Tamara?' The words were out before the thought had really formed in Janet's mind. It was more an intuitive feeling.

'Nothing, really.' She shrugged. 'It's silly. I just have this sense that everything is too good to last. For me, I mean. Not for you, Janet. You have the kind of solidity that is permanent. It's innate in you somehow.' This time her smile was warm. 'It's what I feel about you, anyway.'

'You can count on me, Tamara. I promise you,' Janet replied seriously.

'I know. And it's good to know.'

'I have so much to thank you for.'

She laughed. 'Now don't start that again. Let's go. It's a beautiful afternoon, and I refuse to maunder over the past when we've got so much to look forward to.'

Janet followed her into the hall. The light was dim near the front door. As Tamara reached for the knob, her head and shoulders were outlined against the small-paned window set in the door. Maybe it was the effect of her black hair. Janet had the weird feeling of seeing a dark figure peering out at the light, yet imprisoned in a darkness from which there was no escape. It clutched at her heart and sent a shiver down her spine.

Then the illusion—or whatever it was—broke into fanciful nonsense as Tamara opened the door and walked into the bright afternoon sunshine. All the same, Janet had to give herself a mental shake to get rid of it, and the chill of it didn't leave her until they were walking over the ornamental bridge at the end of the garden.

The summer heat beat down on them. The sky was a brilliant blue and completely cloudless. The built up flowerbed in the centre of the roundabout in front of them was a blaze of colour. There was no darkness, nothing to worry about.

It's Eleanor, Janet reasoned, thinking back over various things Tamara had revealed. Eleanor had cast some pall over Tamara's life, and it wouldn't be dispelled until she was dead and buried. Three of the four months the doctors had given her were gone. Janet hoped Eleanor would prove the doctors right. It would be good to have Tamara and Rory's wedding completely free of that woman.

FORTY-NINE

Eleanor sat on the veranda, watching the grape pickers move along the rows of old vines, harvesting by hand, just as she and Richard had done, side by side, all those years ago. She no longer had the strength to walk to the bench where he had died. There was a limited vintage that year. This was the last vintage for her. She wondered if Paul would remember it. Treasure it. Mark it for special family occasions.

Painful thought. She had enough pain without yearning for the love and respect her sons had once shown her. At least there was no need to stay alert any more, denying herself the relief the tablets brought. They took the edge off everything. She could let her mind drift into dreams, not think of the present at all. Better to remember the good times.

The carer who was keeping watch over her stirred from her chair. 'I think I'll have a cup of tea. Would you like one, Dame Eleanor?'

She nodded. The carer's name eluded her for a moment. Penny. That was it. There were three of them now. Penny and Robyn and Clare. It was too much for any one person, seeing to all her needs twenty-four hours a day, seven days a week. Clare did three days, Penny and Robyn two days each. She liked Clare best. Penny tended to be a bit of a busy bee. Kind-hearted though.

The Angel-On-Call service that supplied the carers was well named. Only an angel would take on this kind of work—washing, showering, toileting, dressing, massaging, fetching and carrying. Their presence took some of the emotional load off Frank and Wilma, as well. She could insist only the hired angels see her at her worst times. It helped in retaining her sense of dignity as a person.

Wilma fussed over tempting her appetite, trying to concoct tasty and interesting meals. It was her way of caring. Bill brought freshly cut flowers from the gardener at the Big House to give her the pleasure of them. Good people. And Frank was always here for her whenever she wanted his company. He was her anchor. He had promised she would have her wish to die here. Near Richard. No hospital at the end.

It was Frank who brought her the cup of tea. 'Told Penny I'd sit with you for a while,' he said, settling into the chair the carer had vacated.

She smiled. 'It's a beautiful morning.'

He nodded, his gaze moving to the grape pickers. 'The last of the old rows. They'll be done today.'

'Yes. The last rows,' she echoed with sad finality.

'They're only vines, Ellie. They shouldn't mean more to you than your children,' he said quietly.

She shook her head. 'My life is wrapped up in those vines, Frank. My life and death.'

'They won't weep for you. Or weep for what might have been.' He heaved a long sigh and looked at her with uncompromising purpose. 'I know you've been holding on to see the grapes picked again, and I have a feeling you'll let go now. I have to tell you, Ellie, it's not right to leave your children with pain in their hearts.'

'I don't want to talk about them, Frank.'

'Then I guess I'm asking you to listen, Ellie.'

Easier to block him out than argue, she decided, turning her gaze to the vineyard again.

'Rory and Tamara are getting married this Saturday.'

It meant nothing to her.

'The wedding is to be held at Peppers Guest House. Four o'clock in the afternoon.'

A wedding? Probably Tamara's way of thumbing her nose at everyone. Her pregnancy must be showing by now. What was it, four, five months?

'They're going to have a marriage celebrant conduct the ceremony on the front lawn, just by the reception area. All the family will be there, Ellie. I could arrange for the Daimler to park quite close.'

The Daimler? For her? It was going to be extremely tiresome if Frank was intent on persuading her to attend.

'It would be a gesture that wouldn't cost you much,' he pressed on in gentle appeal. 'A silent blessing, if you like. No need to talk to anyone. Just you being there would mean a lot, Ellie.'

A lot to whom? she thought bitterly. Paul and David had gone their own way. Tamara and Rory wouldn't give a hoot. Her grandchildren were too young to understand. Frank... She grimaced. She supposed it meant a lot to Frank. A family wedding, peace and goodwill, sins forgiven.

'We all make mistakes,' he said heavily. 'Some we can't ever make right again.'

That was true enough. Impossible to turn back the clock. Too late to change anything now.

'Like Ian.'

The mention of Ian set her nerves on edge. What did Frank mean by bringing up his son now? He never spoke of him.

'I often think about the burden of guilt he carried to his death.'

Shock knifed through her. Had Rory told Frank about Ian?

'How terrible he must have felt in those last moments. The despair, the self-loathing...'

Her heart sank. He knew. And his sadness hurt. It sounded like an old sadness he'd kept to himself for a long, long time. Yet how could that be?

'I know you covered it up to spare me, Ellie. To spare everyone from a shameful scandal. But I've got to say this now. It wasn't Tamara's fault.'

Her hands curled around the ends of the armrests on her chair, gripping tight. Was he about to place the blame on her shoulders? Guilt speared through her, sharpening the pain.

'The day before Ian's funeral, I came across Tamara, crying her heart out,' Frank went on, oblivious to her tension. 'I couldn't get much sense out of her at first. Only the words, "It's my fault. It's my fault." I tried to comfort her. I don't think she remembers spilling it out to me, what my son had done and why she thought it was her fault he had died.'

His voice halted, the knowledge too oppressive even now to speak of it easily. The revelation that it was Tamara who had told him dazed and confused Eleanor. Tamara, before the funeral. And Frank had stood at his son's graveside, knowing it had been suicide, knowing why. He had known all these years and never once spoken or even hinted what he knew.

He sighed heavily. His hand moved in an agitated gesture. 'I was too shocked to help her, Ellie. I let her run away from me. I couldn't ease her shame or her guilt. I couldn't give her back her innocence. I did nothing.'

Shame and guilt. His voice was loaded with it. For being passive. While she... No, she wasn't going to think about the actions she had taken. She had justified them all at the time. What was the point in letting them get at her now?

'When you took Tamara away from here, I thought it was for the best,' Frank went on, his tone one of sad self-mockery. 'A chance to put it all behind her. Time to recover and lead a normal life.'

Relief eased her torment. He didn't blame her for Ian's death. It was only Tamara who concerned him.

'I was wrong.' Pain threaded his voice. 'The hurt went too deep. I didn't know what to do to fix it. She wouldn't let any of us near her. Every time she came home it was like a wounded animal lashing out indiscriminately.'

Evocative words, painting a picture she hadn't really seen before. Whenever she had looked at Tamara, all she had ever seen was black, burning hatred.

'I didn't know about the abortion. I guess you thought it was best at the time. But it must have added to the hurt, Ellie.'

She frowned. It would have been obscene to have Ian's child and pretend it was Rory's. Tamara had accepted that in the end. Why should it have hurt? Yet the hard, flat, chilling expression in her eyes when it was over...

'You were a grown woman when you decided not to have the last baby,' Frank went on, not handing down any moral judgment, just stating the case. 'Tamara was only fourteen. A very impressionable age.'

Fourteen. Had age ever been relevant to Tamara?

'She was wounded, Ellie. Terribly wounded. I think Rory's love is healing her now. I hope so. It grieves me to think of what my son did to her. If my grandson can make her whole again, I can rest easier.'

Tears pricked her eyes. No wonder Frank had approved of Rory and Tamara getting together again. She hadn't realised, hadn't known the burden he'd carried all these years, letting her think she had spared him, suffering in silence, keeping his own counsel. As he'd always done. Frank never gave advice unless asked for it. Though he'd been breaking that personal rule recently, trying to get her to see things his way.

Maybe she should.

He'd given her so much, asking very little in return.

'I want you to rest easier, too. I've got to tell you, Ellie, it was wrong what you did in the boardroom, telling Tamara you wished she'd never been born. Even if you felt it, it was wrong to say it. That girl was crying out for acceptance from you—'

'No!' She turned sharply to him, anger welling up and re-butting his interpretation of what had happened. He couldn't change her view there. It was too stark a memory. 'I won't let you lay that on me, Frank. Tamara was systematically destroying me in front of my sons. And they let her do it.'

He shook his head. 'Rightly or wrongly, she was defending herself. And she gave up her holding in Traverner to appease you.'

'Her hatred of me is so extreme she even went searching through medical records to prove—' she shied away from calling herself a liar and a cheat '—her distorted version of the truth.'

'Was it so distorted, Ellie?' he asked quietly.

'No-one has the right to ask a woman to have a child she doesn't want,' she defended.

He nodded. 'We make mistakes. Then we have to live with them. But an innocent child shouldn't bear the brunt of them, Ellie. Tamara didn't know she was a mistake when you brought her into this world. She's been deeply scarred by knowing it ever since.' He paused, then pointedly added, 'And that wasn't her fault, either. It's time you faced it, Ellie, and made what amends you can.'

She gave a derisive laugh. 'You think going to her wedding will fix everything?'

He sighed and said nothing for a while, staring off into the distance. Eleanor silently fought the ferment of guilt he had stirred. She didn't want to think about it.

'You know, Ellie, Tamara is the one most like you, even to looking for ways around things.'

The comment startled her. 'Tamara...like me?'

Her question drew a sad, ironic smile. 'She's your daugh-

ter. More than your sons are your sons. Paul is like his father. David favours me. Tamara is so like you it sometimes
takes my breath away.'

She stared at him incredulously.

He shook his head at her blindness. 'Her eyes are your
eyes. She has the same black hair you had when you were
young. She's busily organizing everyone, just as you used to
do. She looks at Rory as you once looked at Richard. Energy
radiates from her. Your energy, Ellie. She's all fired up to
make a success of her venture with Janet.'

Max's daughter, she corrected fiercely.

It was as though Frank read her mind. '*Your* daughter. Let
her feel it before you die, Ellie. You do owe her that,' he said
earnestly.

How could she make Tamara feel it when she didn't feel
it herself? Frank was asking the impossible.

'As for Paul and David, Tamara didn't destroy their feeling for you. You've turned them away from you, Ellie, time
and time again, even on Christmas day.'

'It's just another day, Frank,' she snapped.

'No. No, it's not,' he said slowly. 'It's a day for family,
Ellie. It always has been. It always will be. You should have
let them have this last Christmas with you. I know they disappointed you, but...' He paused, then quietly posed the
question. 'Was that their mistake or yours, Ellie?'

Mine, she conceded reluctantly.

'I've been listening to them these past few months. I think
you'd be proud of them if you gave them the chance to be
themselves with you. You'll be leaving Richard's vineyard
in good hands, believe me.'

He was right. Paul was a fine winemaker, and David had
a good head for business.

'Isn't that what you wanted, Ellie? For Richard's sons to
carry on their father's work?' Frank softly prompted.
'Wasn't that what it was all about? For the Traverner line to
go on?'

Yes. Yes, it was, put simply like that. She frowned, feeling crowded by all the other factors Frank was dismissing.

'It's what you've got, Ellie, so why not let the rest go?' he pressed.

The humiliation of defeat burned through her. Tamara making a fool of her, Paul going against her, David letting her down. Pride refused to admit them into her life again. It would be conceding the dreadful debacle in the boardroom was her fault. Too many mistakes to face. Too much pain.

'Let me be, Frank,' she demanded tersely.

He slowly heaved himself to his feet. 'I'm sorry, Ellie. Had to get it off my chest. I'll say no more.'

It was typical of him. He'd said his piece. He was leaving her to live with it. And die with it if she chose.

'I'll go and fetch Penny for you.'

The carer. Who didn't really care in the deepest sense. She couldn't. Getting involved with terminal patients would be too depressing. Her job was to make a dying woman's last days as comfortable as she could.

Frank cared. He wanted to make things right for her before she died. Futile task. There was no medicine for sickness of the soul. Only death could end that. But after death, what then? Was there an afterlife? Rory's curse on her slid into her mind. Would Ian's spirit and that of the aborted child haunt her through eternity? And what of Max? Would she have to answer to him for what she'd done...and not done?

Richard. She clutched at the name, using it as a mantra of protection. Richard would understand. He would forgive the mistakes she had made. She hadn't meant any harm. Not really. She had only done what had to be done to make the vineyard safe for his sons.

Paul and David. They had it now. They didn't need her any more. Tamara had let it go. Appeasing her, Frank said. The one most like her.

She shook her head. Better not to think about that. Tamara

had always been her dark nemesis, haunting her with hatred. Or was she a wounded animal lashing out?

Pain in their hearts.

The child most like her.

Pain...

The Jilton Witch 355

345 Sir Ralph's a studied smile falling away
face in their hands.
His wild tremulous
Julia

FIFTY

'Do you, Rory Francis Buchanan, take this woman...'

Rory smiled. Not so much a woman as an incredibly beautiful, almost fey flowerchild from some other era, dressed in exquisite lace and satin ribbons with a circlet of miniature roses in her hair.

'Tamara Ellen Vandelier...'

Ellen? He'd never known her second name. Who had called her after her mother?

'To be your lawful wedded wife...'

His heart swelled with happiness. His true wife. Not like the contract with Louise.

'For richer for poorer, in sickness and in health...'

He thought of Janet and Jim and knew his love for Tamara would transcend any adversity that came their way.

'Till death do you part?'

Not even death could part them, Rory thought. Their souls were entwined forever. The child in Tamara's womb carried the promise of their mingled genes to the next generation and the next, marching into the future.

'I do,' he said, his eyes shining with love.

'Do you, Tamara Ellen Vandelier, take this man...'

He loved her. He truly did. Above and beyond all the bad

things she'd done. None of it mattered. He saw her as she had always craved to be seen, the dream of herself in another life. But the dream was here and now, in his eyes.

'Rory Francis Buchanan...'

Her heart beat a joyous refrain. Rory...Rory...Rory.

'To be your lawful wedded husband...'

The only one. And she was free to love him. This decent man. Her husband. The father of her child.

'For richer, for poorer, in sickness and in health...'

He'd loved her through the worst there could ever be for them. What they had now was indestructible. He'd proved it to her.

'Till death do you part?'

For a chilling moment, the bright confidence in her mind was dimmed. A black void swept in. Her eyes clung to Rory's, and his golden light pushed it away. He would hold her safe. They belonged together. They had a home. And they were going to have their very own family.

'I do,' she said, and smiled in a glorious burst of happiness.

'I now pronounce you man and wife.'

Gabrielle had to blink back a rush of tears as Rory swept Tamara into an ardent embrace and they kissed, sealing the promises they had made to each other. The crowd of guests who had stood on the lawn for the brief ceremony broke into clapping and murmurs of pleasure. Everything was beautiful.

Tamara, who was usually earthy, looked positively ethereal in the exquisite lace and beribboned dress, and Rory had the strong, handsome air of a golden lion claiming his bride. Around them the flowerbeds were a mass of magnificent colour, marigolds under the jacaranda tree, pastel petunias mixed with blue and white salvia, clumps of cosmos. The path to the wisteria-covered arbour where the photographs were to be taken was bordered by rosebushes, their deep red blooms scenting the air.

'Mum's here.'

Paul and Gabrielle turned startled faces to David. Gabrielle's heart fluttered. Was it good news or bad? Could Eleanor still dominate in the last days of her life?

David nodded towards the driveway. 'Look for yourselves. The Daimler pulled up just as the ceremony started. Uncle Frank is with her. He's getting out of the car now.'

They watched, Gabrielle in considerable trepidation, as the old man headed across the lawn to Rory and Tamara. It couldn't be for another dreadful showdown, she reasoned wildly. Frank Buchanan might have a simple heart and a simple mind, but he was no fool.

'I'm going over,' David said, a determined set to his face.

'No.' Gabrielle shot out a hand to stop him.

'Dammit, Gabrielle! It's probably our only chance to make peace with her.'

'Don't jump in, David,' she advised urgently. 'Uncle Frank is coming for Tamara. It's her day.'

'But...' He looked distressed and anxious.

Paul clasped his shoulder. 'We can follow. We're her brothers.'

Please let it be good, Gabrielle prayed, as she turned to watch Frank Buchanan greet the newlyweds—his grandson, his new granddaughter-in-law. Let it be a gracious gift. *Let it be fair. As fair as this day should be for Tamara.*

Eleanor felt her heart contract as they approached the car, Rory looking grimly protective, Tamara... How strange she should choose a dress so like the one for her own wedding to Richard, the handkerchief-point skirt edged with satin ribbon, the lace sleeves caught prettily with ribbons at the elbow. The photographs of her first wedding had never been on show after her marriage to Max. Impossible for

Tamara to have seen them. She looked just like—Eleanor closed her eyes in pain—her daughter.

The car door opened. 'Ellie.' A warning plea from Frank.

She took a deep breath and opened her eyes. Tamara slid onto the seat beside her. No hatred today, but her expression was wary, watchful, waiting for the reason behind the summons.

'Thank you for giving me this time,' Eleanor started stiffly.

'Uncle Frank asked me to,' came the blunt reply.

It was no more than she could expect, given their history together. Eleanor tried to loosen her voice to a more appealing tone. 'I'm sorry your father isn't here to see you. Max would have been very proud of you, Tamara.'

She wasn't touched. 'It's kind of you to say so.'

'He was a kind and generous man. He was not unhappy with me, you know.'

'I know. I tried to compete with you for his attention. I always failed.'

'He did love you, Tamara.'

She said nothing. They both knew where Max's attention had been directed and why. Eleanor recognised whatever she said now would be too little, too late. The reaching-out point had passed, unfulfilled. She remembered Richard once saying there were three things that could never be taken back—the spoken word, the shot arrow and the lost opportunity. A multitude of those lay between herself and Tamara.

She touched the lacquered box she had brought with her, the one hope of something that might be shared, might be found acceptable, a link. 'I thought you might like the jewellery Max gave me. You are his daughter.'

'He bought it for you, not me.'

'I would like to give it to you.'

Tamara shook her head. 'I want nothing to remind me of

those years.' Her eyes were softly mocking. 'I don't expect you to understand, but I feel reborn today.'

Free of the past to which Eleanor was tied.

She did understand.

She had given nothing. There was nothing. It had gone beyond amends, beyond apology and forgiveness. She had created the void between them, and it was unbridgeable. She made the effort to give up graciously.

'Then I can only wish you and Rory a long life and happiness together.'

Tamara's black eyes intensified as they searched for a gleam or flicker of anything other than sincerity. 'Thank you,' she said at last, her voice little more than a husky whisper. 'I wish... I wish it could have been different.'

Eleanor managed a rueful smile. 'My mistake. Thank you for giving Traverner to Paul and David, Tamara.'

'It's their roots,' she dismissed quickly. 'Will you speak to them? They need—'

'Yes. But only briefly. I won't spoil your new birthday.'

'I'm glad you came—' a shaky little smile, the glisten of tears '—to give me good wishes. Thank you.'

She ducked out of the car.

No goodbye.

'Paul, David,' Tamara called, 'come and say hello to your mother.'

Your mother.

Disowned as Tamara had been disowned.

But it was justice, not hatred. Eleanor knew she had to let it go at that. There was no other choice. For the first time in her life, she regretted, truly regretted the course she had taken with Tamara. The bond of hatred might have been a bond of love she could have held precious. Frank was right. Of her three children, the daughter she had spurned was most like her.

* * *

Rory hugged Tamara close as they walked up the path to the arbour. 'Are you all right?' he murmured, watching the Daimler move off, taking Eleanor back to her refuge.

'Yes.' She gave him a shining look. No shadows. 'She doesn't hate me any more. I'm free, Rory.'

He laughed, relieved and elated that Tamara at last felt released from the oppression of her mother's ill will. 'You're not free of me, my love. We've just tied an irrevocable knot.'

'But that's how we want it. And she even wished us a long life and happiness together.'

He swung her around to face him, wanting to drink in the incandescent beauty of her vibrant face. 'I'll always carry this image of you,' he promised. 'When we're old and grey, I'll still see you like this, Tamara. My bride, my wife, on our wedding day.'

'Mind that you do, Rory Buchanan.' She laughed. 'I'll settle for you remembering it for the next few months as I get lumpier and lumpier with our baby.'

'More and more beautiful with our baby.'

'Well, just for insurance, we're going to have a lot of photos taken. What we're going to have from now on are good memories, Rory.'

'Yes,' he heartily agreed. 'Only good memories.'

FIFTY-ONE

Paul left it until eleven o'clock to visit his mother. Usually by then she was resting comfortably. When he arrived at the old homestead he sought out his uncle first, finding him on the back veranda, perusing the newspaper.

'How's Mum this morning, Uncle Frank?'

'Ah, Paul.' He smiled benevolently. 'A fairly peaceful night. She'll be pleased to see you.'

'Okay to go right in, then?'

'Yes, I would think so. The nurse is sitting by your mother's bed. Might be an idea to check with her.'

Paul waved an acknowledgment and headed for his mother's bedroom. He tapped lightly on the door before opening it and stepping inside. The room had a hospital air about it, a mobile tray stacked with medicines, a stand for the morphine drip his mother controlled, an oxygen machine with a tube running to a ventilator mask, all supervised by a registered nurse in a starched white uniform.

His mother's eyes were closed, and she lay completely still, so fragile now, barely more than skin and bone. It felt terribly wrong, this dragged-out process of dying, the gradual diminishment of the woman she had been. It would have been more merciful if she had gone at four months, as the doctors had predicted. Yet if there hadn't been the extra time with her... Paul couldn't help feeling grateful to have had the opportunity to forge a new understanding, a closer relationship than they'd ever had before. It was the same for David.

The nurse gave him a nod and a smile and vacated her chair beside the bed, gesturing for him to take it. Unless requested to stay, she always left the room to allow for private visits, although the door remained ajar for an urgent call to be heard.

The photographs on the bedside table caught Paul's eye as he moved quietly forward. They were something new. There was a lovely shot of Tamara on her wedding day. But the other... He frowned. His parents on their wedding day? He couldn't remember having seen it before. It was definitely a bridal photograph, though, with his mother wearing a short veil and carrying a bouquet.

He paused by the chair, suddenly struck by the similarities in the photographs. Tamara looked like his mother. Their dresses almost matched in style, and they had the same luminous expression on their faces. He picked up the frames, comparing the two young women with a sense of wonder that he had never noticed how alike they were.

'It shows how much she is my daughter, doesn't it?'

The rueful comment tugged at him. His mother's eyes were open, alive and alert.

'Do you want to see Tamara, Mum?' he asked directly. 'If I asked her to come, I think she would.'

An ironic smile. 'We've said our goodbyes, Paul.'

He privately acknowledged there was no meeting ground. Too much between them. He found it a sad situation, but there was nothing he could do. Neither of them wanted to talk about it.

'Is she still happy?'

'Very,' he quickly affirmed. 'The three of them—Gabrielle, Sharon and Tamara—have tripped off to

Newcastle today to buy baby things.' He smiled. 'No doubt they'll drool over them.'

'Yes. It's an exciting time. The first baby.' Her eyes clouded. 'I hope there won't be any complications with the birth.'

'Why should there be?'

Her eyelids drooped. Her fingers plucked at the bed-clothes. She looked sad. 'It would be terrible if she lost the baby.'

Paul sat and took her frail, fretting hand in his, warmly fondling it. He knew she was thinking of the abortion, the physical and emotional effect it might have had on Tamara. Whatever the rights and wrongs of that decision, it couldn't be changed now. He tried to ease the guilt she felt.

'You mustn't worry, Mum. Everything's fine. Gabrielle would have told me if Tamara was having any medical problems. They talk incessantly about the pregnancy.'

His mother slowly relaxed. 'I'm glad she's got someone to talk to.'

'You can rest assured of that, Mum.'

Her gaze flicked to him. 'I rewrote my will, Paul. As you said, Tamara should get the Big House. I know she won't want it, but I've left it to her. Perhaps you could suggest to her it would bring in a good income as a function centre. Or whatever.'

'Yes, well...' He took a deep breath. 'We have a problem there, Mum. As a matter of fact, it's one of the things I want to discuss with you. I received a quote from a plumber this morning. Irene wants to tear up some of the ballroom and put in a pool.'

'What?' Blank incredulity.

Paul winced and explained. 'In the past six months she's turned the place into a sort of a temple. Now she wants a pool for people to walk into and have their sins washed away.'

His mother rolled her eyes. 'Mad as a hatter. We'll have to get her out.'

Paul raised his eyebrows. 'Easier said than done. You've let her have free rein all this time. She thinks the place is hers, possession being nine-tenths of the law.'

'Ridiculous! I'll deal with it right now. Get me the Big House on that phone, Paul.'

He smiled. It was good to see she was her old imperious self again. He pressed the necessary buttons, and after a few moments a voice answered.

'Mother Irene's Temple. This is Sister Shirley speaking. How may I help you?'

'Good God!' The appalled words fell out. His mother's eyes rounded in glazed horror, then narrowed with blazing purpose. 'This is Dame Eleanor Vandelier, the owner of your so-called temple. You will fetch Mother Irene to this telephone immediately, Sister Shirley.'

'Oh! Yes, Dame Eleanor. Right away, Dame Eleanor.' The words came out in jerky gasps, followed by the click of the receiver being put down.

His mother glared at him. 'That puffed-up, prurient preacher! I gave her the means to hold her precious prayer meetings, and she makes a Hollywood production of it!'

Paul barely smothered a grin. His mother was certainly back to form, however briefly. He hoped it wouldn't drain too much of what little energy she had. He refrained from comment, allowing her to regain her breath for the next salvo. The brilliant flash of her eyes told him she was working up to it.

Shirley Doggitt's voice issued forth again. 'Dame Eleanor, I'm terribly sorry. Mother Irene said she can't speak to an unrepentant sinner, but she'll pray you'll be redeemed be-fore—um, before...'

'Sister Shirley, you tell Mother Irene I'll have the police there before this day is out to evict the lot of you. If that doesn't fetch her to the phone, believe you me—' her teeth were gnashing '—you'd better start packing.'

'Oh! Oh!' It sounded as though Sister Shirley was in danger of swallowing her tongue. 'I'll tell her,' she gobbled. The receiver was dropped with a clunk this time.

'If you want them out, I'll handle it, Mum,' Paul soothed. 'No need for you to get all worked up.'

'That witch of a woman needs burning at the stake,' she fumed. 'Her and her damned candles. That's what killed Louise, you know. It was a pity Irene didn't go with her.'

Paul preferred to let that incident slip into bygones. 'It's not worth getting upset, Mum. Tell me what you want done, and I'll do it.'

'No. I put Irene there. She'll hear it from me. Then you can see my will is carried out, Paul.'

Steely resolve.

Paul didn't argue, but he was concerned. Her colour was up, and she was clearly stressed. He wondered if he should fetch the nurse. Then Irene's voice galvanised both of them.

'I will not allow you to threaten my people, Eleanor.'

'Then get them and yourself out of my house, Irene,' his mother retorted with blistering authority. 'You have abused my hospitality, taking advantage of my illness to play God. It stops now.'

'Blasphemer! This is the temple of Jehovah, and you have no power over it. I am His servant, and He has given it unto me to hold it sacred.'

The scornful defiance was like a red rag to a bull. Paul could see his mother metaphorically pawing the ground, nostrils steaming. 'You raving hypocrite! God would spit in your eye before he gave you anything. You hear me and you hear me good!'

'He will shrivel your filthy tongue. He will strike you dead.'

It sparked the charge. 'He can strike me dead as soon as he likes, and I'll be grateful for it. But it won't make a blind bit of difference to you, Irene. The Big House will go to Tamara. That's my will, and my will shall be done.'

'The whore...'

'Say one more word against Tamara and you'll be out of there tonight, emulating the lilies of the field.' Eleanor's head came up. 'I suggest you apply yourself to finding some other temple to ply your sick brand of religion. I'll give you one week, Irene.' Her eyes flared with savage satisfaction as she elaborated. 'Seven days to create another world for yourself somewhere else. There's a godly act for you.'

'You mock—'

'I'll do more than mock. If you're not gone from the Big House by then, you'll be evicted. Those are my orders.'

She signalled to Paul to disconnect. He did it swiftly. She was gasping for breath. He reached for the ventilator mask, switched on the oxygen and helped settle the mask over her nose and mouth. 'I'll get the nurse,' he said.

She grasped his wrist and shook her head, staying him. He waited, worrying that the effort of taking control had proved too much for her and she might collapse and die in front of him. Her eyes clung to his, commanding his acquiescence to her wish. He gently stroked her arm, needing to touch, to show his caring.

'I love you, Mum,' he said softly. 'I shouldn't have let you do that.'

She dragged her other hand up and pulled the mask below her chin. 'My mistake. Did me good to fix it. Had to make it free. For Tamara.'

'I'll make sure of it, Mum. Rest now.'

'Yes. Love you, too.'

'I know.'

She fumbled with the mask.

He helped her adjust it then leaned over and kissed her forehead. 'Bye for now, Mum. Take care.'

Her hand trailed from his and she closed her eyes. Paul waited a few more moments. She seemed all right. He left quietly and found the nurse in the kitchen with Wilma Guthrie. He gave her a quick report and she hurried to the bedroom to keep watch.

Paul stepped to the back veranda before leaving. 'You'll let me know if Mum wants me, won't you, Uncle Frank?'

The newspaper rustled. 'You can count on me, Paul. Any trouble?'

'No. No trouble.'

He gave his uncle a goodbye salute, privately hoping that Irene would give him trouble. Booting her out of the Big House would bring him considerable satisfaction.

FIFTY-TWO

Die, die, die... The command throbbed in Irene's mind, gathering power. Eleanor would not live out the hour, let alone a day or a week. She had defied and mocked Jehovah. Even before the blasphemer had finished speaking, the breath was being sucked out of her. Irene had heard the gasping.

Eleanor was a dead woman.

But Tamara... Irene's exultation fragmented as it was hit by the memory of Tamara bursting into her cottage like an evil whirlwind, using the power of darkness to torment and confuse and tempt like the daughter of Satan she was. A sword to cut down those who had deprived them was the promise she had held out with her forked tongue. It was Tamara herself who would deprive God's chosen of the temple.

The whore had known it all along, biding her time, plotting for the downfall of all Irene had achieved, calling herself the avenging sword. Another lie. Tamara had not foreseen the revelation God had granted, the holy vision of Irene receiving the gift of the avenging sword, purified by the pillar of fire. The power surged again, feeding off the certainty that God's will would triumph. He would show the way.

In a trance of divine truth, Irene emerged from the library. Her most favoured disciple, Sister Shirley, rushed to accost her, needing the embrace of faith and love. Her chest was heaving with distress, her hands flying in fretful gestures.

'Oh, Mother Irene, she said such awful things. Can she really put us out?'

'You heard a sinner wailing in her death throes, Sister Shirley. Have no fear.' She hugged the huge mass of Shirley's warm quivering flesh, squashing it into quiet submission. No Jezebel could take this from her. 'Jehovah will provide,' she declared benevolently.

Shirley sighed in relief. 'You are so wise, Mother Irene.' Then in a flush of excitement she drew back and waved towards the centre of the ballroom. 'We can still have the christening pool?'

Irene walked to the grandly carved chair she had placed directly under the apex of the dome. She could see the pool, extending from the foyer to this place of grace. Sinners would come to be cleansed and rise up from the holy water to sit in this chair. There they would be bathed anew in the light of Jehovah. The ultimate redemption.

'Nothing can stop it,' she declared with ringing conviction. 'I will get a starting date from the plumber.'

'Oh, goody!' Shirley clapped her hands in delight.

Irene went upstairs, where the plumber was fixing a leaking pipe in one of the bathrooms. He was one of the new brethren, eager to help in turning the temple into all it could be. Tamara would not be allowed to stand in the way of the righteous.

Irene did not interrupt the plumber at work. She watched, enthralled, as he used a blowtorch to solder the broken pipe. The jet of flame reminded her of the pillar of fire. It was a sign. The instrument of God's will was at hand.

FIFTY-THREE

What a lovely, lovely day, Tamara thought, brimming over with happiness, and the excitement would stretch for hours yet. Janet was going to drop in for afternoon tea, after her meeting with Rory. Then Rory would come home. It would be just as much fun showing off her purchases as buying them.

'Park in the driveway, Gabrielle,' she instructed. 'We won't have so far to carry everything.'

'Are you having some plumbing done, Tamara?' Sharon asked, her head swivelling towards a pick-up truck parked on the side of the road. It had the logo of a plumbing company emblazoned on the driver's door.

'No.'

'No-one in it. Maybe he's broken down.'

'Or gone for a pee,' Tamara suggested.

They all laughed, high-spirited after the delight of shopping for a baby and a very enjoyable lunch together. Gabrielle brought the car to a halt, and they piled out, loaded with shopping bags. Tamara moved ahead to unlock the front door.

'Let's take everything straight into the nursery. We'll lay it all out for Janet to see.'

'For us to see again, you mean,' Gabrielle said with a grin.

'It's making me clucky,' Sharon declared. 'There's nothing as seductive as baby clothes. They're so tiny and exquisite.'

'I think David would prefer sexy lingerie,' Tamara teased, opening the door and holding it wide for them. 'Slinky red satin and lace is a definite turn-on.'

Sharon laughed. 'Believe me, David doesn't need any encouragement. I bet Rory doesn't, either.'

'No, it's amazing. I'm totally out of shape and I swear Rory finds it more exciting.'

'There's nothing more intimate than you carrying his child,' Gabrielle advised, her lovely blue eyes twinkling. 'I used to watch Paul's face when he felt the baby move. The seven wonders of the world were nothing in comparison.'

'It's marvellous, isn't it?' Tamara heaved a blissful sigh as she closed the door. 'Who'd have thought pregnancy could be such a pleasure? I expected it to be the pits.'

She led them down the hall to the room that was now the nursery. It was already fully equipped. She and Rory had had a wonderful time selecting a bassinette and a cot and a changing table and a rocking chair. They'd papered the walls with Disney characters and hung fascinating mobiles from the ceiling. A line of soft toys adorned the windowsill.

'Oh, look at them!' Sharon cried in delight. 'I adore the panda bear.'

'I insisted on that one. Black and white is definitely my style,' Tamara said archly. 'Class is better than quantity, I told Rory. He chose the floppy dog. And the elephant. And the giraffe. I think he would have bought the whole soft toy department if I hadn't called a halt.'

'One besotted father coming up,' Gabrielle said with a knowing nod.

Tamara laughed, secure in the knowledge that Rory was going to be the best father in the world. She started unpacking the beautiful clothes she had bought, booties and bonnets and matinee jackets, tiny singlets and pretty bibs and embroidered nighties. Sharon and Gabrielle laid them out in sets on the changing table. The bunny rugs were still in the bags when the doorbell sounded.

Tamara shoved the bags at Sharon and Gabrielle. 'That'll be Janet. Lay the rugs over the cot rails for her to see. I'll let her in.'

Bubbling with anticipation, Tamara waltzed out of the nursery. Janet was earlier than she had expected, but that was good. It gave them more time to have fun with Gabrielle and Sharon. It was so great to have friends to share things with. The support Gabrielle and Sharon had given her these past few months had shown her what having a family was all about, and she resolved to plan days like this on a regular basis, even after the baby was born.

With Janet, as well. She'd been going over vineyard figures with Rory today, but Tamara was intent on teaching her there was time for sheer joy in life apart from business. If she could have chosen a sister, it would be Janet, Tamara decided. They shared an understanding that encompassed so much of their lives, needs, dreams, and the natural empathy that came from the empty loneliness they had known.

Tamara grinned, hugging her stomach. She certainly wasn't empty, and loneliness was well in the past now. Life was beautiful and full of riches. She was still grinning in warm welcome to Janet as she opened the door.

There was a moment of blank surprise. Irene? What was she pointing at her?

Fire hitting her. Searing. Sizzling. Hair. Skin. She threw up her arms to protect her face. Too late. Pain. Burning. Clothes. She was ablaze. Screaming, turning, beating. Pain...

Rory, Rory, Rory...

The baby...oh, please, the baby...

Rory...

It's coming...the blackness...hold me safe...falling...
pain...falling...the black void taking me...taking me...not
my baby...please...not my baby...

FIFTY-FOUR

Gabrielle ran down the hall, her heart pumping madly with shock, Sharon's screams in her ears. She launched herself at the blazing figure on the floor, heedless of any danger to herself, smothering the fire with the bunny rugs she was holding when the screaming started.

'Get water, Sharon! Get water,' she cried. 'We've got to cool her down.'

'Oh, God! Look at her!' Sharon staggered to the open door and retched on the front porch.

'There's no time to be sick.' Gabrielle scrambled to her feet to yank Sharon inside to help.

'It's Irene. She's running to the truck.'

'Forget Irene. Tamara needs us.'

'Yes.' She was gasping and shuddering, but she tottered inside to face what had to be done. 'Water,' she repeated dazedly.

'The kitchen is closest,' Gabrielle advised curtly and knelt to gently turn Tamara's head on its side in the hope of keeping airways open for her to breathe. The horror of touching the burnt and blackened flesh brought bile to her mouth, but she swallowed it, forcing her mind to remember the first aid instructions for a burn victim.

Maintaining airways was vital. Tamara was still breathing. Cool the body. Remove clothes. Take off any jewellery—rings, watch. The burnt flesh would swell and weep. At least the fire was out, but her clothes were smouldering. 'Keep dousing her with water while I ring for an ambulance,' she yelled at Sharon, scrambling to her feet.

'Is she still alive?'

'Yes. Though God knows how.'

A sense of urgency made her run to the telephone. She tapped in the emergency number as Sharon raced to Tamara with a saucepan of water. Gabrielle noticed Sharon was as white as a sheet, but at least she'd gone past hysterics and was trying to do her best.

'Ambulance. Burn victim,' she answered the emergency operator and was instantly connected to the right service. She tried to be as quick and as accurate as she could in replying to the questions asked. The advice given was no more than she already knew. She hung up and ran to Tamara, kneeling beside her, uncaring of the puddle of water around her. As carefully as she could, she started removing the remnants of clothes.

'Ambulance will only be ten minutes,' she informed Sharon. 'Keep the water coming.'

'Why did Irene do it? Has she gone mad?'

'I don't know.' It flashed into her mind that Louise had burnt, too.

'The baby,' Sharon cried. 'What about the baby?'

'We've got to think of Tamara first. Get moving, Sharon.'

Gabrielle didn't want to think at all. She set herself the task of doing what she could, one bit at a time, clamping down on translating what she was seeing into the Tamara she had known. It would be terrible if she lived and terrible if she died. Gabrielle prayed she wouldn't regain consciousness for a while. The pain and shock would be too dreadful.

The wedding ring had to come off. Tamara had been so beautiful on her wedding day. It wasn't fair. It was the worst cruelty of all, coming now. She'd only begun to be happy with Rory. And the baby. What was happening to the baby?

'I'd better shift your car, Gabrielle,' Sharon suggested.

'Yes. Do it.'

Rory would be demented. His own mother attacking Tamara like this, putting their child at risk. Who would tell him? Paul. It would have to be Paul. He would look after Rory, make sure he didn't do anything foolish. She would call Paul as soon as the ambulance officers came.

The car, roaring up the driveway.

The ambulance arriving.

She could stop. More experienced help taking over from her.

'Tell them the helicopter had better land at Peppers Guest House. Too many trees here,' one of the officers yelled.

'Helicopter?' Sharon echoed, shrinking against the wall for support as they went about their business.

'With paramedics,' came the matter-of-fact reply. 'It's already been called. She'll be flown straight to the John Hunter Hospital at Newcastle for treatment.'

'How long before it comes?' Gabrielle asked, staggering to the telephone again. Her legs were like jelly. Shock catching up with her.

'Should be waiting for us on the back lawn at Pepper's by the time we get there.'

She got Paul on the line, told him what had happened. 'I'll go with her, Paul. You get Rory and bring him to the John Hunter. We can't wait.'

They wrapped Tamara in a sterile sheet and lifted her onto a stretcher. Oxygen was being administered through nasal prongs. Gabrielle followed as they carried her to the ambulance.

'Will you clean up, Sharon?' she asked tremulously. 'It would be terrible for Rory to come home to...'

'Yes. I'll do it. You did the...the worst, Gabrielle.'

They both had tears in their eyes.

'I'll call David at the vineyard when...when I know something.'

'Tell them she's twenty-eight weeks, Gabrielle. Tell them...' She broke into sobbing.

'I'll tell them,' Gabrielle promised.

The baby. If Tamara died, could they save the baby?

FIFTY-FIVE

Rory had to acknowledge it was just as well Paul was driving. It would save time at the other end, Paul had argued. Save an accident, too, Rory now realised. Concentrating on the road would have been beyond him. His mind was shot to pieces.

Tamara had suffered so much at the hands of his family. Now this, this ultimate cruelty, striking so viciously, so void of any humanity. His mother—his mad mother, merciless in her screwed-up hellfire religion, uncaring of the hurt she inflicted. So many hurts.

It was like some hideous pattern pulsing at him in flashes that revealed a truth of monstrous proportions. His mother, the evil influence behind all the dreadful things that had happened in his life. They jabbed into his mind. Tamara so sickeningly abused under her roof, his father driven to an obscene secrecy, driven to blow himself up in his plane, Cathy running away to the most final escape route of all, Louise burnt to death in the cottage, Tamara attacked...

Though Tamara was still alive. She had to pull through. It couldn't stop here. Not when they'd come so far and had so much to live for. And there was the baby to give her the will to live. Their child. Their dreams.

He vaguely heard Janet in the back seat, calling the hospital on her mobile telephone, but he knew they wouldn't give out details. They never did in critical cases. They knew he was coming. They'd wait until he got there before anything definite was said.

He tried to will his strength to Tamara. He had to hold her safe. He'd promised. For it to be his own mother the danger—not Eleanor— The shock, the devastation of it went soul-deep. *Hold on, my darling*, he pleaded. *We'll beat her together. All we have to do is stand together. And I'll give you justice.*

If it was the last thing he ever did, he'd deliver hellfire to the woman who practised it. Tamara wouldn't be touched by her again. Nor their children. He'd make their world safe for them.

Janet called out directions to Paul. Signs to the hospital. Almost there. Adrenaline pumped through Rory. Tamara was his life. Only a few more moments and he'd be with her. He'd talk her through it, love her through it, make her know that nothing mattered but being together.

Paul drove the car straight up to the emergency entrance. Rory was out and running in an instant. He heard car doors banging shut, Paul and Janet following. Then Gabrielle was in front of him, stopping him, Gabrielle, her face streaked with tears. He grabbed her arms, begging for good news, but he knew, he knew...

'I'm sorry, Rory.'

'No, no...' He shook his head even as an iron fist clamped around his heart.

'They tried everything. We were still in the helicopter. They tried, Rory, but she...she stopped breathing and they couldn't revive her.'

'Tamara...' He couldn't believe it. Tamara, so vibrant and vital. It wasn't possible for it to end like this. 'I must go to her. Where is she?'

'No, Rory.' Gabrielle's expressive eyes were full of horror.

'Tamara wouldn't want that. You mustn't. I...I identified her for you. There's no need...'

'I can't not be with her, Gabrielle,' he argued, too anguished to listen. 'I must see her. I must...' Tamara was alone. It was all wrong. He hadn't been with her when she'd needed him most. He had to bring her back, had to hold her hand...

'Janet, tell him,' Gabrielle appealed frantically. 'Tell him it's not...it's not Tamara any more.'

She burst into weeping, and Paul quickly drew her into his embrace. 'Rory, listen to her, for God's sake!' he said gruffly. 'Gabrielle knows. She was there.'

'For Tamara's sake,' Janet put in fiercely, inserting herself between them and grabbing the lapels of Rory's suitcoat to force his attention. 'Tamara told me what you said to her on your wedding day, that you'd always remember her as she was then. You've got to do it, Rory. I know all your instincts are crying out to go to her, but it's not fair. It's not right.'

She didn't understand. His love for Tamara was indestructible. If he could just reach out to her... 'She's my wife, Janet. My Tamara, no matter what. I don't care how she looks.'

'*She* would care.'

'No.' He shook his head in anguished denial, tugging at Janet's staying hands. But they gripped harder and beat at him.

'Stop thinking of what you want. There's only one thing left you can do for Tamara, Rory, and you must do it,' she commanded, jolting him with her urgent intensity.

'For her you must hold her in your mind,' she went on, hammering him. 'Hold her memory safe. It's what she'd want, Rory. The good memories. Only the good ones.'

Hold her safe. It was what he'd failed to do. Failed... He shut his eyes tight as the scream shrieked through him. Tamara, the ache, the yearning, the unbearable emptiness, the life that had been ripped from them.

'There's still the baby, Rory.'

Gabrielle's voice, reminding him of the other life Tamara had carried, the happiness of their baby growing, moving. He groaned and opened his eyes, driven to know what Gabrielle meant by her words, tortured by the spectre of their child dying, too.

'Still the baby?' He must have misheard, misunderstood. Impossible for it to survive in the circumstances. Dead, both dead. Only the memories.

Gabrielle, facing him again, her hands lifted, appealing, offering, her wet eyes clinging to his, pleading for his belief. 'They rushed Tamara into surgery. It had to be quick. They only had eight minutes from when—when she died to save the baby. They did it, Rory. There's a good chance...'

Deep breath. *Let it be true. Let me have some part of her.* He forced himself to speak, to ask, 'Our child is alive?'

'So far so good,' Gabrielle assured him optimistically. 'But go and see for yourself, Rory. They've put the baby in a humidicrib, under constant monitoring to make sure it has every chance. The nurse at the desk will get someone to take you there.'

Alive, with a good chance of surviving. He could hardly take it in. Their baby, a survivor against all odds. Like Tamara.

'I'll come with you,' Janet said, clasping his hand.

He looked at her distractedly.

'I need to see Tamara's baby, too, Rory,' she appealed softly.

He nodded. He was not the only one suffering the loss. Death, birth...they needed the affirmation of life going on. He gripped Janet's hand. She had always been a true friend to him, like a sister to Tamara.

A nurse showed them the way. Footsteps echoing along corridors. Hollow sounds. Everything so hollow now. They entered a large ward fitted out with several humidicribs. The nurse led them to one. It was labelled Buchanan.

The baby was tiny. Incredibly, perfectly formed. Tamara's black hair.

The nurse lifted the lid of the crib and smiled at Rory. 'You may touch if you like.'

The agony of grief eased a little as he reached in and tentatively ran featherlight fingertips over the soft, warm body. Alive. A gift. Tamara's gift of love to him. Their child.

FIFTY-SIX

Eleanor drifted in and out of consciousness. She heard a tap on the door, David's voice softly calling, a chair moving. It was difficult to stir herself. She felt so weak. But she wanted to talk to David again. Paul had been here this morning. She had to give David time, too.

Richard's sons.

Paul, always the leader, right from when they were little boys. Such good playmates together, rarely fighting, Paul taking the blame if they got caught out in mischief. They were easy children, happy children. They'd all been happy when Richard was alive.

Happy now, even Tamara. Paul had said so. And she'd finally done something right for Tamara, getting Irene out of the Big House. No reminder of the bad times.

Her hand was cold. Where was Frank? He'd promised to hold it, stay with her to the end. Not much strength left. But there was something she had to do. Hadn't she heard David's voice? Yes, David had come to visit her. She had to make the effort to concentrate, open her eyes.

'David,' she called.

'I'll get him for you,' the nurse said, rising from her chair.

Voices at the door. They both came in, Frank and David.

They sat down on either side of her. Frank took her hand again, warm, gentle, soothing.

'It's good to see you, David,' she said.

'Mum...'

He looked distressed. He'd barely met her eyes. He was holding himself in check, worrying, trying to hide it. She had not lost her awareness of body language yet, and David was invariably more transparent than Paul. He'd never been able to lie to her.

'Tell me what's wrong, David,' she invited, wanting to put him at ease.

He threw an anguished look at Frank. They must have discussed the problem outside her hearing, wanting to save her any concern. But that wasn't right. She was his mother.

'Let me help, David,' she pressed.

He shook his head, the composure he'd tried to maintain crumbling. Biting his lips. Throat convulsing. 'No-one can help, Mum.'

'Tamara died a little while ago, Ellie,' Frank said quietly.

Died? That couldn't be so. She must have heard wrongly. Yet there were tears in David's eyes. And Frank had his stoic face on. Her heart fluttered. 'Did you say Tamara...'

'Yes, Ellie.' Frank nodded gravely. 'She's gone. From all of us. Leaving the pain behind.'

She tried to cling to disbelief, turning to David, wanting him to make something different of what she had heard.

'It's true,' he said flatly.

Her mind grappled with a flood of questions. 'How? Why?' she cried.

'Let it go, Ellie,' Frank gently urged.

'No.' Her hands clawed at the bedclothes in agitation. Her eyes darted to David, desperate for knowledge. 'It didn't just happen. There must be...' She gasped for breath, reached for the will and the authority to enforce what she wanted one more time. 'Tell me, David.'

He fought her for several seconds, but he couldn't contain

it. 'Irene attacked her this afternoon. She went to Rory's house with a blow torch and when Tamara opened the door...'

'Fire,' she moaned.

'Sharon and Gabrielle did all they could, but the burns were so bad... It must have been shock. I don't know. She died before they arrived at the hospital.'

Fire. Irene. Irene and her temple. A guilty horror seized her. She turned her head to her brother.

'It's my fault, Frank. I told Irene to get out of the Big House. I told her it was for Tamara.'

He looked so old and weary, yet still he squeezed her hand comfortingly. 'You didn't aim the blowtorch, Ellie.'

'I pulled the trigger. It's my fault. I should have realised...'

'We all should have realised much more than we did,' he said heavily. 'Blame lies in many places, Ellie. Don't take it all upon yourself.'

There was no balm for her guilt, her careless arrogance. The crime had been committed, so many crimes, and there was no calling any of them back. Too late for amends. Always too late with Tamara. She had truly loved Rory. Something could be—must be done for Rory.

'Irene. She's mad, Frank. How will Rory cope with this?'

'Not to worry,' he soothed. 'I'll take care of Irene.'

'The baby,' she moaned.

'They saved the baby. Rory's with it now.'

A thread of hope, of solace. Frank's future saved. Rory would have the child. But Tamara. She closed her eyes as grief tightened her chest. The daughter she should have loved... Too late, too late... And this, the punishment for the words not spoken, the turning away, the spurned opportunities.

Her lost child, dead now because of her. Frank didn't know the secrets she'd kept, the silence, letting Irene get away with too much. Irene, who had watched what Ian had done to Tamara and held it over his head while indulging her own secret desires. Tamara suffering for it, Tamara dying for it. The guilt and the grief were too heavy to bear, too heavy...

'David...'

'Yes, Mum?'

'Forgive me.'

'There's nothing to forgive. I love you, Mum.'

'I love you.'

David, Paul...if only Tamara could have said it, too. Foolish thought. She hadn't deserved it, hadn't earned it. Tamara had served her with justice but hadn't received it herself.

'Justice. There has to be justice, Frank,' she pleaded.

'I'll see to it, Ellie. Rest easy now. I promise you, justice will be done.'

The strong resolve in his voice assured her it would be so. Frank was like an oak tree, solid, reliable, staunch in his beliefs. His word was his bond. He was her brother, through everything, to the end.

If she rested, would Tamara come for her, forgive her? Was there another life on the other side of death, light after the darkness?

Richard, I have a daughter. Don't let her be alone, Richard. She needs not to be alone. I want to be there for her. Her name is Tamara. She's my daughter...

FIFTY-SEVEN

$\diagdown\diagdown\diagup$

Frank chose to walk. They'd walked everywhere in the old days, and he was comfortable with it. No haste tonight. Time didn't matter at all. The sense of a long cycle closing sat heavily on his mind.

His gaze was drawn to the familiar night sky. He and Joyce had courted under these stars. Richard and Ellie. He was the only one left. The thought came to him that maybe it would be fitting for him to go, too. He pondered it for a while, then slowly shook his head. The children needed him to smooth the passing over to the new cycle. To add to their burden would not be fair at such a time as this. They'd asked him to be the bridge. He had accepted.

It was good they were all pulling together now. He was proud of them. And pleased that Janet had the Selby vineyard again. Like old times. Though it hadn't been the old-timers who had achieved it.

It was painful to think of Tamara, home for so short a time yet giving so much. The only consolation was she would live on in the child. Frank nodded to himself. Another reason for him to keep going. He wanted to see Tamara's baby thriving, being given its just due in the family, loved and cherished.

He reached the sliprail fence and paused. He'd helped

Richard put it up. Ellie bringing them a picnic lunch. The memory of his little sister blurred into the vivid face of Tamara. Two of a kind. Was there a meeting place after death? His sense of rightness felt there had to be one, where mistakes were finally put in perspective and torment was laid to rest.

He walked on, treading the road he had to take tonight. He was glad Irene wasn't of his blood. No real kin at all. Though it must cut deep with Rory, knowing she was his mother. It probably didn't help to say there was nothing of Irene in him, but it was true enough. Irene was evil, no milk of human kindness in her, no caring for anyone but herself. Rory was intrinsically good.

Strange how genes could skip a generation. Rory was very like Joyce in looks and in nature, one of the sweetest women who ever lived, though feisty when her dander was up about something. Frank wished Rory had known his grandmother. Joyce had died too young, far too young.

They hadn't known she had a weak heart until Ian was born and the doctors had advised no more children. Ian had only been thirteen when she died. A bad age to lose a mother. Not that any age was good. Frank had often wondered if Joyce would have seen through Irene's facade of virtue and somehow stopped that ill-fated marriage.

So much grief had ensued from it, death and destruction—Ian, poor little Cathy, Louise, Tamara. It was a miracle the baby had survived. He had to protect Rory and the baby from any more of it. To his way of thinking, simple solutions were always best. He had no doubts about his course tonight.

It would inevitably mean more involvement with officialdom, but he accepted that reality. The paperwork had to be done, satisfaction given to the proper authorities. He hoped it could be delayed until tomorrow. Tonight...tonight was very personal. The wrongs had to be righted in every sense, a clean slate for the children to imprint their own lives, untainted by influences that belonged to another time.

He thought of them gathered together in Rory's house. There was strength and comfort in sympathetic company. He'd told David what to do, to take Sharon and wait for the others to return from the hospital, to stay with Rory and hold him safe. A vigil had to be kept. They would know, they would see, they would understand when the vigil was over.

The Big House was illuminated from every angle, making it stand out like a beacon. Once such light had meant Max was holding a grand party and he wanted everyone in the valley to know it. Now it was an aggrandisement of Irene's obscene religion, a temple of pseudo light and redemption.

To Frank it represented overweening pride and ambition that had been heedless of the cost of human suffering, lives trampled over, lives crippled, lives taken. An empty house in all that really mattered. A haunted house. The children didn't want it. Ellie had turned her back on it at the end of her life. A house with no heart.

He turned down the long avenue of poplars. Straight ahead of him was the huge stone fountain, its ostentatious spray resembling a silvery cobweb under lights. Several vehicles were parked in the circular driveway. Frank smiled grimly. Irene's evening prayer meeting was about to get a visitation worthy of the Old Testament.

Her temple was an abomination. Frank had his own beliefs about God. They were not reflected in any formal religion he knew. Somehow the important principles of caring and sharing got lost amidst pomp and ceremony. To his mind, God had no need of mansions or cathedrals or temples to proclaim His power and greatness. Such values were man-made, nothing to do with God at all. It didn't do man any good, either, setting himself above others. Pride and ambition.

His gaze travelled up the massive columns that supported the portico framing the double front doors. Louise had coveted this image of greatness. In pursuing it, she had died. Tamara had been innocently born into this house, and because Irene coveted it Tamara had died. Frank walked up the steps, determined to end the long train of evil that had brought so much misery.

The right-hand door was unlocked. He opened it wide and left it that way. The apron foyer gave him a clear view into the ballroom where Irene was holding court from Ellie's chair, placed directly under the centre of the overhead dome. In front of her a small congregation sat on chairs from the formal dining room. His entrance didn't interrupt Irene's Bible reading, but a few heads turned to see who had come.

Frank ignored the gathering. He proceeded to unbolt the other front door and open it wide. This action brought the reading to a halt. It also raised a buzz of murmuring amongst Irene's misguided minions. The whispers stopped as he walked into the ballroom. Frank did a count of heads as people turned in their chairs to stare at him. He halted at the foot of the short aisle that led to where Irene sat in self-glorified authority.

Frank Buchanan was a well-known figure. He bore his seventy-six years well, still tall and unstooped, broad-shouldered, barrel-chested, his legs as solid as tree trunks, his craggy face weather-beaten, yet stamped with a strength of character that few would question, his iron grey hair adding to his air of an elder statesman who had power to wield if he chose to.

Irene did not greet or welcome him. She stared at him, boldly defying whatever reason had brought him here. He stared back as the faces of his family marched through his mind, last and longest of all his little sister Ellie, who had tried to right a wrong and whose last minutes of life had been riven by guilt for what this creature of darkness had done.

'Dame Eleanor Buchanan Traverner Vandelier,' he said slowly, giving each name respectful weight, 'is dead.'

Gasps from the gullible followers.

Smug satisfaction on Irene's face. 'We will pray for her soul,' she unctuously proclaimed.

'You will all leave this house,' Frank commanded, a quiet steel in his voice that was rarely heard but intensely effective when it was. 'Those of you who have come to this meeting, go now. Those who have taken up residence here, go and pack your belongings and leave in the minibus my sister provided.'

It brought Irene to her feet. 'You have no authority here, Frank Buchanan.'

'If I have to drive these strangers from my sister's house with a whip, I will, Irene. Let no-one doubt it.' He cast a resolute look around the mesmerised spectators. 'Start moving. I want this house cleared within the hour.'

Chair legs scraped on the polished parquet flooring.

Irene promptly sat. 'I shall not leave.'

Hesitation amongst the ranks.

'You may choose as you please, Irene,' Frank conceded, having anticipated precisely this stance from her. 'I will not allow anyone else to stay.'

'In respect for Dame Eleanor's passing, and the distraught state of mind of her brother, we will not continue this prayer meeting. Go in God's grace, my sisters and brothers. Sister Shirley, Sister Nora and Sister Miriam will remain with me.'

Her arrogance didn't bother him. The favoured few could wait until after the others had left. His edict, backed by Irene's permission, produced the desired result of getting rid of those who did not live in the house with her. Most of them scuttled out, only too relieved to escape what was shaping up as a family argument that was none of their business. He walked to the portico to watch the vehicles depart, checking he had the numbers right.

There was no live-in staff to worry about. Irene's antics

had driven them away months ago. He waited until the last set of tail-lights turned onto the public road, then went to the ballroom to deal with the three deluded women who had obediently and loyally remained in their chairs, supporting the dangerous fanatic who dominated them.

He picked up one of the vacated chairs, set it in the middle of the makeshift aisle and sat down, prepared to be patient. The faithful three sat with bowed heads, either praying for deliverance or passively waiting for an axe to fall. Irene glared at him, clearly infuriated by his intrusion but knowing he had a physical advantage over her and not quite daring to test it.

Frank didn't hold with violence of any kind. It was abhorrent to him. His threat of a whip had been purely metaphorical. He did not intend to lay a hand on anyone. Nevertheless, Irene would be destroyed tonight. She had shown no mercy. She would get none. This day of grief would end in justice.

'Shirley, Miriam, Nora,' he addressed them gravely, 'I am sorry you have uprooted yourselves from your normal lives to reside in this house with Irene. It was not a wise decision.'

'They serve the will of Jehovah,' Irene snapped at him.

'This woman you call mother went to my grandson's home this afternoon and murdered his wife, Tamara.'

Their heads jerked up.

'Liar!' Irene screeched. 'Father of lies!'

'She drove there in a plumber's truck,' Frank continued, unruffled by Irene's response. 'When Tamara opened the door to her, Irene attacked her with a blowtorch, burning her so badly she died on the way to hospital.'

He was aware of shocked reactions from the trio to whom his speech was directed, but he kept his gaze focused on Irene, whose grip on the situation was visibly cracking.

'Jehovah strikes down all who would defile His temple,' she screeched at him. 'Their lot is hellfire and damnation. I am His instrument. I hold the avenging sword.'

'This cruel and callous act was witnessed by both Gabrielle and Sharon Traverner,' he stated unequivocally. 'After Irene ran off they were desperately engaged in trying to save Tamara's life and that of her child. Tamara was seven months pregnant.'

One of the women burst into tears.

'Sister Shirley, weep not for the whore,' Irene commanded in a whip-cracking tone.

'The police have not yet been notified of the crime,' Frank informed them. 'They shall be, very shortly. The family has had to bear two deaths within hours of each other. It was too much to deal with all at once.'

'Mother Irene.' It was a sobbing cry from the one Irene had addressed as Sister Shirley, a very overweight young woman 'Please tell us it isn't true.'

Irene lifted her head in proud zeal. 'The daughters of Satan give way to the righteous. The black souls burn, as it is written in the holy book. I have made the temple safe from them.'

Frank waited a few moments for Irene's guilt to sink in and the shock and horror to grow. Then he nailed home the position. 'If you are innocent of any knowledge of this crime, go and do as I ordered earlier. Pack your possessions and leave as quickly as you can. If you stay here with Irene, you will be charged with aiding and abetting a murderer.'

Irene's eyes flashed imperiously. 'They assist the Chosen One. I am the keeper of the flame for Jehovah. It is their duty and their privilege to serve me.'

'You will be serving a prison sentence if you stay,' Frank warned. 'You will be found guilty by association to one of the most heinous murders ever perpetrated. There will be no escape from public censure. For the rest of your lives, you will be reviled and condemned for what was done this day. Is that what you want?'

'Rory was always nice to me. He stood up for me,' Sister

Shirley cried, tears streaming down her face as she struggled to her feet. 'If you did this, Irene, you are no mother.'

'I am the mother of believers,' Irene hurled at her. 'Desert me and Jehovah will cast you into darkness.'

'She did it,' Frank quietly confirmed.

Irene leaned forward, her face jutting out as she flouted his earthly ignorance. 'I am the Hand of God.'

'And I am the hand of justice, Irene,' Frank replied, relentless in pursuing his purpose. 'Make no mistake about it, any of you. I will see justice done in this matter. My family will not suffer at the hands of this woman again.'

Sister Shirley quivered. 'Louise burnt, too. I can't stay. I can't!' She burst into more weeping and blundered off towards the staircase.

The others rose shakily from their chairs and followed her, their faith crushed by the weight of evidence and Irene's failure to rebut the accusation. Irene shrieked a stream of biblical invective after them, but their steps did not falter. Curses were rained down on Frank's head. He let them flow over him, unperturbed and unmoved by anything Irene could do or say. She opened her Bible and read in a shrill, declaiming voice. He sat in silence, waiting.

When the three women came downstairs with their bags, he followed them to the back entrance of the house and watched them go to one of the garages. A few minutes later the minibus emerged and was driven off. He listened until the sound of the engine was lost in distance.

Having emptied the house of innocent people, he strolled to the gardener's shed, took Ellie's set of master keys for the Big House and its environs out of his trouser pocket, found the one that unlocked the shed door, opened it and pocketed the keys. Two full cans of petrol were stored for filling up the tractor mower. He carried them out, leaving the door open. Given Irene's state of mind, she wouldn't care about anything being stolen. Neither did he.

It didn't take long to return to the house. Irene was still

reading the Bible from her chair of authority in the ball-room. He dribbled the petrol from one can through the various hallways and up the staircase. With very deliberate intent, he circled the ballroom with the other, leaving no loophole for escape, trailing a last line to the open front doors.

Irene was still babbling from the Bible, having shown no awareness whatsoever of what he was doing. He walked to her and dropped Ellie's keys by her chair. Still she read on, ignoring his presence and his actions.

'Irene, I'm going to burn this house to the ground,' he said loudly. 'Do you want to burn with it?'

She looked up, her eyes glazed with her own mad fire. 'I sit in Jehovah's chair. You have no power over me. The will of God will triumph.'

'I take it you're staying.'

'Nothing can make me leave this holy temple.'

'That's what I figured. So be it.'

He walked out to the portico, struck a match, tossed it into the trail of petrol, saw the first explosion of flame, then turned his back on it and proceeded down the steps, away from the crackle of fire behind him.

The air was sweet in the open night. He didn't retrace his route down the avenue of poplars, choosing to avoid any incoming traffic by walking across the rolling lawns to the fence that separated the grounds of the Big House from the fields of Traverner vines. He slipped through the rails and looked back.

The beacon of light was no longer white. It was red and black. The peace of the night was broken by exploding glass and the roar of a blaze consuming everything in its path. He'd heard that smoke usually suffocated people before fire got them. He hoped it wasn't the case with Irene. She should feel what she had inflicted on Tamara before she died. Either way, it was over, the pain and death she had brought into his family.

The fire would bring people soon. They might even try to stop it, but it was too big to be put out now. The house would be gutted. What was left standing could be bull-dozed and trucked away. Given a week or two, the Big House and all it had stood for would be nothing but ashes in the wind. It was the closing of a cycle that had started with Richard's death and ended with Ellie's.

Satisfied he had laid the past to rest as best he could, Frank resumed the journey to the old homestead where people would expect him to be. He came across the garden bench Ellie had placed to mark Richard's death. He sat and rested for a while, gazing at the rows of old vines planted long before he was born.

Their gnarled wood was bare of leaves. Winter was fast approaching. They looked dead, but Frank knew they weren't. He'd been watching the cycle of the seasons all his life. These old vines would burst into bud come the spring.

And spring would come for the children, too. It was the natural turn of things. Cut away the deadwood, and the vine flourished with a renewal of life.

He nodded, content. The future would take care of itself now. He looked at the red haze in the sky. The deadwood had been cut away.

FIFTY-EIGHT

'No caterpillars, Daddy,' Liam said gravely, eyeing the young leaves on the vines they passed.

'No, not a one that I can see,' Rory agreed, smiling at his four-year-old son.

Liam grinned back, his brilliant black eyes—Tamara's eyes—sparkling with triumphant delight. 'The little wasps must have got them.'

'I reckon they did.'

'Grandpa told me...'

Rory half-listened to the story of problems with the caterpillars in former years, related to Liam by his great-grandfather. He kept smiling and nodding and occasionally commenting, loving the way Liam soaked in knowledge and revelled in it. He was very much Tamara's child, so eager to embrace all life had to offer. He radiated joy in it.

Rory felt she was still with him, always would be, her voice echoing in his mind.

I have this dream of you taking our child into the vineyard with you and teaching it all you know, giving it the heritage I was denied, sharing your love of it, the kind of bonding I wish I'd known.

Their son. Inextricably part of her and part of him.

Tamara would approve of his marriage to Janet. A mother to Liam. A loving mother. Tamara had wanted that so much herself. He hoped he and Janet would have children, too. They both liked the idea of a big family. It would be good for Liam to have brothers and sisters, giving him a sense of family beyond Rory's life span. He didn't want Tamara's child to know the loneliness Tamara had felt.

Rory was comfortable with Janet. It wasn't a marriage of passion. They had both known a love that crossed all barriers, and they respected each other's memories. What they shared was warm companionship based on a deep understanding of each other's needs and on solid friendship. It was good.

Janet had loved Liam from the day he was born. To her, too, he was an extension of Tamara, a child to be cherished and given all Tamara would have given him. He was a happy little boy, confident of his place in the world he inhabited.

'Daddy, my legs are getting tired. Will you give me a piggyback?'

'Well, we can't have you getting too tired to play with your cousins.' Rory crouched down for Liam to hug his neck as he hoisted the little boy up on his back. 'How's that?'

'I like being up high, Daddy. I can see all the vineyard.' The love of it was in his voice. He belonged here, and he knew he did. 'Is Grandpa going to be at Uncle Paul's?'

'Yes. It's his birthday, remember? He's eighty years old today.'

Paul and Gabrielle had organised a family party. Frank Buchanan's eightieth birthday was an occasion to celebrate and a way of thanking him for simply being there for them.

Rory thought back to the burning of the Big House. It was generally believed Irene had done it. Only the family knew whose hand had been behind the cauterising act that had begun the process of healing.

Destroy...

It was what Tamara had set out to do, yet with her cour-

age and drive to start a new life, she had seeded a new life
for all of them. Birth and rebirth.

'Have we got a birthday present for Grandpa?'

'Yes.'

'Can I give it to him, Daddy?'

'Yes, Liam. You can give it to him.'

Rory smiled. He knew his grandfather needed no other
gift than Liam himself, the child who was the embodiment
of the continuation of the family, the future. More than that,
Liam held both Tamara and Eleanor in him, bonded in love,
not hatred, and all the more precious for it to the man who
had tried to bring mother and daughter together.

Rory had forgiven Eleanor. He now knew the devastation
of heart and soul that came with the sudden loss of the one
whose love gave life meaning. He could very easily have
acted in a destructive fashion if his grandfather had not
moved so quickly and decisively to eliminate the source of
pain.

Life did move on if one let it. Tamara had taught him that,
to put the worst behind him and look for the good. And
there were so many good things to live for.

Though sometimes, when he smelled roses, the image of
Tamara on their wedding day came to him so poignantly, it
was as though, if he swung around quickly, she would be
there, laughing at him and saying she was free.

It hurt.

But it was a good memory.

Like everything about Tamara...

Unforgettable.

SUSAN WIGGS

Jesse Morgan is a man hiding from the pain of the past, a man who has vowed never to give his heart again. Keeper of a remote lighthouse along a rocky and dangerous coast, he has locked himself away from everything but his bitter memories. Now the sea has given him a second chance.

THE LIGHTKEEPER

"A classic beauty-and-the-beast love story that will stay in your heart long after you've turned the last page. A poignant, beautiful romance." —Kristin Hannah

Available in October 1997
at your favorite retail outlet.

MIRA BOOKS

The Brightest Stars in Women's Fiction.™

She was innocent...of everything but love

PRESUMED GUILTY

Someone was sleeping in Miranda Wood's bed. But he wasn't really sleeping—he was dead. There was no one who would believe she hadn't murdered her former lover, least of all the dead man's brother. But Chase Tremain couldn't help but fall for her—even when it was clear that someone wanted to keep them apart...forever.

TESS GERRITSEN

Available October 1997 at your favorite retail outlet.

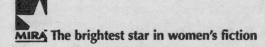

MIRA The brightest star in women's fiction

MTG2

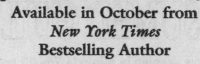

Indiscreet

Camilla Ferrand wants everyone, especially her dying grandfather, to stop worrying about her. So she tells them that she is engaged to be married. But with no future husband in sight, it's going to be difficult to keep up the pretense. Then she meets the very handsome and mysterious Benedict Ellsworth who generously offers to accompany Camilla to her family's estate—as her most devoted fiancé.

But at what cost does this *generosity* come?

From the bestselling author of *Impulse*

CANDACE CAMP

Available in November 1997
at your favorite retail outlet.

"Candace Camp also writes for Silhouette® as Kristen James

MIRA **The brightest star in women's fiction**

MCCIND